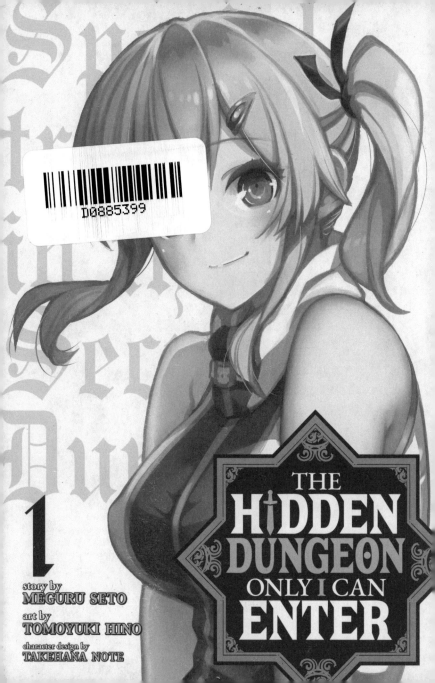

D0885399

1

THE HiDDEN DUNGEON ONLY I CAN ENTER

story by
MEGURU SETO

art by
TOMOYUKI HINO

character design by
TAKEHANA NOTE

CONTENTS

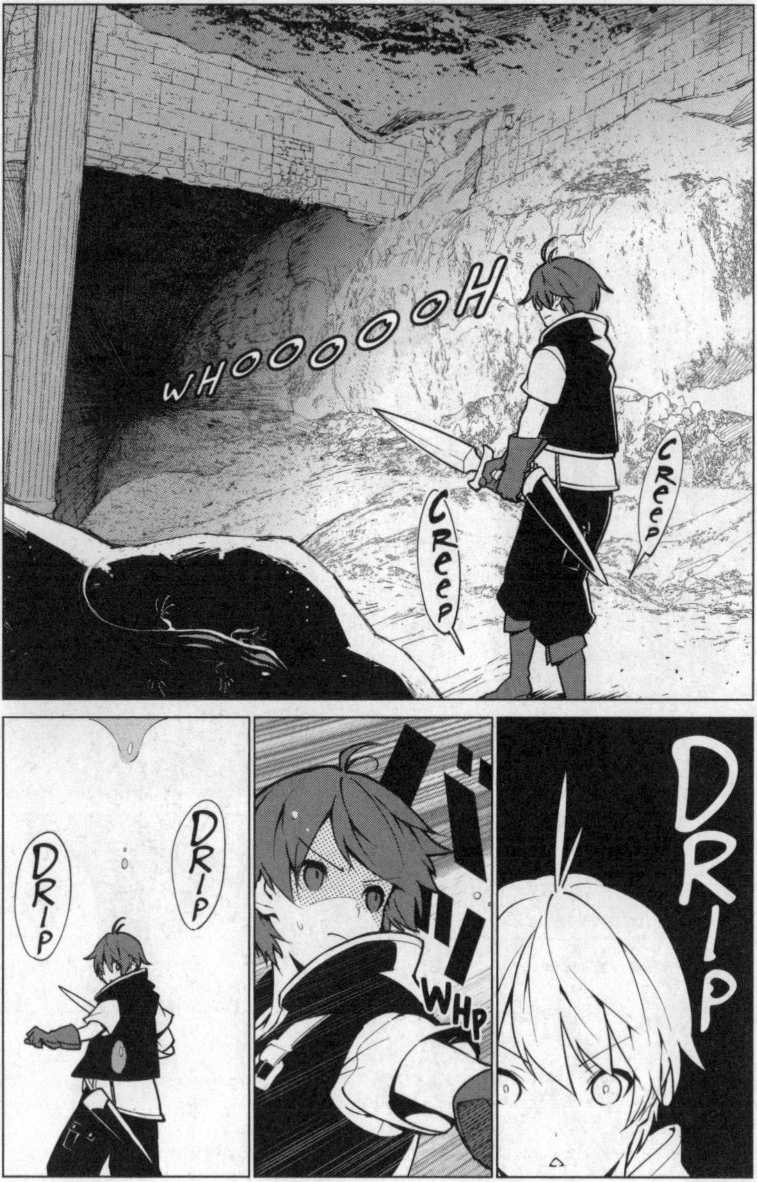
WHOOOOOOH
Creep
Creep
DRIP
WHP
DRIP
DRIP

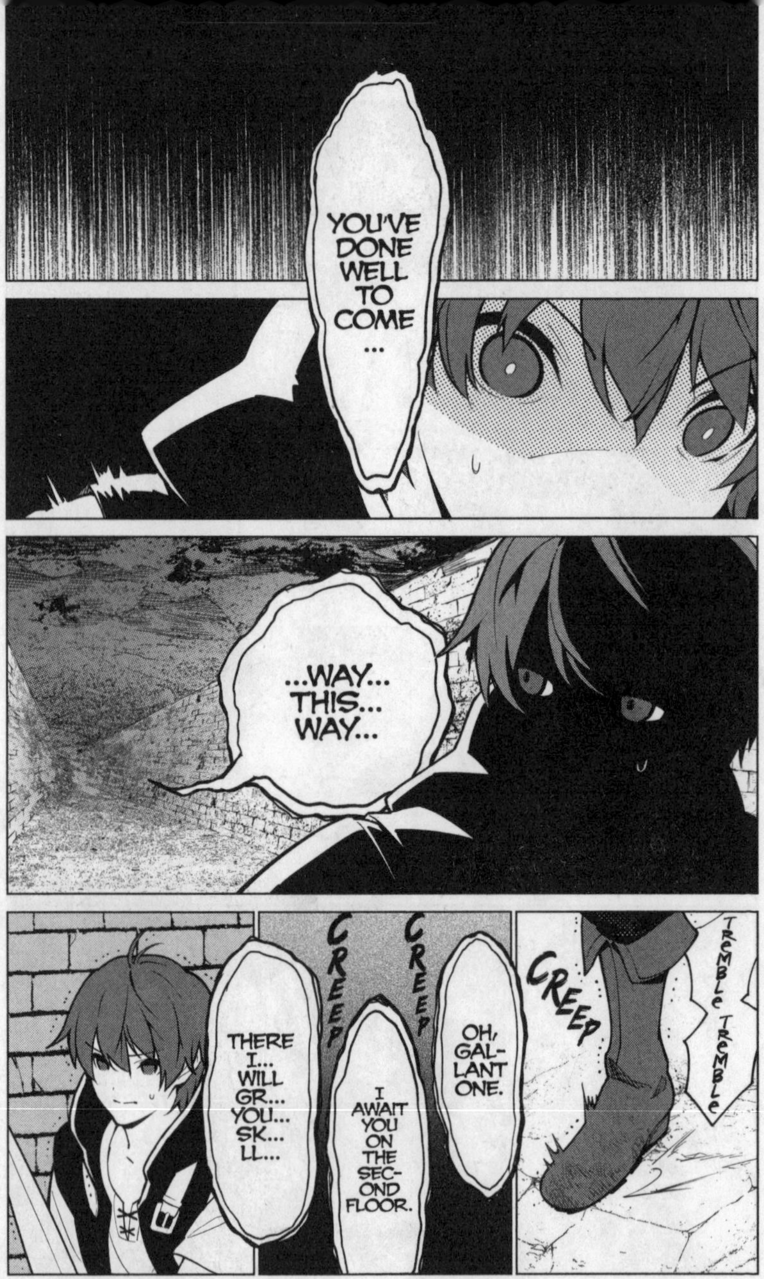
YOU'VE DONE WELL TO COME ...
...WAY... THIS... WAY...
TREMBLE TREMBLE
CREEP
CREEP
CREEP
OH, GAL-LANT ONE.
I AWAIT YOU ON THE SEC-OND FLOOR.
THERE I... WILL GR... YOU... SK... LL...

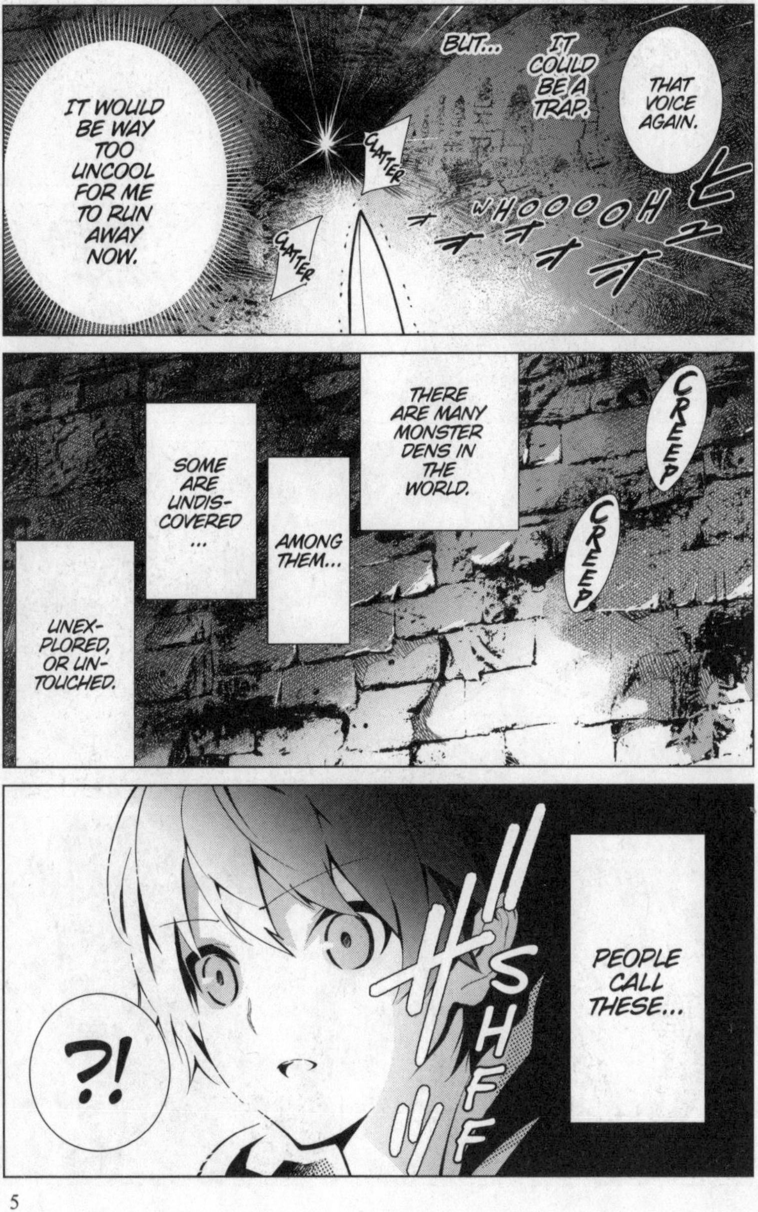
THAT VOICE AGAIN.
IT COULD BE A TRAP.
BUT...
WHOOOOH
CLATTER
CLATTER
IT WOULD BE WAY TOO UNCOOL FOR ME TO RUN AWAY NOW.
CREEP
CREEP
THERE ARE MANY MONSTER DENS IN THE WORLD.
AMONG THEM...
SOME ARE UNDIS-COVERED ...
UNEX-PLORED, OR UN-TOUCHED.
PEOPLE CALL THESE...
SHFF
?!

Chapter 1: The Great Sage Skill

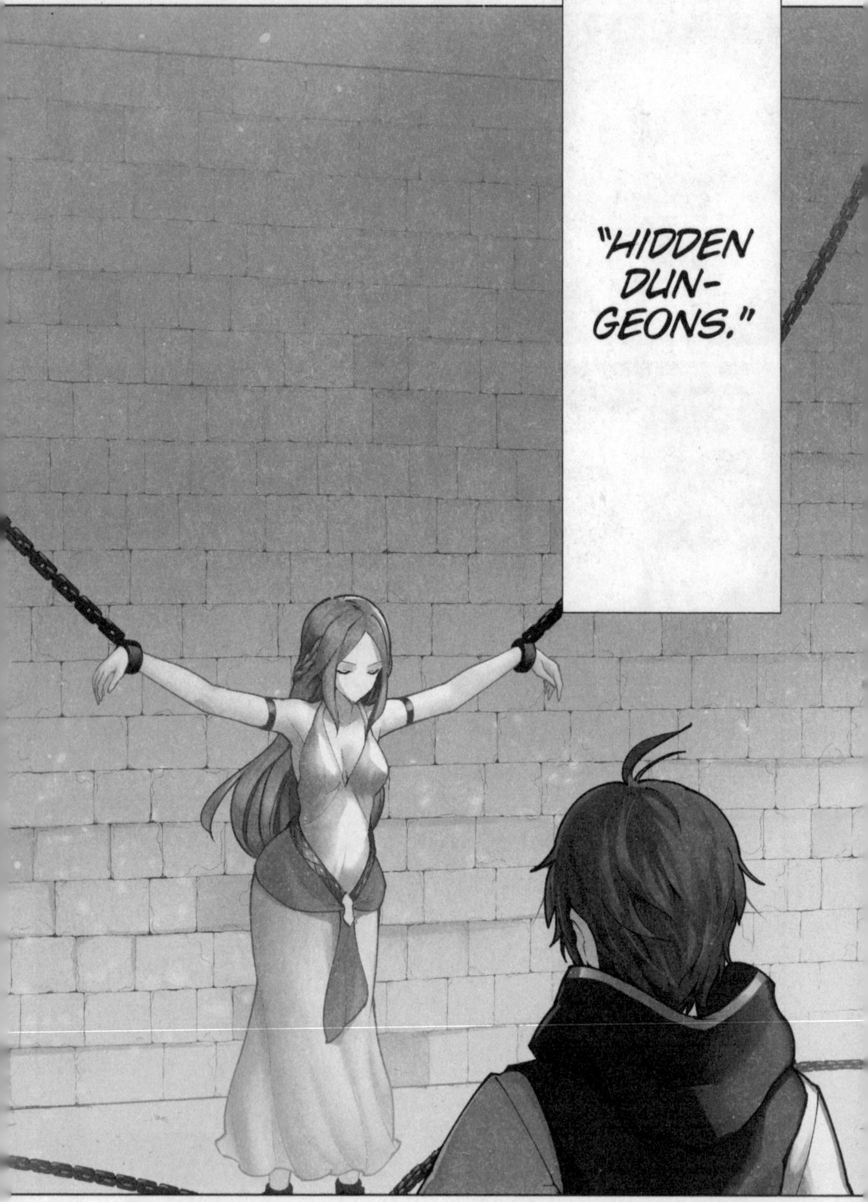
"HIDDEN DUN-GEONS."

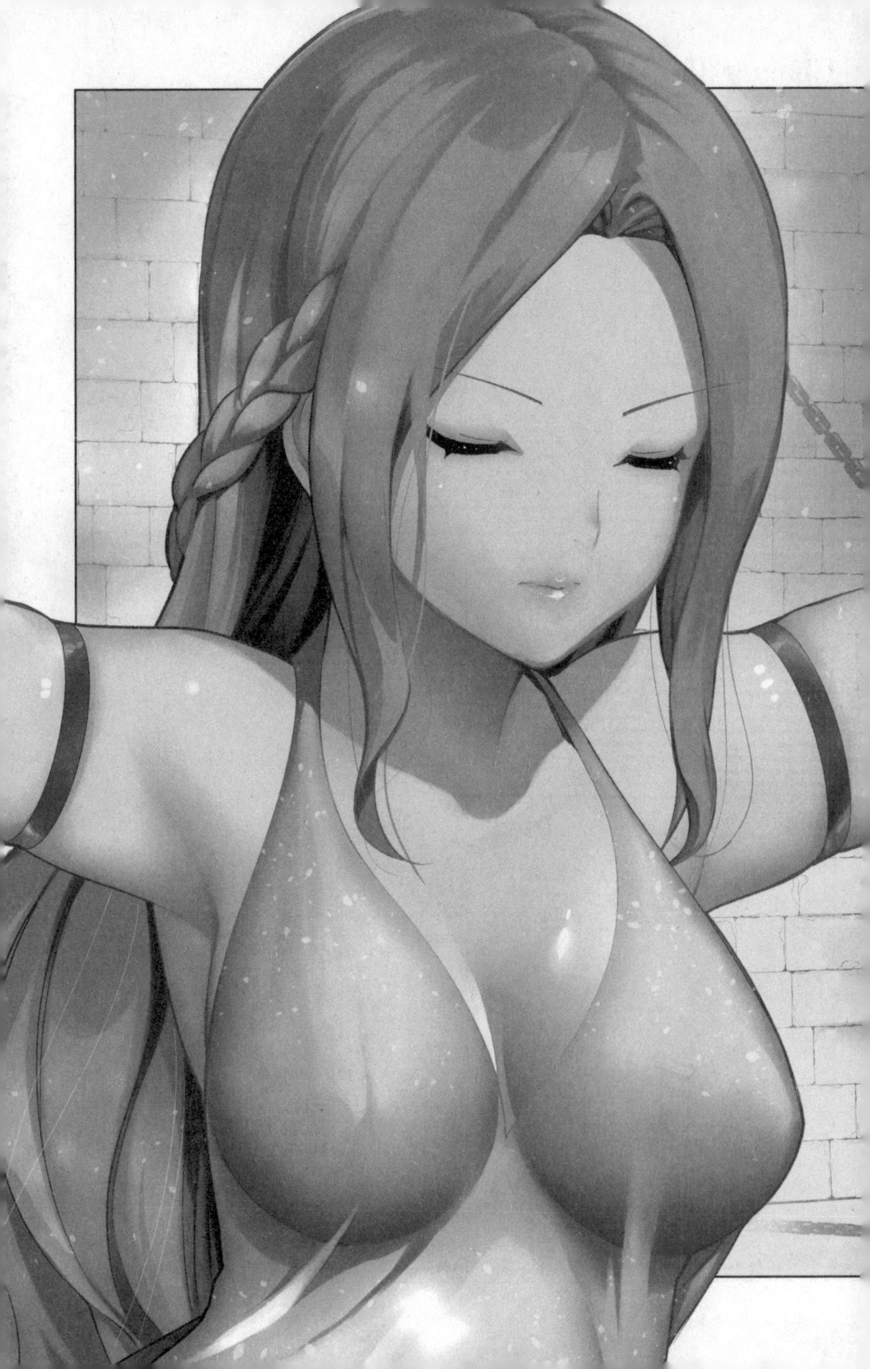

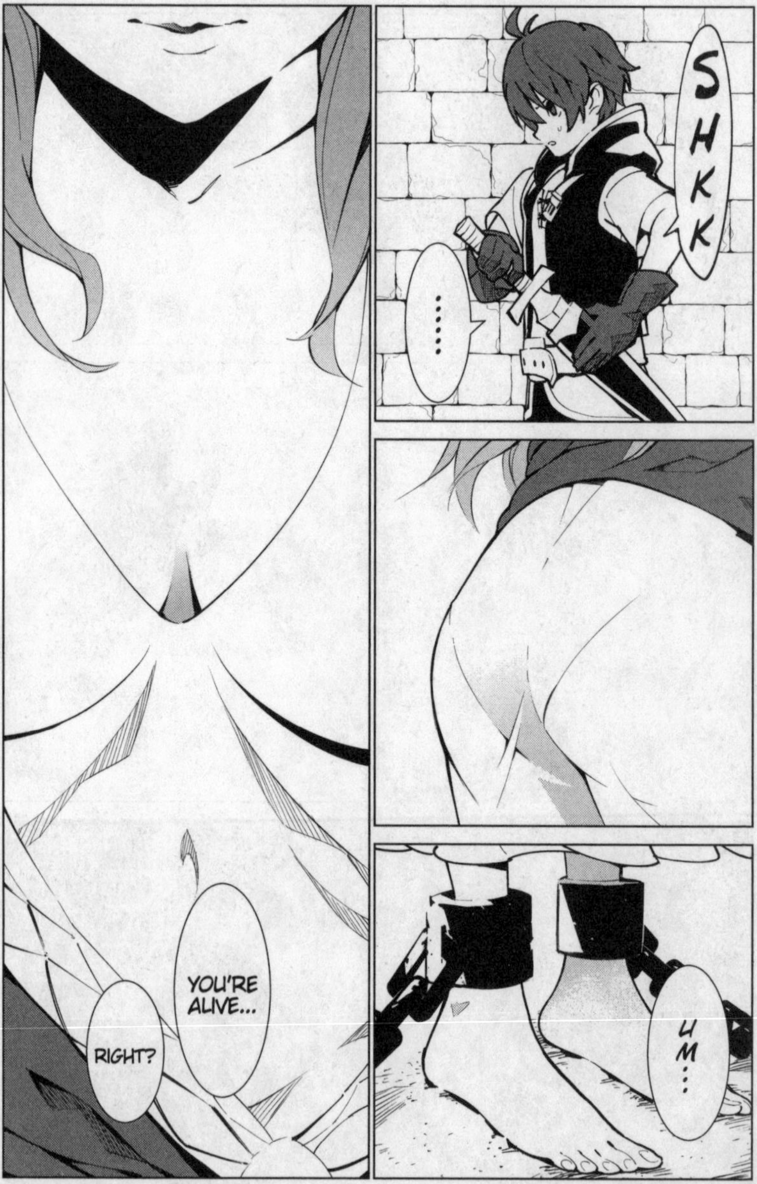
SHKK
......
UM...
YOU'RE ALIVE...
RIGHT?

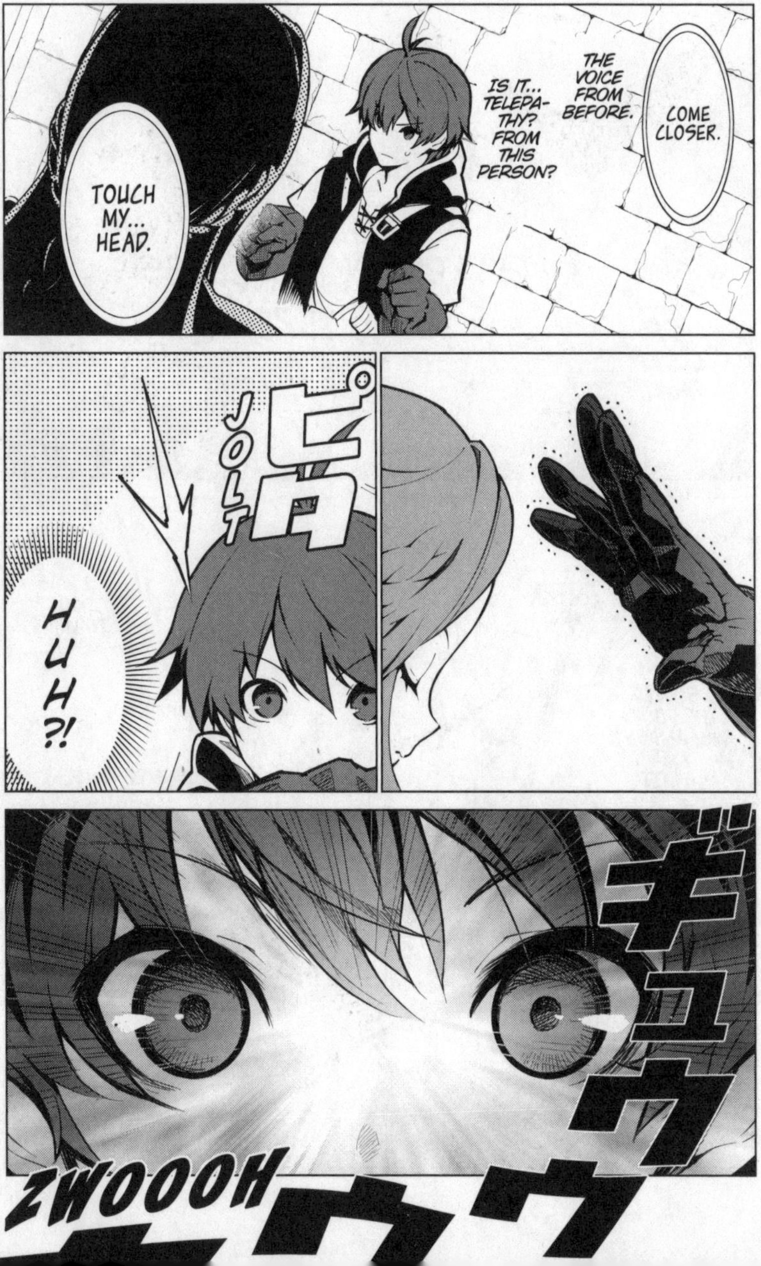
COME CLOSER.
THE VOICE FROM BEFORE.
IS IT... TELEPATHY? FROM THIS PERSON?
TOUCH MY... HEAD.
ピク
JOLT
HUH?!
ZWOOOH

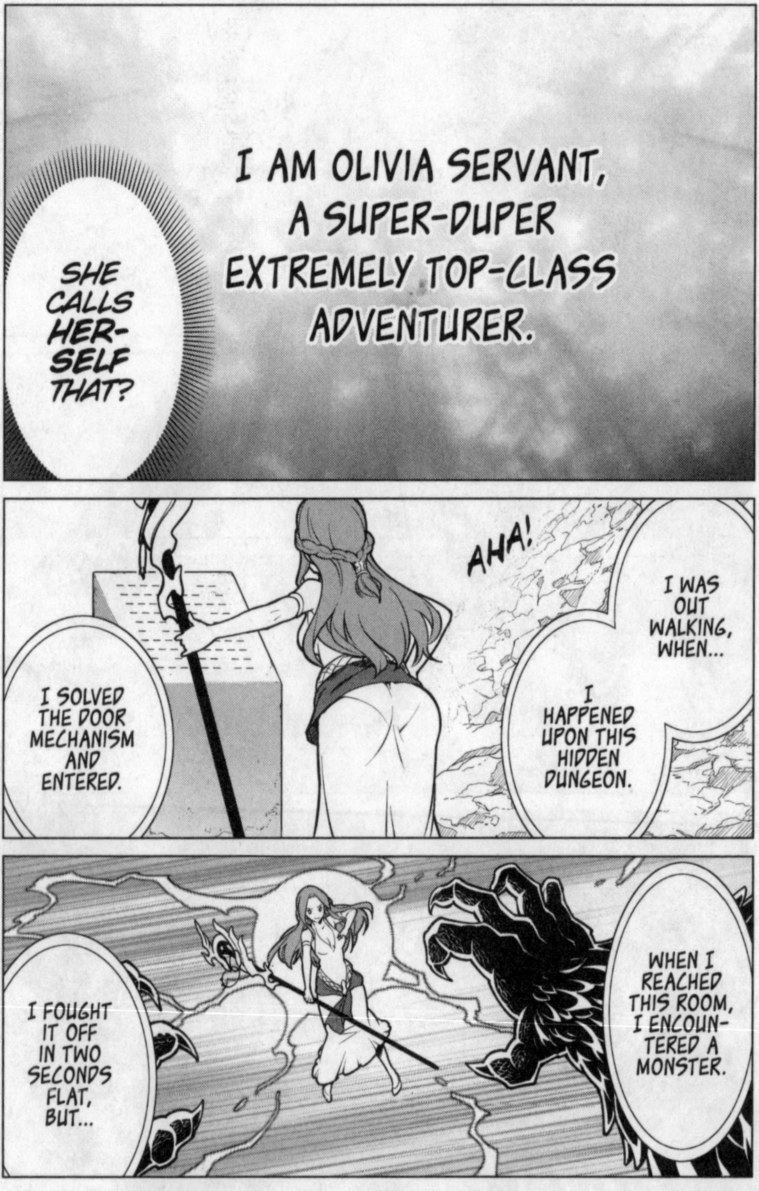
I AM OLIVIA SERVANT, A SUPER-DUPER EXTREMELY TOP-CLASS ADVENTURER.
SHE CALLS HER-SELF THAT?
I WAS OUT WALKING, WHEN...
I HAPPENED UPON THIS HIDDEN DUNGEON.
AHA!
I SOLVED THE DOOR MECHANISM AND ENTERED.
WHEN I REACHED THIS ROOM, I ENCOUN-TERED A MONSTER.
I FOUGHT IT OFF IN TWO SECONDS FLAT, BUT...

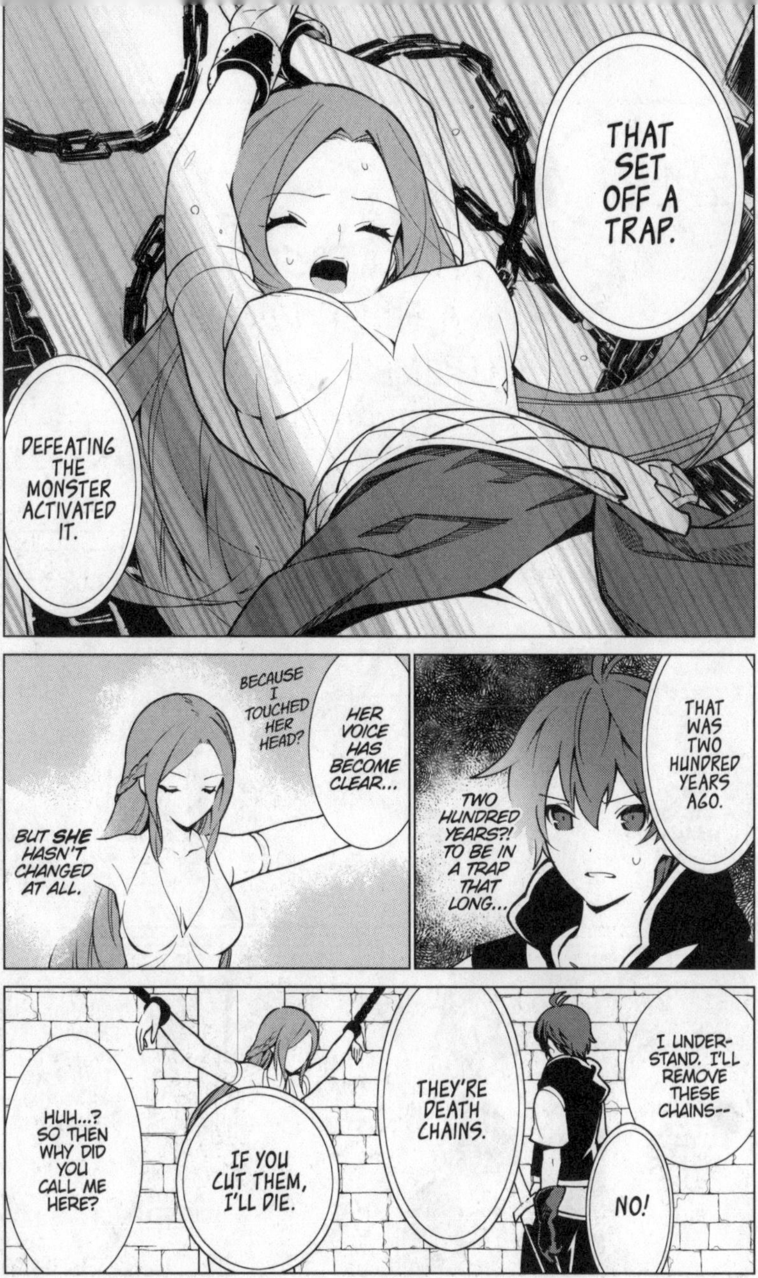
THAT SET OFF A TRAP.
DEFEATING THE MONSTER ACTIVATED IT.
THAT WAS TWO HUNDRED YEARS AGO.
TWO HUNDRED YEARS?! TO BE IN A TRAP THAT LONG...
HER VOICE HAS BECOME CLEAR...
BECAUSE I TOUCHED HER HEAD?
BUT SHE HASN'T CHANGED AT ALL.
I UNDER-STAND. I'LL REMOVE THESE CHAINS--
NO!
THEY'RE DEATH CHAINS.
IF YOU CUT THEM, I'LL DIE.
HUH...? SO THEN WHY DID YOU CALL ME HERE?

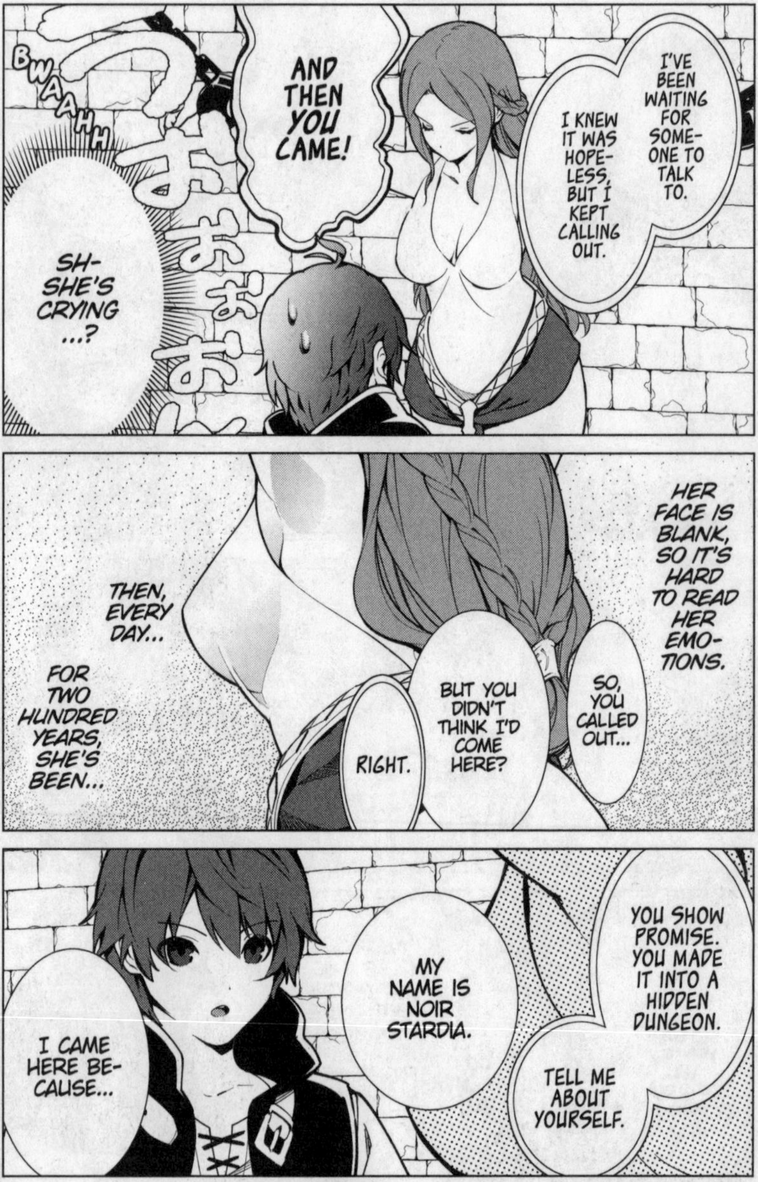
I'VE BEEN WAITING FOR SOME-ONE TO TALK TO.
I KNEW IT WAS HOPE-LESS, BUT I KEPT CALLING OUT.
AND THEN YOU CAME!
BWAAHH
SH-SHE'S CRYING ...?
HER FACE IS BLANK, SO IT'S HARD TO READ HER EMO-TIONS.
SO, YOU CALLED OUT...
BUT YOU DIDN'T THINK I'D COME HERE?
RIGHT.
THEN, EVERY DAY...
FOR TWO HUNDRED YEARS, SHE'S BEEN...
YOU SHOW PROMISE. YOU MADE IT INTO A HIDDEN DUNGEON.
TELL ME ABOUT YOURSELF.
MY NAME IS NOIR STARDIA.
I CAME HERE BE-CAUSE...

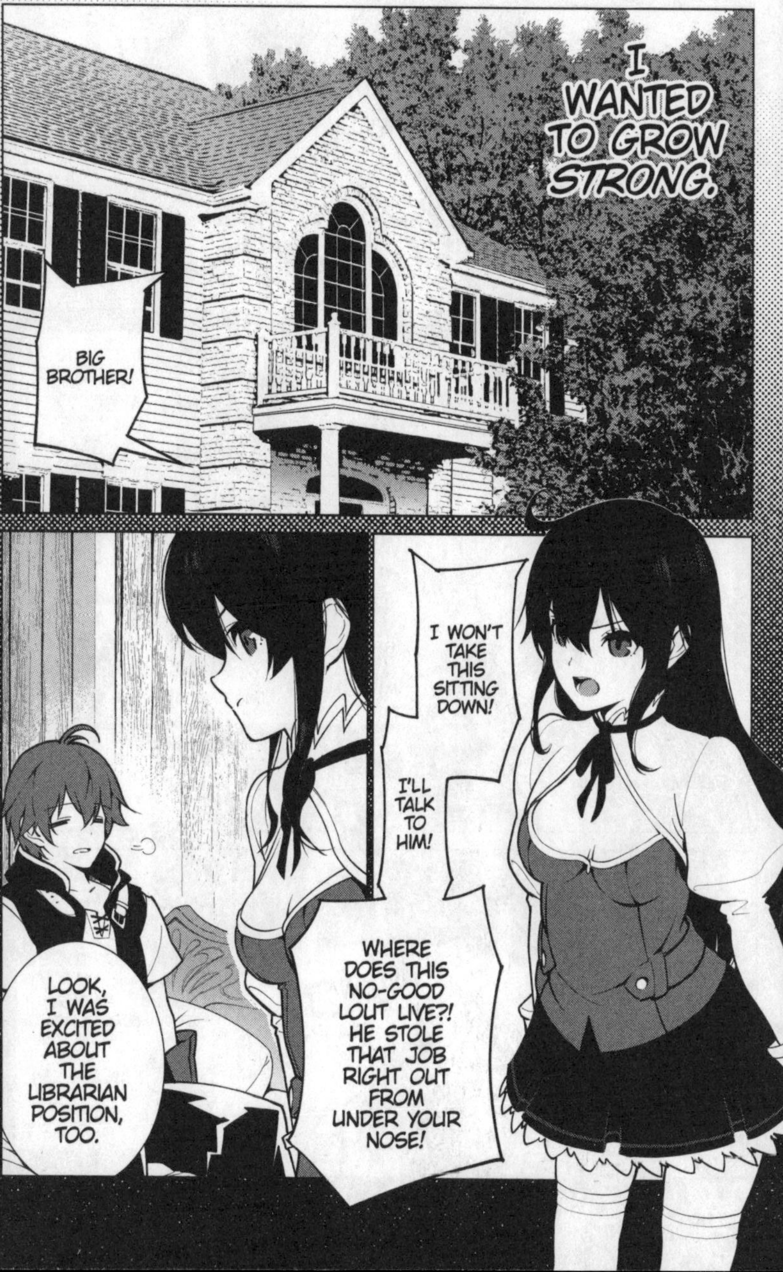
I WANTED TO GROW STRONG.
BIG BROTHER!
I WON'T TAKE THIS SITTING DOWN!
I'LL TALK TO HIM!
WHERE DOES THIS NO-GOOD LOUT LIVE?! HE STOLE THAT JOB RIGHT OUT FROM UNDER YOUR NOSE!
LOOK, I WAS EXCITED ABOUT THE LIBRARIAN POSITION, TOO.

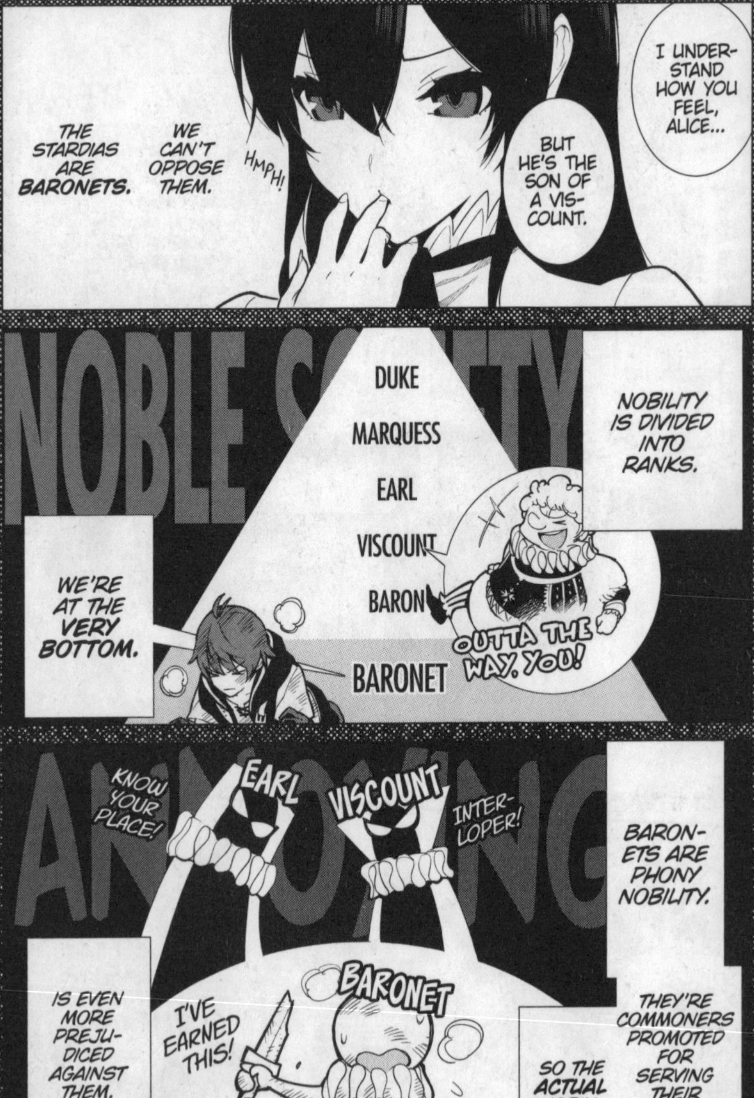
I UNDER-STAND HOW YOU FEEL, ALICE...
BUT HE'S THE SON OF A VIS-COUNT.
HMPH!
WE CAN'T OPPOSE THEM.
THE STARDIAS ARE BARONETS.
NOBILITY IS DIVIDED INTO RANKS.
DUKE
MARQUESS
EARL
VISCOUNT
BARON
BARONET
OUTTA THE WAY, YOU!
WE'RE AT THE VERY BOTTOM.
BARON-ETS ARE PHONY NOBILITY.
THEY'RE COMMONERS PROMOTED FOR SERVING THEIR COUNTRY.
SO THE ACTUAL NOBILI-TY...
VISCOUNT
INTER-LOPER!
EARL
KNOW YOUR PLACE!
BARONET
I'VE EARNED THIS!
IS EVEN MORE PREJU-DICED AGAINST THEM.

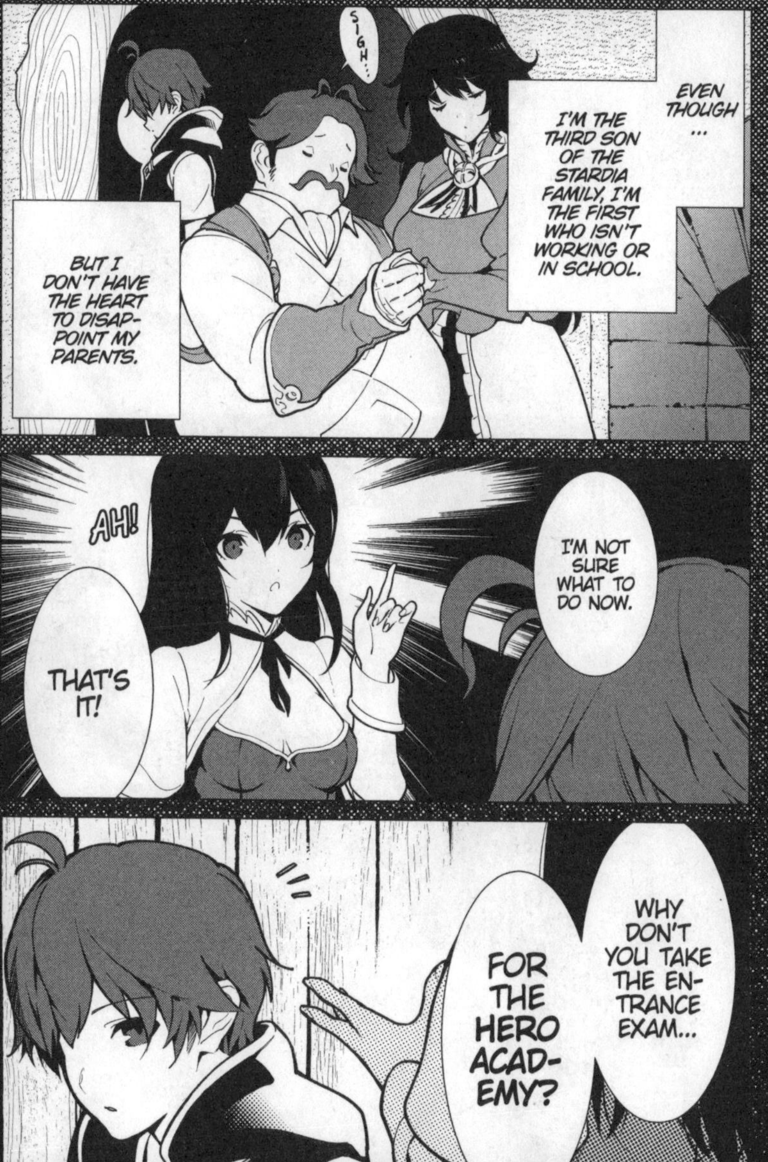
EVEN THOUGH...
I'M THE THIRD SON OF THE STARDIA FAMILY, I'M THE FIRST WHO ISN'T WORKING OR IN SCHOOL.
SIGH...
BUT I DON'T HAVE THE HEART TO DISAPPOINT MY PARENTS.
I'M NOT SURE WHAT TO DO NOW.
AH!
THAT'S IT!
WHY DON'T YOU TAKE THE ENTRANCE EXAM...
FOR THE HERO ACADEMY?

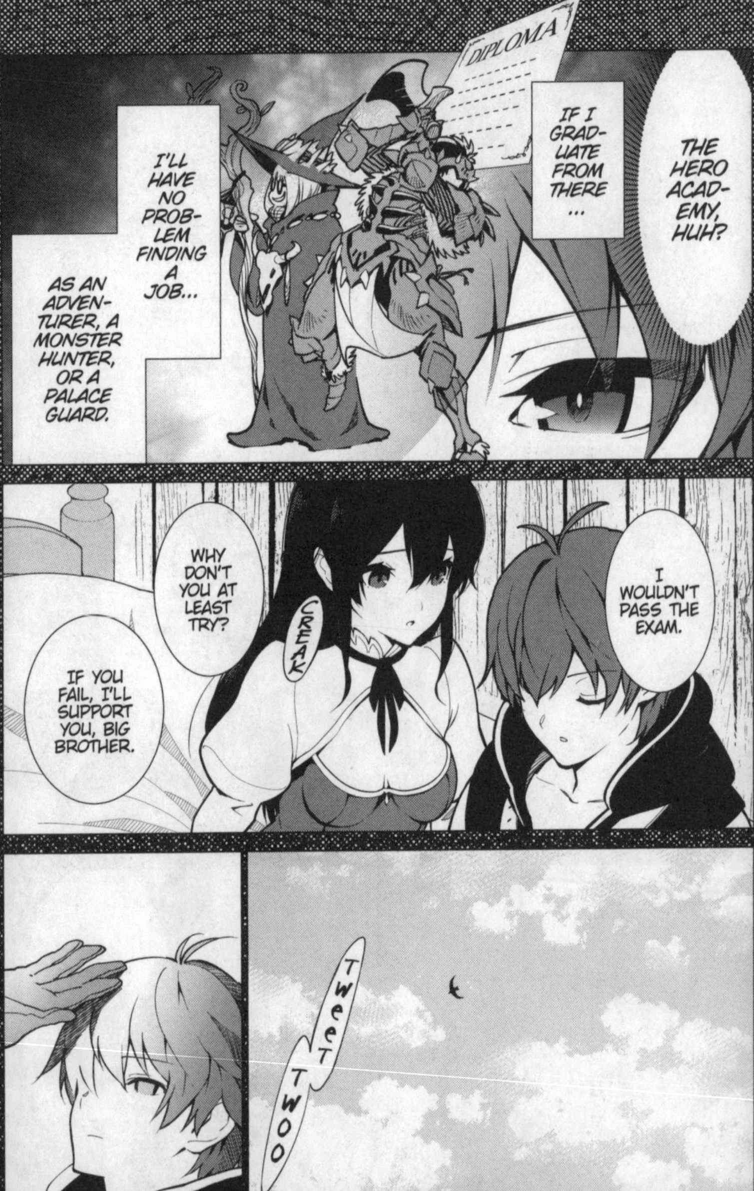
DIPLOMA
THE HERO ACADEMY, HUH?
IF I GRADUATE FROM THERE ...
I'LL HAVE NO PROBLEM FINDING A JOB...
AS AN ADVENTURER, A MONSTER HUNTER, OR A PALACE GUARD.
I WOULDN'T PASS THE EXAM.
CREAK
WHY DON'T YOU AT LEAST TRY?
IF YOU FAIL, I'LL SUPPORT YOU, BIG BROTHER.
TWEET TWOO

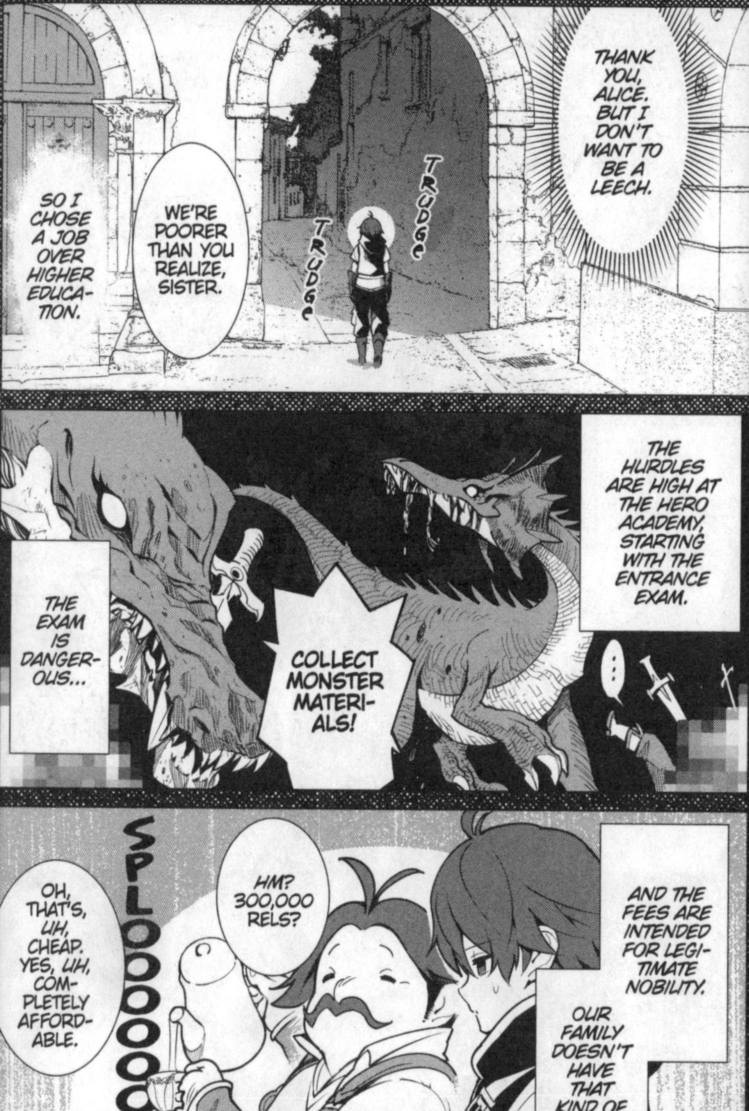
THANK YOU, ALICE. BUT I DON'T WANT TO BE A LEECH.
TRUDGE
TRUDGE
WE'RE POORER THAN YOU REALIZE, SISTER.
SO I CHOSE A JOB OVER HIGHER EDUCATION.
THE HURDLES ARE HIGH AT THE HERO ACADEMY, STARTING WITH THE ENTRANCE EXAM.
...
COLLECT MONSTER MATERIALS!
THE EXAM IS DANGEROUS...
AND THE FEES ARE INTENDED FOR LEGITIMATE NOBILITY.
OUR FAMILY DOESN'T HAVE THAT KIND OF MONEY.
HM? 300,000 RELS?
OH, THAT'S, UH, CHEAP. YES, UH, COMPLETELY AFFORDABLE.
SPLOOOOOOOSH

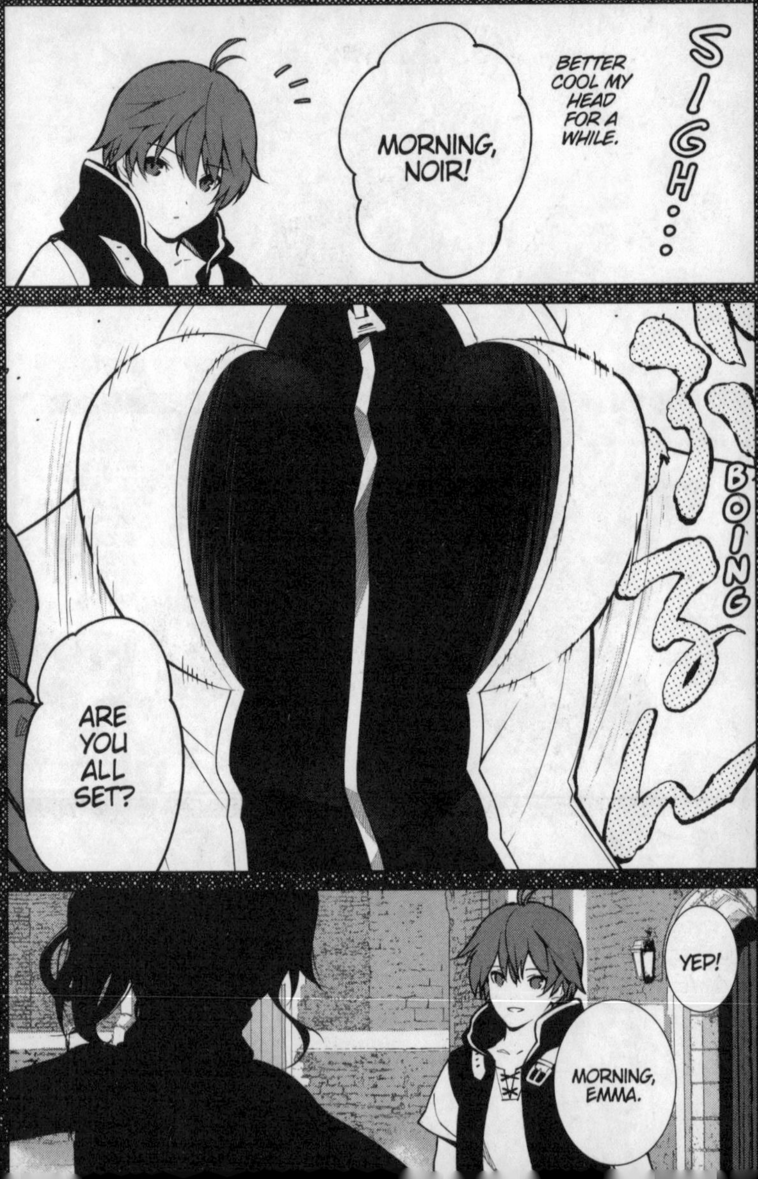
SIGH...
BETTER COOL MY HEAD FOR A WHILE.
MORNING, NOIR!
BOING
ARE YOU ALL SET?
YEP!
MORNING, EMMA.

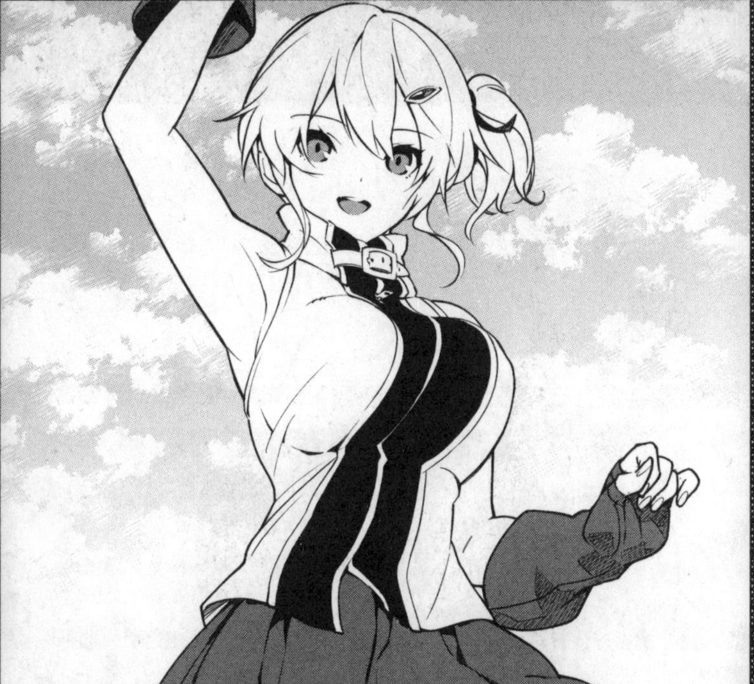

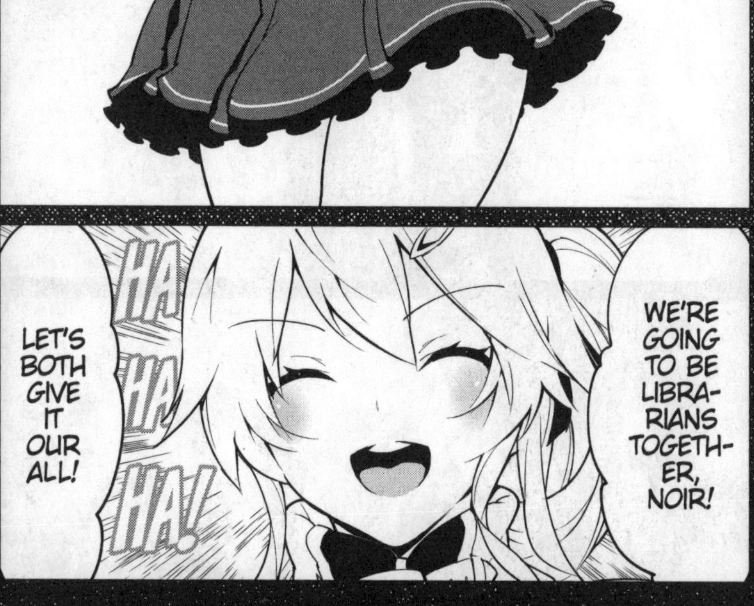
WE'RE GOING TO BE LIBRARIANS TOGETHER, NOIR!
HA HA HA!
LET'S BOTH GIVE IT OUR ALL!

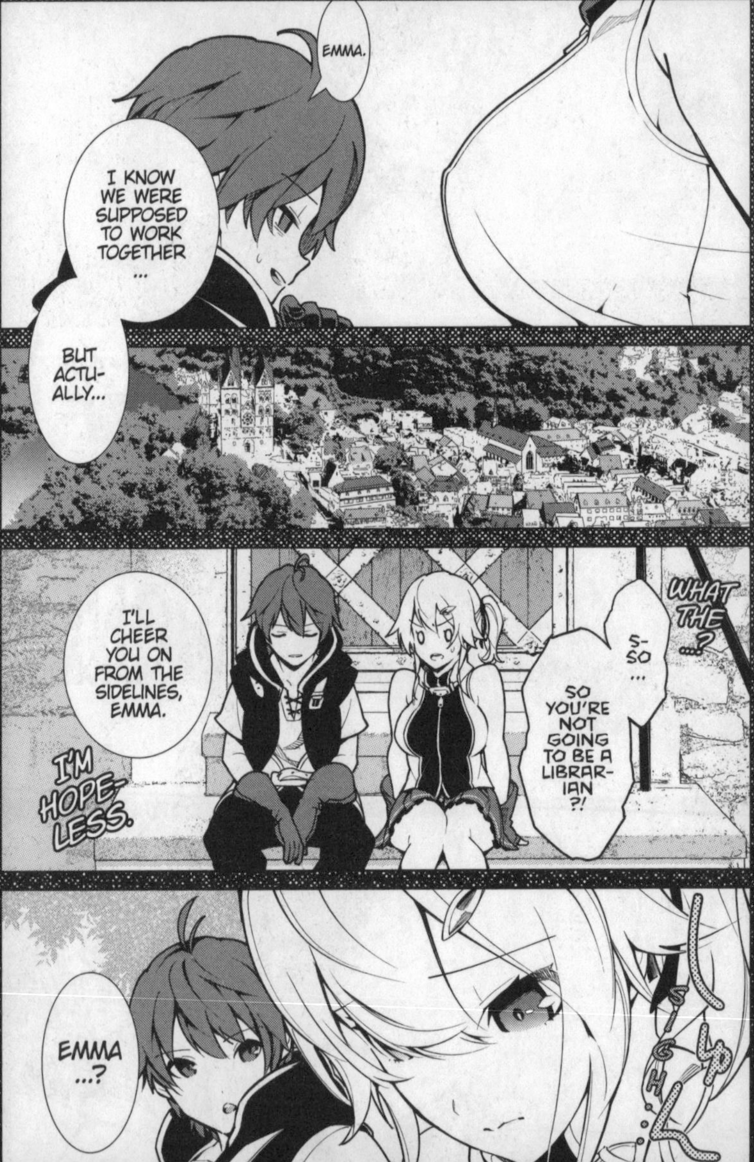
EMMA.
I KNOW WE WERE SUPPOSED TO WORK TOGETHER ...
BUT ACTU-ALLY...
WHAT THE ...?
S-SO ...
SO YOU'RE NOT GOING TO BE A LIBRAR-IAN?!
I'LL CHEER YOU ON FROM THE SIDELINES, EMMA.
I'M HOPE-LESS.
EMMA ...?

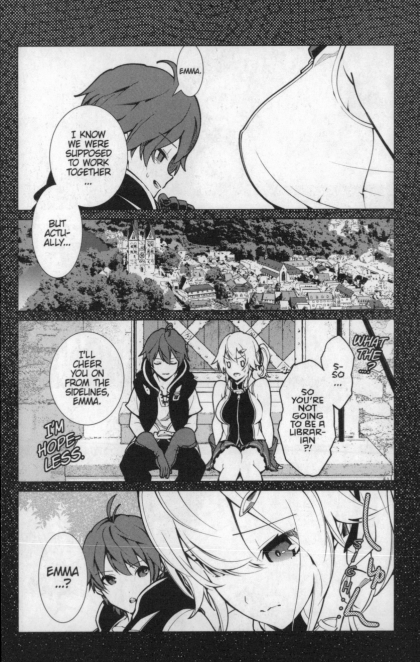

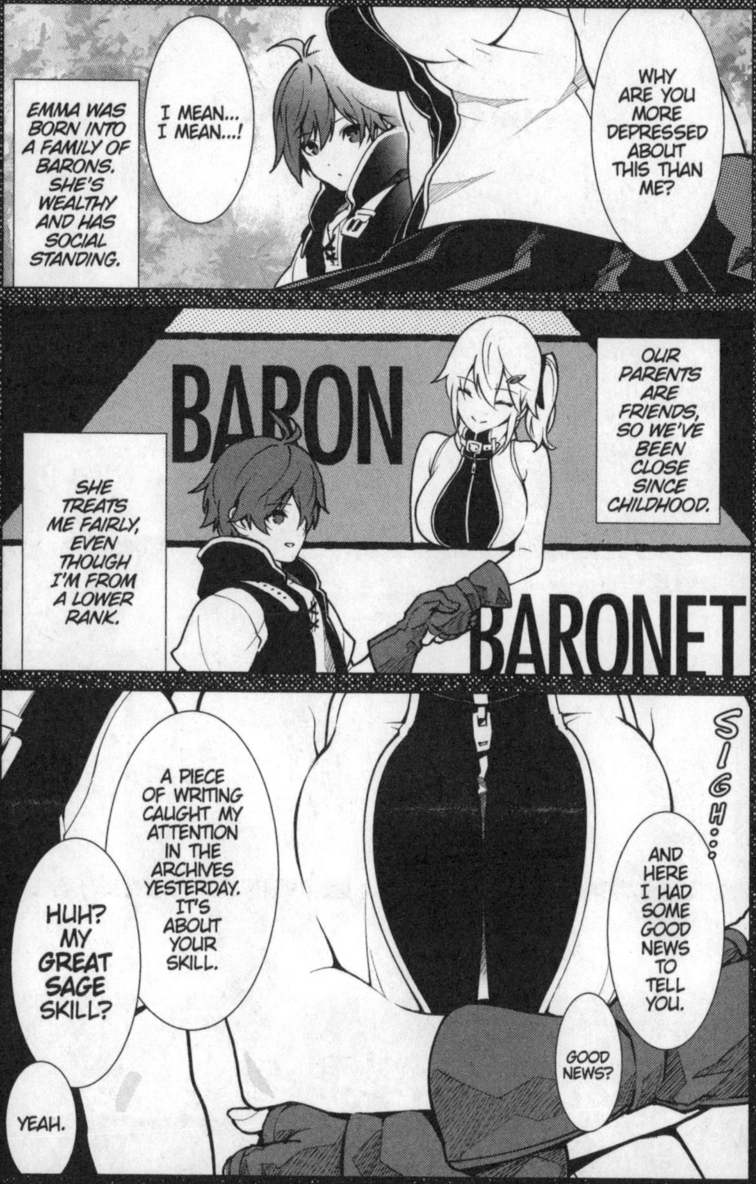
WHY ARE YOU MORE DEPRESSED ABOUT THIS THAN ME?
I MEAN... I MEAN...!
EMMA WAS BORN INTO A FAMILY OF BARONS. SHE'S WEALTHY AND HAS SOCIAL STANDING.
OUR PARENTS ARE FRIENDS, SO WE'VE BEEN CLOSE SINCE CHILDHOOD.
BARON
SHE TREATS ME FAIRLY, EVEN THOUGH I'M FROM A LOWER RANK.
BARONET
SIGH...
AND HERE I HAD SOME GOOD NEWS TO TELL YOU.
GOOD NEWS?
A PIECE OF WRITING CAUGHT MY ATTENTION IN THE ARCHIVES YESTERDAY. IT'S ABOUT YOUR SKILL.
HUH? MY GREAT SAGE SKILL?
YEAH.

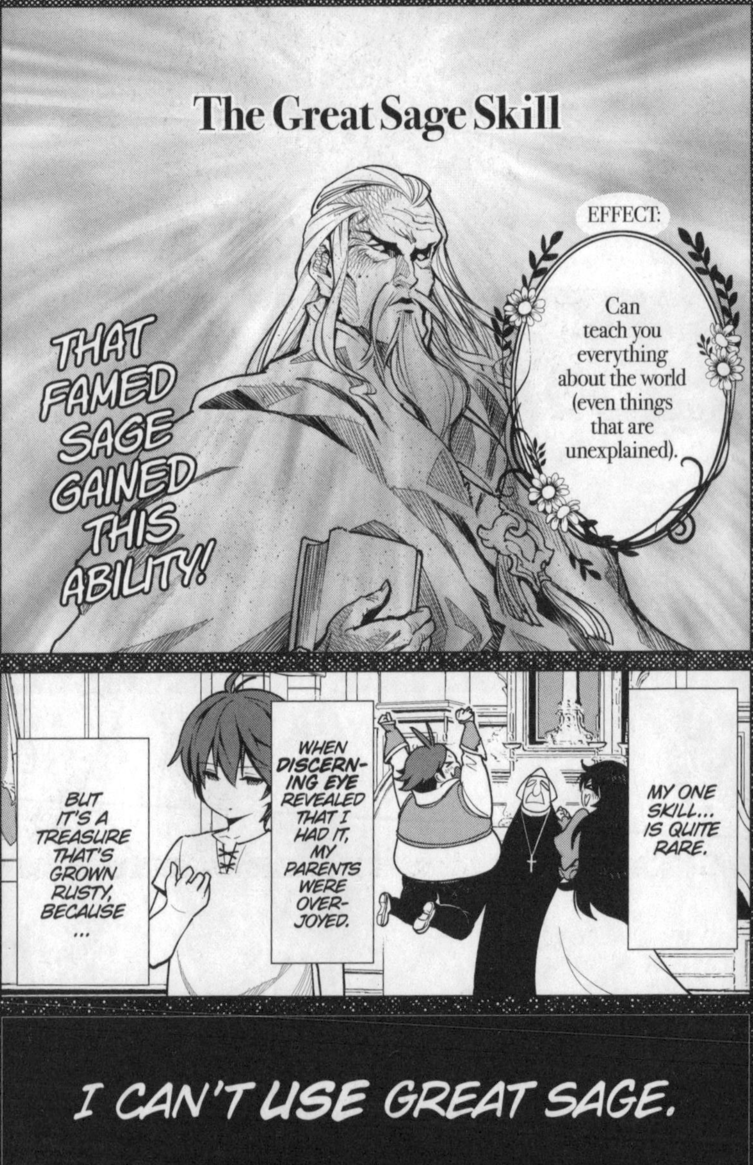
The Great Sage Skill
EFFECT:
Can teach you everything about the world (even things that are unexplained).
THAT FAMED SAGE GAINED THIS ABILITY!
MY ONE SKILL... IS QUITE RARE.
WHEN DISCERNING EYE REVEALED THAT I HAD IT, MY PARENTS WERE OVERJOYED.
BUT IT'S A TREASURE THAT'S GROWN RUSTY, BECAUSE...
I CAN'T USE GREAT SAGE.

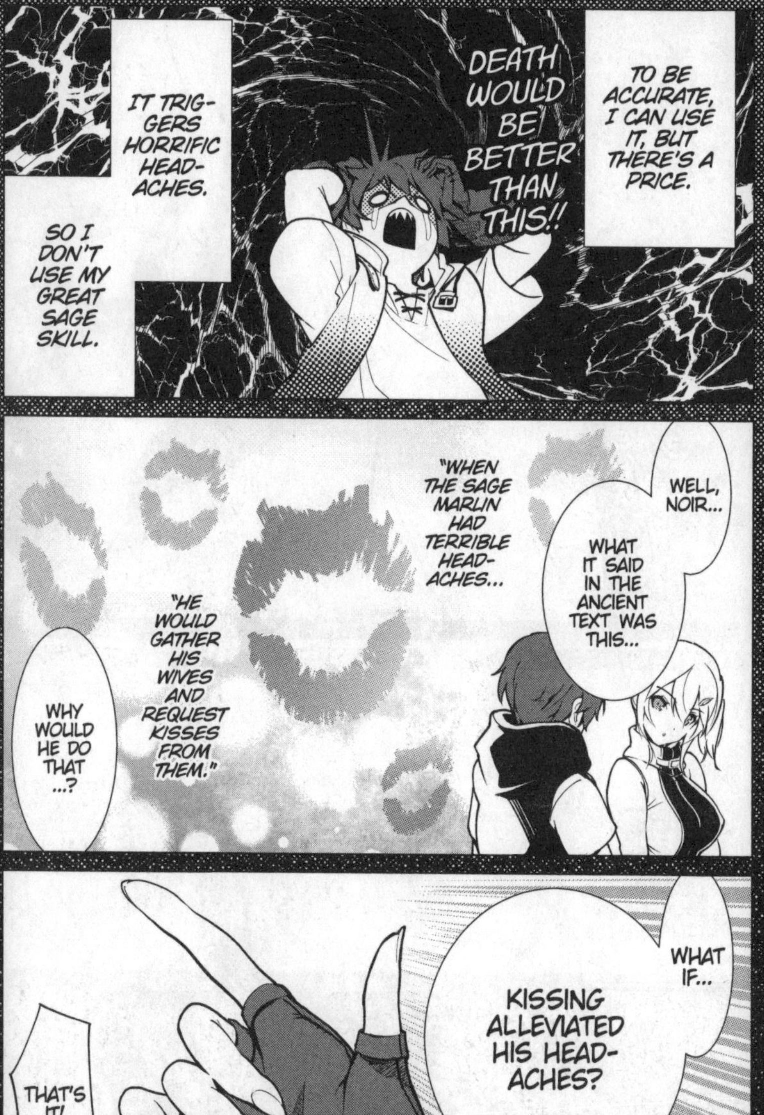
TO BE ACCURATE, I CAN USE IT, BUT THERE'S A PRICE.
DEATH WOULD BE BETTER THAN THIS!!
IT TRIGGERS HORRIFIC HEADACHES.
SO I DON'T USE MY GREAT SAGE SKILL.
WELL, NOIR...
WHAT IT SAID IN THE ANCIENT TEXT WAS THIS...
"WHEN THE SAGE MARLIN HAD TERRIBLE HEADACHES...
"HE WOULD GATHER HIS WIVES AND REQUEST KISSES FROM THEM."
WHY WOULD HE DO THAT ...?
WHAT IF...
KISSING ALLEVIATED HIS HEADACHES?
THAT'S IT!

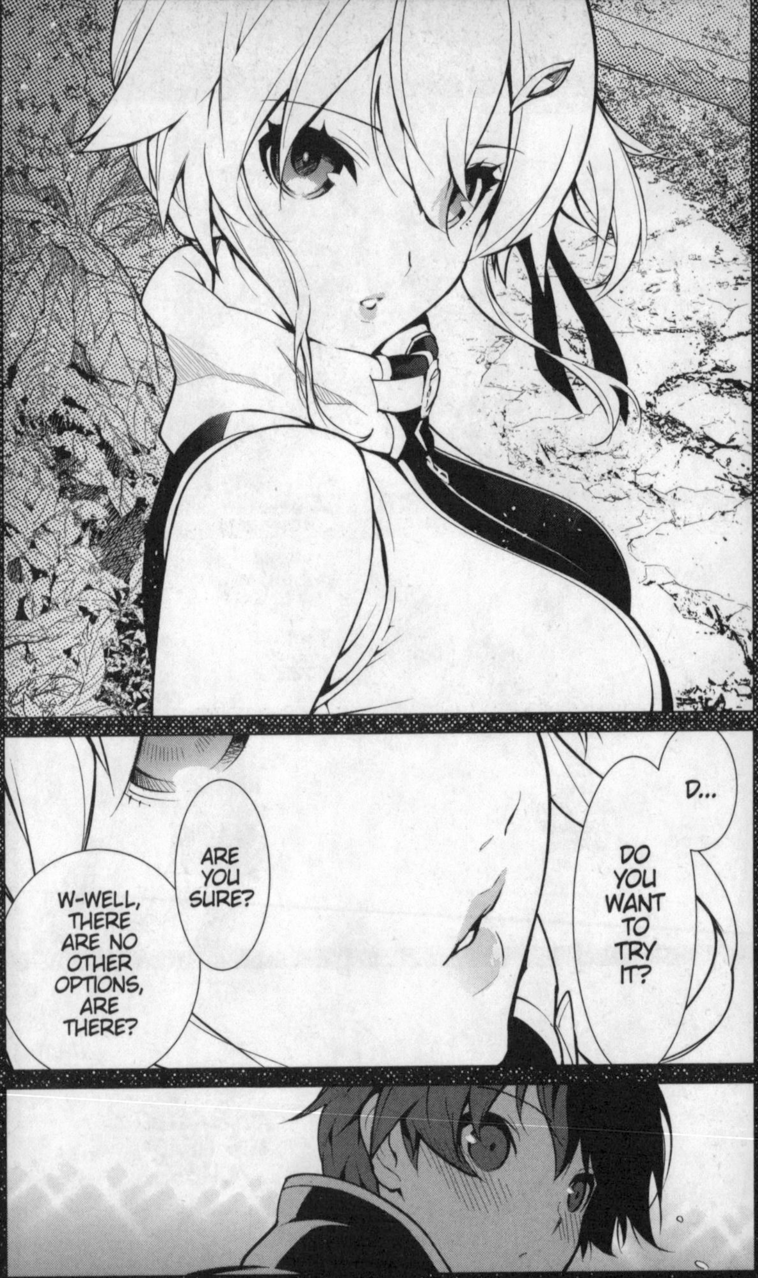
D...
DO YOU WANT TO TRY IT?
ARE YOU SURE?
W-WELL, THERE ARE NO OTHER OPTIONS, ARE THERE?

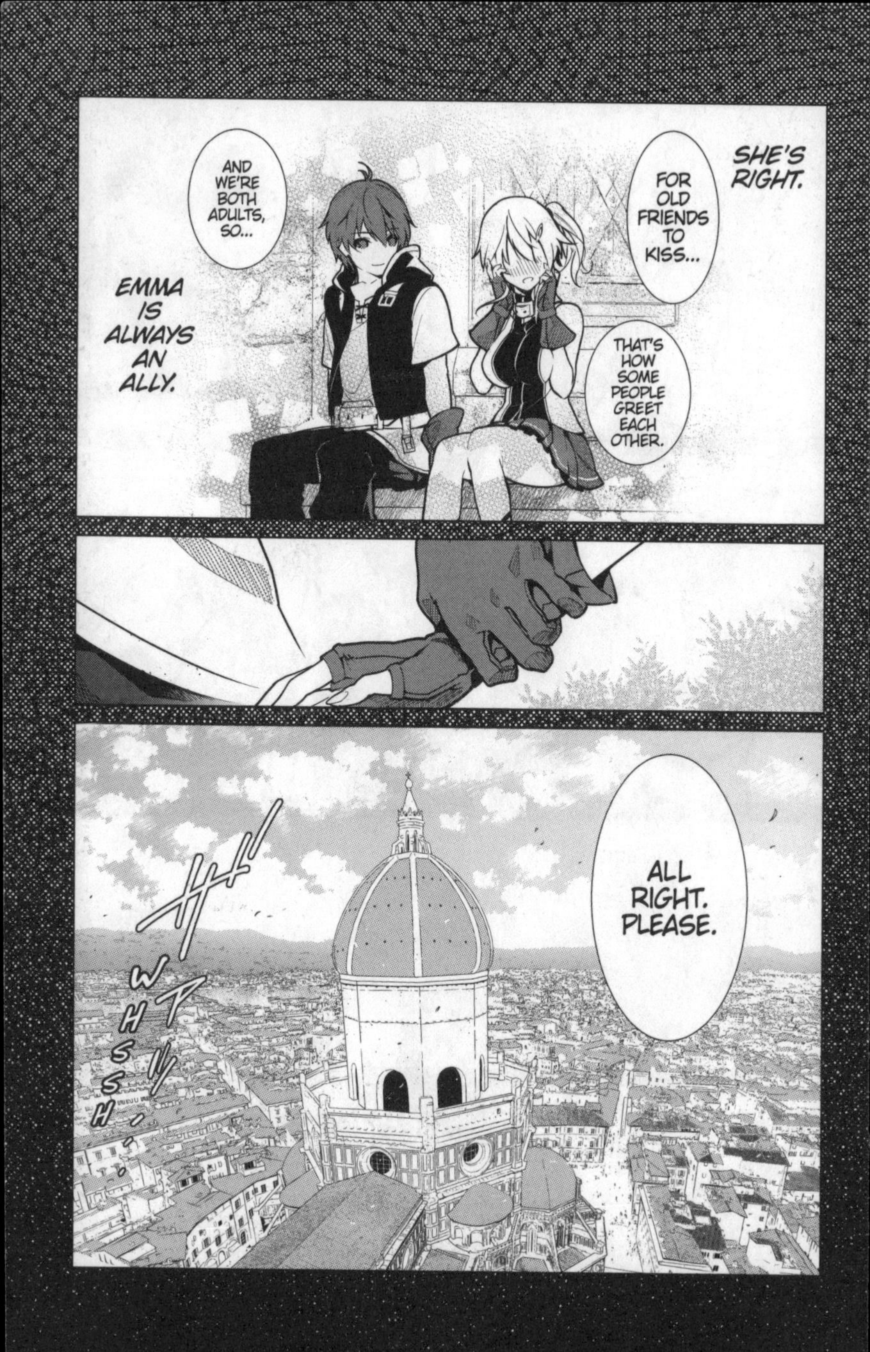
SHE'S RIGHT.
FOR OLD FRIENDS TO KISS...
THAT'S HOW SOME PEOPLE GREET EACH OTHER.
AND WE'RE BOTH ADULTS, SO...
EMMA IS ALWAYS AN ALLY.
ALL RIGHT. PLEASE.
WHSSH...

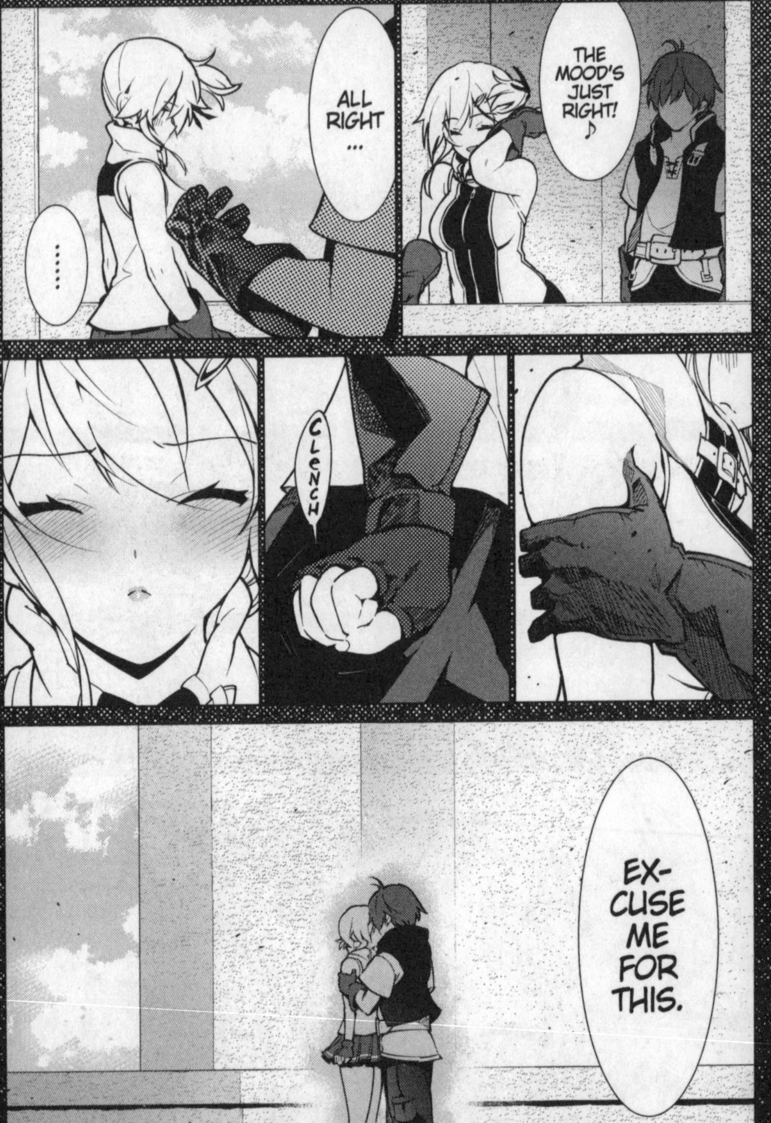
THE MOOD'S JUST RIGHT! ♪
ALL RIGHT ...
......
CLENCH
EX-CUSE ME FOR THIS.

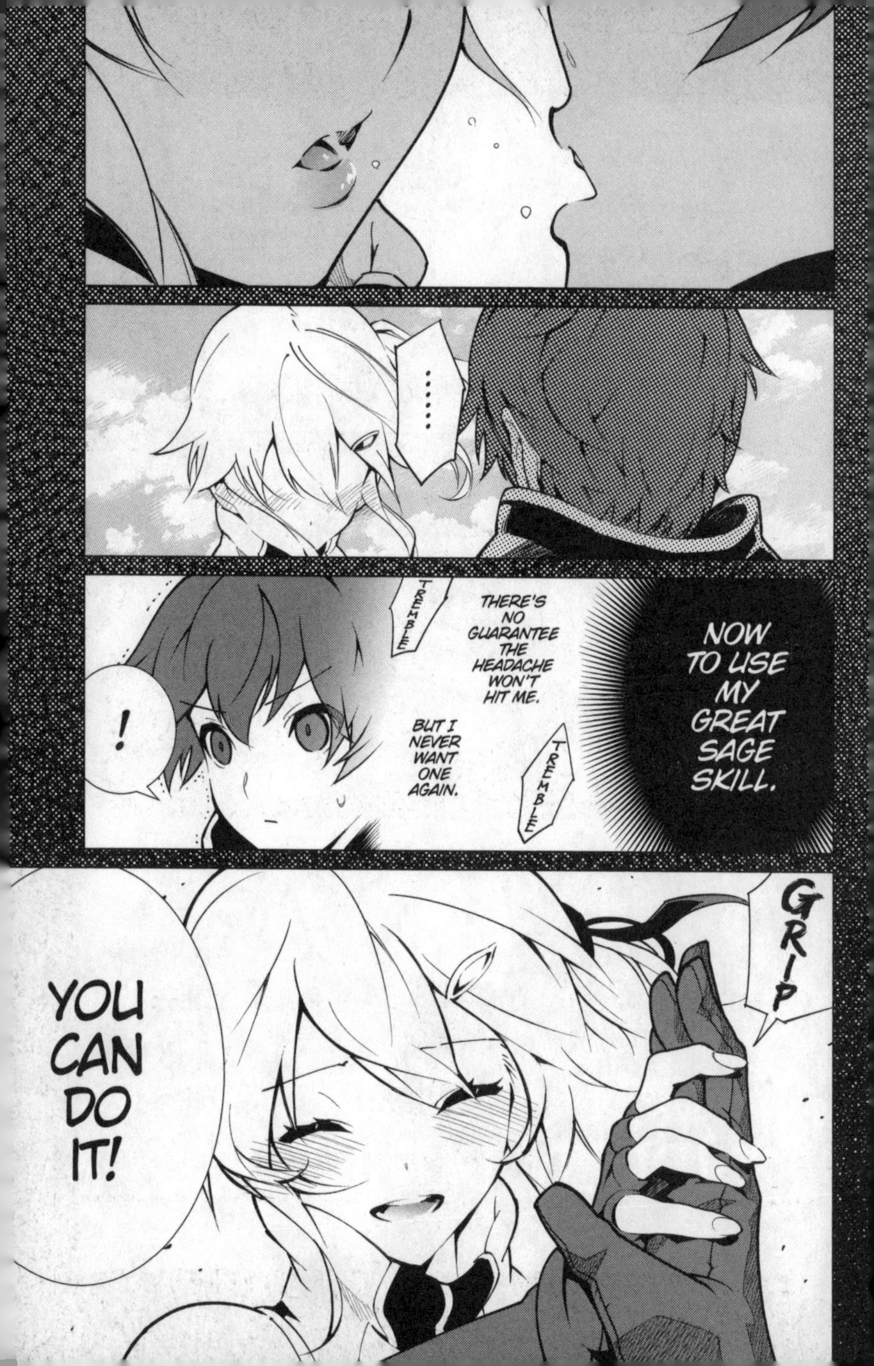
......
NOW TO USE MY GREAT SAGE SKILL.
TREMBLE
THERE'S NO GUARANTEE THE HEADACHE WON'T HIT ME.
BUT I NEVER WANT ONE AGAIN.
TREMBLE
!
GRIP
YOU CAN DO IT!

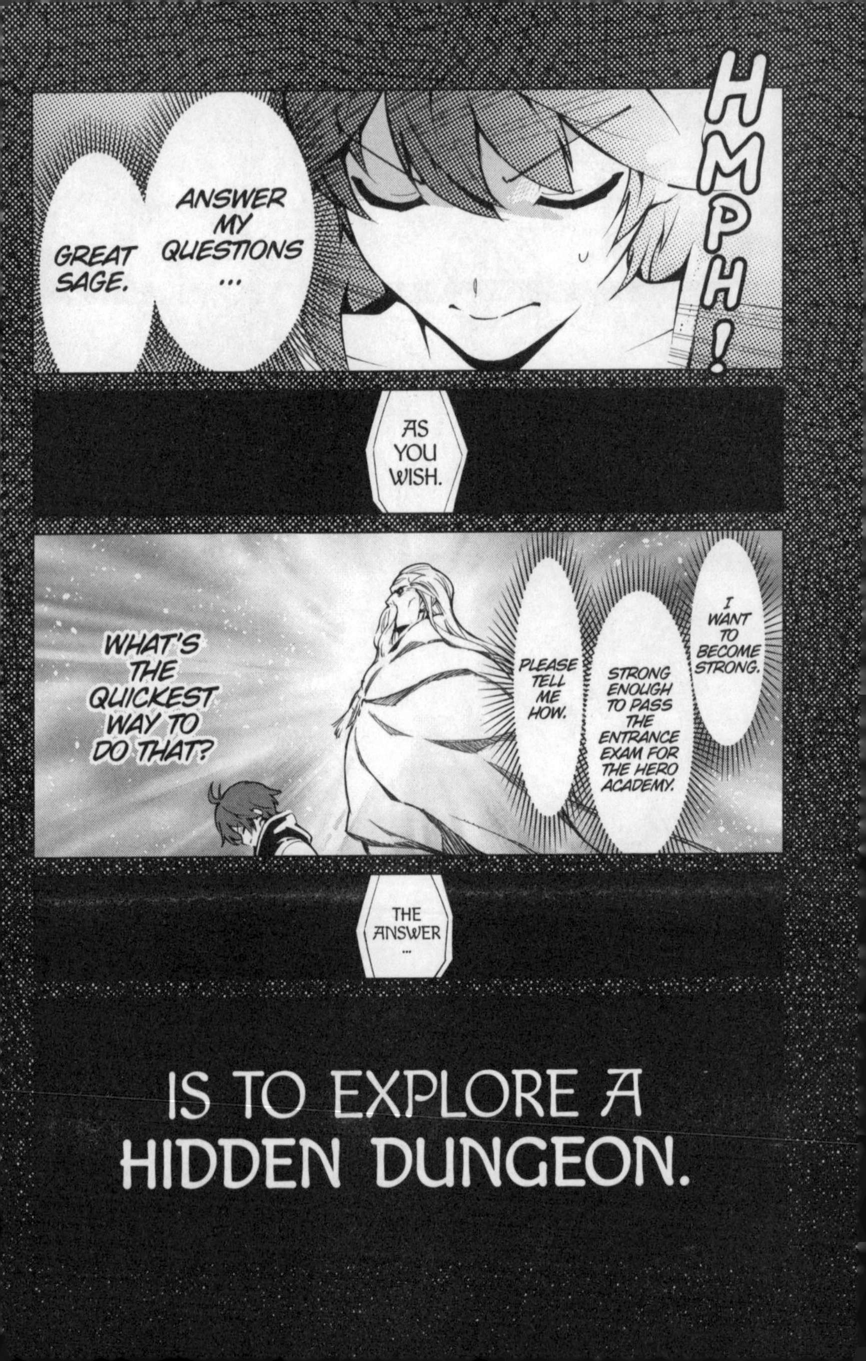
HMPH!
ANSWER MY QUESTIONS ...
GREAT SAGE.
AS YOU WISH.
I WANT TO BECOME STRONG.
STRONG ENOUGH TO PASS THE ENTRANCE EXAM FOR THE HERO ACADEMY.
PLEASE TELL ME HOW.
WHAT'S THE QUICKEST WAY TO DO THAT?
THE ANSWER ...
IS TO EXPLORE A HIDDEN DUNGEON.

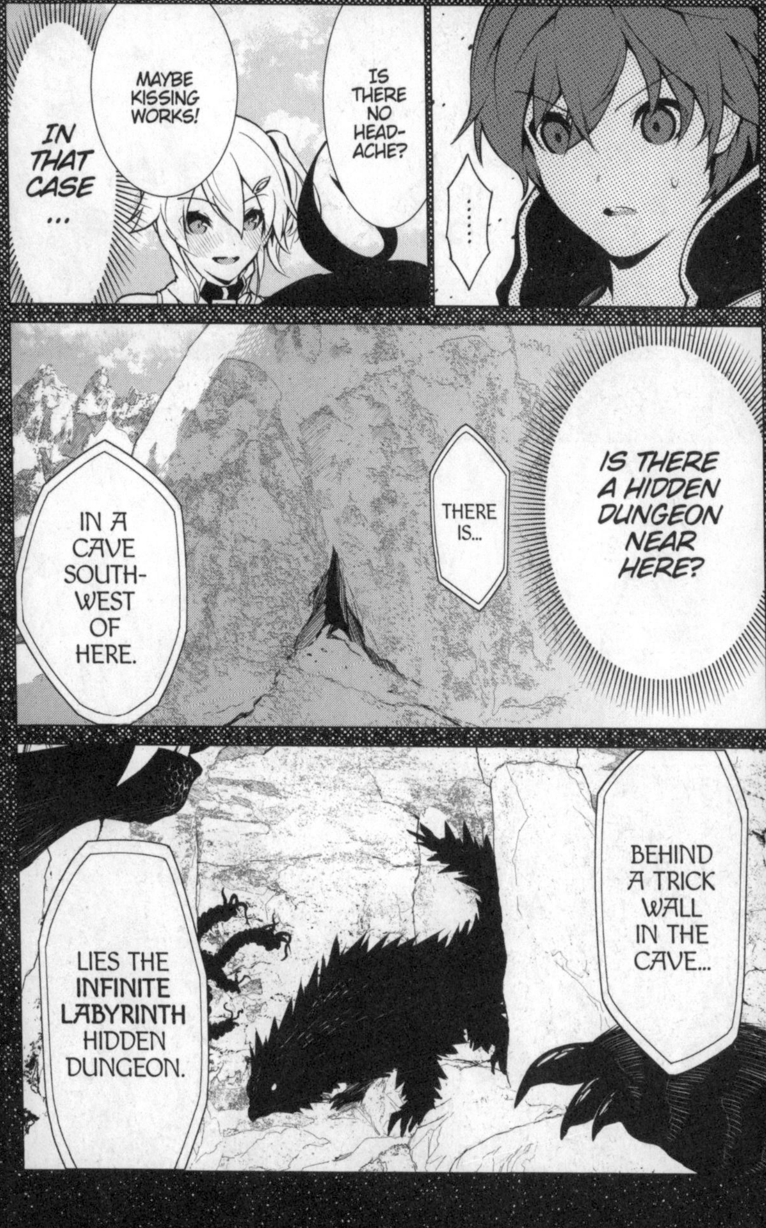
……
IS THERE NO HEAD-ACHE?
MAYBE KISSING WORKS!
IN THAT CASE …
IS THERE A HIDDEN DUNGEON NEAR HERE?
THERE IS...
IN A CAVE SOUTH-WEST OF HERE.
BEHIND A TRICK WALL IN THE CAVE...
LIES THE **INFINITE LABYRINTH** HIDDEN DUNGEON.

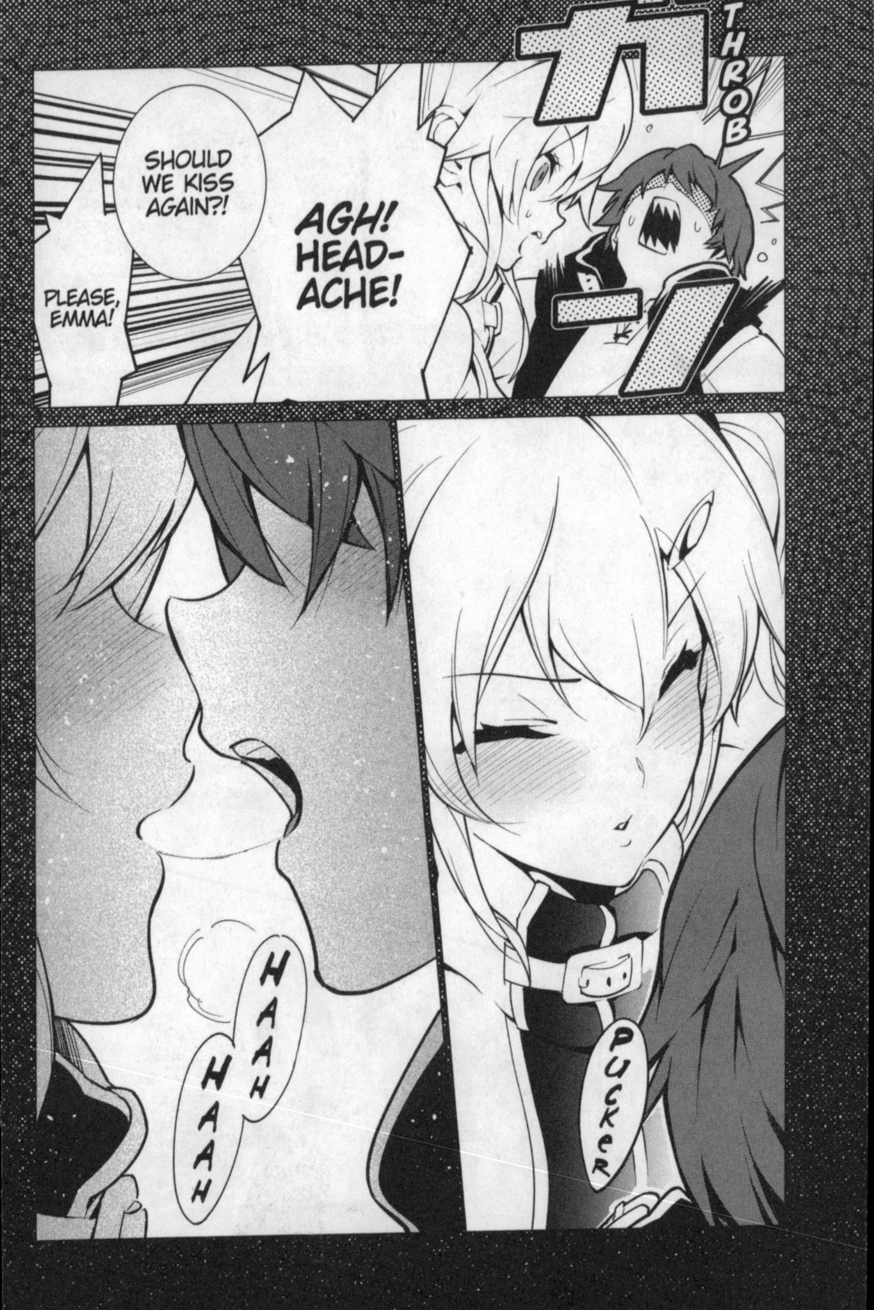
THROB
AGH! HEAD-ACHE!
SHOULD WE KISS AGAIN?!
PLEASE, EMMA!
PUCKER
HAAH HAAH

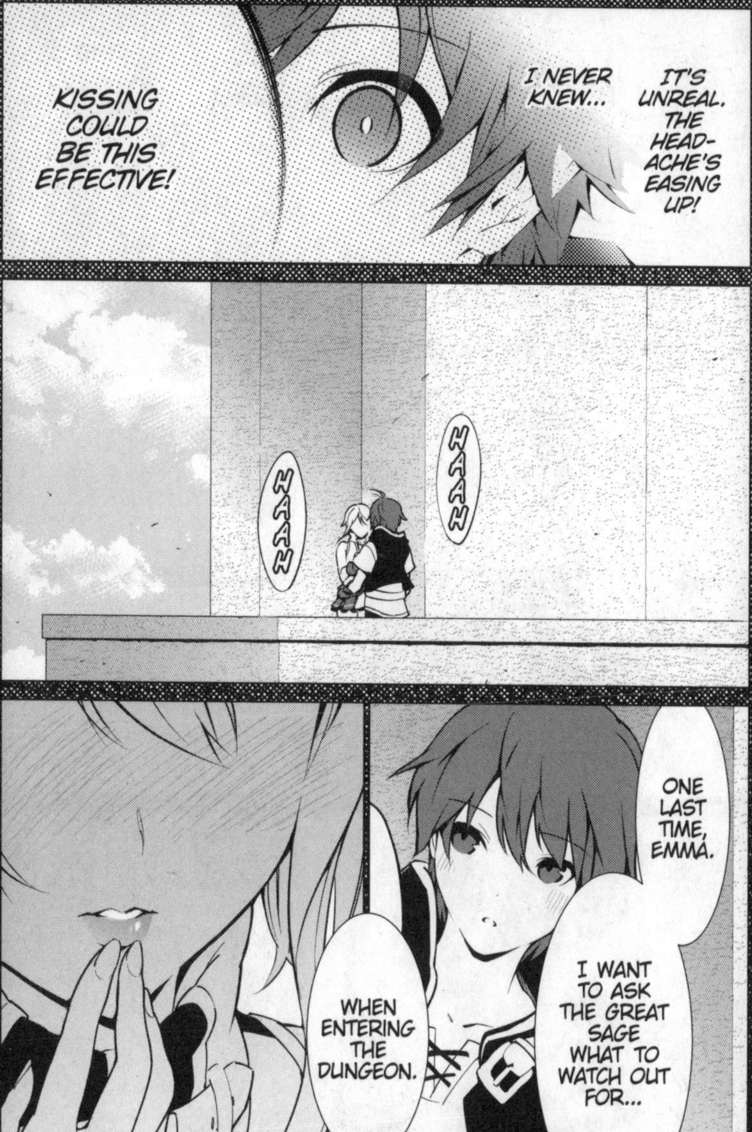
IT'S UNREAL. THE HEAD-ACHE'S EASING UP!
I NEVER KNEW...
KISSING COULD BE THIS EFFECTIVE!
HAAAH
HAAAH
ONE LAST TIME, EMMA.
I WANT TO ASK THE GREAT SAGE WHAT TO WATCH OUT FOR...
WHEN ENTERING THE DUNGEON.

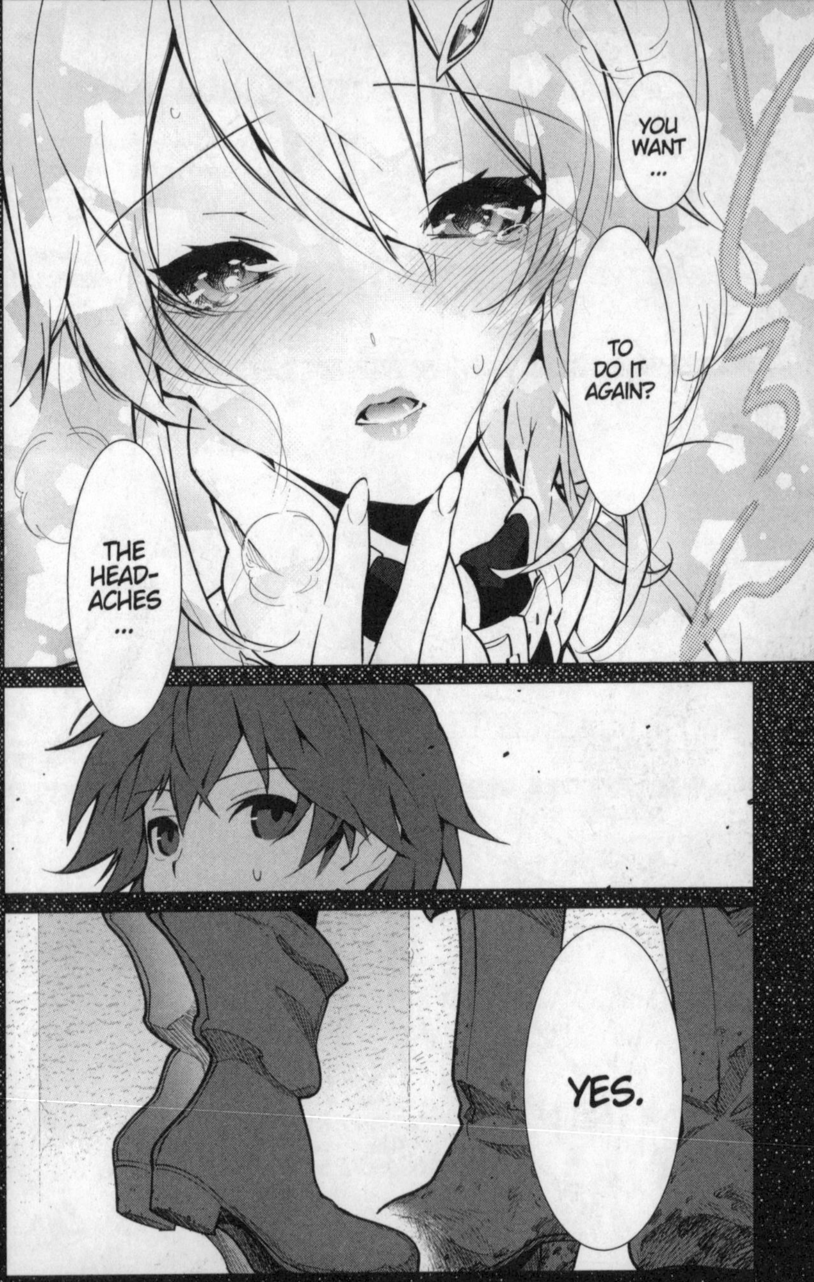
YOU WANT ...
TO DO IT AGAIN?
THE HEAD-ACHES ...
YES.

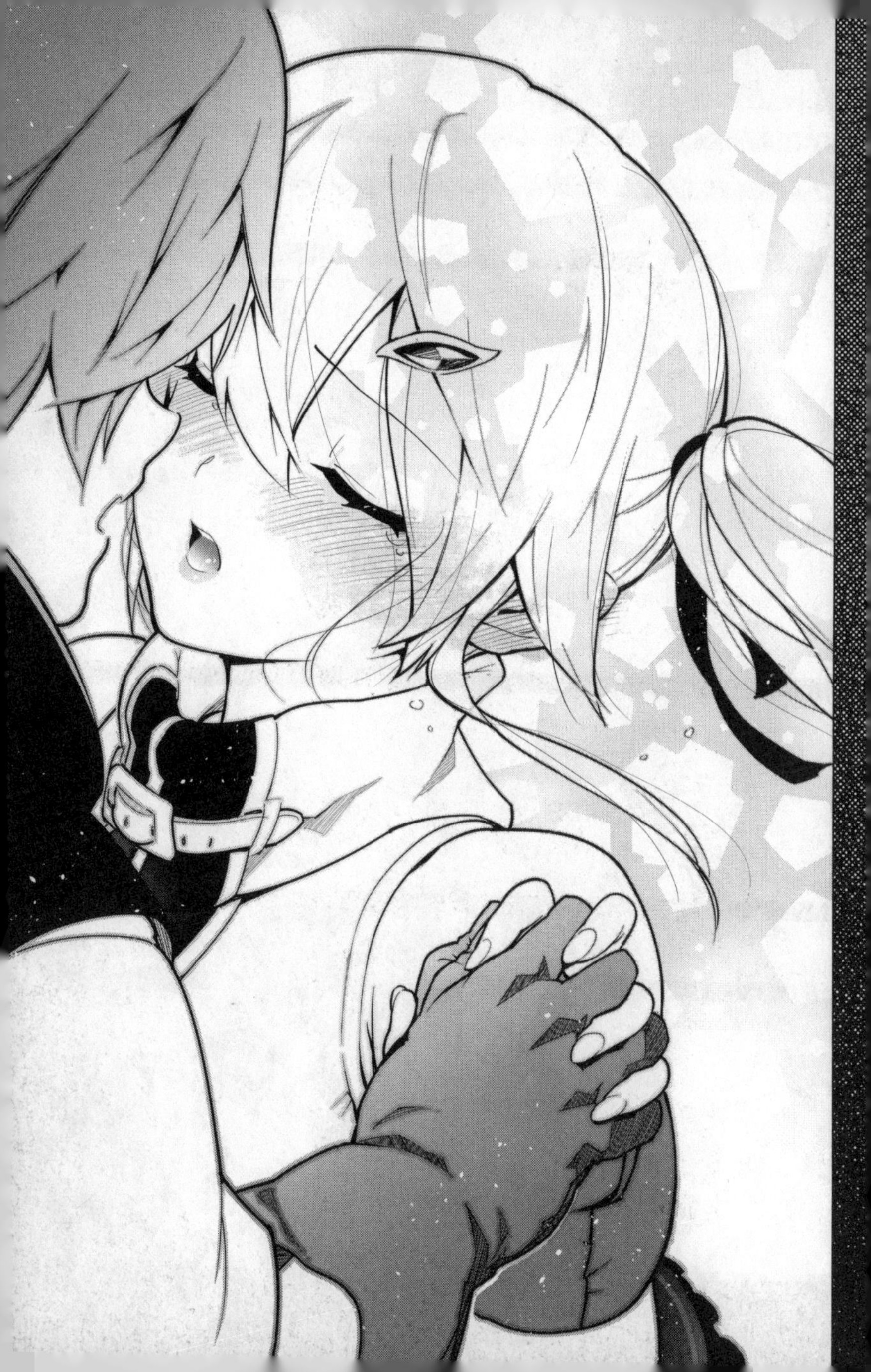

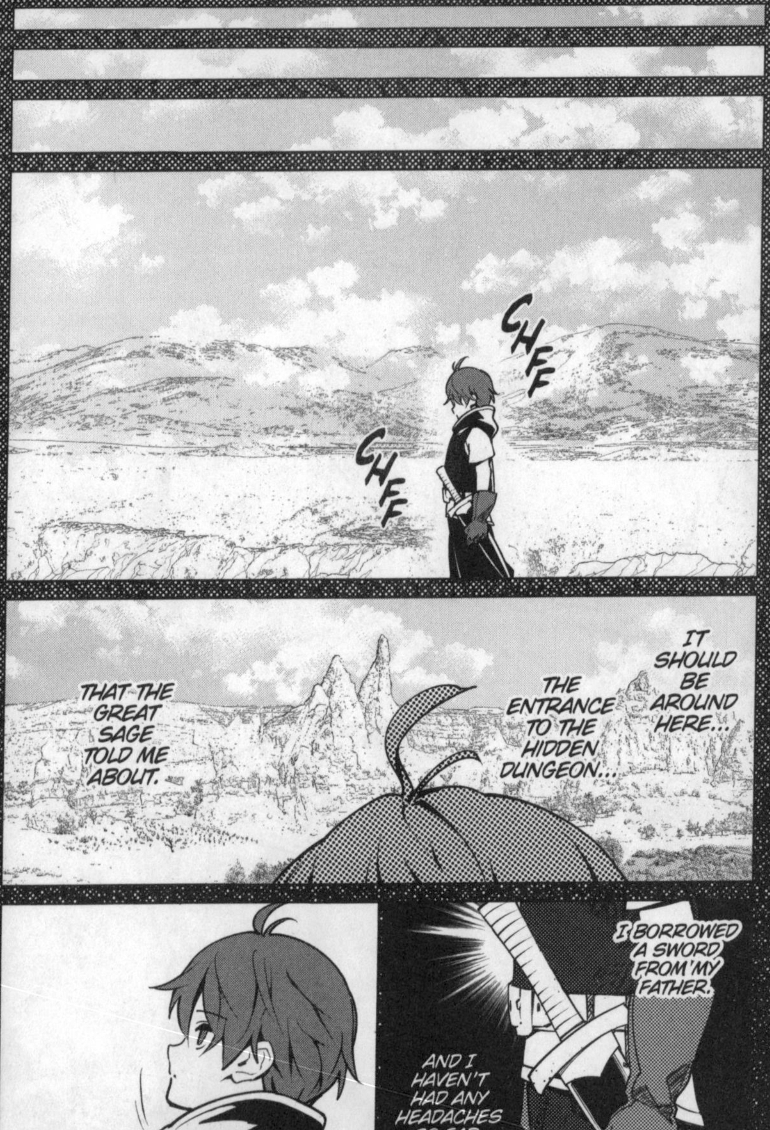
CHFF
CHFF
IT SHOULD BE AROUND HERE...
THE ENTRANCE TO THE HIDDEN DUNGEON...
THAT THE GREAT SAGE TOLD ME ABOUT.
I BORROWED A SWORD FROM MY FATHER.
AND I HAVEN'T HAD ANY HEADACHES SO FAR.

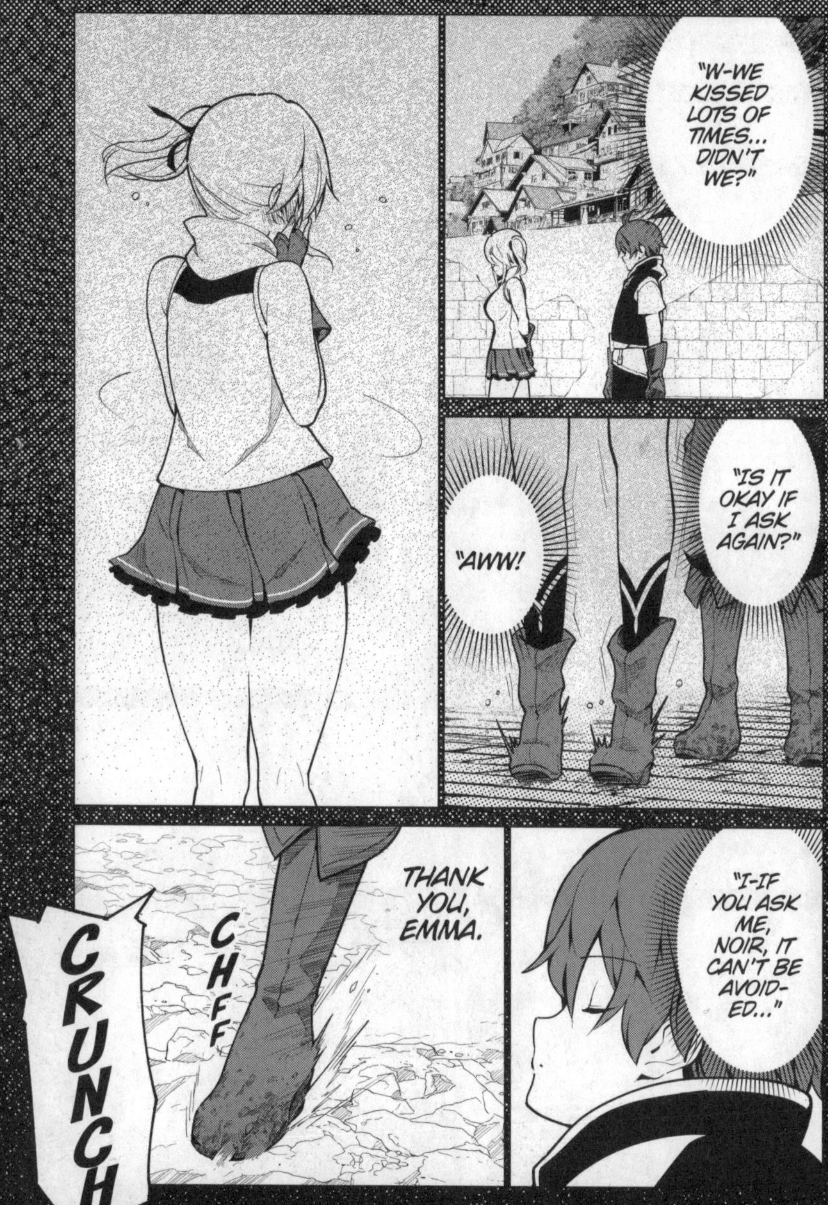
"W-WE KISSED LOTS OF TIMES... DIDN'T WE?"
"IS IT OKAY IF I ASK AGAIN?"
"AWW!
"I-IF YOU ASK ME, NOIR, IT CAN'T BE AVOIDED..."
THANK YOU, EMMA.
CHFF
CRUNCH

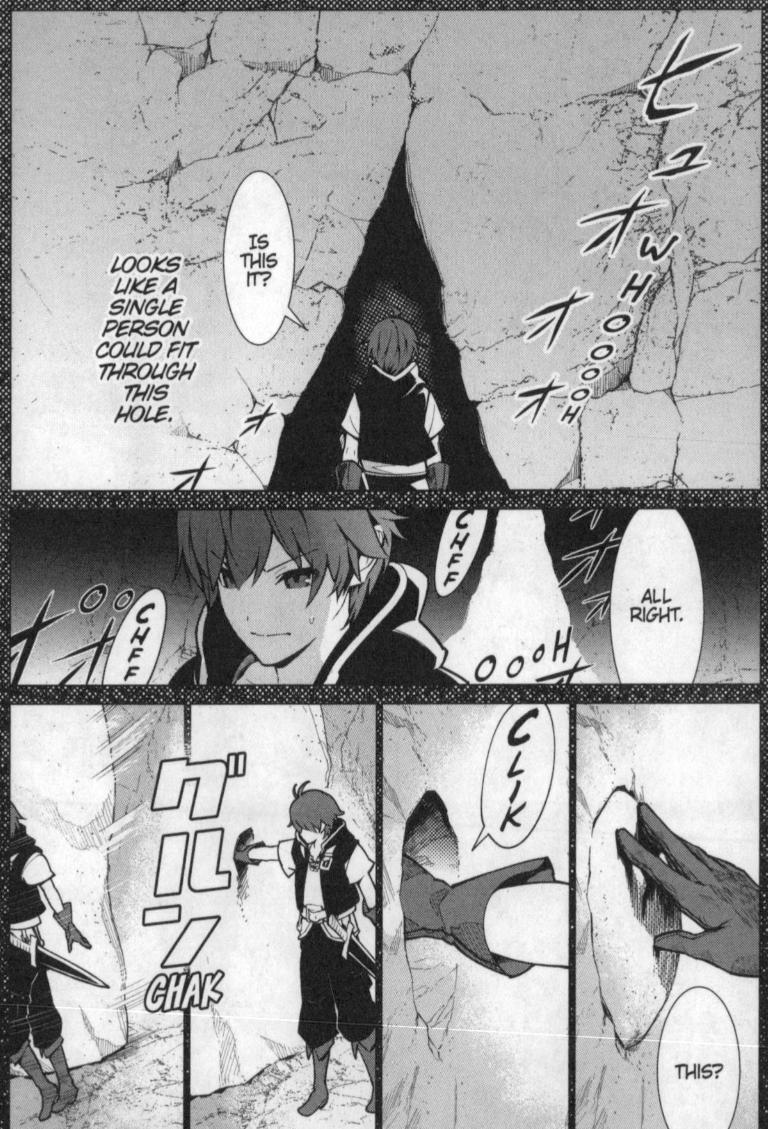
WHOOOOOOH
IS THIS IT?
LOOKS LIKE A SINGLE PERSON COULD FIT THROUGH THIS HOLE.
ALL RIGHT.
OOOH
CHFF
CHFF
THIS?
CLIK
CHAK

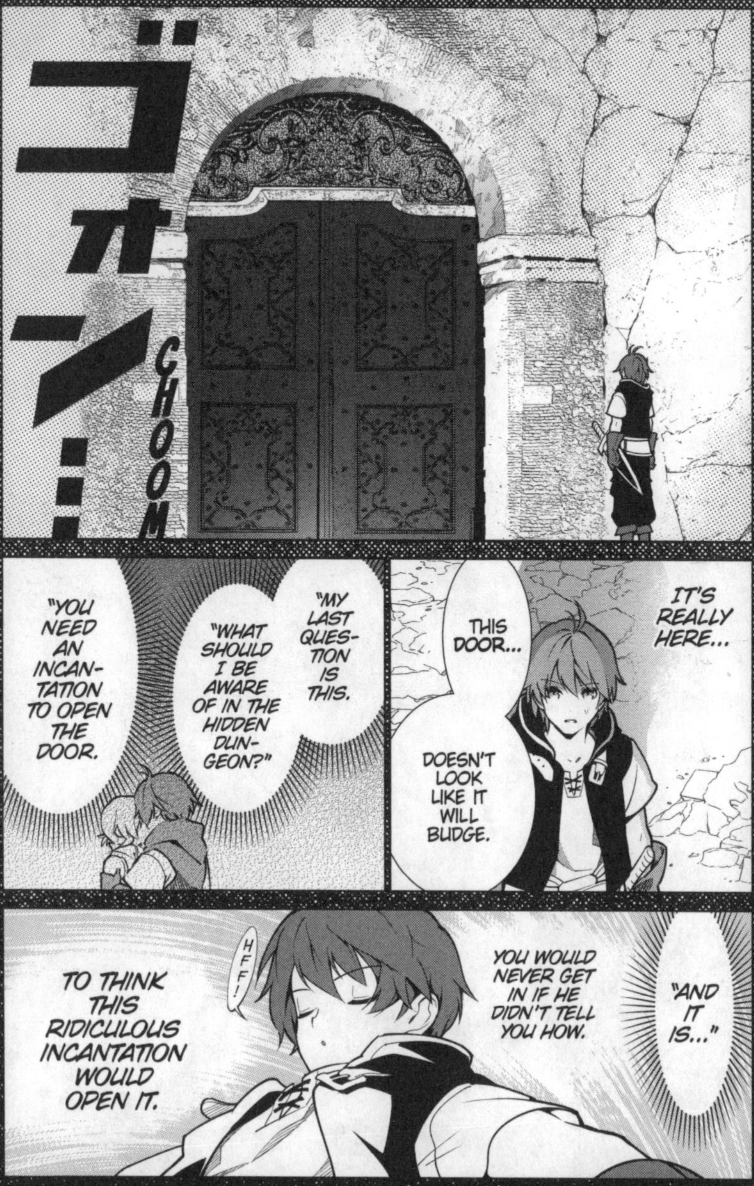
ゴオン…
CHOOM
IT'S REALLY HERE...
THIS DOOR...
DOESN'T LOOK LIKE IT WILL BUDGE.
"MY LAST QUESTION IS THIS.
"WHAT SHOULD I BE AWARE OF IN THE HIDDEN DUNGEON?"
"YOU NEED AN INCANTATION TO OPEN THE DOOR.
"AND IT IS..."
YOU WOULD NEVER GET IN IF HE DIDN'T TELL YOU HOW.
HFF!
TO THINK THIS RIDICULOUS INCANTATION WOULD OPEN IT.

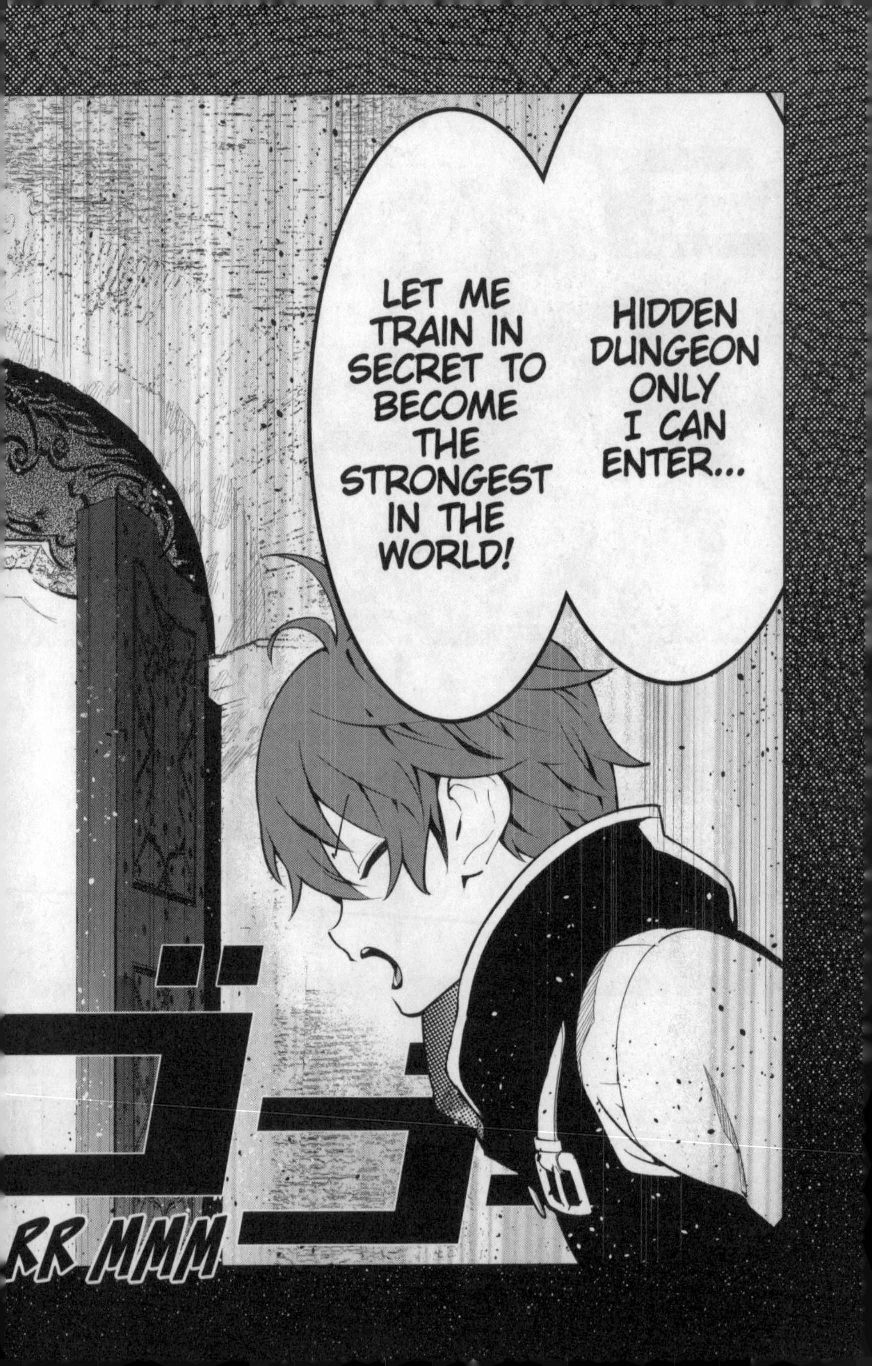
HIDDEN DUNGEON ONLY I CAN ENTER...
LET ME TRAIN IN SECRET TO BECOME THE STRONGEST IN THE WORLD!
RR MMM

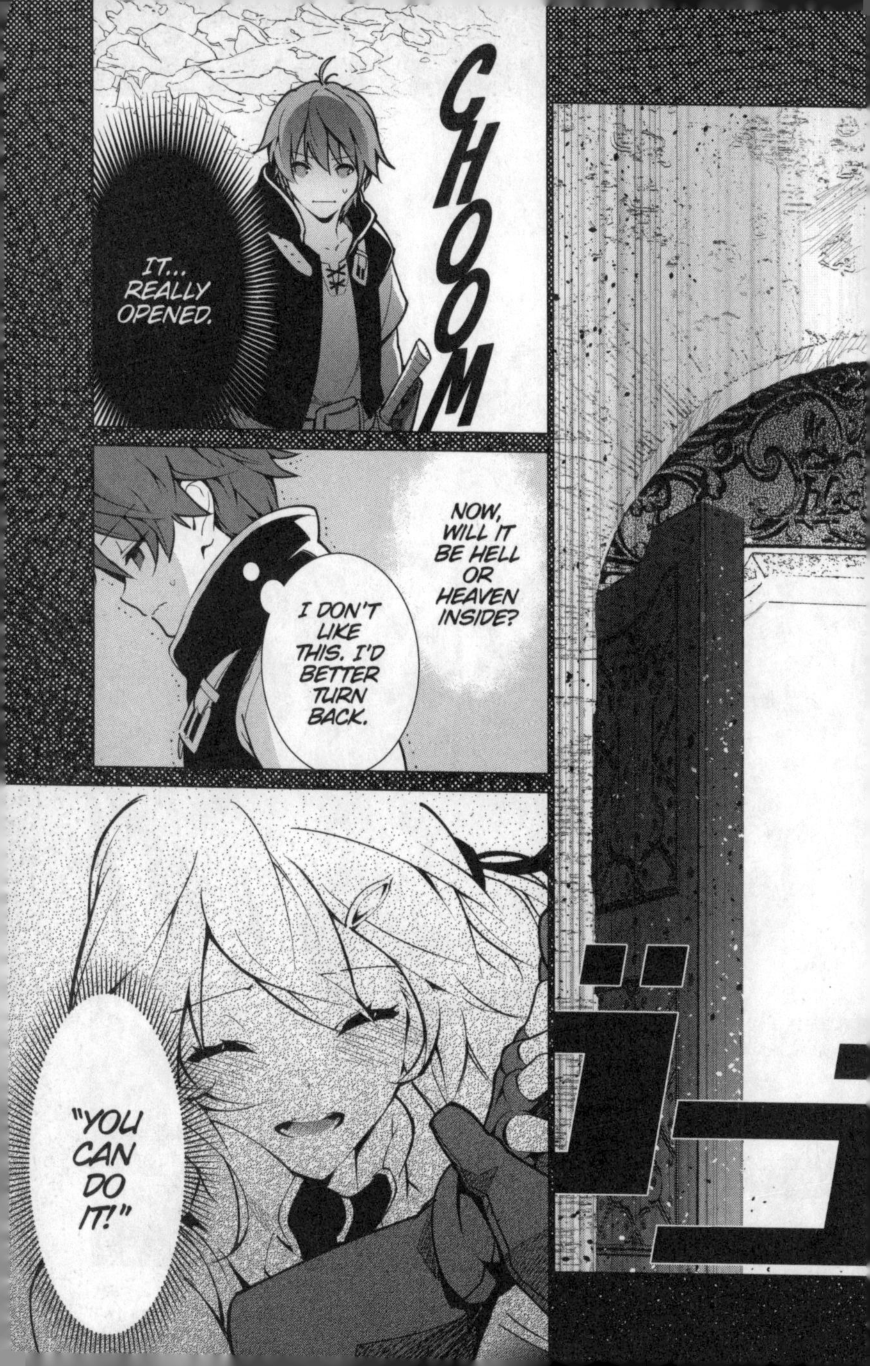
CHOOM
IT... REALLY OPENED.
NOW, WILL IT BE HELL OR HEAVEN INSIDE?
I DON'T LIKE THIS. I'D BETTER TURN BACK.
"YOU CAN DO IT!"

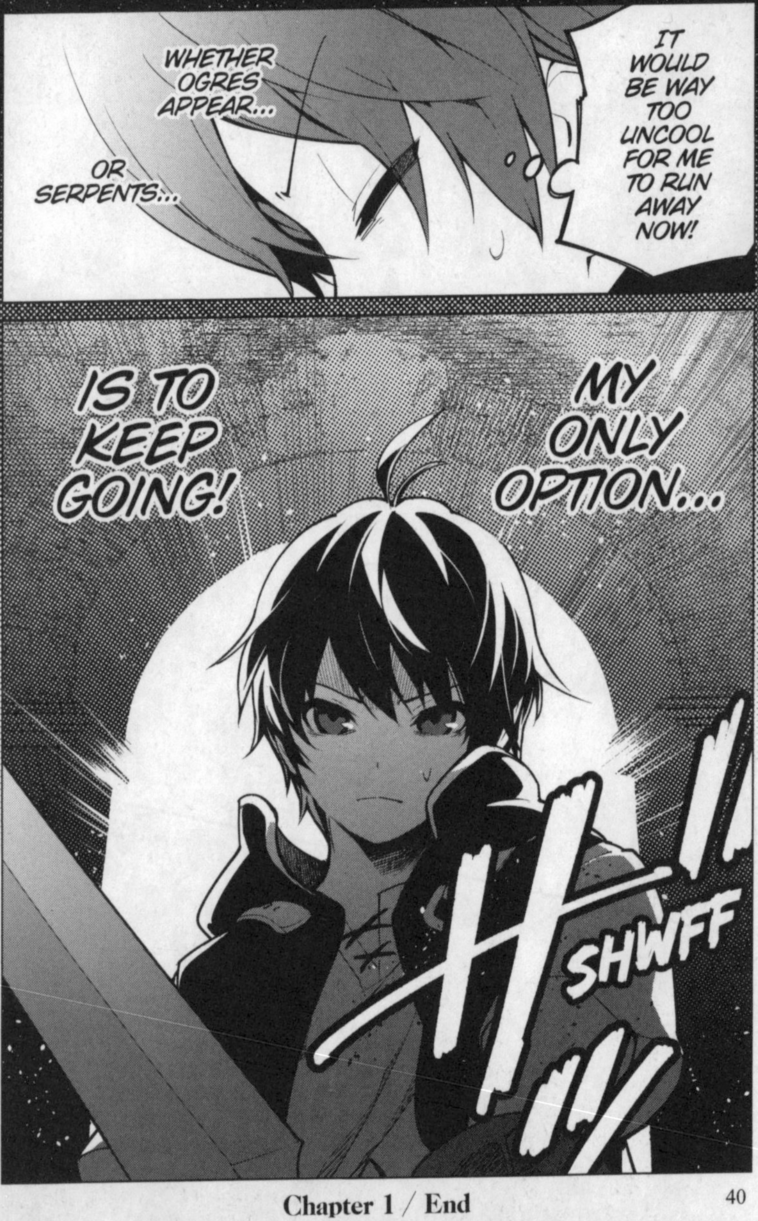

Chapter 1 / End

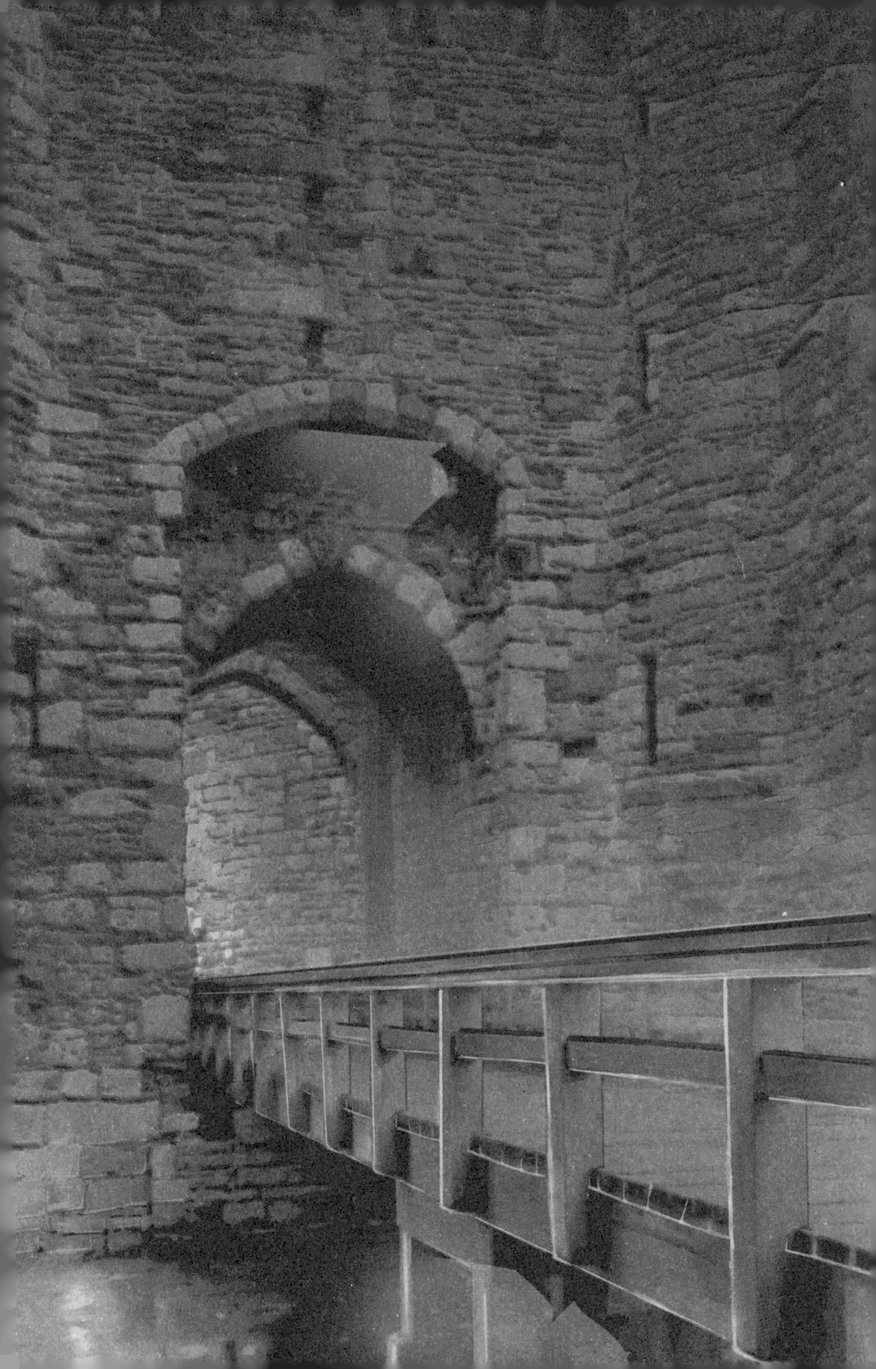

THE HIDDEN DUNGEON ONLY I CAN ENTER

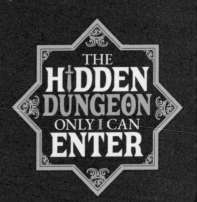

Chapter 2: The Get Creative Skill

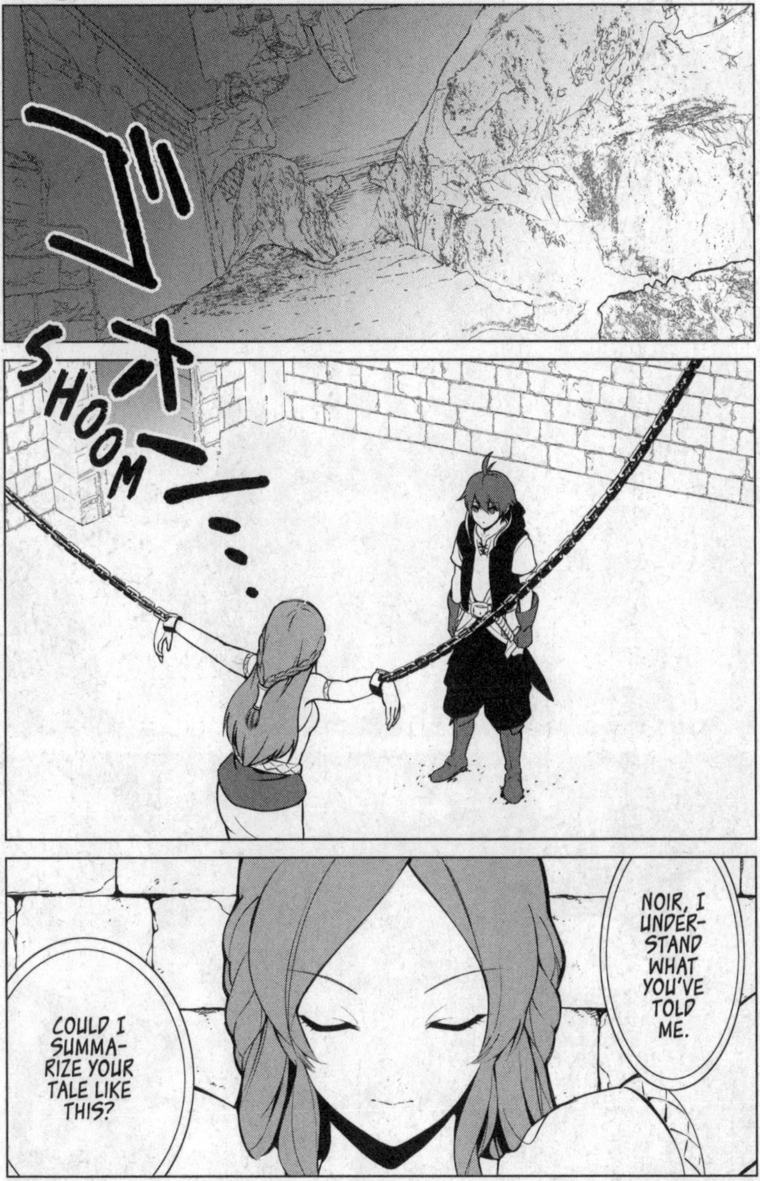
SHOOM
NOIR, I UNDER-STAND WHAT YOU'VE TOLD ME.
COULD I SUMMA-RIZE YOUR TALE LIKE THIS?

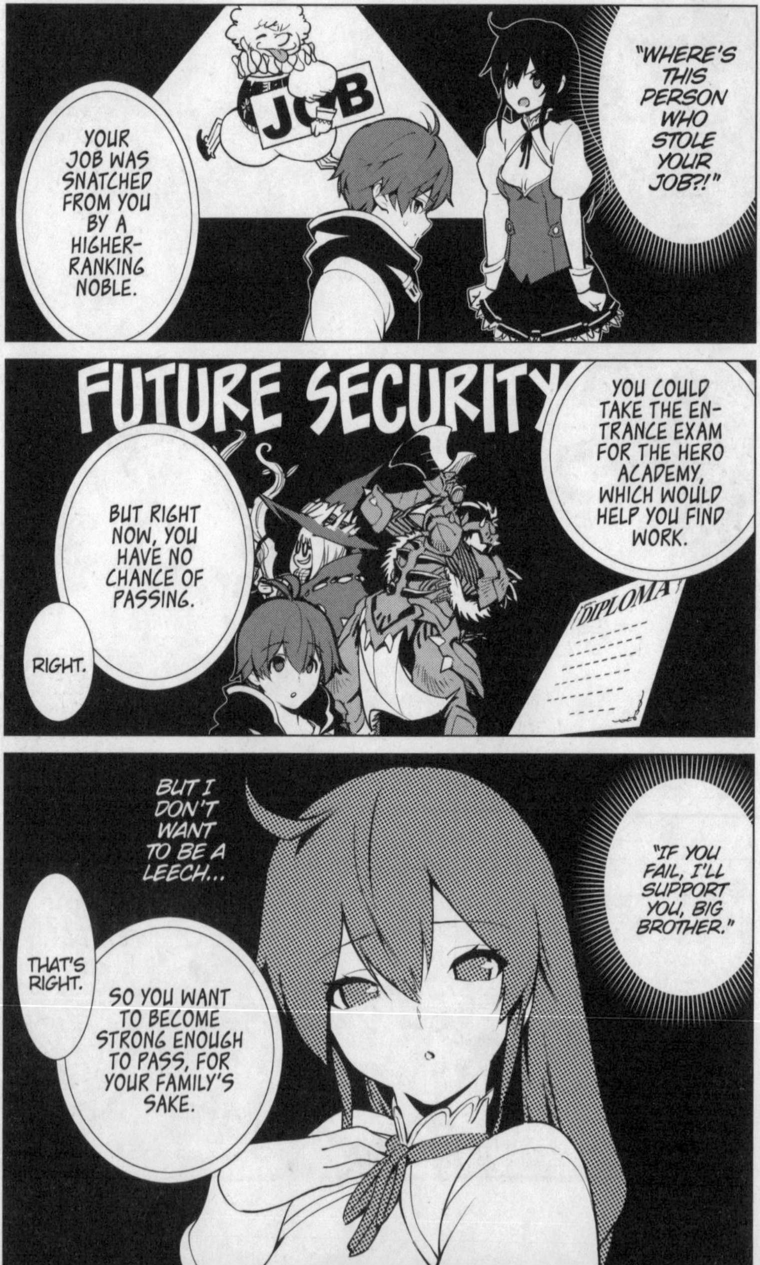
"WHERE'S THIS PERSON WHO STOLE YOUR JOB?!"
JOB
YOUR JOB WAS SNATCHED FROM YOU BY A HIGHER-RANKING NOBLE.
YOU COULD TAKE THE EN-TRANCE EXAM FOR THE HERO ACADEMY, WHICH WOULD HELP YOU FIND WORK.
FUTURE SECURITY
DIPLOMA
BUT RIGHT NOW, YOU HAVE NO CHANCE OF PASSING.
RIGHT.
"IF YOU FAIL, I'LL SUPPORT YOU, BIG BROTHER."
BUT I DON'T WANT TO BE A LEECH...
SO YOU WANT TO BECOME STRONG ENOUGH TO PASS, FOR YOUR FAMILY'S SAKE.
THAT'S RIGHT.

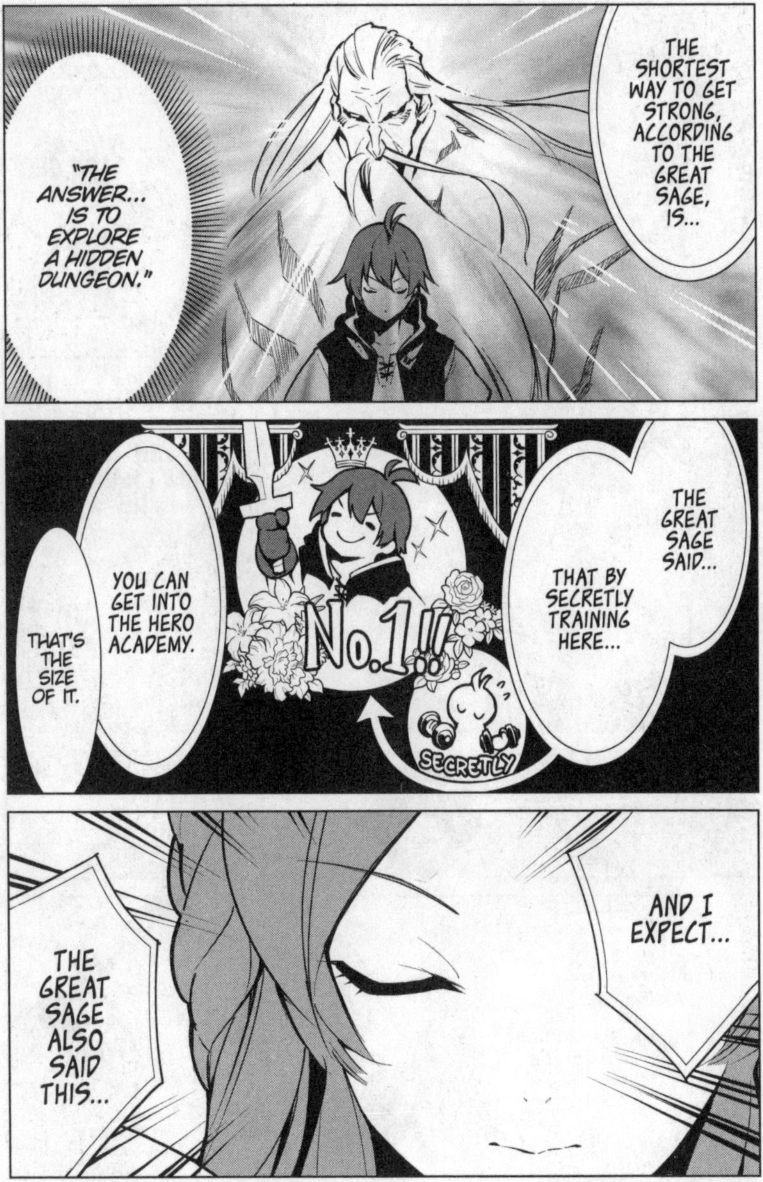
THE SHORTEST WAY TO GET STRONG, ACCORDING TO THE GREAT SAGE, IS...
"THE ANSWER... IS TO EXPLORE A HIDDEN DUNGEON."
THE GREAT SAGE SAID...
THAT BY SECRETLY TRAINING HERE...
SECRETLY
No.1!!
YOU CAN GET INTO THE HERO ACADEMY.
THAT'S THE SIZE OF IT.
AND I EXPECT...
THE GREAT SAGE ALSO SAID THIS...

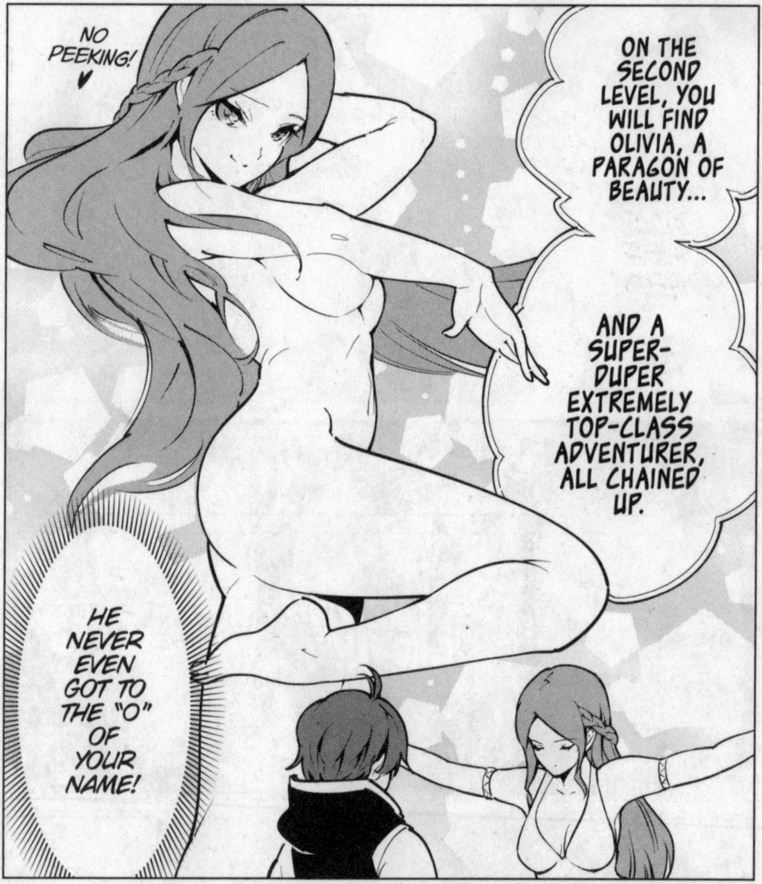
ON THE SECOND LEVEL, YOU WILL FIND OLIVIA, A PARAGON OF BEAUTY...
AND A SUPER-DUPER EXTREMELY TOP-CLASS ADVENTURER, ALL CHAINED UP.
NO PEEKING! ♥
HE NEVER EVEN GOT TO THE "O" OF YOUR NAME!

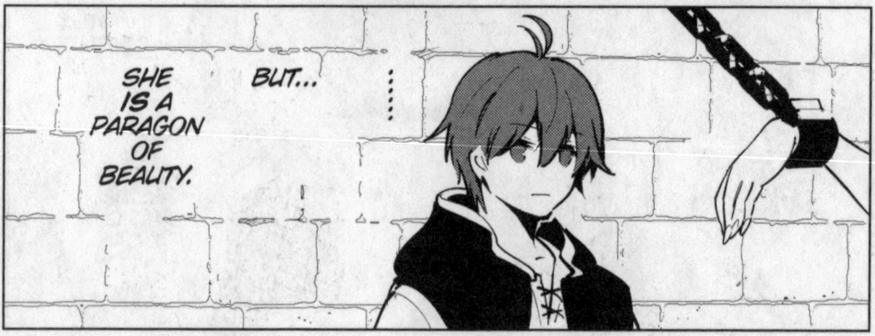
......
BUT...
SHE IS A PARAGON OF BEAUTY.

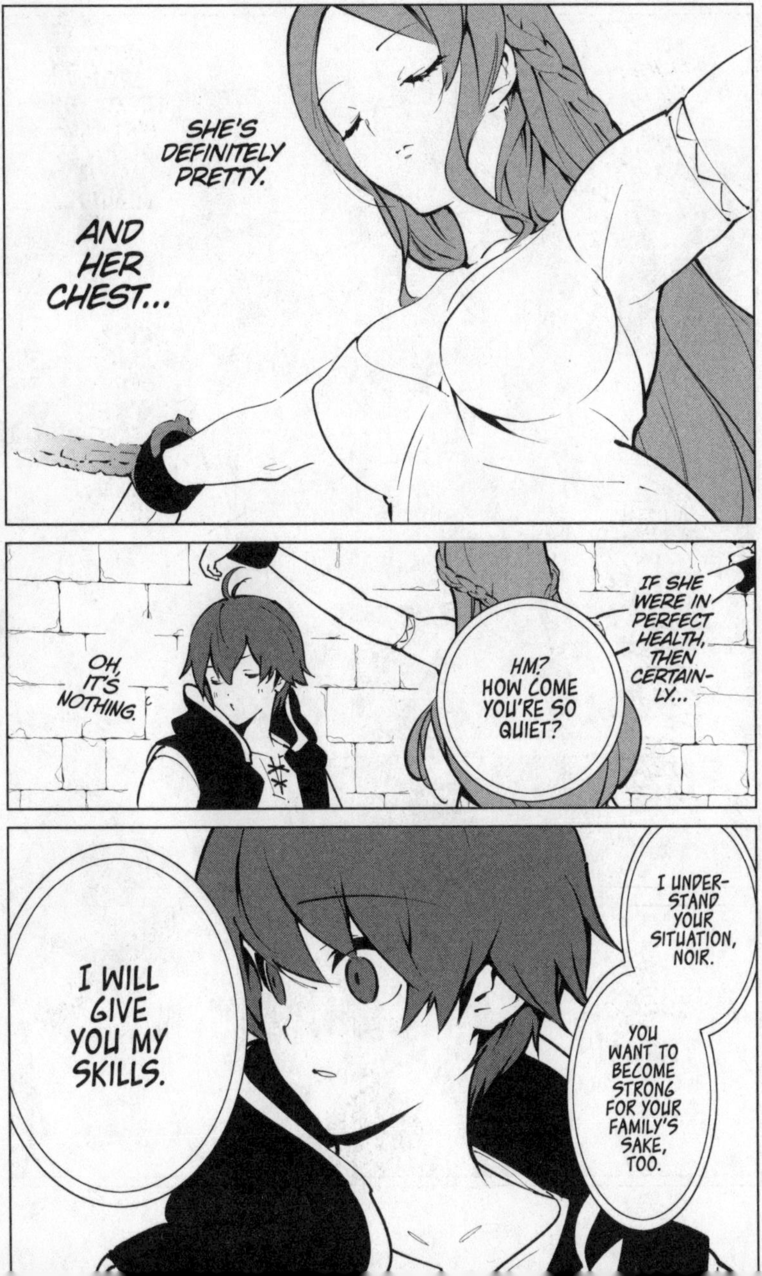
SHE'S DEFINITELY PRETTY.
AND HER CHEST...
IF SHE WERE IN PERFECT HEALTH, THEN CERTAINLY...
HM? HOW COME YOU'RE SO QUIET?
OH, IT'S NOTHING.
I UNDERSTAND YOUR SITUATION, NOIR.
YOU WANT TO BECOME STRONG FOR YOUR FAMILY'S SAKE, TOO.
I WILL GIVE YOU MY SKILLS.

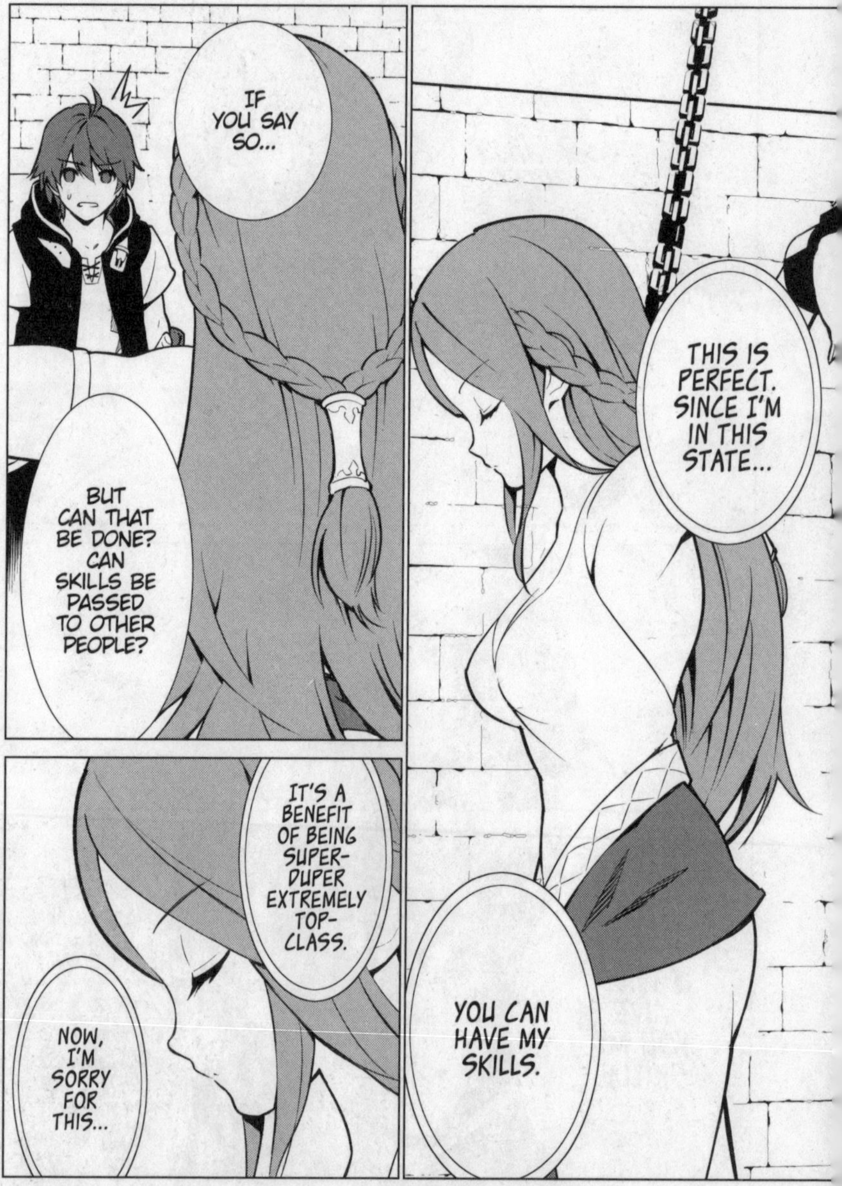
THIS IS PERFECT. SINCE I'M IN THIS STATE...
YOU CAN HAVE MY SKILLS.
IF YOU SAY SO...
BUT CAN THAT BE DONE? CAN SKILLS BE PASSED TO OTHER PEOPLE?
IT'S A BENEFIT OF BEING SUPER-DUPER EXTREMELY TOP-CLASS.
NOW, I'M SORRY FOR THIS...

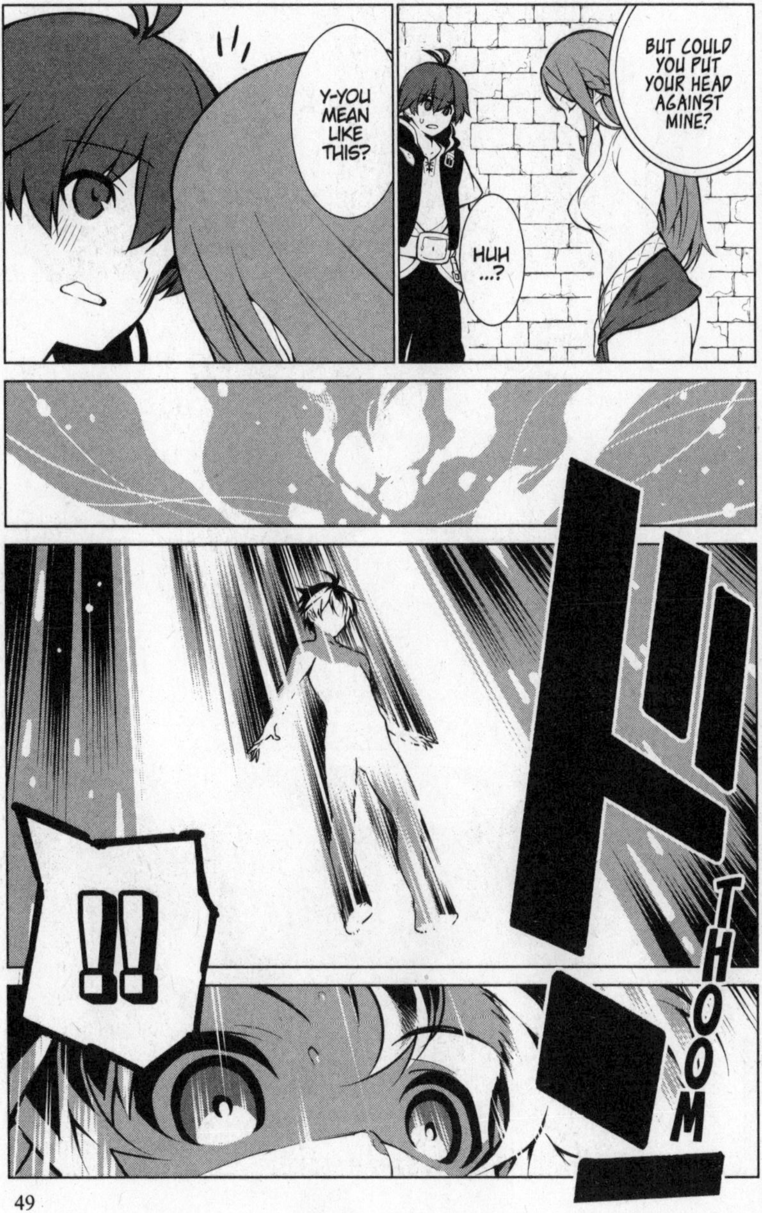
BUT COULD YOU PUT YOUR HEAD AGAINST MINE?
HUH ...?
Y-YOU MEAN LIKE THIS?
THOOM
!!

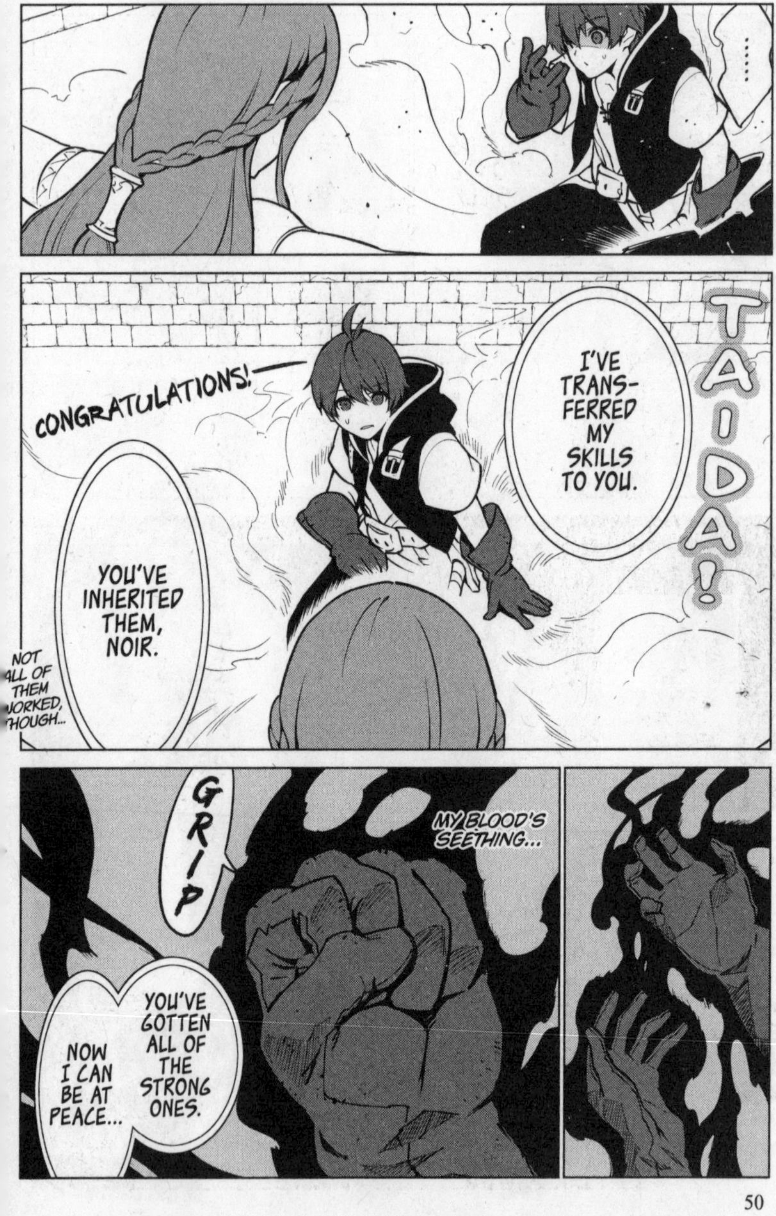
......
TAIDA!
I'VE TRANSFERRED MY SKILLS TO YOU.
CONGRATULATIONS!
YOU'VE INHERITED THEM, NOIR.
NOT ALL OF THEM WORKED, THOUGH...
GRIP
MY BLOOD'S SEETHING...
YOU'VE GOTTEN ALL OF THE STRONG ONES.
NOW I CAN BE AT PEACE...

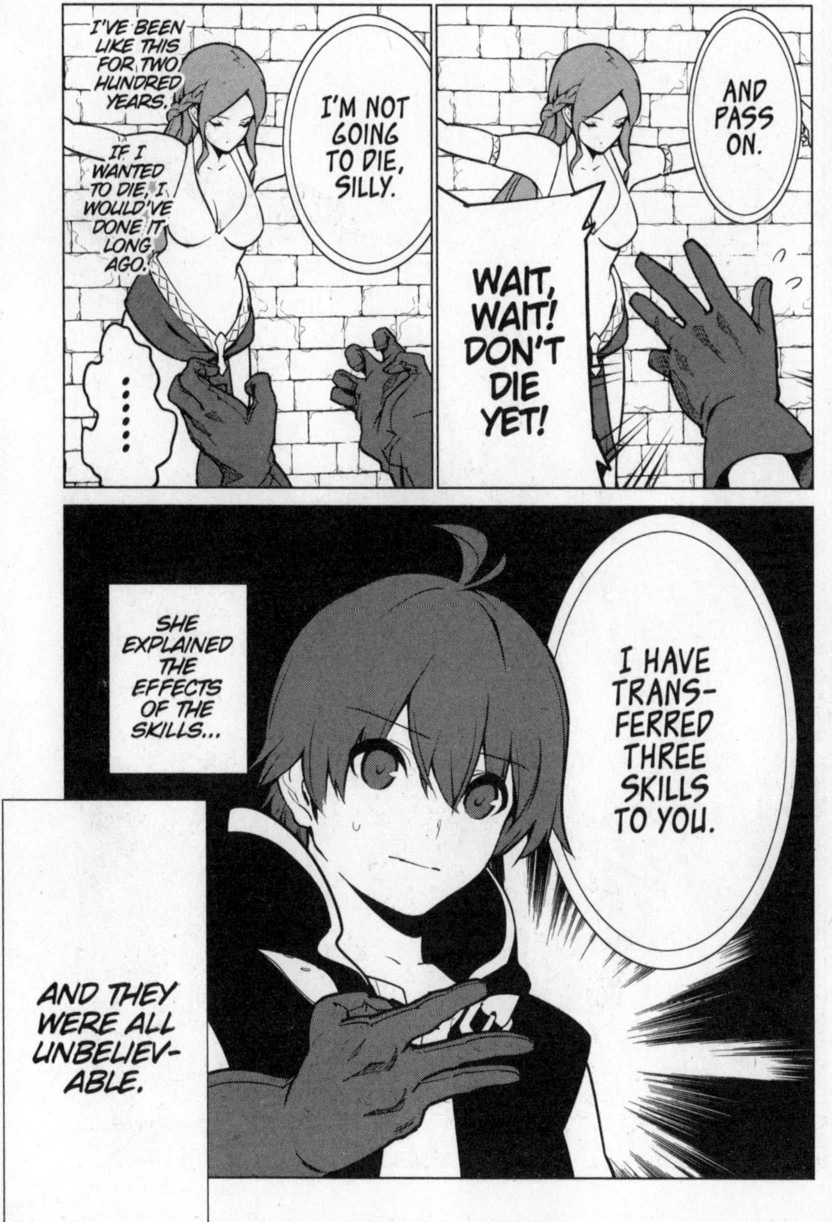
AND PASS ON.
WAIT, WAIT! DON'T DIE YET!
I'M NOT GOING TO DIE, SILLY.
I'VE BEEN LIKE THIS FOR TWO HUNDRED YEARS.
IF I WANTED TO DIE, I WOULD'VE DONE IT LONG AGO.
......
I HAVE TRANSFERRED THREE SKILLS TO YOU.
SHE EXPLAINED THE EFFECTS OF THE SKILLS...
AND THEY WERE ALL UNBELIEVABLE.

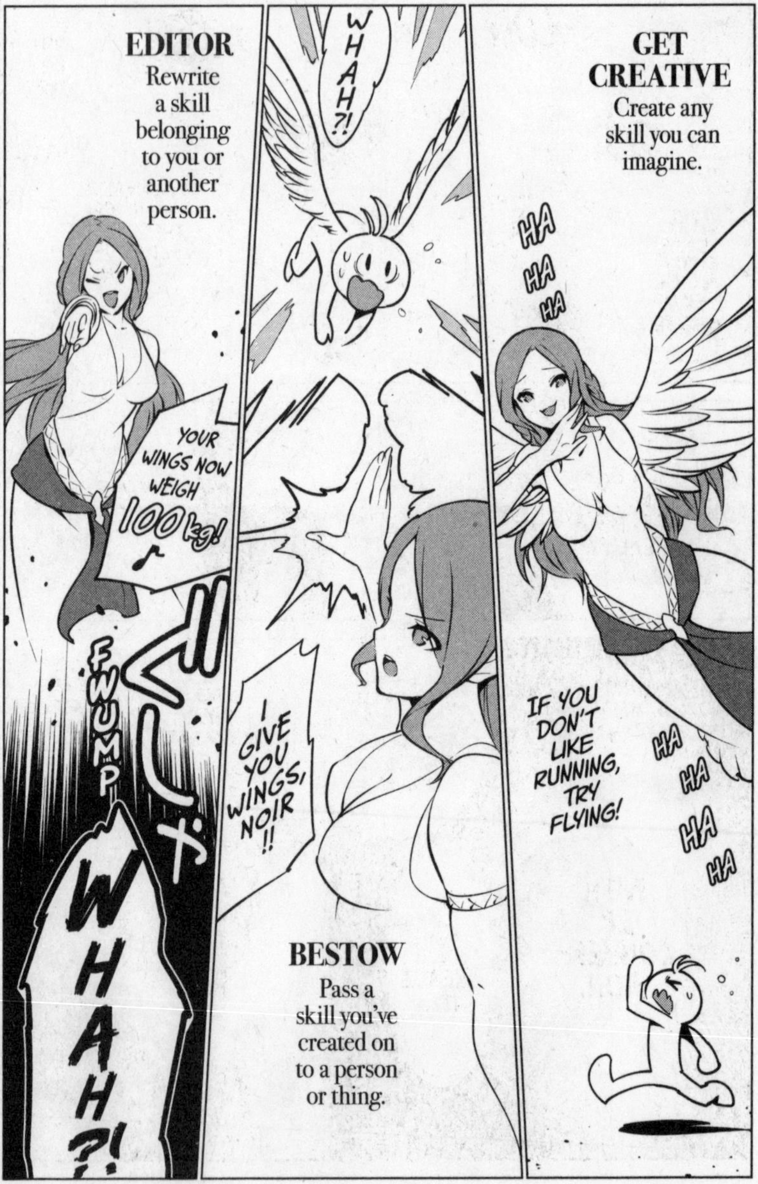
GET CREATIVE
Create any skill you can imagine.
HA HA HA
IF YOU DON'T LIKE RUNNING, TRY FLYING!
HA HA HA HA
WHAH?!
I GIVE YOU WINGS, NOIR!!
BESTOW
Pass a skill you've created on to a person or thing.
EDITOR
Rewrite a skill belonging to you or another person.
YOUR WINGS NOW WEIGH 100kg! ♪
FWUMP
WHAH?!

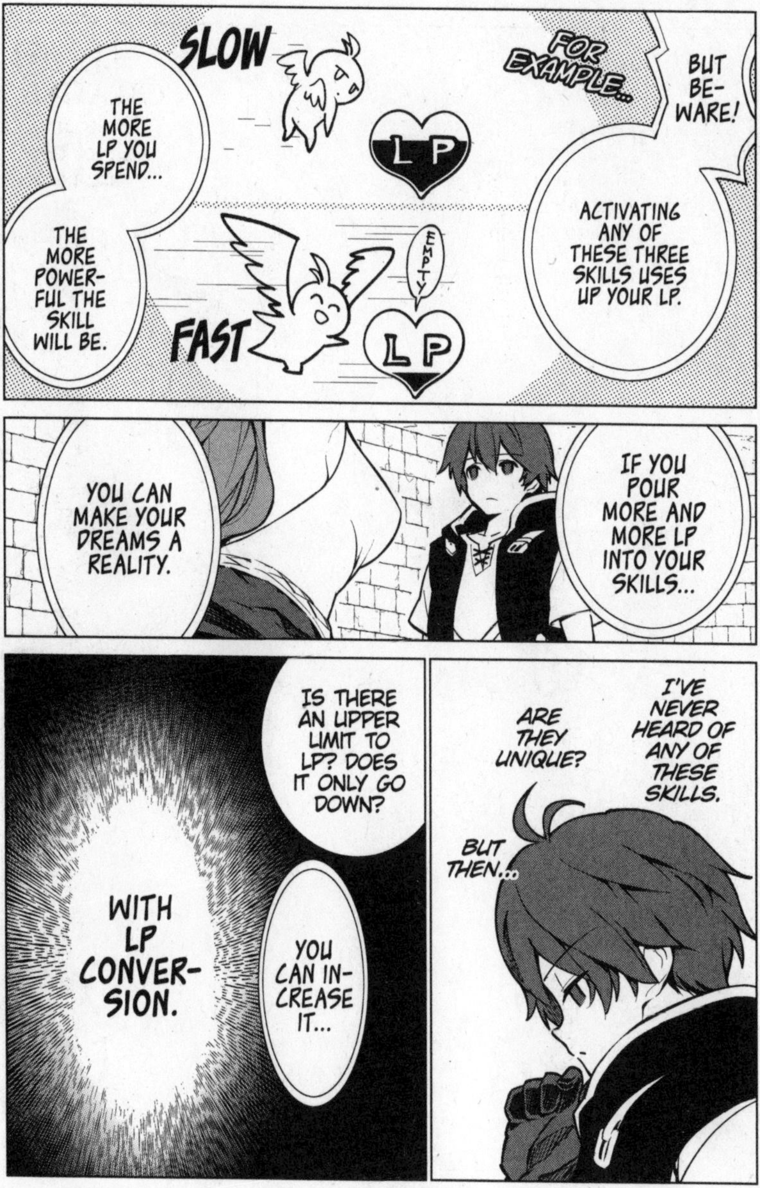
BUT BE-WARE!
ACTIVATING ANY OF THESE THREE SKILLS USES UP YOUR LP.
FOR EXAMPLE...
LP
SLOW
EMPTY
LP
FAST
THE MORE LP YOU SPEND...
THE MORE POWER-FUL THE SKILL WILL BE.
IF YOU POUR MORE AND MORE LP INTO YOUR SKILLS...
YOU CAN MAKE YOUR DREAMS A REALITY.
I'VE NEVER HEARD OF ANY OF THESE SKILLS.
ARE THEY UNIQUE?
BUT THEN...
IS THERE AN UPPER LIMIT TO LP? DOES IT ONLY GO DOWN?
YOU CAN IN-CREASE IT...
WITH LP CONVER-SION.

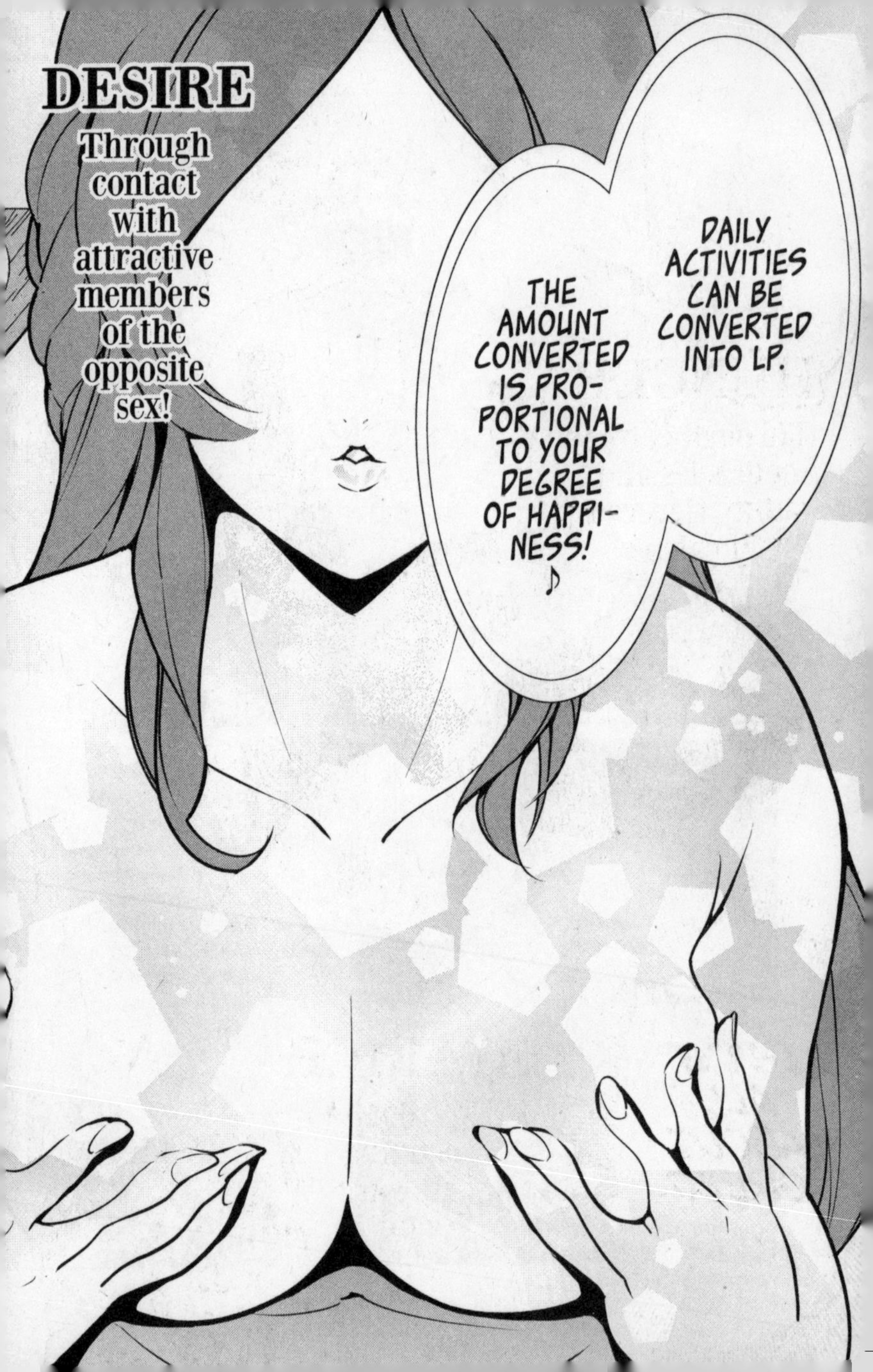
DAILY ACTIVITIES CAN BE CONVERTED INTO LP.
THE AMOUNT CONVERTED IS PROPORTIONAL TO YOUR DEGREE OF HAPPINESS! ♪
DESIRE
Through contact with attractive members of the opposite sex!

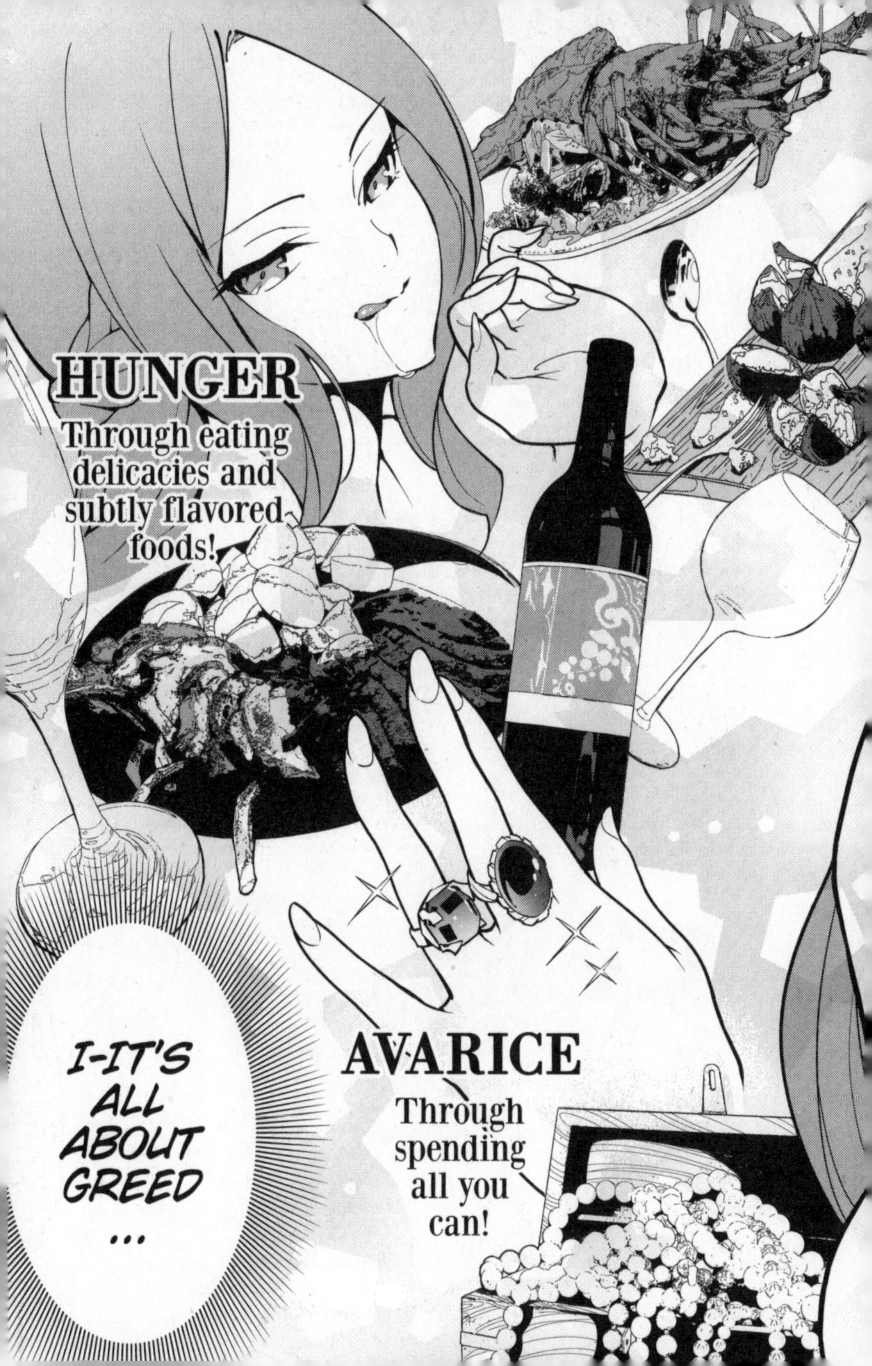
HUNGER
Through eating delicacies and subtly flavored foods!
AVARICE
Through spending all you can!
I-IT'S ALL ABOUT GREED ...

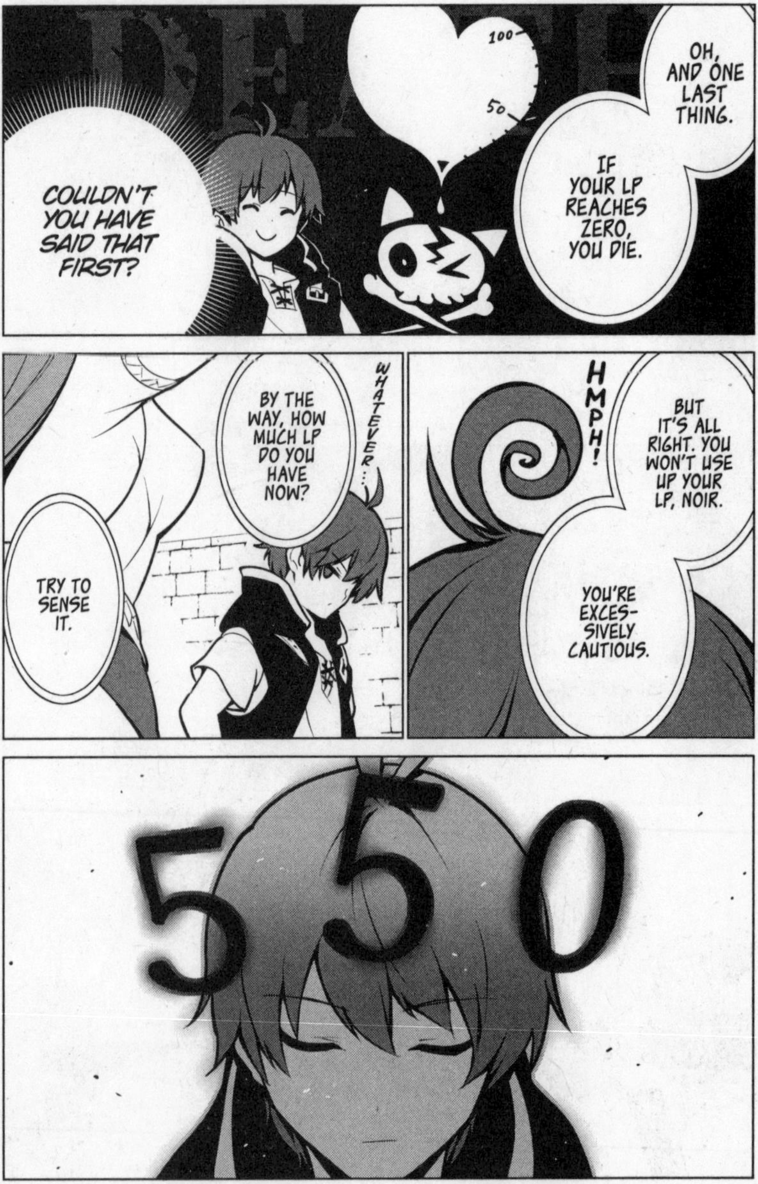
OH, AND ONE LAST THING.
IF YOUR LP REACHES ZERO, YOU DIE.
100
50
COULDN'T YOU HAVE SAID THAT FIRST?
BUT IT'S ALL RIGHT. YOU WON'T USE UP YOUR LP, NOIR.
HMPH!
YOU'RE EXCES-SIVELY CAUTIOUS.
WHATEVER...
BY THE WAY, HOW MUCH LP DO YOU HAVE NOW?
TRY TO SENSE IT.
550

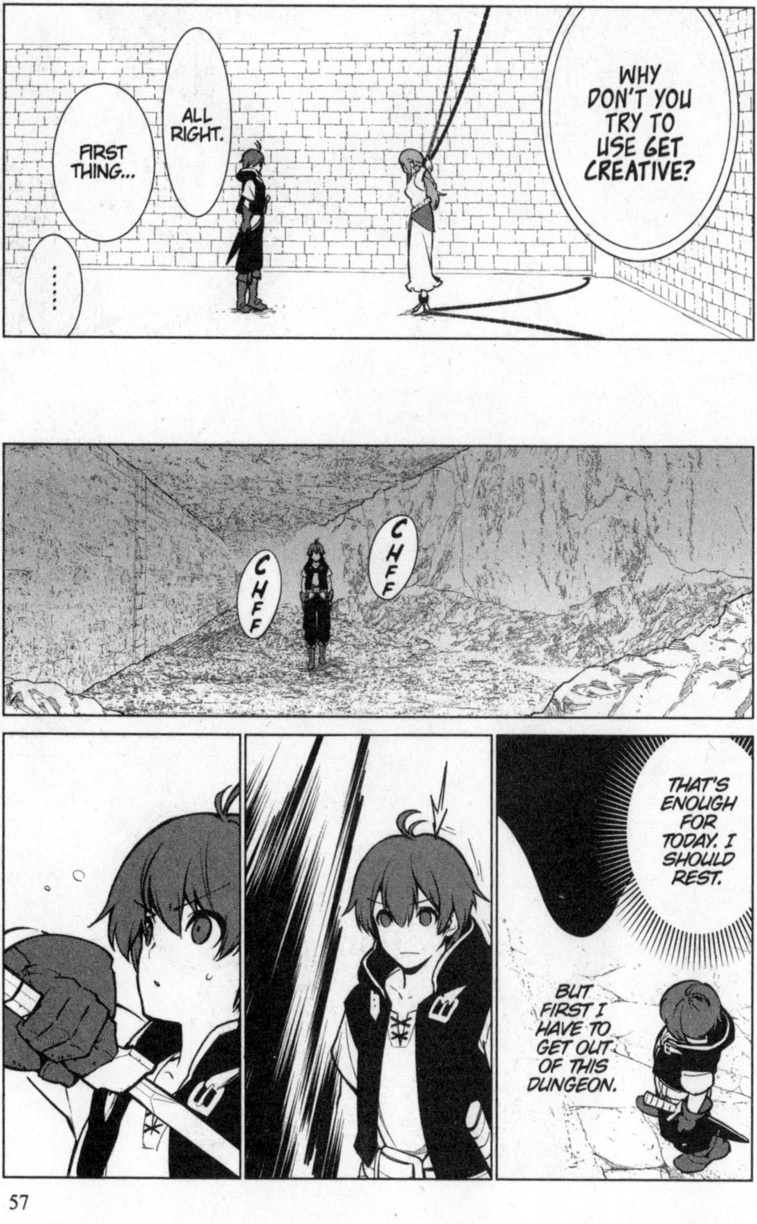
WHY DON'T YOU TRY TO USE GET CREATIVE?
ALL RIGHT.
FIRST THING...
......
CHFF
CHFF
THAT'S ENOUGH FOR TODAY. I SHOULD REST.
BUT FIRST I HAVE TO GET OUT OF THIS DUNGEON.

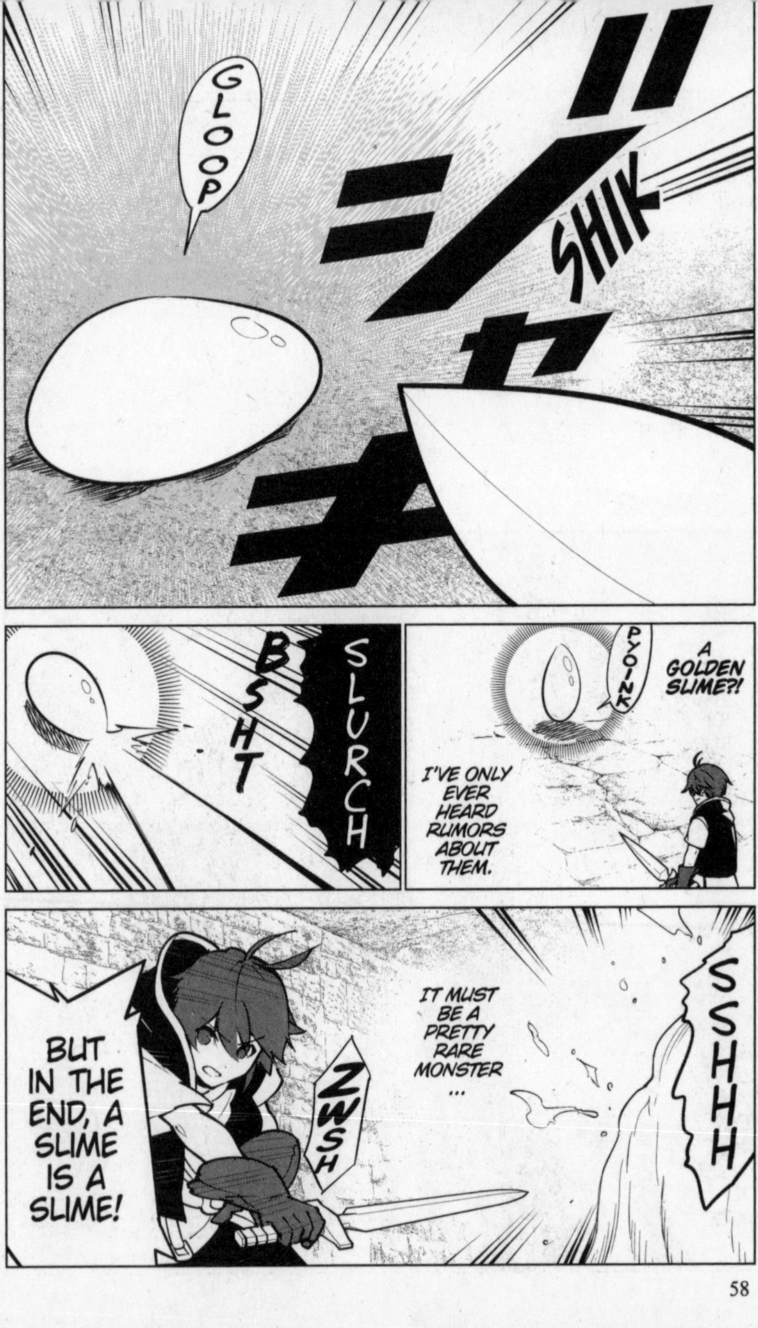
GLOOP
SHIK
A GOLDEN SLIME?!
PYOINK
I'VE ONLY EVER HEARD RUMORS ABOUT THEM.
SLURCH
BSHT
SSHHH
IT MUST BE A PRETTY RARE MONSTER ...
ZWSH
BUT IN THE END, A SLIME IS A SLIME!

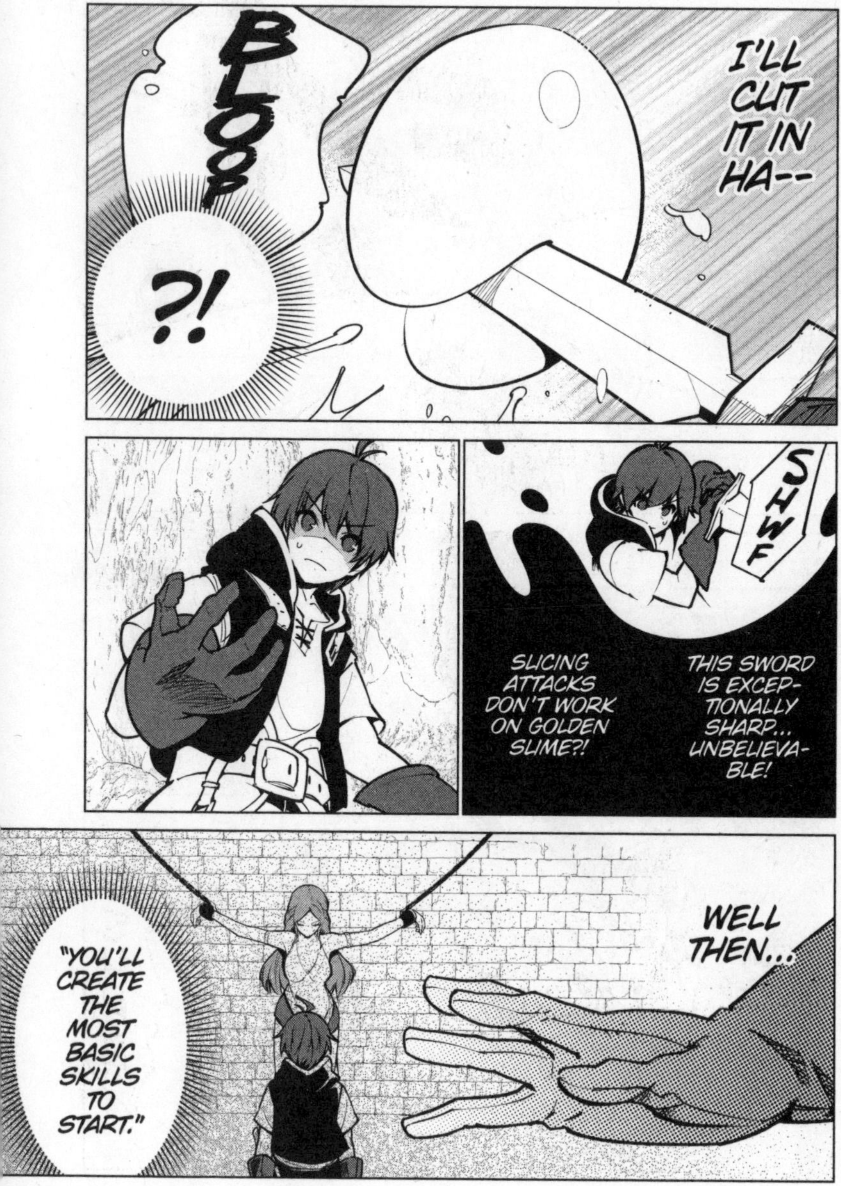
I'LL CUT IT IN HA--
BLOOP
?!
SHWF
THIS SWORD IS EXCEP-TIONALLY SHARP... UNBELIEVA-BLE!
SLICING ATTACKS DON'T WORK ON GOLDEN SLIME?!
WELL THEN...
"YOU'LL CREATE THE MOST BASIC SKILLS TO START."

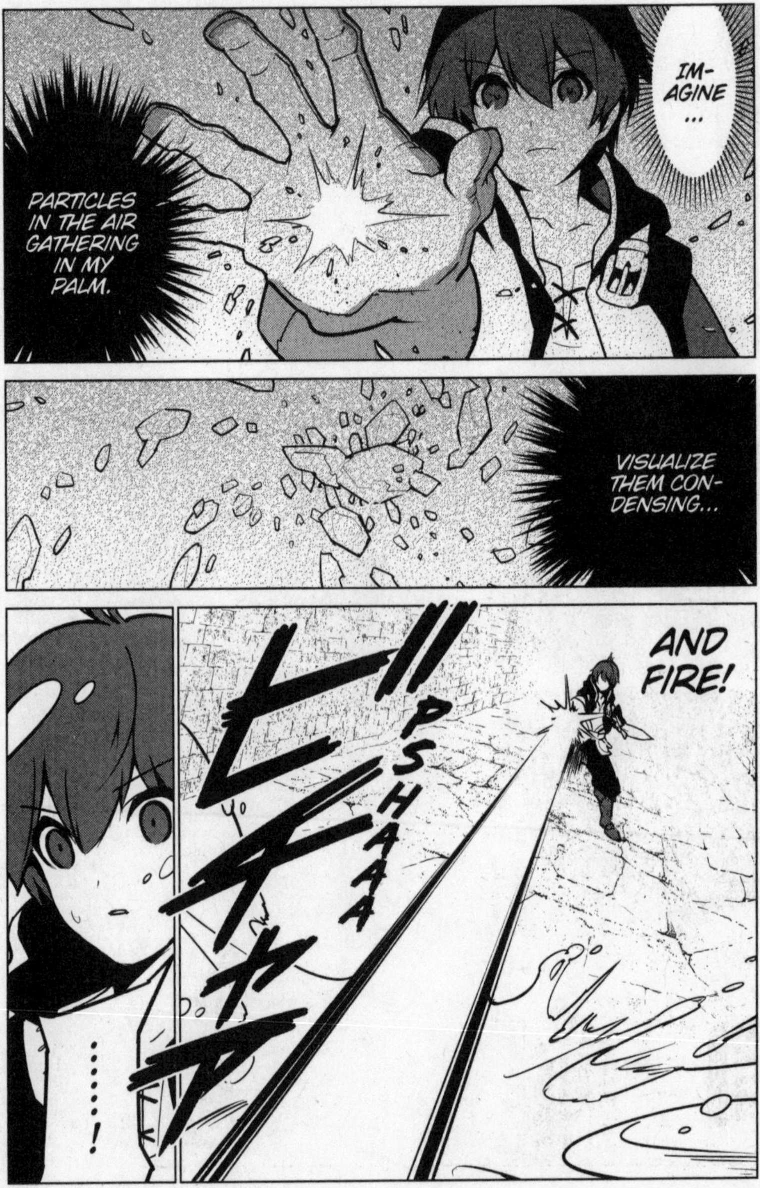
IM-
AGINE
...
PARTICLES
IN THE AIR
GATHERING
IN MY
PALM.
VISUALIZE
THEM CON-
DENSING...
AND
FIRE!
PSHAAAA
......!

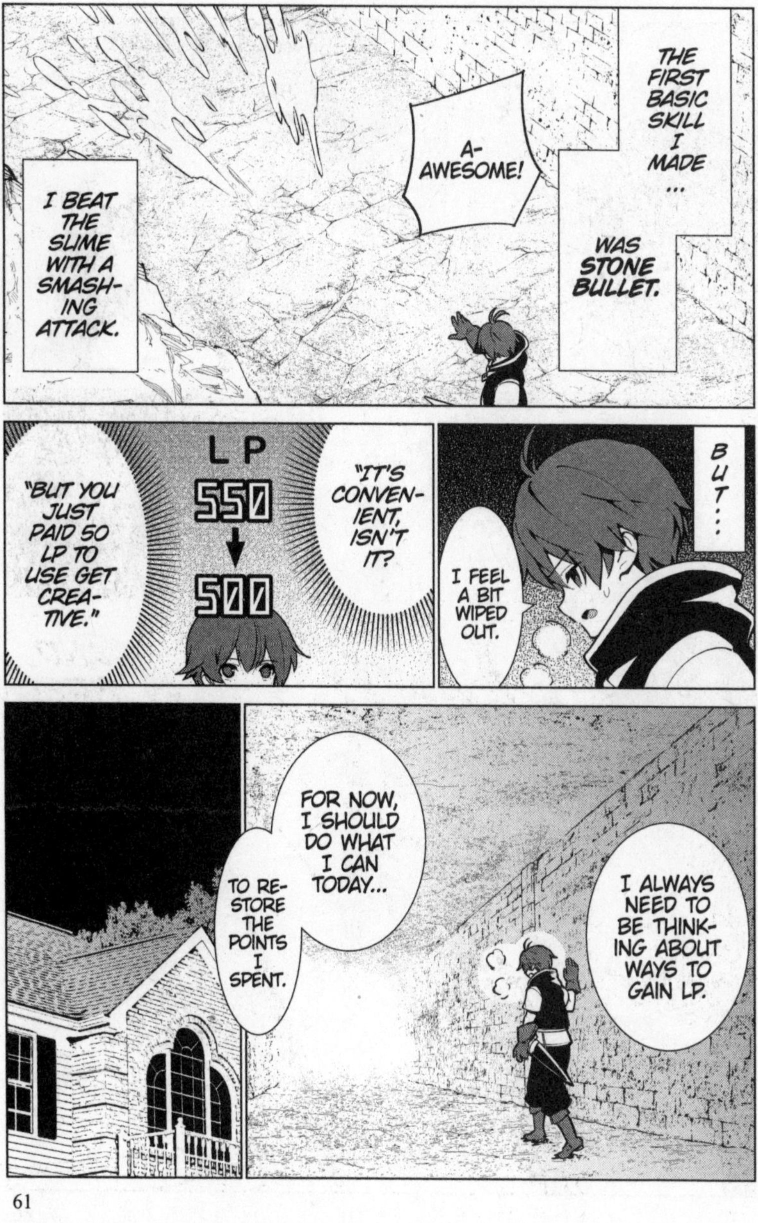
THE FIRST BASIC SKILL I MADE...
WAS STONE BULLET.
A-AWESOME!
I BEAT THE SLIME WITH A SMASHING ATTACK.
BUT...
I FEEL A BIT WIPED OUT.
"IT'S CONVENIENT, ISN'T IT?
LP
550
500
"BUT YOU JUST PAID 50 LP TO USE GET CREATIVE."
I ALWAYS NEED TO BE THINKING ABOUT WAYS TO GAIN LP.
FOR NOW, I SHOULD DO WHAT I CAN TODAY...
TO RESTORE THE POINTS I SPENT.

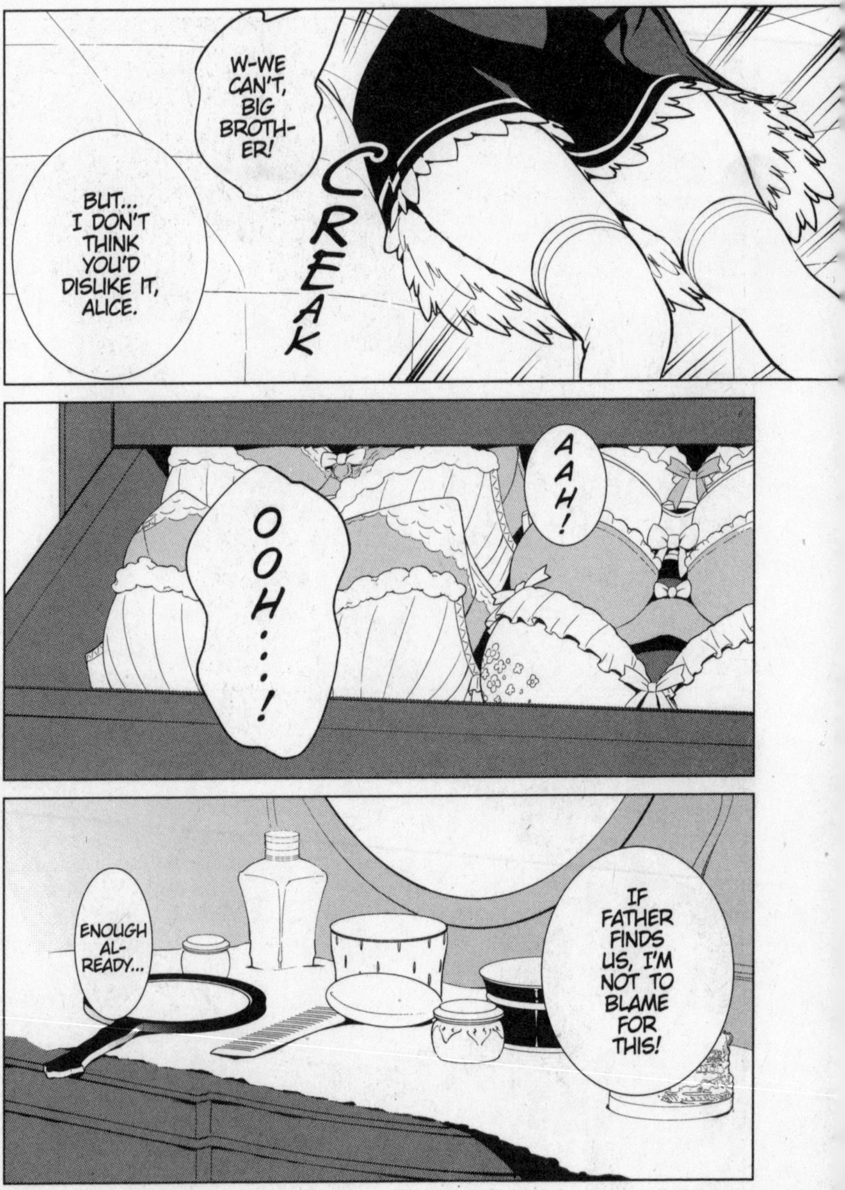
W-WE CAN'T, BIG BROTH-ER!
CREAK
BUT... I DON'T THINK YOU'D DISLIKE IT, ALICE.
AAH!
OOH...!
IF FATHER FINDS US, I'M NOT TO BLAME FOR THIS!
ENOUGH AL-READY...

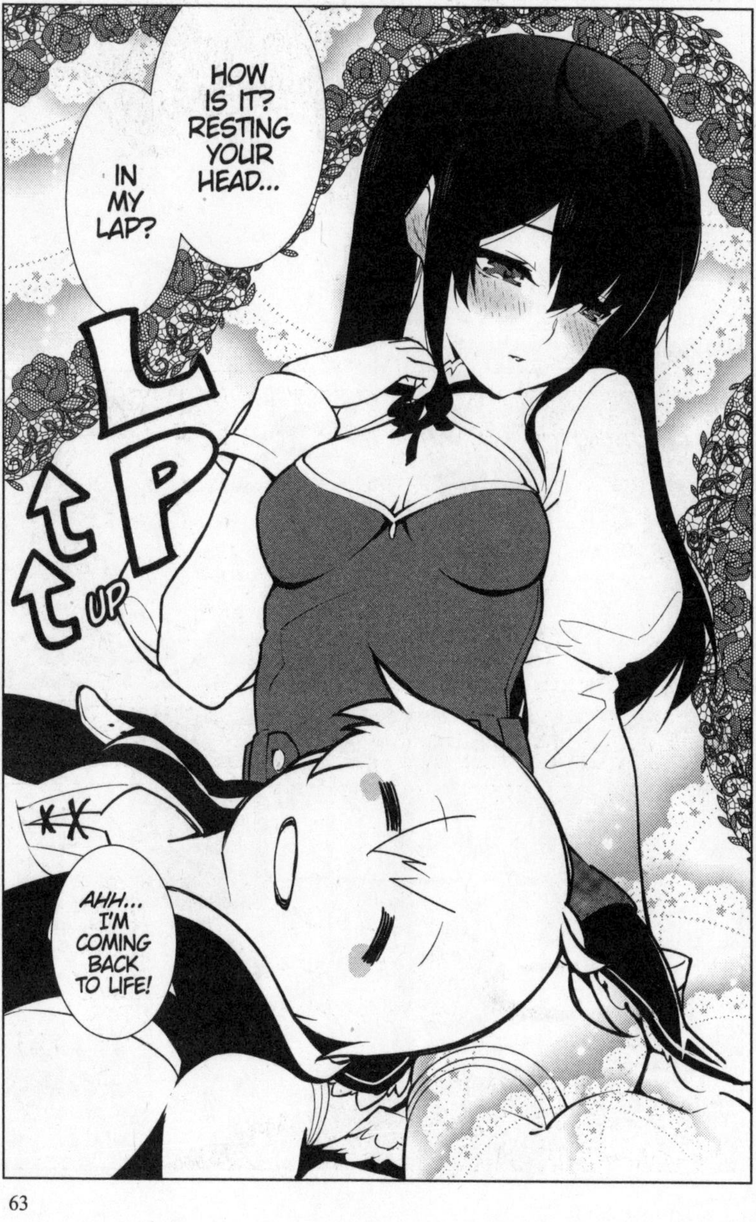
HOW IS IT? RESTING YOUR HEAD...
IN MY LAP?
UP
AHH... I'M COMING BACK TO LIFE!

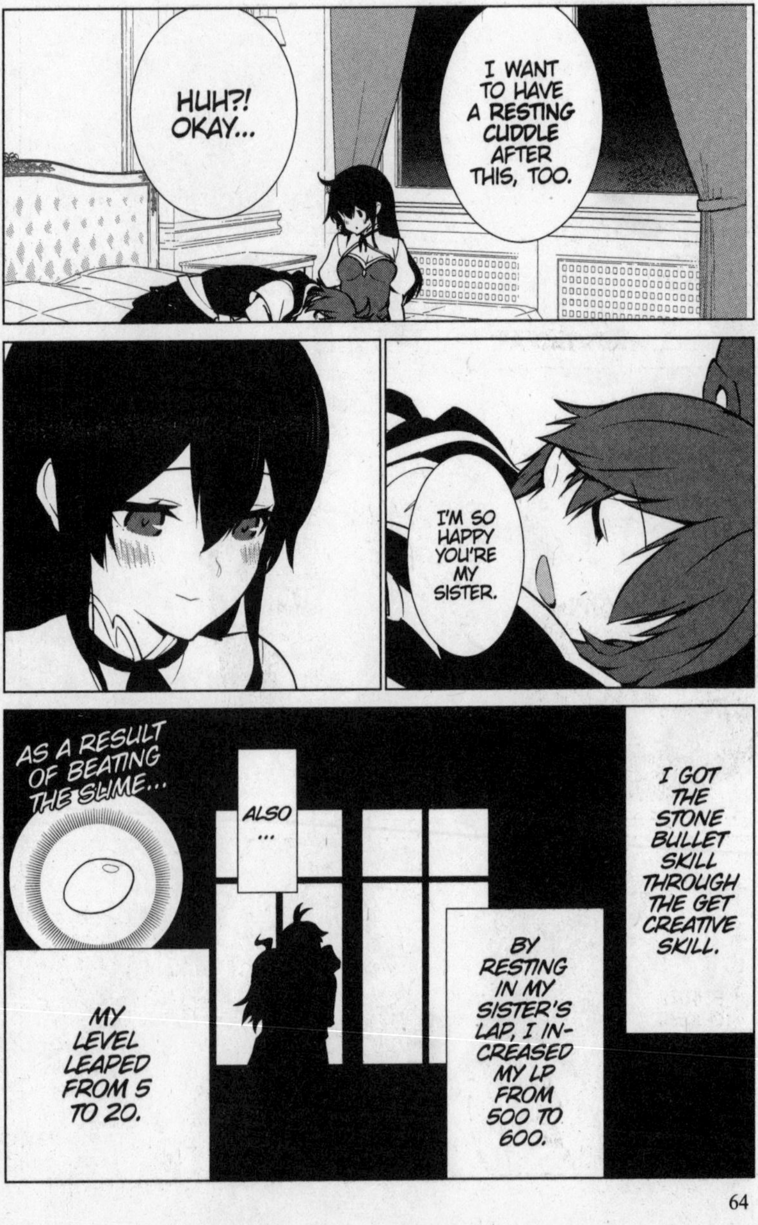
I WANT TO HAVE A RESTING CUDDLE AFTER THIS, TOO.
HUH?! OKAY...
I'M SO HAPPY YOU'RE MY SISTER.
AS A RESULT OF BEATING THE SLIME...
MY LEVEL LEAPED FROM 5 TO 20.
I GOT THE STONE BULLET SKILL THROUGH THE GET CREATIVE SKILL.
ALSO...
BY RESTING IN MY SISTER'S LAP, I IN-CREASED MY LP FROM 500 TO 600.

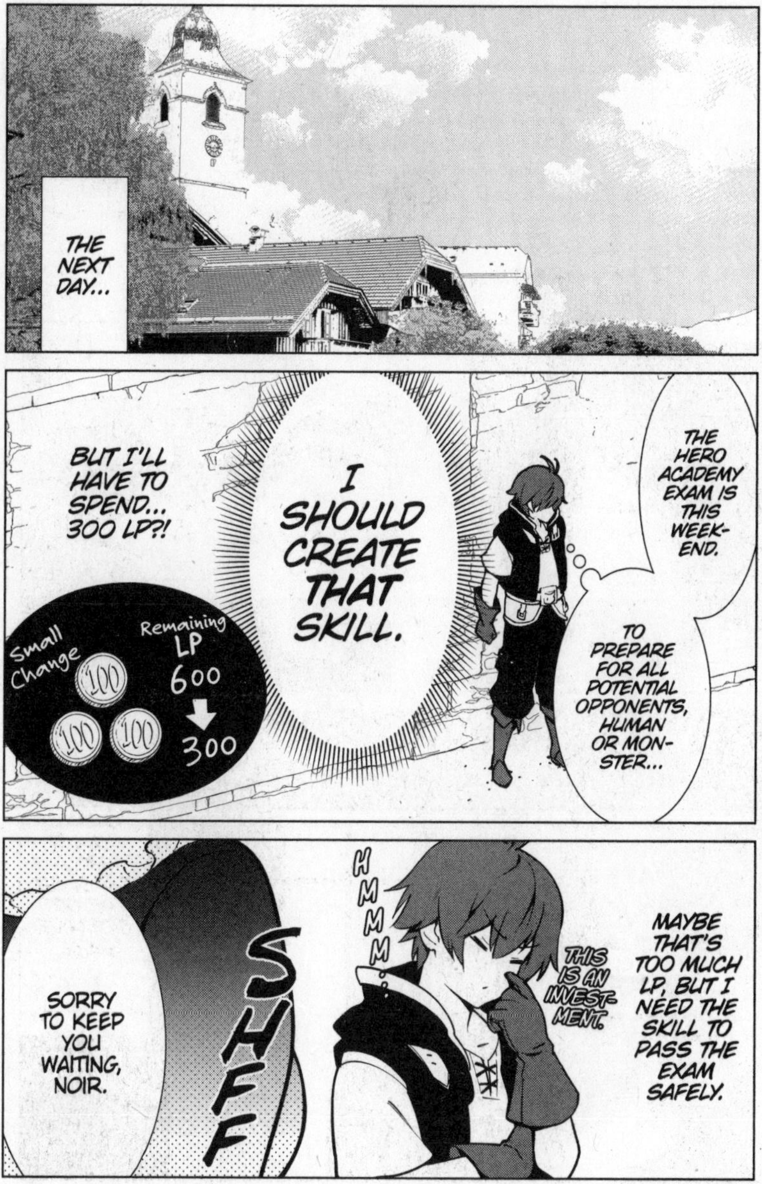
THE NEXT DAY...
THE HERO ACADEMY EXAM IS THIS WEEK-END.
TO PREPARE FOR ALL POTENTIAL OPPONENTS, HUMAN OR MON-STER...
I SHOULD CREATE THAT SKILL.
BUT I'LL HAVE TO SPEND... 300 LP?!
Remaining LP 600 300
Small Change 100 100 100
MAYBE THAT'S TOO MUCH LP, BUT I NEED THE SKILL TO PASS THE EXAM SAFELY.
THIS IS AN INVEST-MENT.
HMMM...
SHFF
SORRY TO KEEP YOU WAITING, NOIR.

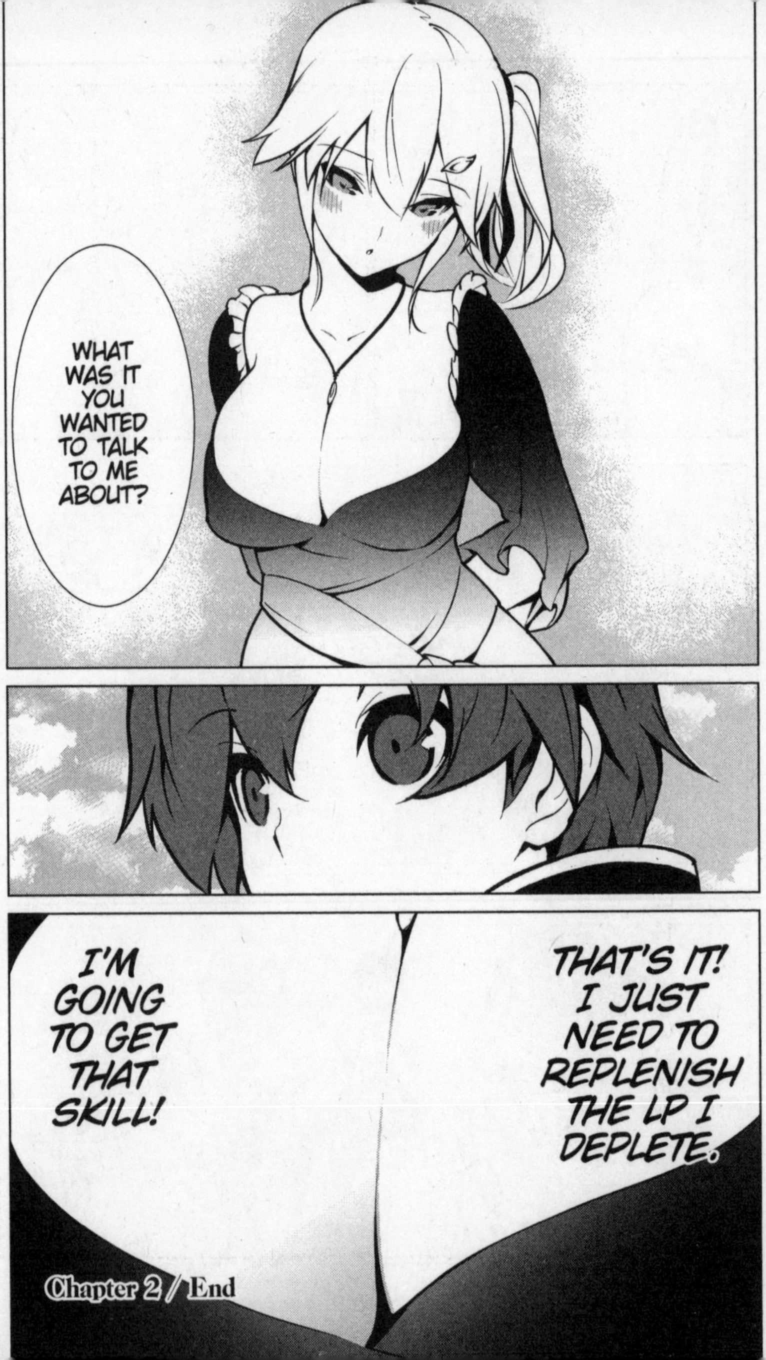
WHAT WAS IT YOU WANTED TO TALK TO ME ABOUT?
THAT'S IT! I JUST NEED TO REPLENISH THE LP I DEPLETE.
I'M GOING TO GET THAT SKILL!
Chapter 2 / End

◆EMMA LAST NIGHT◆

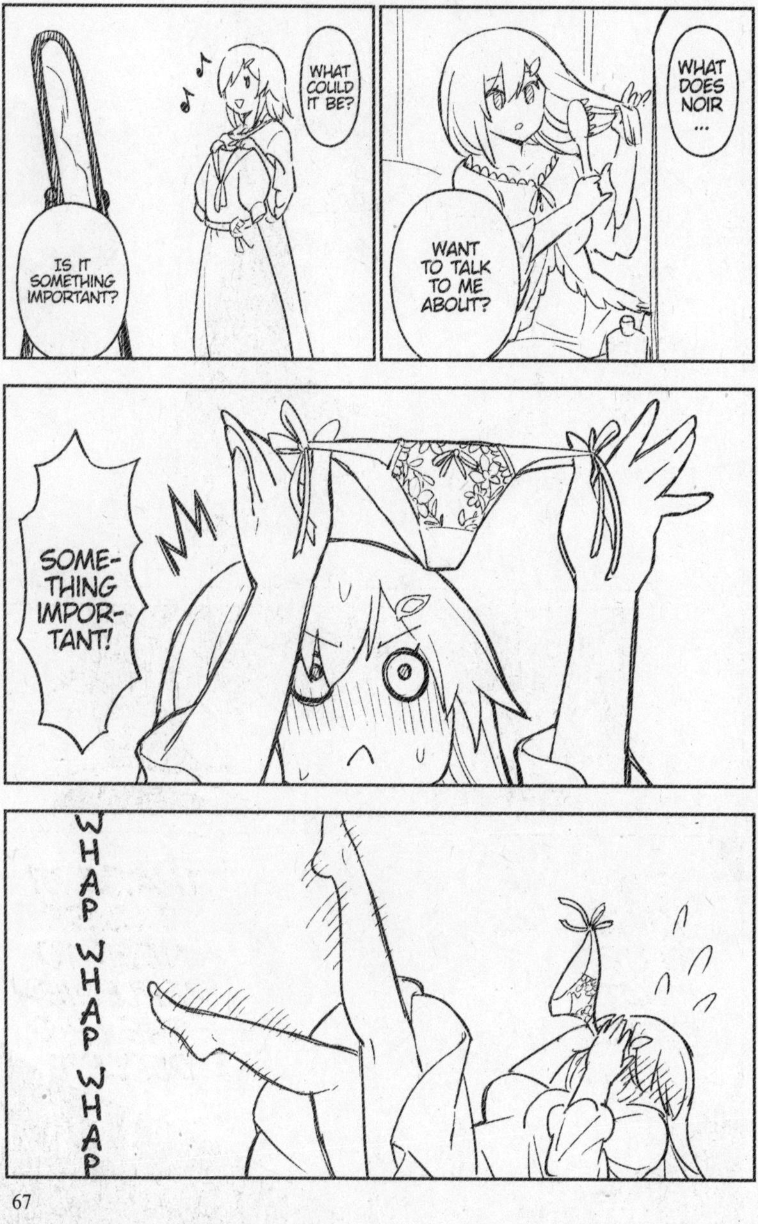
WHAT DOES NOIR ...
WANT TO TALK TO ME ABOUT?
WHAT COULD IT BE?
IS IT SOMETHING IMPORTANT?
SOME-THING IMPOR-TANT!
WHAP WHAP WHAP

THE HIDDEN DUNGEON ONLY I CAN ENTER

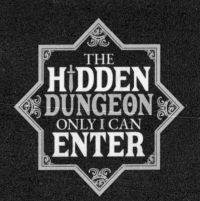

Chapter 3: Discerning Eye

SORRY TO KEEP YOU WAITING, NOIR.

WHAT WAS IT YOU WANTED TO TALK TO ME ABOUT?

SURE.

THANKS TO YOU, I FOUND A HIDDEN DUNGEON.

AND THANKS FOR THE KISSES, TOO...

TRULY.

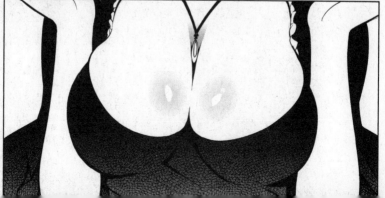

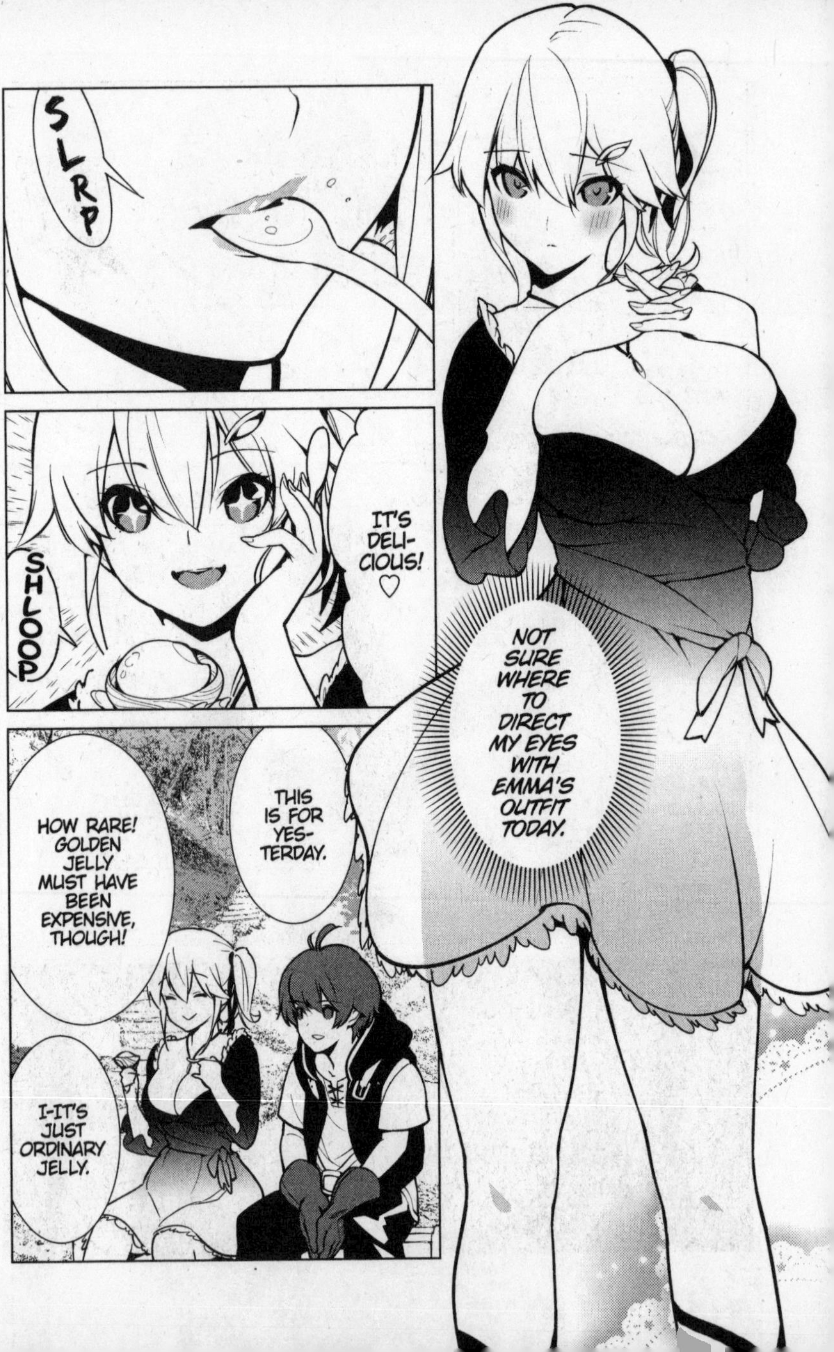
NOT SURE WHERE TO DIRECT MY EYES WITH EMMA'S OUTFIT TODAY.
SLRP
IT'S DELI-CIOUS! ♡
SHLOOP
THIS IS FOR YES-TERDAY.
HOW RARE! GOLDEN JELLY MUST HAVE BEEN EXPENSIVE, THOUGH!
I-IT'S JUST ORDINARY JELLY.

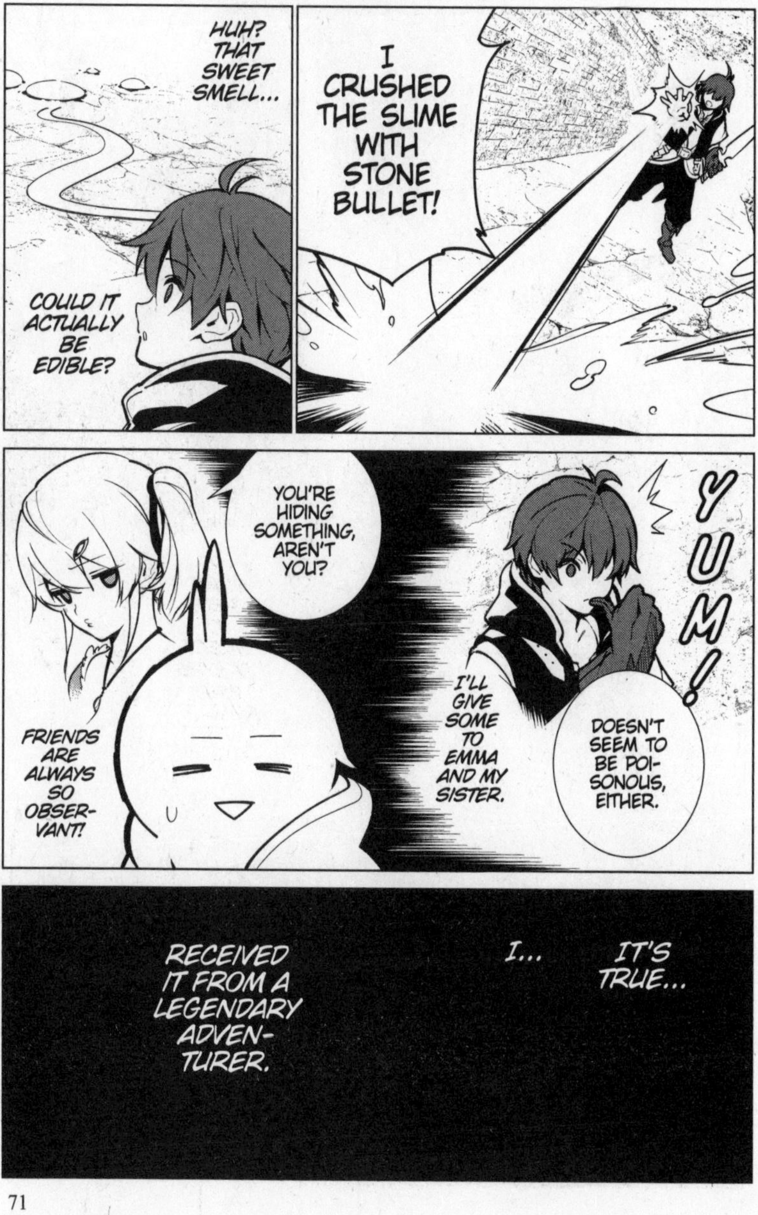
I CRUSHED THE SLIME WITH STONE BULLET!
HUH? THAT SWEET SMELL...
COULD IT ACTUALLY BE EDIBLE?
YUM!
DOESN'T SEEM TO BE POI-SONOUS, EITHER.
I'LL GIVE SOME TO EMMA AND MY SISTER.
YOU'RE HIDING SOMETHING, AREN'T YOU?
FRIENDS ARE ALWAYS SO OBSERVANT!
IT'S TRUE...
I...
RECEIVED IT FROM A LEGENDARY ADVENTURER.

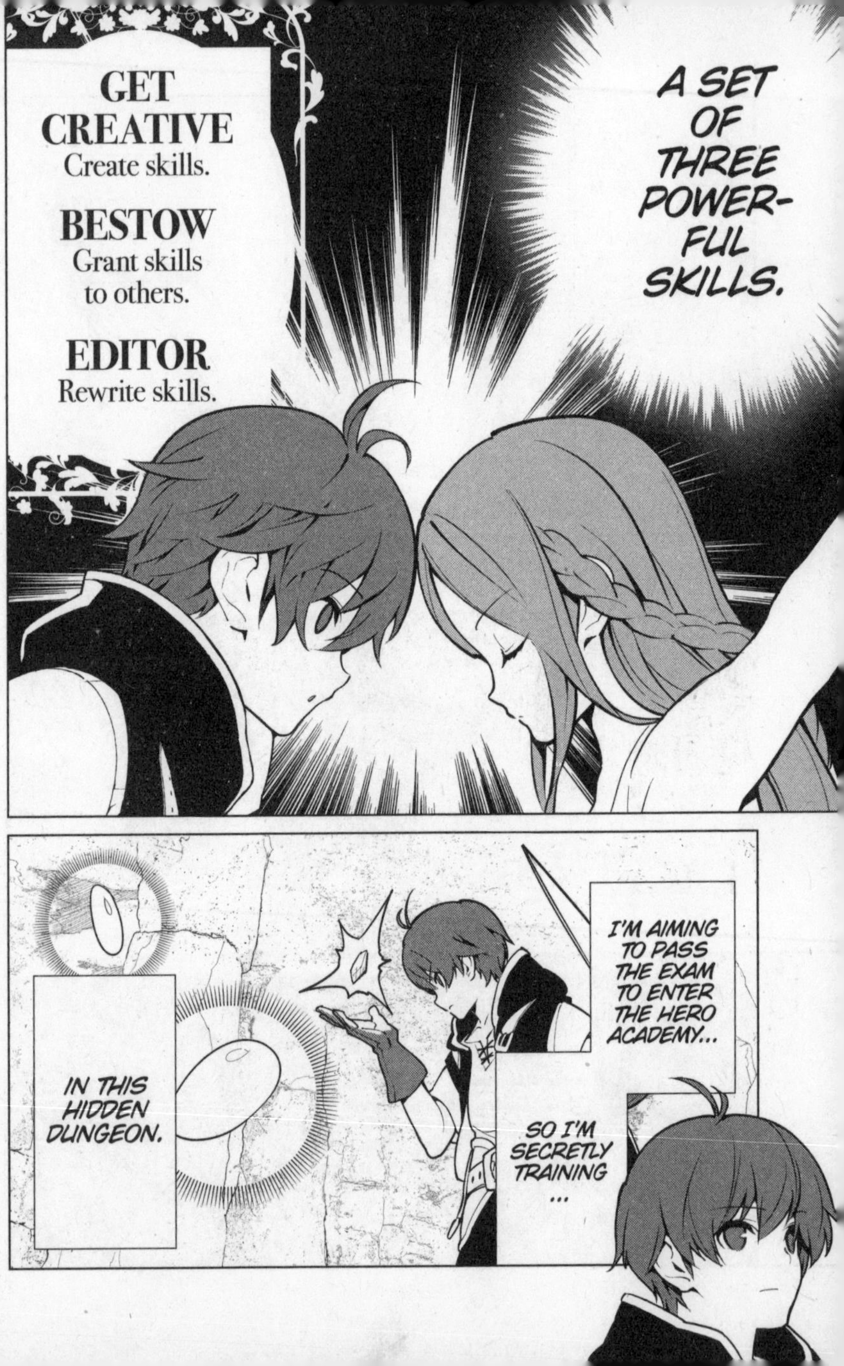
A SET OF THREE POWER-FUL SKILLS.
GET CREATIVE
Create skills.
BESTOW
Grant skills to others.
EDITOR
Rewrite skills.
I'M AIMING TO PASS THE EXAM TO ENTER THE HERO ACADEMY...
SO I'M SECRETLY TRAINING...
IN THIS HIDDEN DUNGEON.

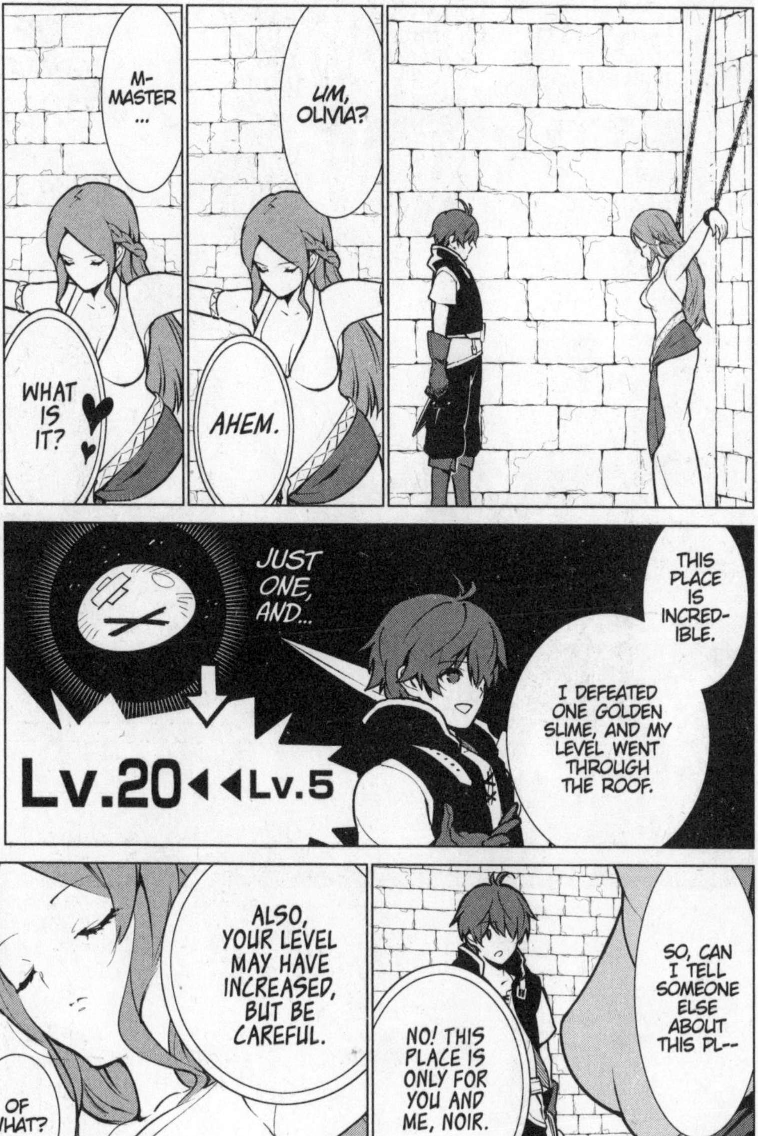

UM, OLIVIA?
AHEM.
M-MASTER...
WHAT IS IT?
THIS PLACE IS INCREDIBLE.
I DEFEATED ONE GOLDEN SLIME, AND MY LEVEL WENT THROUGH THE ROOF.
JUST ONE, AND...
Lv.20 ◂◂Lv.5
SO, CAN I TELL SOMEONE ELSE ABOUT THIS PL--
NO! THIS PLACE IS ONLY FOR YOU AND ME, NOIR.
ALSO, YOUR LEVEL MAY HAVE INCREASED, BUT BE CAREFUL.
OF WHAT?

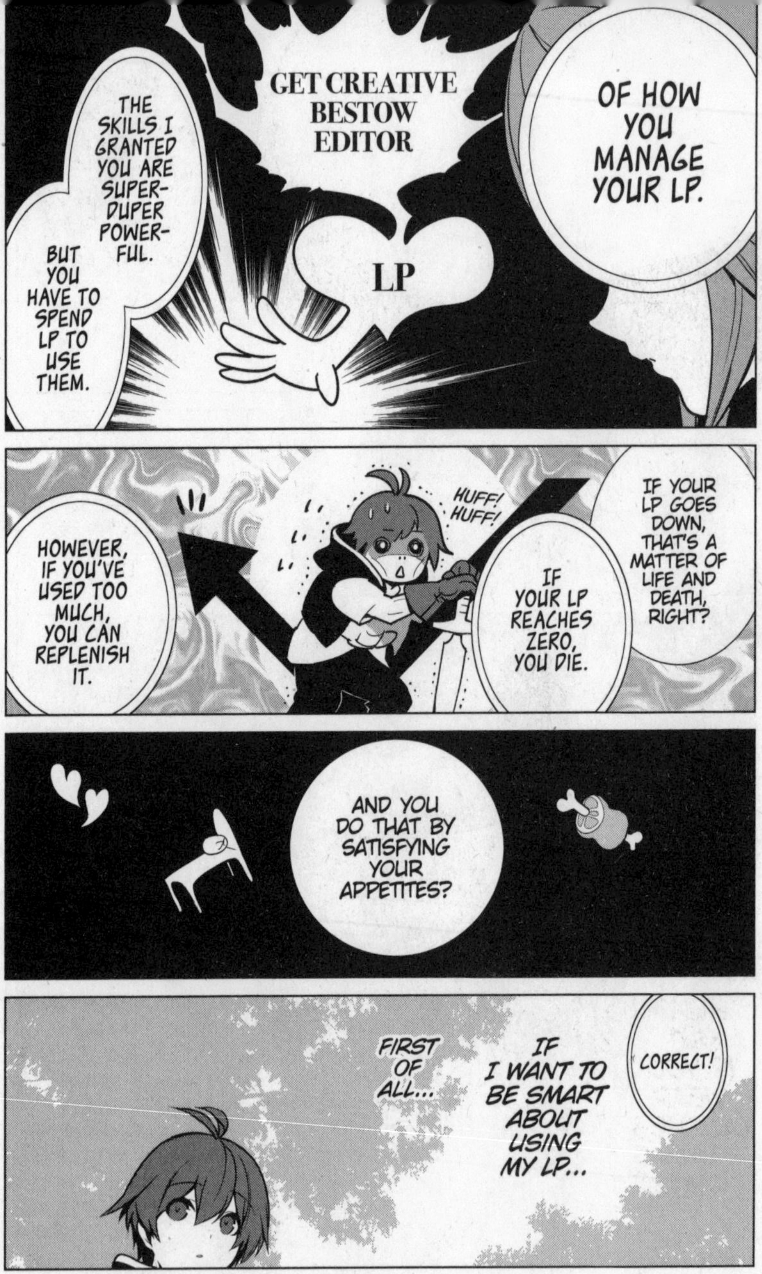
OF HOW YOU MANAGE YOUR LP.
GET CREATIVE BESTOW EDITOR
THE SKILLS I GRANTED YOU ARE SUPER-DUPER POWERFUL.
BUT YOU HAVE TO SPEND LP TO USE THEM.
LP
IF YOUR LP GOES DOWN, THAT'S A MATTER OF LIFE AND DEATH, RIGHT?
HUFF! HUFF!
IF YOUR LP REACHES ZERO, YOU DIE.
HOWEVER, IF YOU'VE USED TOO MUCH, YOU CAN REPLENISH IT.
AND YOU DO THAT BY SATISFYING YOUR APPETITES?
CORRECT!
IF I WANT TO BE SMART ABOUT USING MY LP...
FIRST OF ALL...

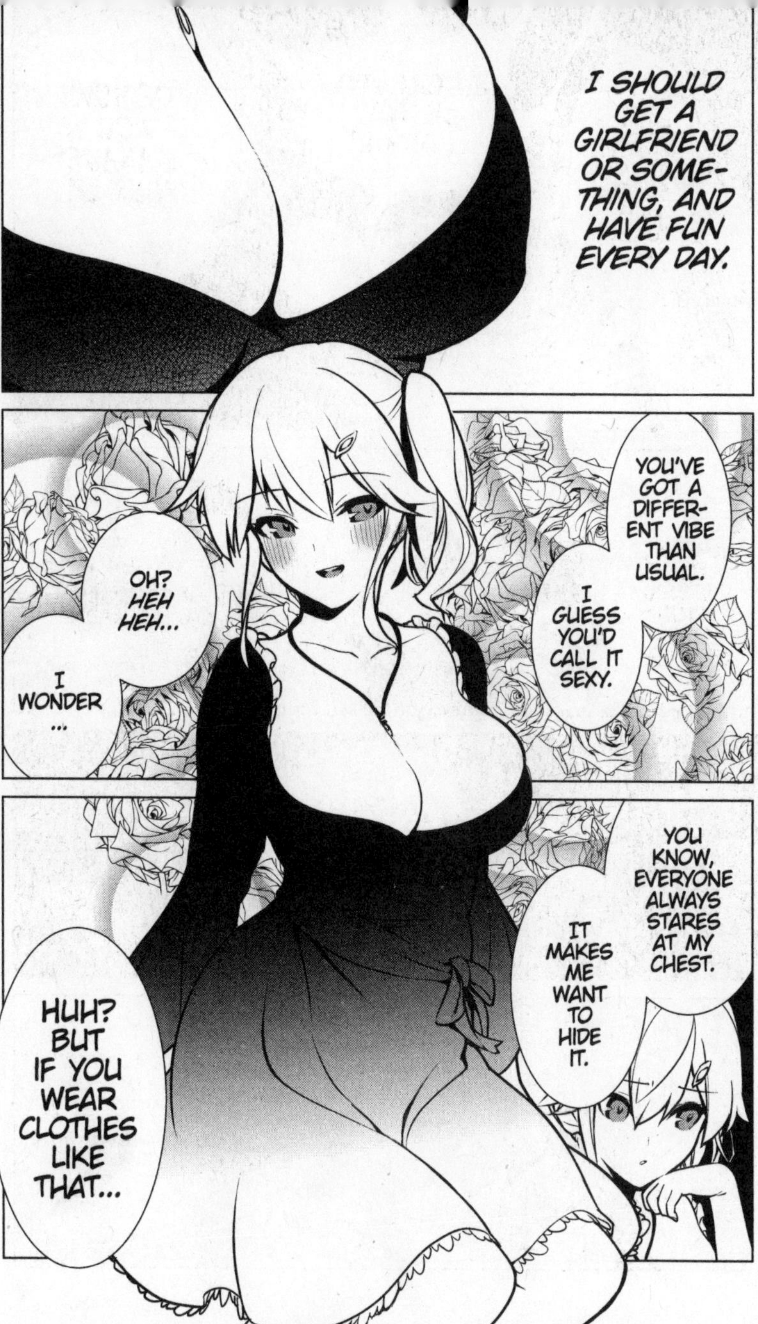
I SHOULD GET A GIRLFRIEND OR SOMETHING, AND HAVE FUN EVERY DAY.
YOU'VE GOT A DIFFERENT VIBE THAN USUAL.
I GUESS YOU'D CALL IT SEXY.
OH? HEH HEH...
I WONDER...
YOU KNOW, EVERYONE ALWAYS STARES AT MY CHEST.
IT MAKES ME WANT TO HIDE IT.
HUH? BUT IF YOU WEAR CLOTHES LIKE THAT...

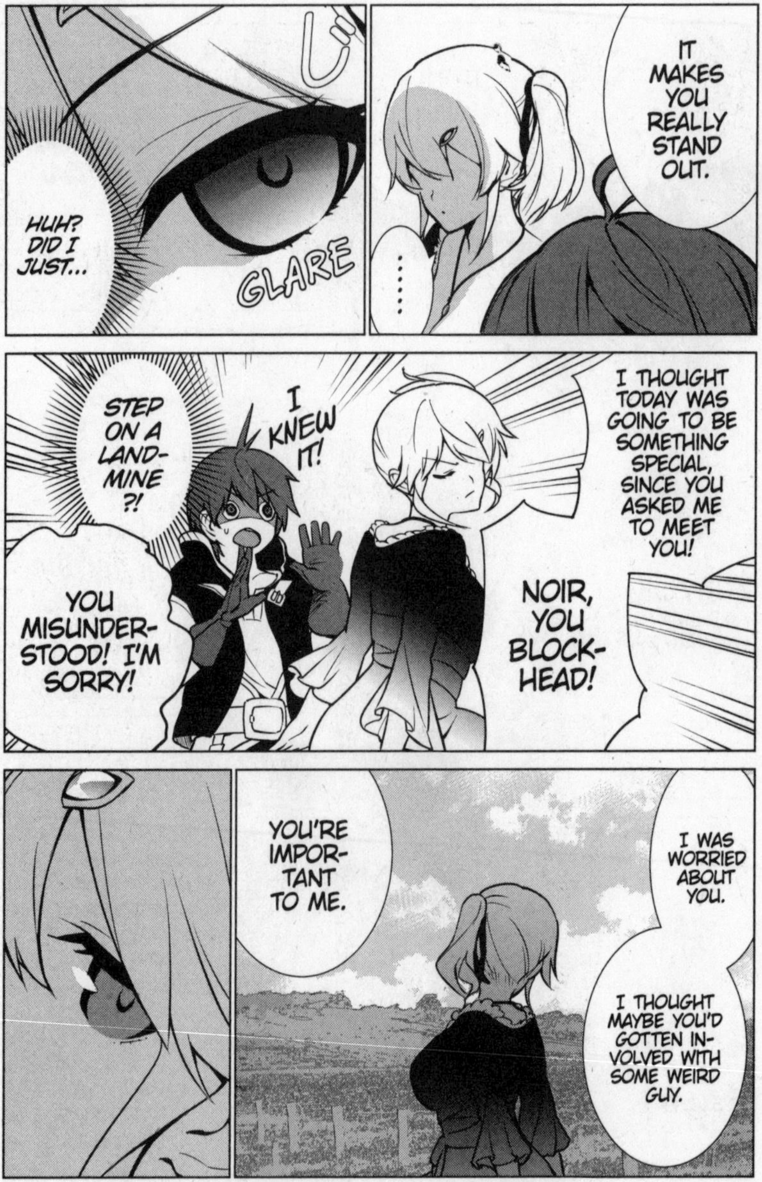
IT MAKES YOU REALLY STAND OUT.
......
HUH? DID I JUST...
GLARE
I THOUGHT TODAY WAS GOING TO BE SOMETHING SPECIAL, SINCE YOU ASKED ME TO MEET YOU!
NOIR, YOU BLOCK-HEAD!
I KNEW IT!
STEP ON A LAND-MINE?!
YOU MISUNDER-STOOD! I'M SORRY!
I WAS WORRIED ABOUT YOU.
I THOUGHT MAYBE YOU'D GOTTEN IN-VOLVED WITH SOME WEIRD GUY.
YOU'RE IMPOR-TANT TO ME.

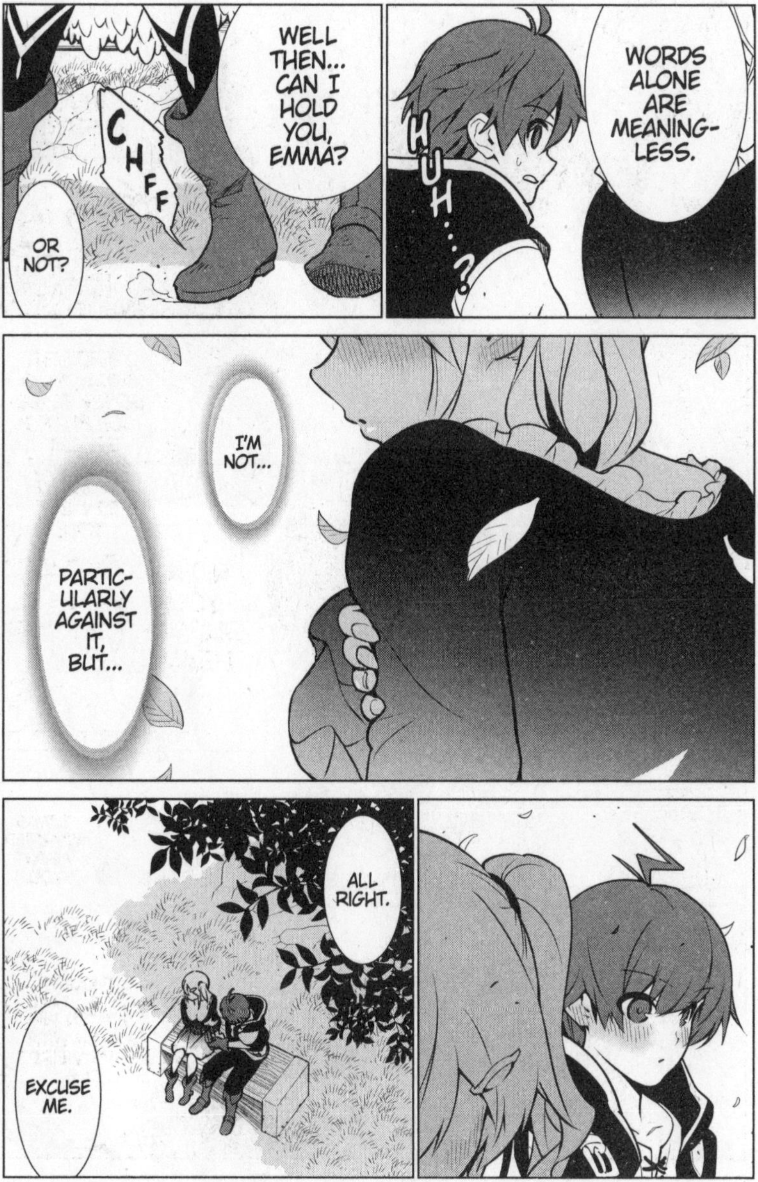
WORDS ALONE ARE MEANING-LESS.
HUH...?
WELL THEN... CAN I HOLD YOU, EMMA?
CHFF
OR NOT?
I'M NOT...
PARTIC-ULARLY AGAINST IT, BUT...
ALL RIGHT.
EXCUSE ME.

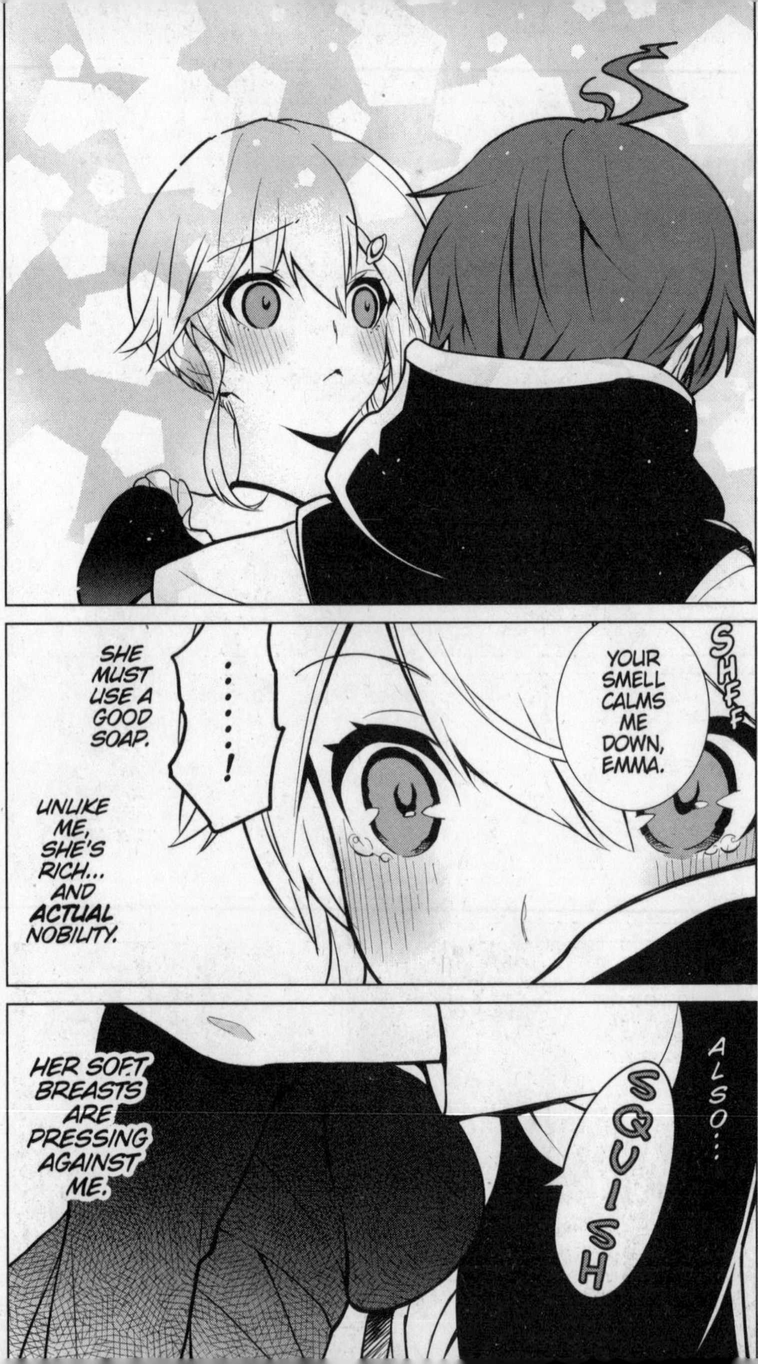
SHFF
YOUR SMELL CALMS ME DOWN, EMMA.
......!
SHE MUST USE A GOOD SOAP.
UNLIKE ME, SHE'S RICH... AND ACTUAL NOBILITY.
ALSO...
SQUISH
HER SOFT BREASTS ARE PRESSING AGAINST ME.

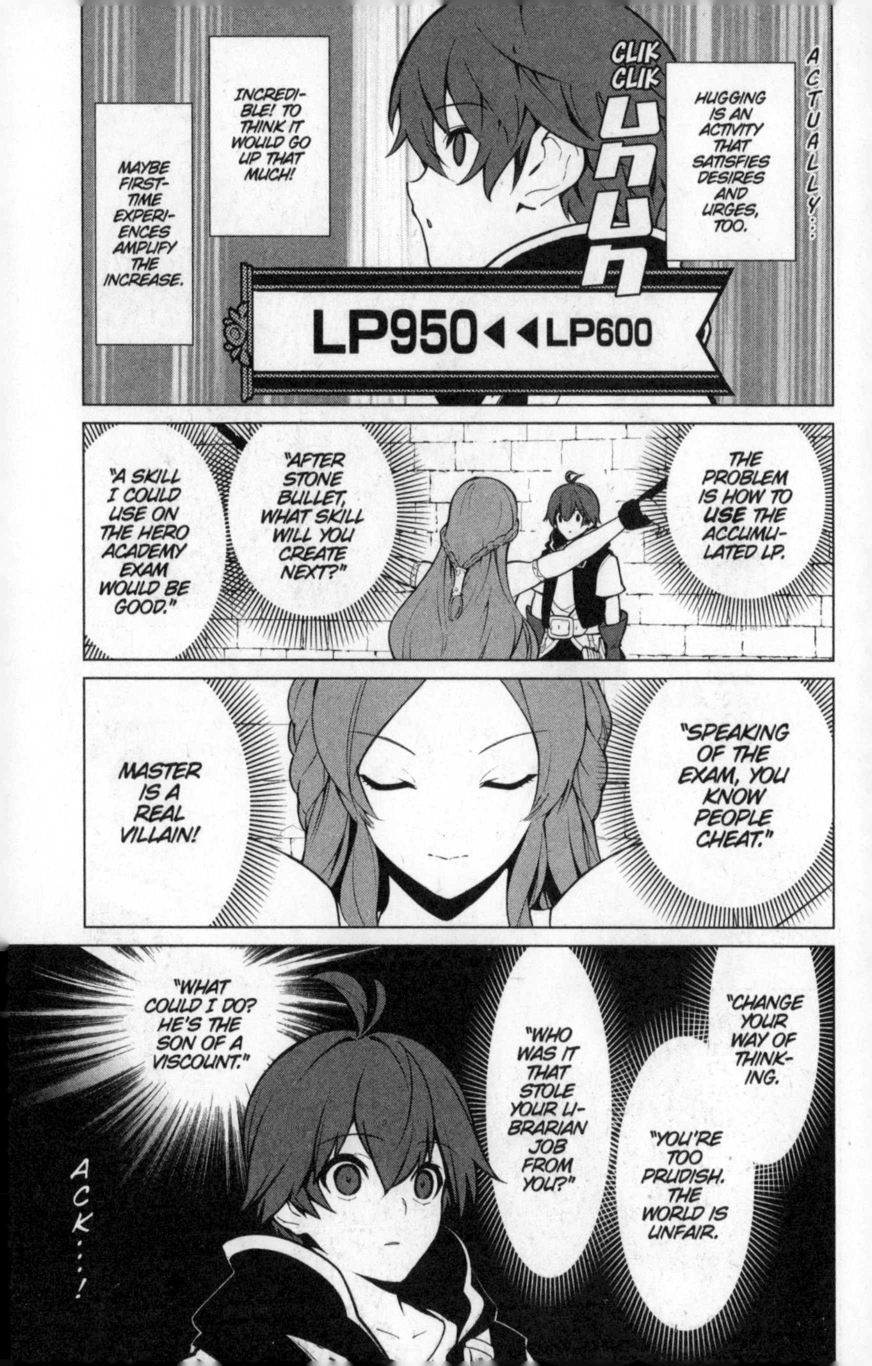
ACTUALLY...
HUGGING IS AN ACTIVITY THAT SATISFIES DESIRES AND URGES, TOO.
CLIK CLIK
INCREDIBLE! TO THINK IT WOULD GO UP THAT MUCH!
MAYBE FIRST-TIME EXPERIENCES AMPLIFY THE INCREASE.
LP950 ◀◀ LP600
THE PROBLEM IS HOW TO USE THE ACCUMULATED LP.
"AFTER STONE BULLET, WHAT SKILL WILL YOU CREATE NEXT?"
"A SKILL I COULD USE ON THE HERO ACADEMY EXAM WOULD BE GOOD."
"SPEAKING OF THE EXAM, YOU KNOW PEOPLE CHEAT."
MASTER IS A REAL VILLAIN!
"CHANGE YOUR WAY OF THINKING.
"YOU'RE TOO PRUDISH. THE WORLD IS UNFAIR.
"WHO WAS IT THAT STOLE YOUR LIBRARIAN JOB FROM YOU?"
"WHAT COULD I DO? HE'S THE SON OF A VISCOUNT."
ACK...!

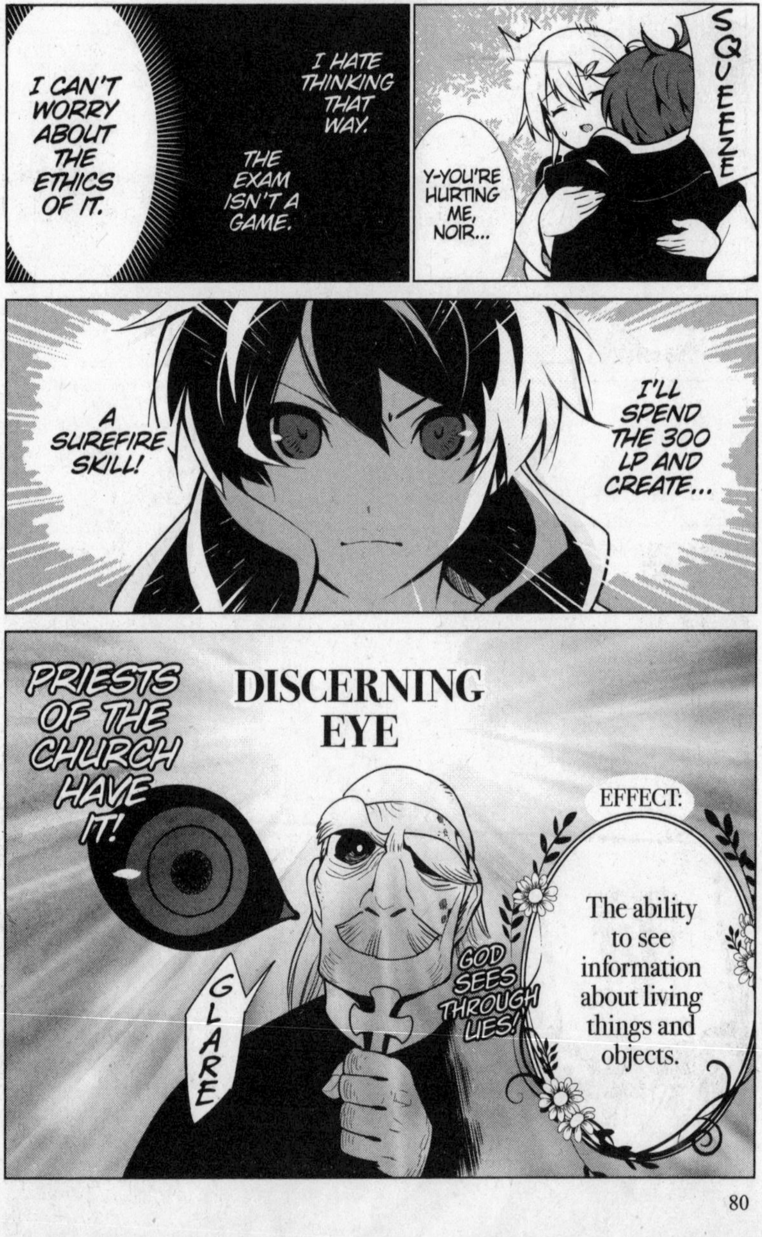
SQUEEZE
Y-YOU'RE HURTING ME, NOIR...
I HATE THINKING THAT WAY.
THE EXAM ISN'T A GAME.
I CAN'T WORRY ABOUT THE ETHICS OF IT.
I'LL SPEND THE 300 LP AND CREATE...
A SUREFIRE SKILL!
DISCERNING EYE
EFFECT:
The ability to see information about living things and objects.
PRIESTS OF THE CHURCH HAVE IT!
GOD SEES THROUGH LIES!
GLARE

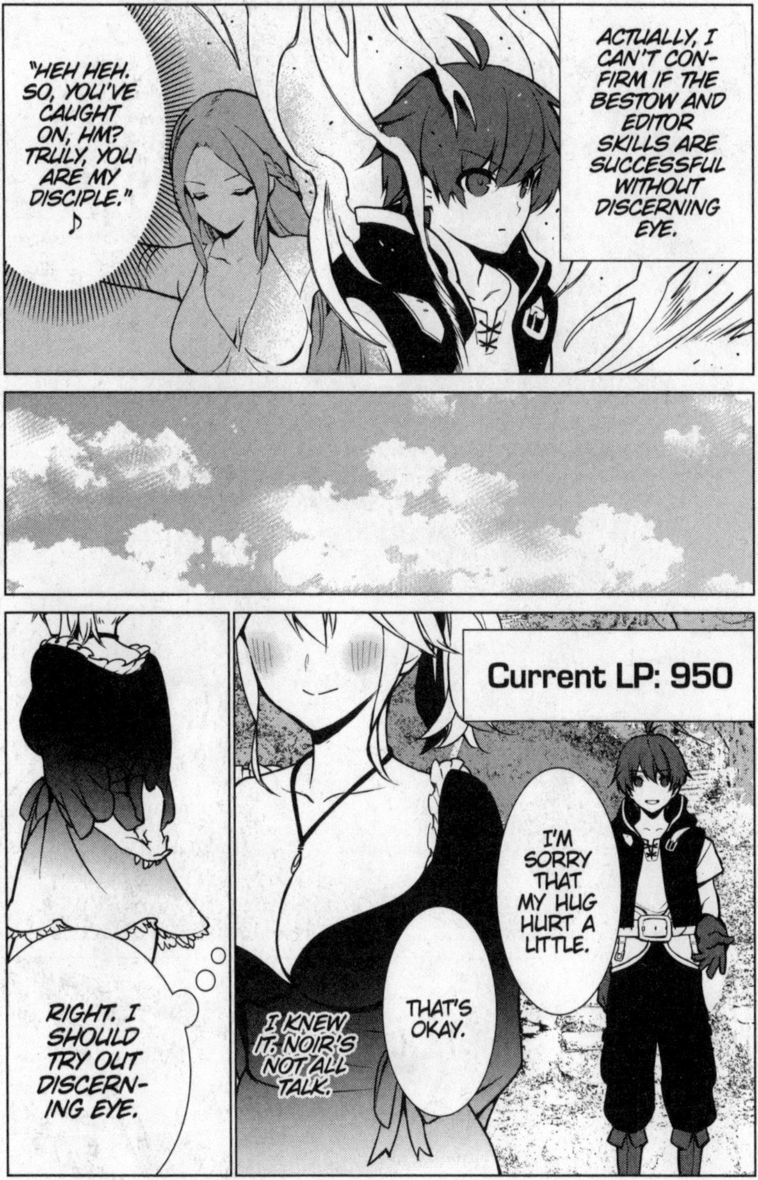
ACTUALLY, I CAN'T CONFIRM IF THE BESTOW AND EDITOR SKILLS ARE SUCCESSFUL WITHOUT DISCERNING EYE.
"HEH HEH. SO, YOU'VE CAUGHT ON, HM? TRULY, YOU ARE MY DISCIPLE." ♪
Current LP: 950
I'M SORRY THAT MY HUG HURT A LITTLE.
THAT'S OKAY.
I KNEW IT. NOIR'S NOT ALL TALK.
RIGHT. I SHOULD TRY OUT DISCERNING EYE.

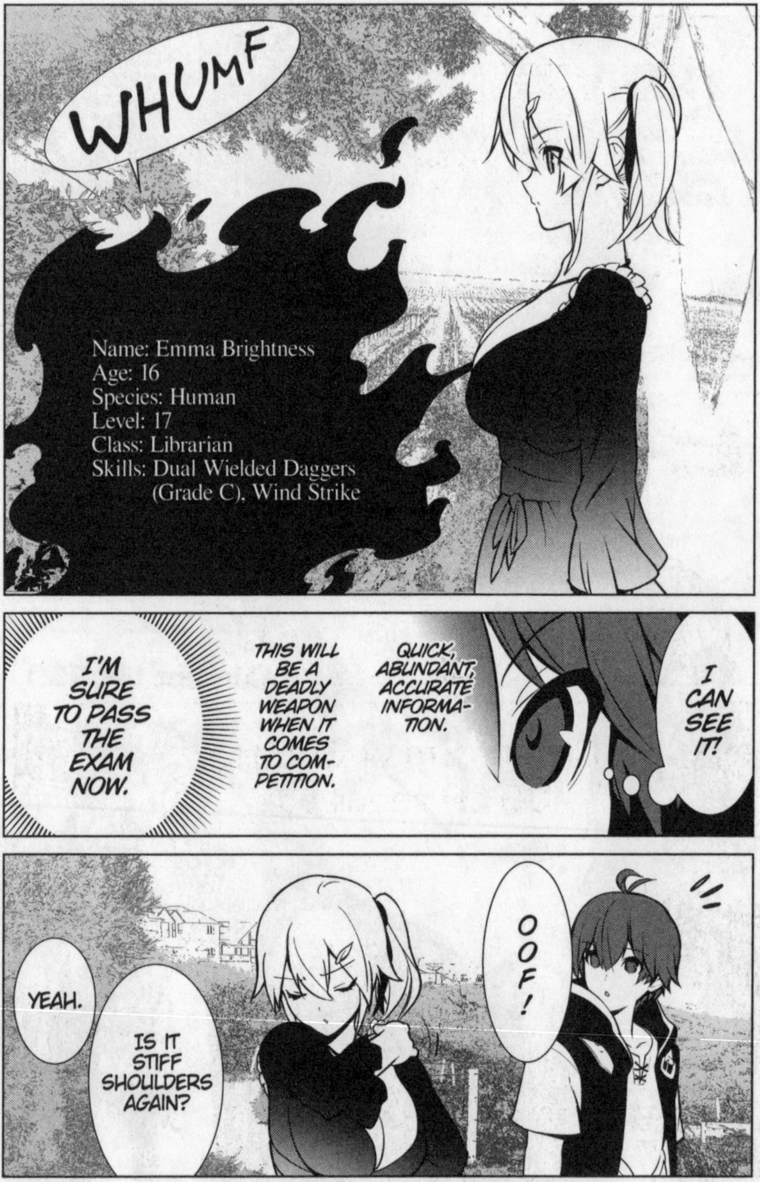
WHUMF
Name: Emma Brightness
Age: 16
Species: Human
Level: 17
Class: Librarian
Skills: Dual Wielded Daggers (Grade C), Wind Strike
I CAN SEE IT!
QUICK, ABUNDANT, ACCURATE INFORMATION.
THIS WILL BE A DEADLY WEAPON WHEN IT COMES TO COMPETITION.
I'M SURE TO PASS THE EXAM NOW.
OOF!
IS IT STIFF SHOULDERS AGAIN?
YEAH.

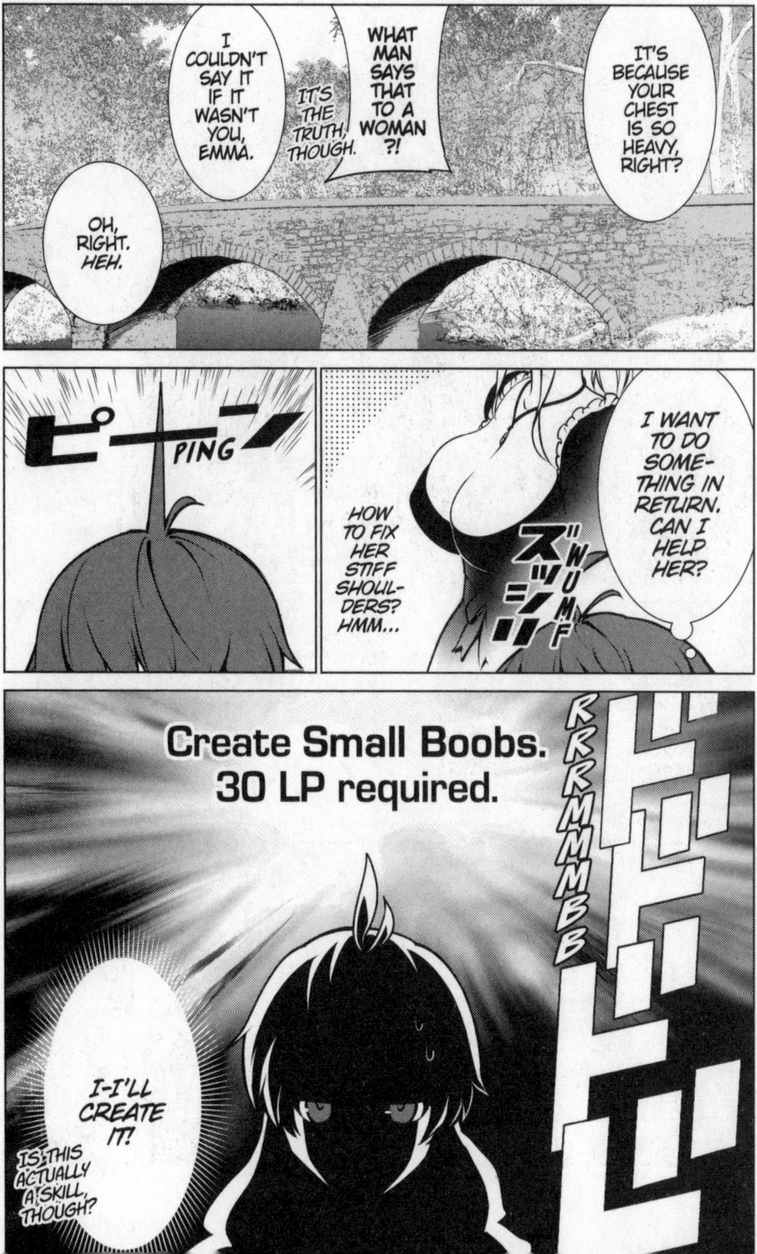
IT'S BECAUSE YOUR CHEST IS SO HEAVY, RIGHT?
WHAT MAN SAYS THAT TO A WOMAN?!
IT'S THE TRUTH, THOUGH.
I COULDN'T SAY IT IF IT WASN'T YOU, EMMA.
OH, RIGHT. HEH.
I WANT TO DO SOMETHING IN RETURN. CAN I HELP HER?
WUMF
HOW TO FIX HER STIFF SHOULDERS? HMM...
PING
RRRMMMBB
Create Small Boobs.
30 LP required.
I-I'LL CREATE IT!
IS THIS ACTUALLY A SKILL, THOUGH?

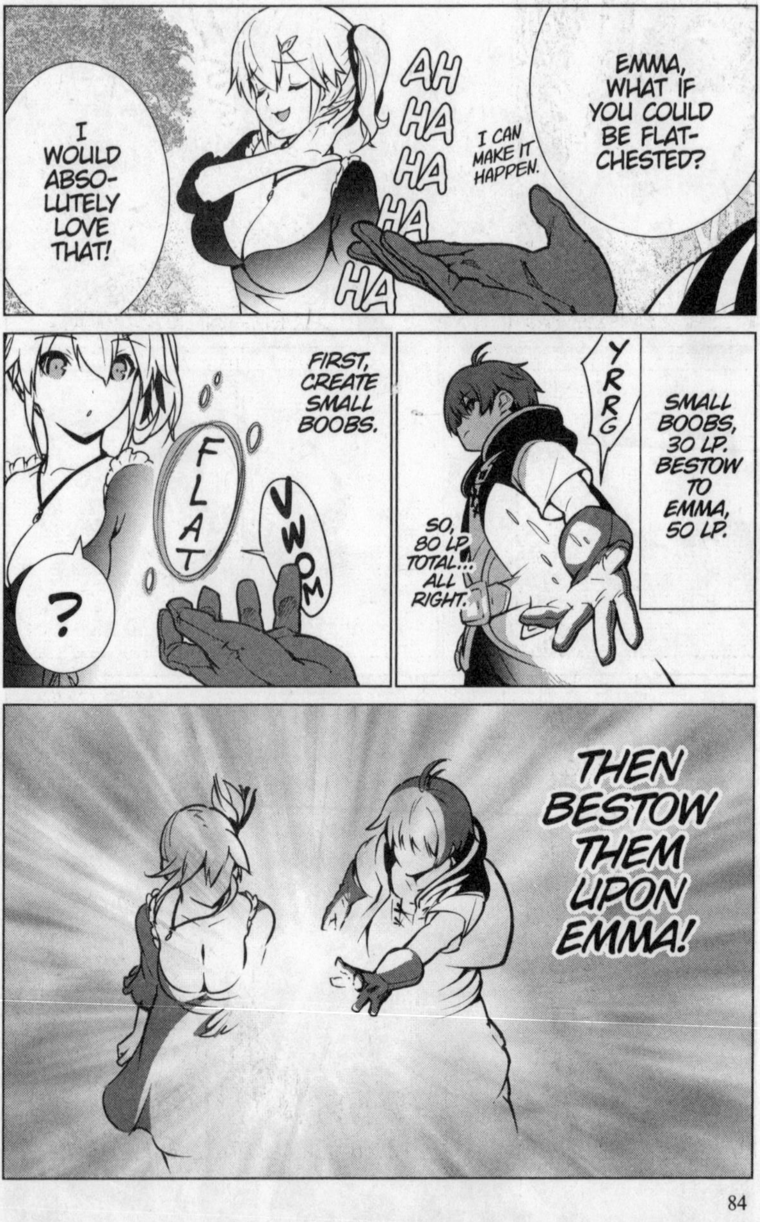
EMMA, WHAT IF YOU COULD BE FLAT-CHESTED?
I CAN MAKE IT HAPPEN.
AH HA HA HA HA HA
I WOULD ABSOLUTELY LOVE THAT!
YRRG
SMALL BOOBS, 30 LP. BESTOW TO EMMA, 50 LP.
SO, 80 LP TOTAL... ALL RIGHT.
FIRST, CREATE SMALL BOOBS.
FLAT
VWOM
?
THEN BESTOW THEM UPON EMMA!

WHUH?

HSSS

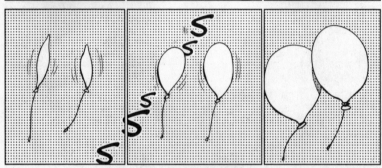

SSS

SWUF

SHRRRUF

THIS SKILL SET IS UN-BELIEVABLE, MASTER...

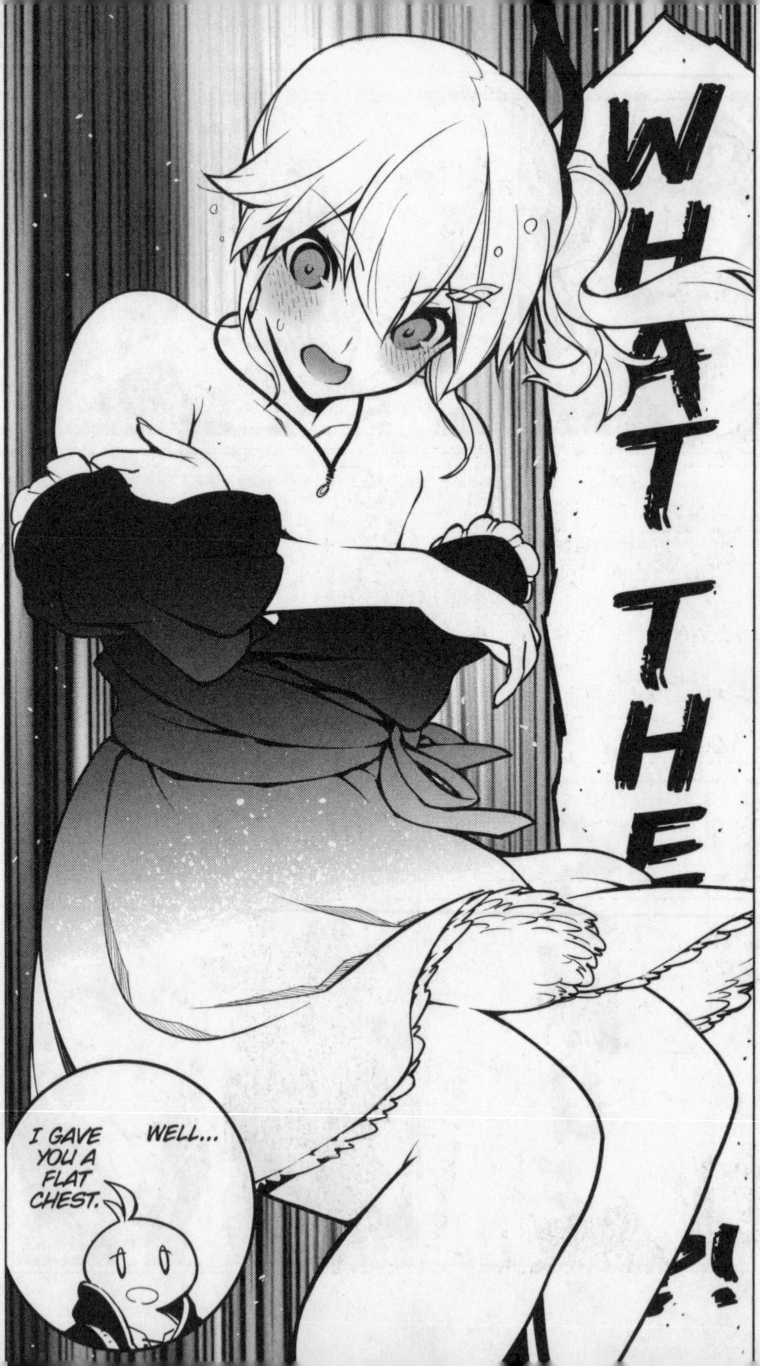
WHAT THE
?!
WELL...
I GAVE YOU A FLAT CHEST.

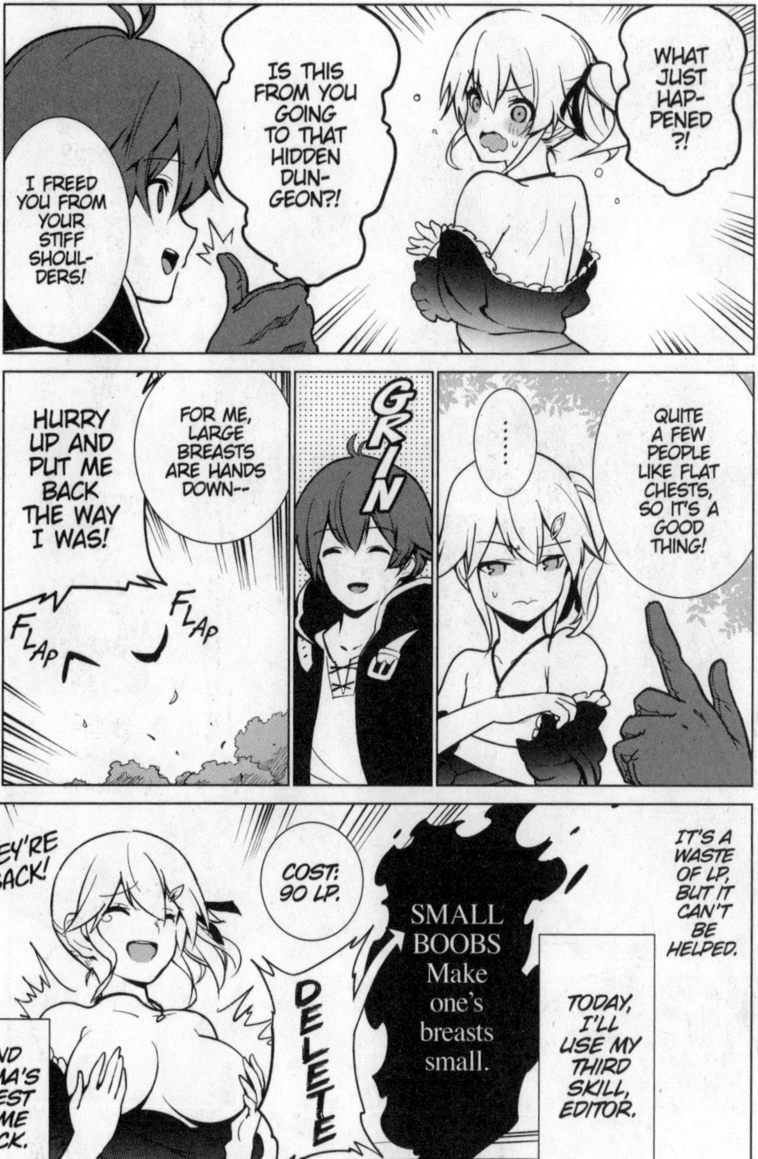
WHAT JUST HAP-PENED?!
IS THIS FROM YOU GOING TO THAT HIDDEN DUN-GEON?!
I FREED YOU FROM YOUR STIFF SHOUL-DERS!
QUITE A FEW PEOPLE LIKE FLAT CHESTS, SO IT'S A GOOD THING!
......
GRIN
FOR ME, LARGE BREASTS ARE HANDS DOWN--
HURRY UP AND PUT ME BACK THE WAY I WAS!
FLAP
FLAP
IT'S A WASTE OF LP, BUT IT CAN'T BE HELPED.
TODAY, I'LL USE MY THIRD SKILL, EDITOR.
SMALL BOOBS Make one's breasts small.
DELETE
COST: 90 LP.
THEY'RE BACK!
AND EMMA'S CHEST CAME BACK.

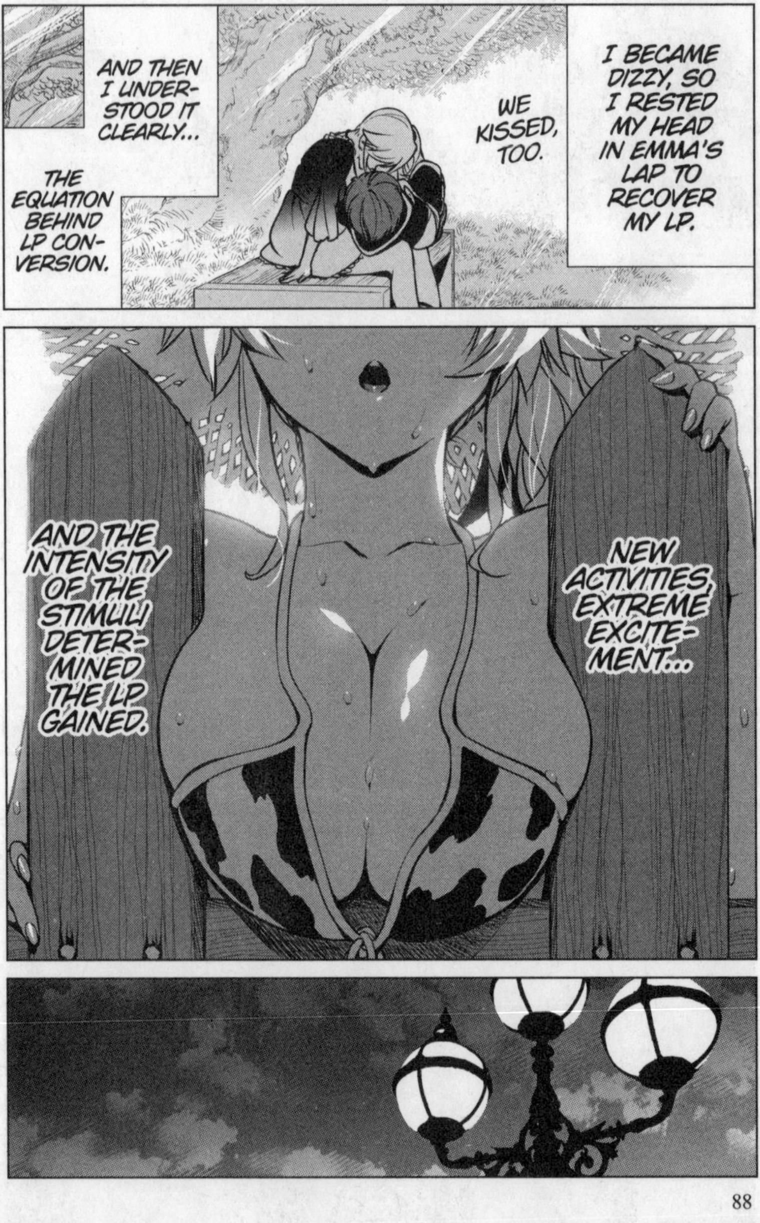
I BECAME DIZZY, SO I RESTED MY HEAD IN EMMA'S LAP TO RECOVER MY LP.
WE KISSED, TOO.
AND THEN I UNDER-STOOD IT CLEARLY...
THE EQUATION BEHIND LP CON-VERSION.
NEW ACTIVITIES, EXTREME EXCITE-MENT...
AND THE INTENSITY OF THE STIMULI DETER-MINED THE LP GAINED.

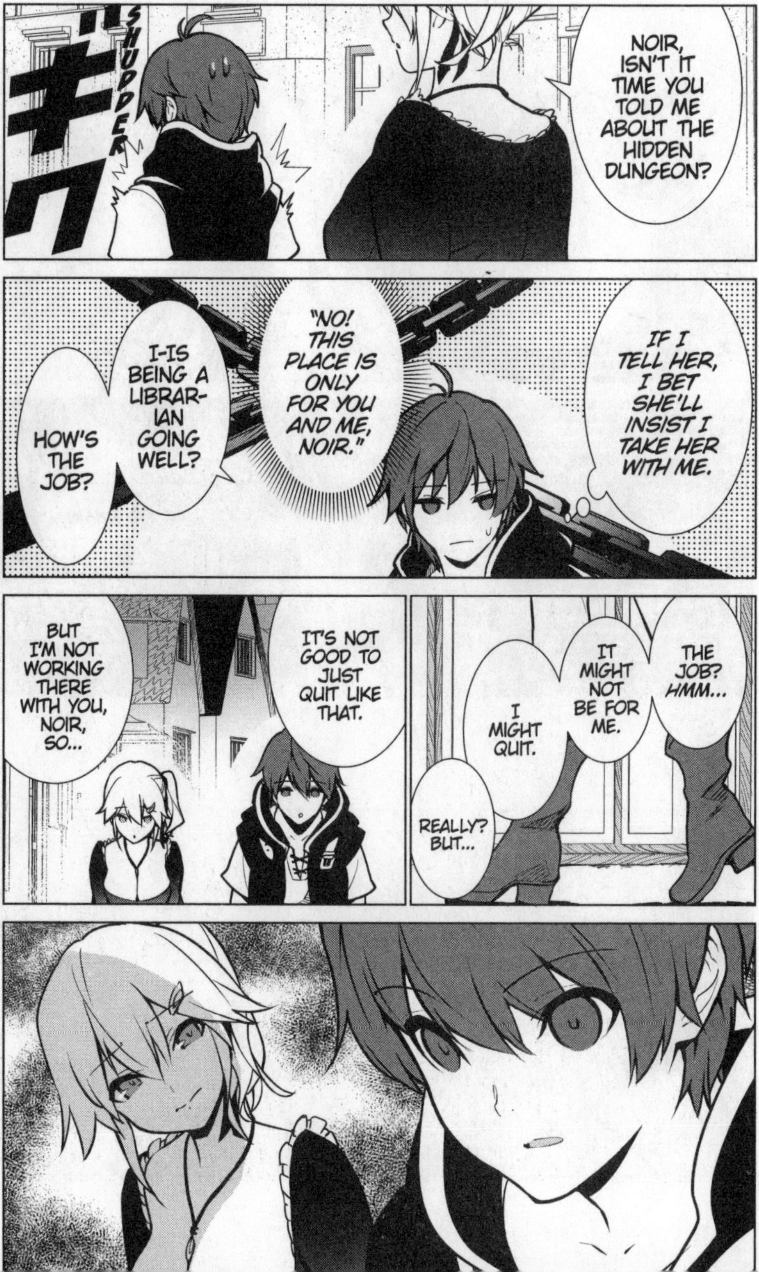
NOIR, ISN'T IT TIME YOU TOLD ME ABOUT THE HIDDEN DUNGEON?
SHUDDER
ギク
IF I TELL HER, I BET SHE'LL INSIST I TAKE HER WITH ME.
"NO! THIS PLACE IS ONLY FOR YOU AND ME, NOIR."
I-IS BEING A LIBRARIAN GOING WELL?
HOW'S THE JOB?
THE JOB? HMM...
IT MIGHT NOT BE FOR ME.
I MIGHT QUIT.
REALLY? BUT...
IT'S NOT GOOD TO JUST QUIT LIKE THAT.
BUT I'M NOT WORKING THERE WITH YOU, NOIR, SO...

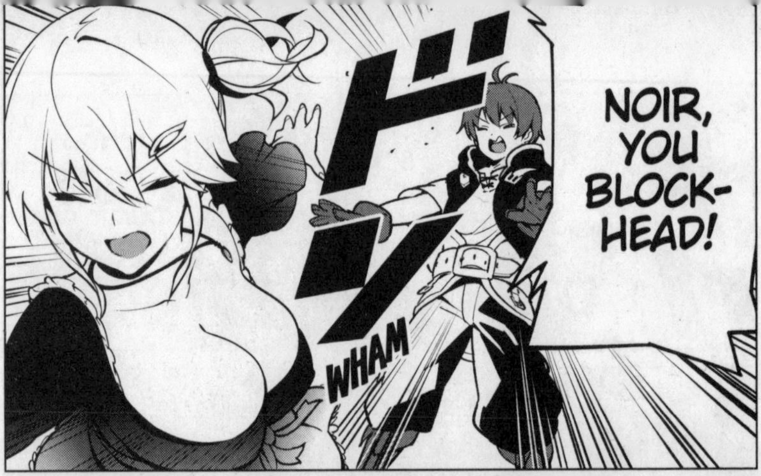
NOIR, YOU BLOCK-HEAD!
WHAM

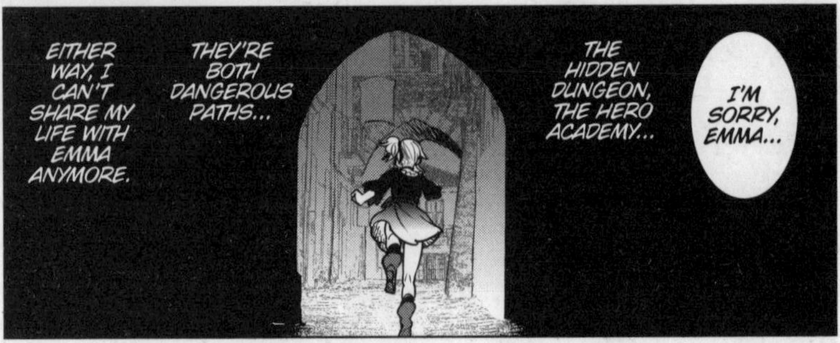
I'M SORRY, EMMA...
THE HIDDEN DUNGEON, THE HERO ACADEMY...
THEY'RE BOTH DANGEROUS PATHS...
EITHER WAY, I CAN'T SHARE MY LIFE WITH EMMA ANYMORE.

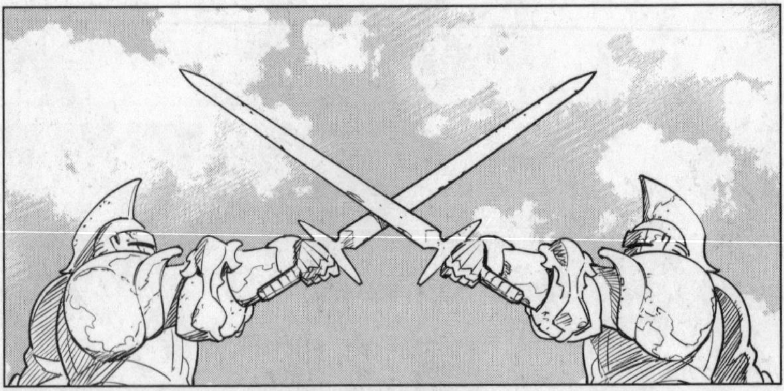

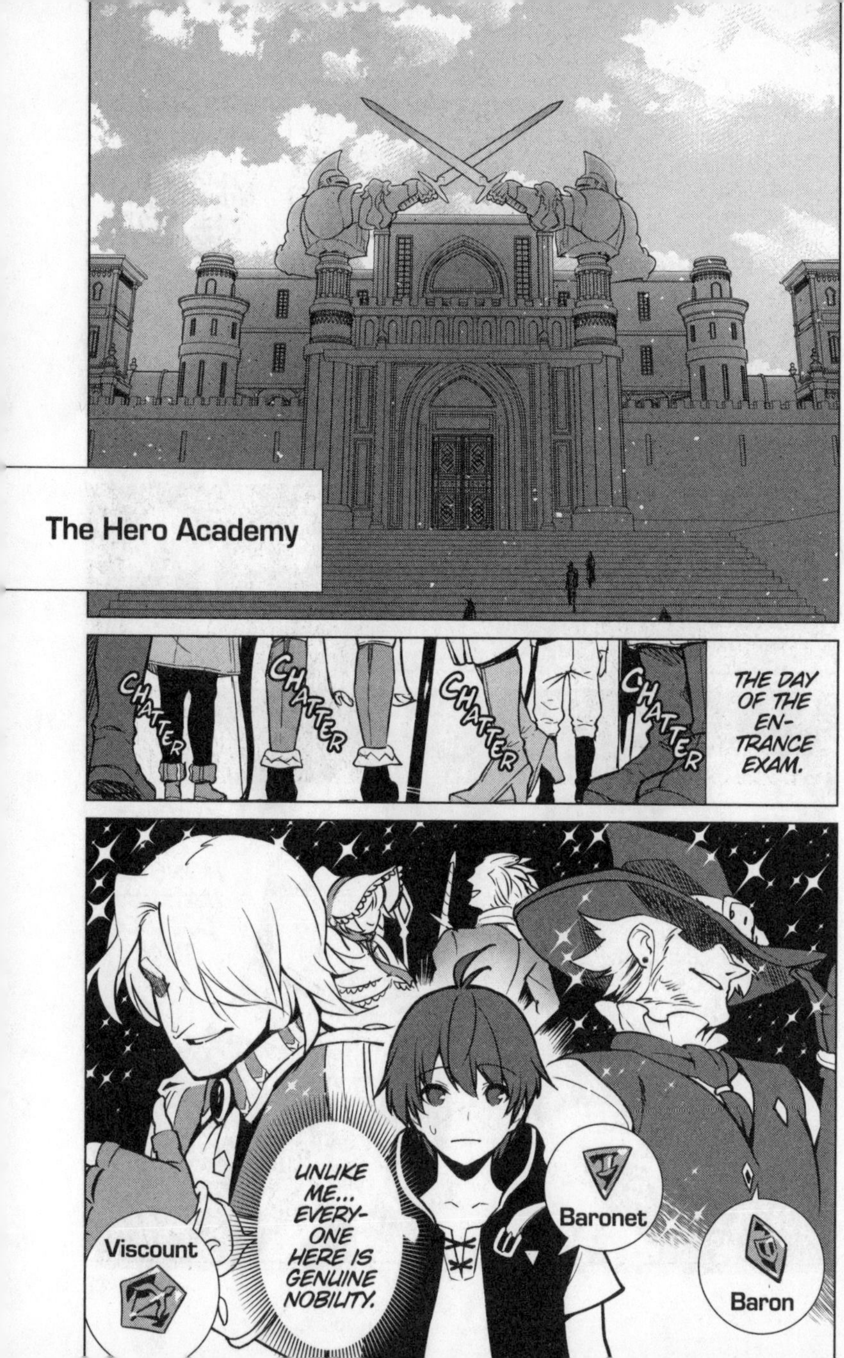
The Hero Academy
THE DAY OF THE EN-TRANCE EXAM.
CHATTER
CHATTER
CHATTER
CHATTER
UNLIKE ME... EVERY-ONE HERE IS GENUINE NOBILITY.
Baronet
Baron
Viscount

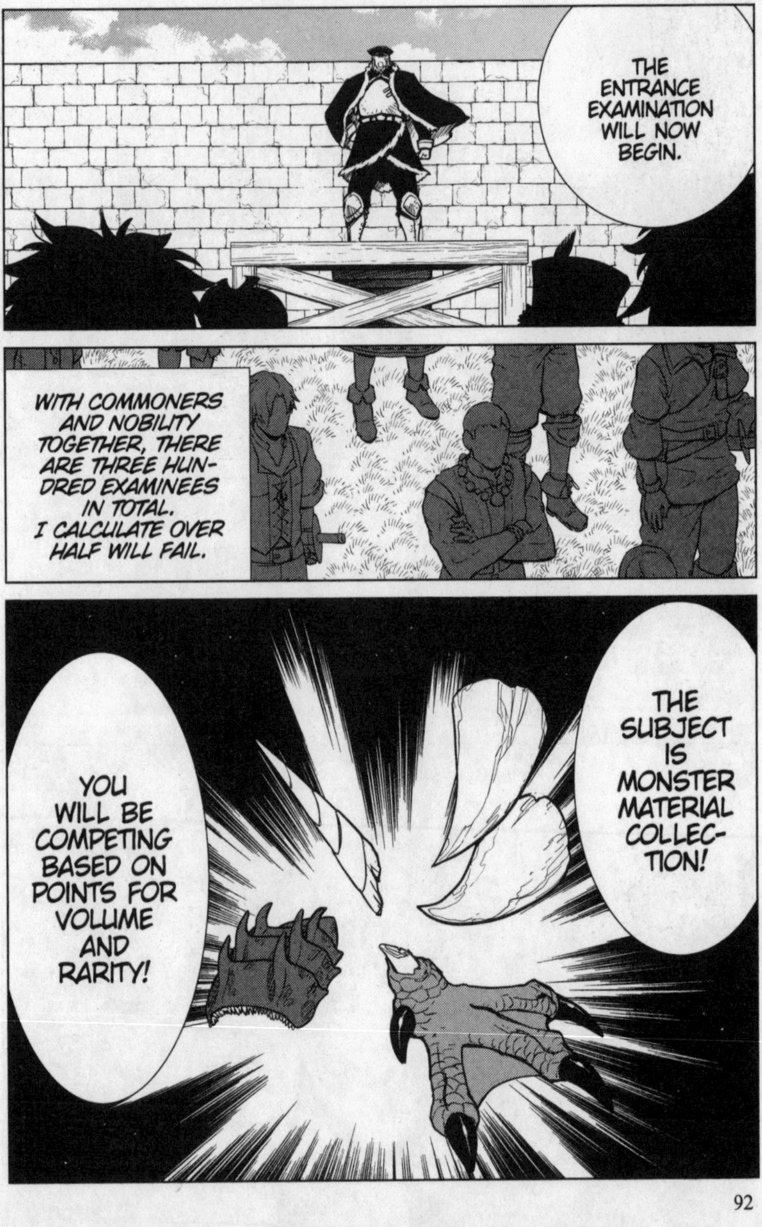
THE ENTRANCE EXAMINATION WILL NOW BEGIN.
WITH COMMONERS AND NOBILITY TOGETHER, THERE ARE THREE HUN-DRED EXAMINEES IN TOTAL. I CALCULATE OVER HALF WILL FAIL.
THE SUBJECT IS MONSTER MATERIAL COLLEC-TION!
YOU WILL BE COMPETING BASED ON POINTS FOR VOLUME AND RARITY!

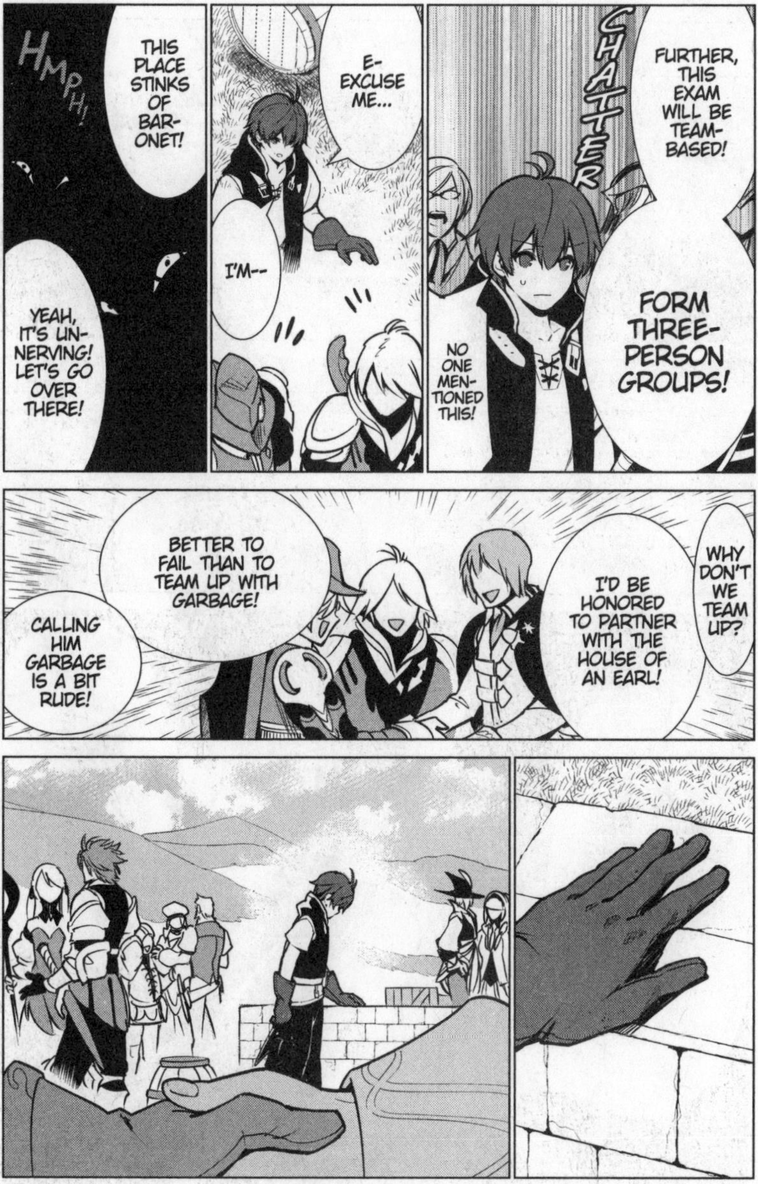
CHATTER
FURTHER, THIS EXAM WILL BE TEAM-BASED!
FORM THREE-PERSON GROUPS!
NO ONE MENTIONED THIS!
E-EXCUSE ME...
I'M--
HMPH!
THIS PLACE STINKS OF BARONET!
YEAH, IT'S UNNERVING! LET'S GO OVER THERE!
WHY DON'T WE TEAM UP?
I'D BE HONORED TO PARTNER WITH THE HOUSE OF AN EARL!
BETTER TO FAIL THAN TO TEAM UP WITH GARBAGE!
CALLING HIM GARBAGE IS A BIT RUDE!

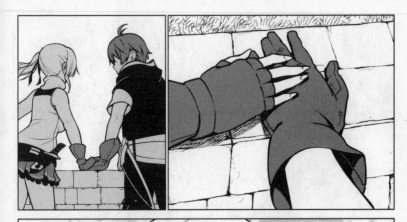

WHAT'S WITH THE FACE?

EMMA?

WHAT ARE YOU DOING HERE?

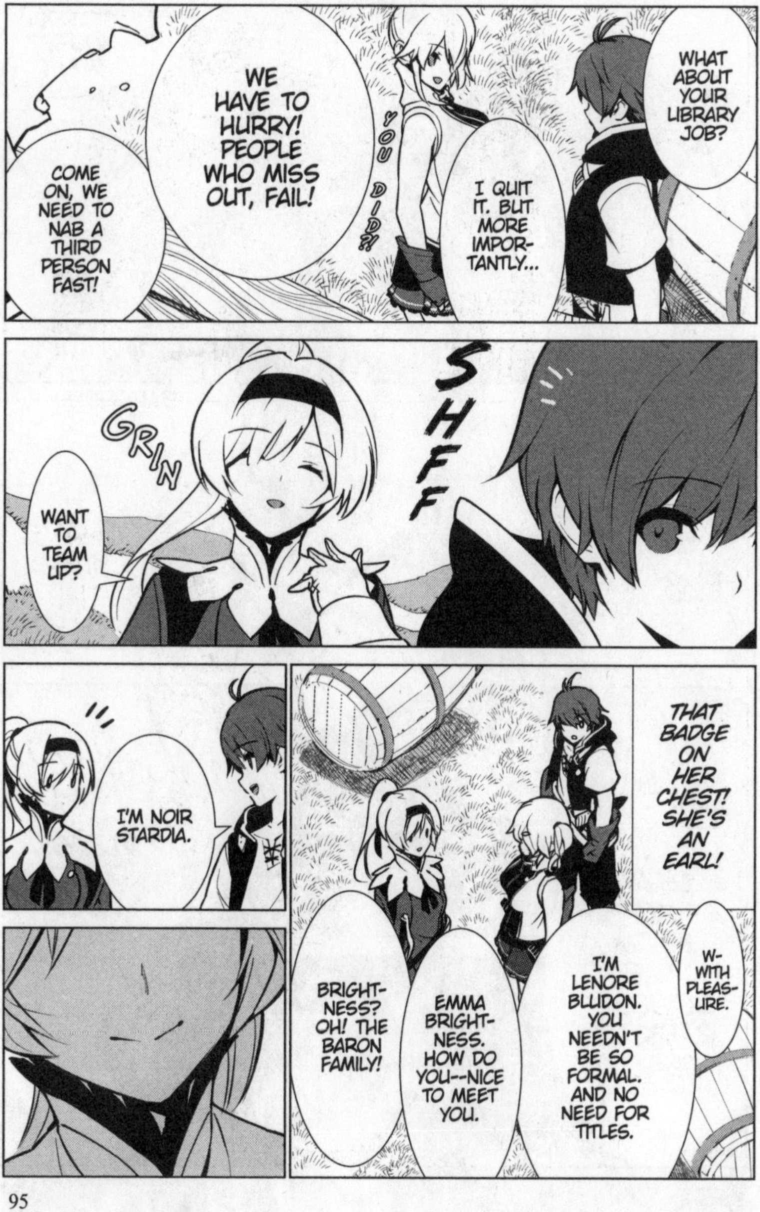
WHAT ABOUT YOUR LIBRARY JOB?
I QUIT IT. BUT MORE IMPORTANTLY...
YOU DID?!
WE HAVE TO HURRY! PEOPLE WHO MISS OUT, FAIL!
COME ON, WE NEED TO NAB A THIRD PERSON FAST!
SHFF
GRIN
WANT TO TEAM UP?
THAT BADGE ON HER CHEST! SHE'S AN EARL!
W-WITH PLEASURE.
I'M LENORE BLUDON. YOU NEEDN'T BE SO FORMAL. AND NO NEED FOR TITLES.
EMMA BRIGHTNESS. HOW DO YOU--NICE TO MEET YOU.
BRIGHTNESS? OH! THE BARON FAMILY!
I'M NOIR STARDIA.

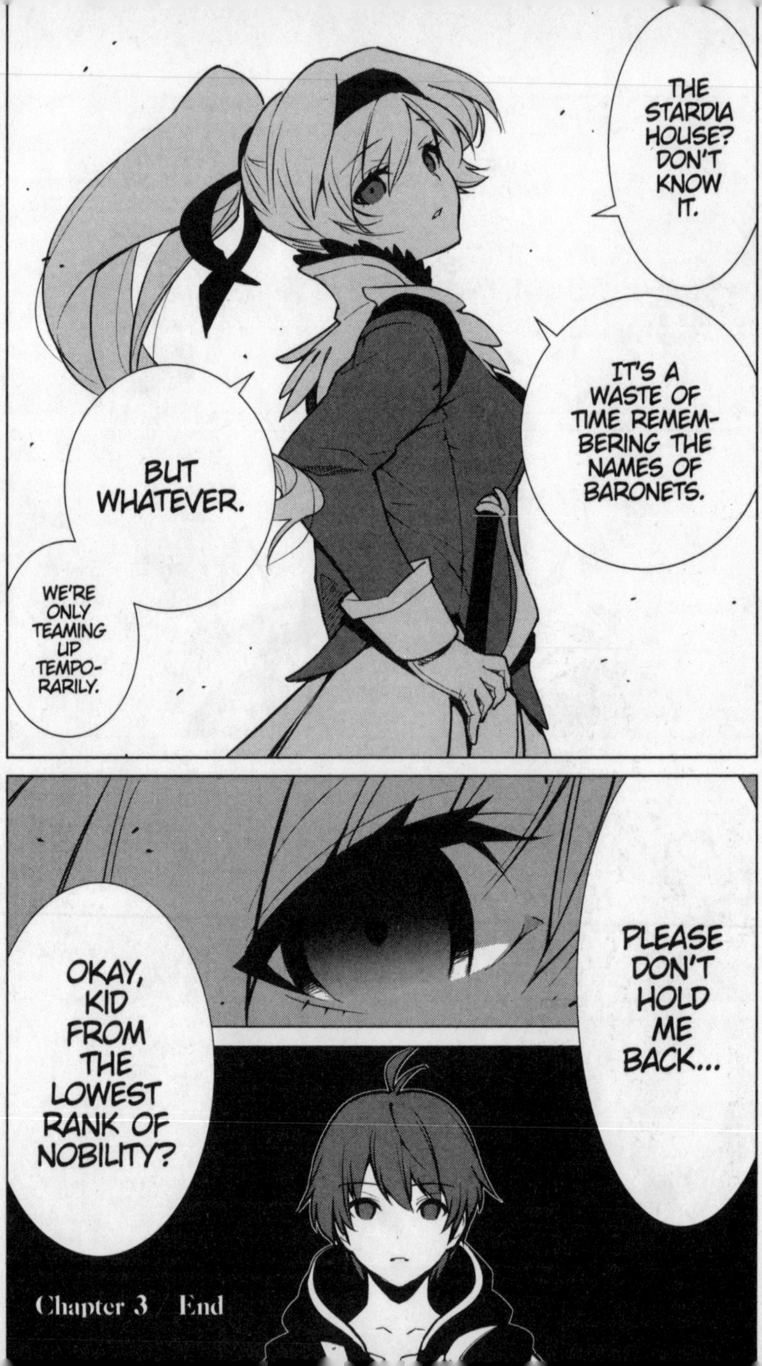
THE STARDIA HOUSE? DON'T KNOW IT.
IT'S A WASTE OF TIME REMEMBERING THE NAMES OF BARONETS.
BUT WHATEVER.
WE'RE ONLY TEAMING UP TEMPORARILY.
PLEASE DON'T HOLD ME BACK...
OKAY, KID FROM THE LOWEST RANK OF NOBILITY?
Chapter 3 / End

THE HIDDEN DUNGEON ONLY I CAN ENTER

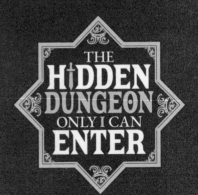

Chapter 4: Stone Bullet, Improved

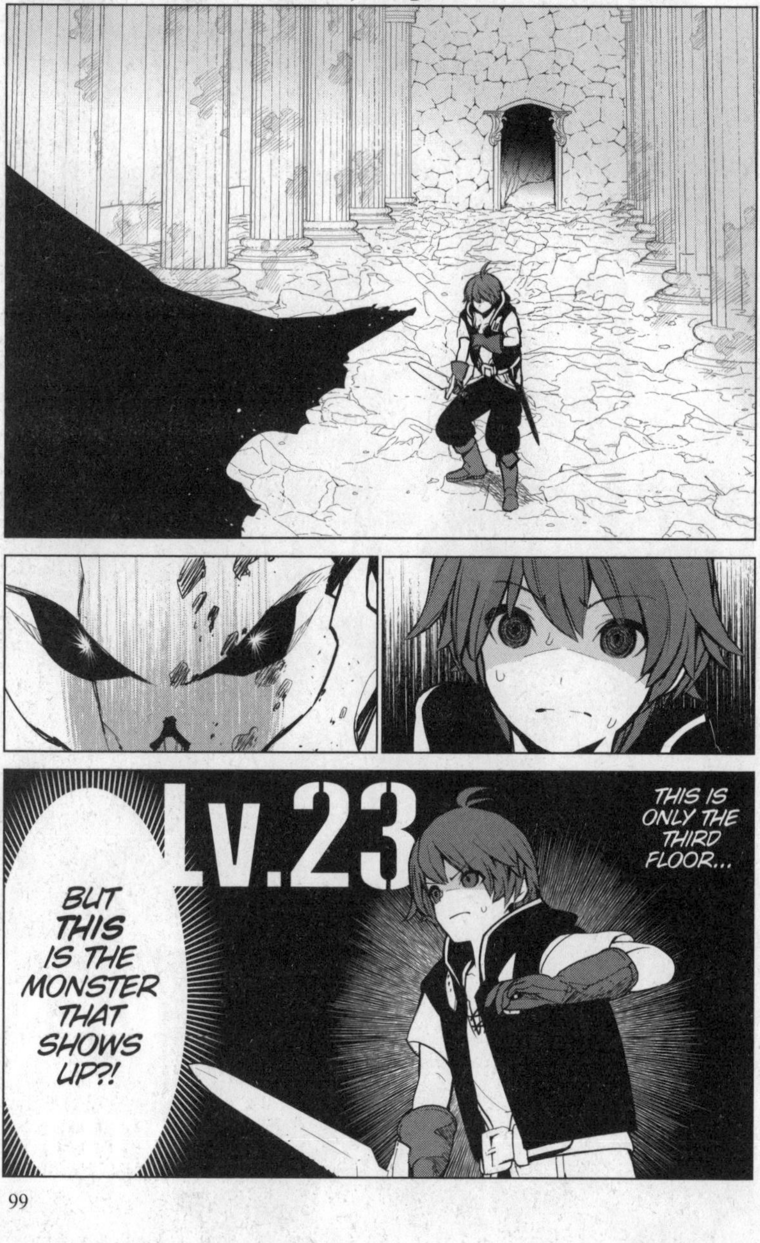
THIS IS ONLY THE THIRD FLOOR...
Lv.23
BUT THIS IS THE MONSTER THAT SHOWS UP?!

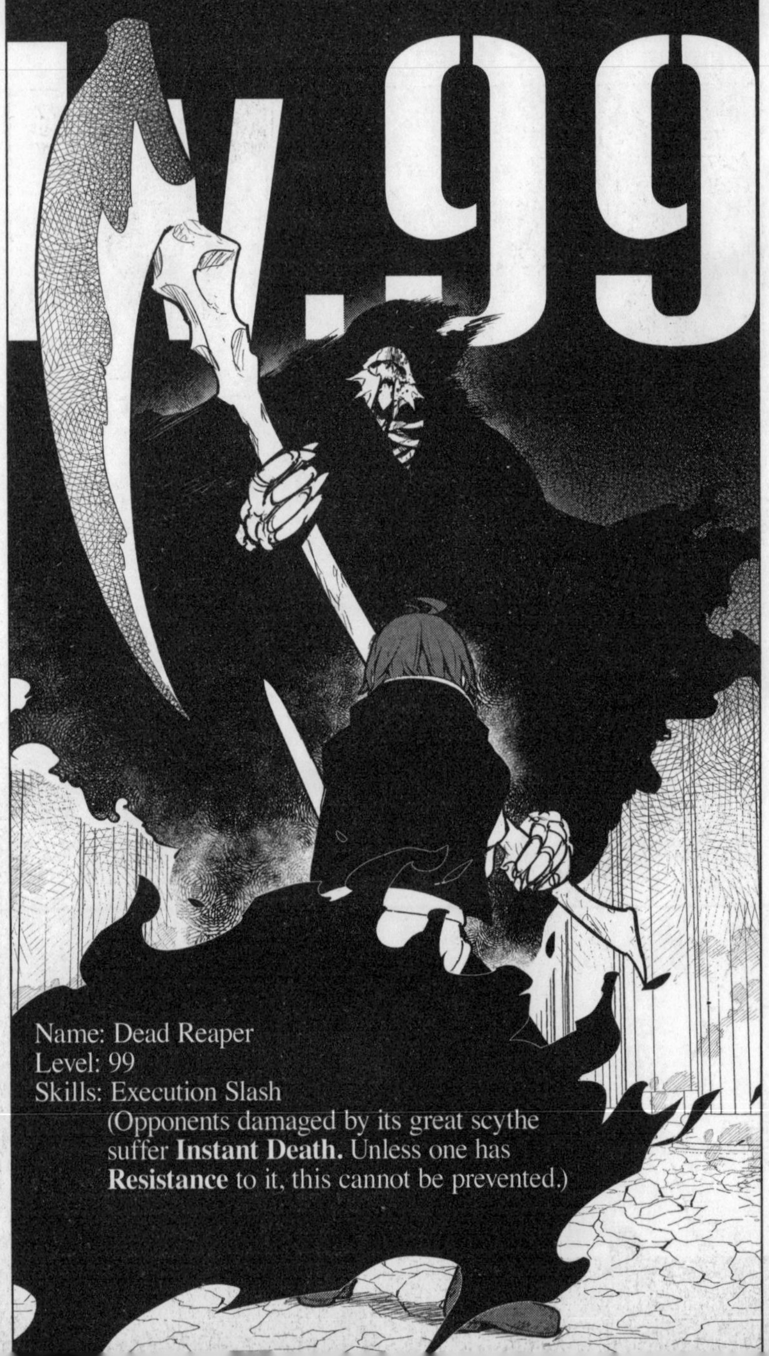
V.99
Name: Dead Reaper
Level: 99
Skills: Execution Slash
(Opponents damaged by its great scythe suffer **Instant Death.** Unless one has **Resistance** to it, this cannot be prevented.)

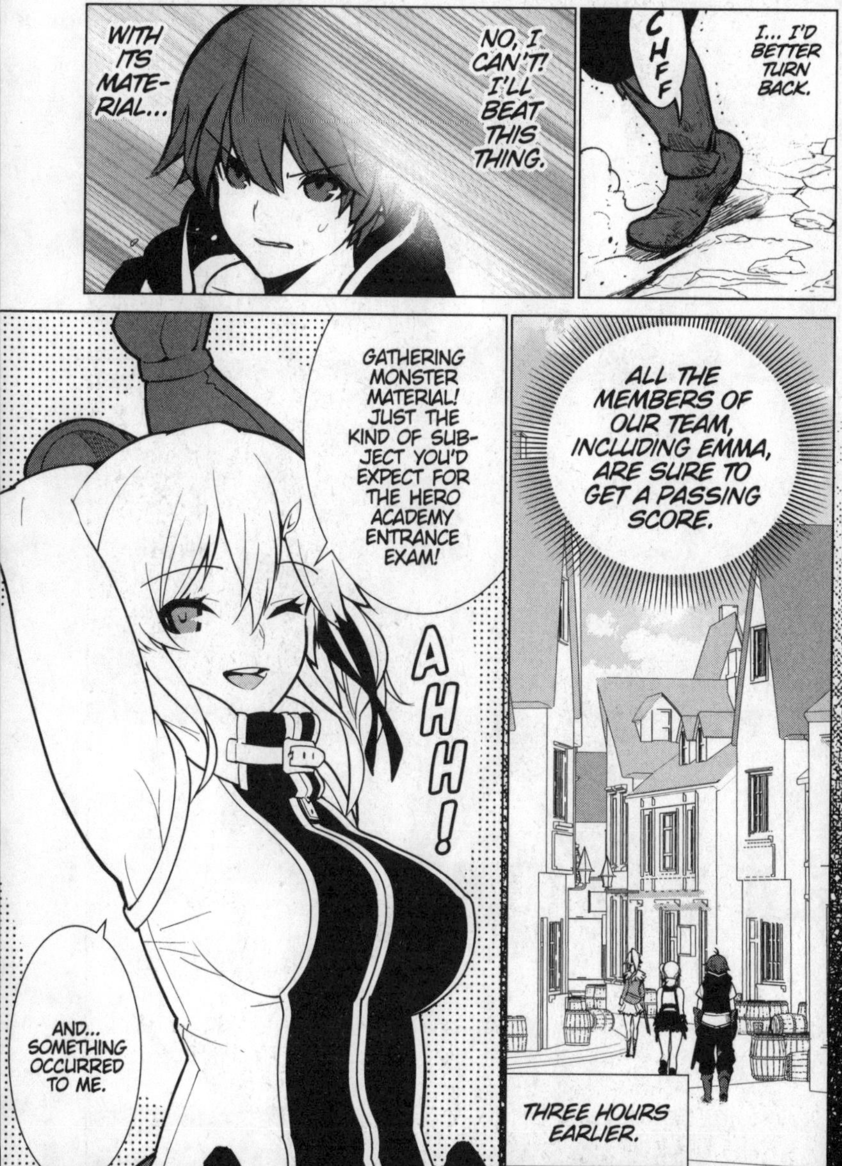
I... I'D BETTER TURN BACK.
CHFF
NO, I CAN'T! I'LL BEAT THIS THING.
WITH ITS MATE-RIAL...
ALL THE MEMBERS OF OUR TEAM, INCLUDING EMMA, ARE SURE TO GET A PASSING SCORE.
THREE HOURS EARLIER.
GATHERING MONSTER MATERIAL! JUST THE KIND OF SUB-JECT YOU'D EXPECT FOR THE HERO ACADEMY ENTRANCE EXAM!
AHHH!
AND... SOMETHING OCCURRED TO ME.

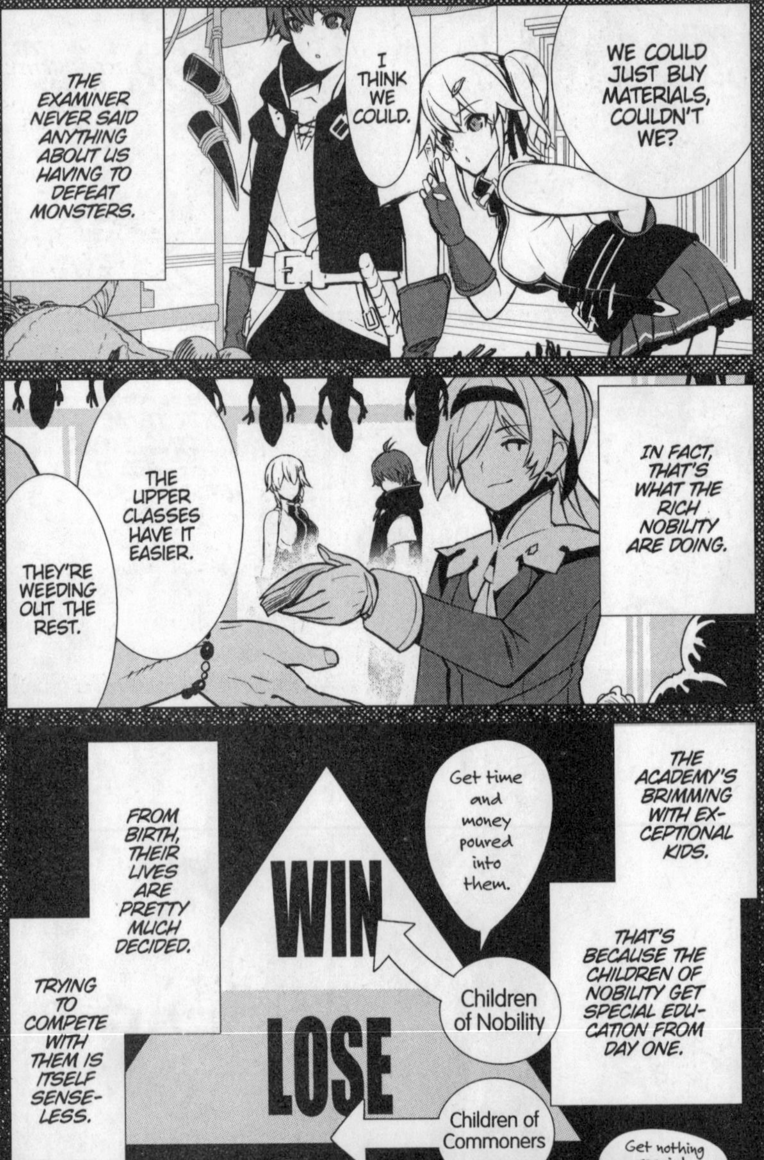
WE COULD JUST BUY MATERIALS, COULDN'T WE?
I THINK WE COULD.
THE EXAMINER NEVER SAID ANYTHING ABOUT US HAVING TO DEFEAT MONSTERS.
IN FACT, THAT'S WHAT THE RICH NOBILITY ARE DOING.
THE UPPER CLASSES HAVE IT EASIER.
THEY'RE WEEDING OUT THE REST.
THE ACADEMY'S BRIMMING WITH EX-CEPTIONAL KIDS.
THAT'S BECAUSE THE CHILDREN OF NOBILITY GET SPECIAL EDU-CATION FROM DAY ONE.
Get time and money poured into them.
Children of Nobility
WIN
Get nothing special.
Children of Commoners
LOSE
FROM BIRTH, THEIR LIVES ARE PRETTY MUCH DECIDED.
TRYING TO COMPETE WITH THEM IS ITSELF SENSE-LESS.

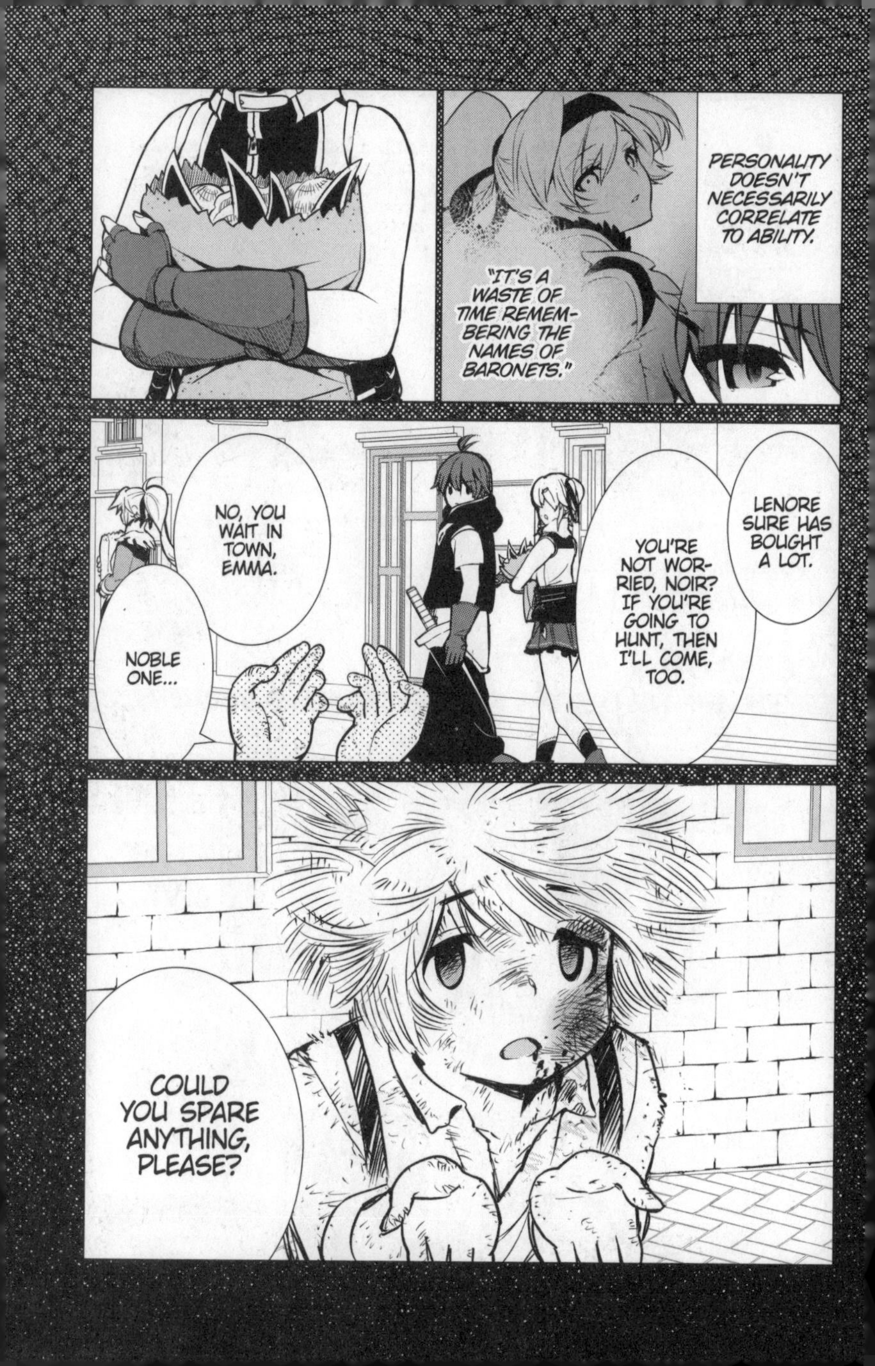
PERSONALITY DOESN'T NECESSARILY CORRELATE TO ABILITY.
"IT'S A WASTE OF TIME REMEMBERING THE NAMES OF BARONETS."
LENORE SURE HAS BOUGHT A LOT.
YOU'RE NOT WORRIED, NOIR? IF YOU'RE GOING TO HUNT, THEN I'LL COME, TOO.
NO, YOU WAIT IN TOWN, EMMA.
NOBLE ONE...
COULD YOU SPARE ANYTHING, PLEASE?

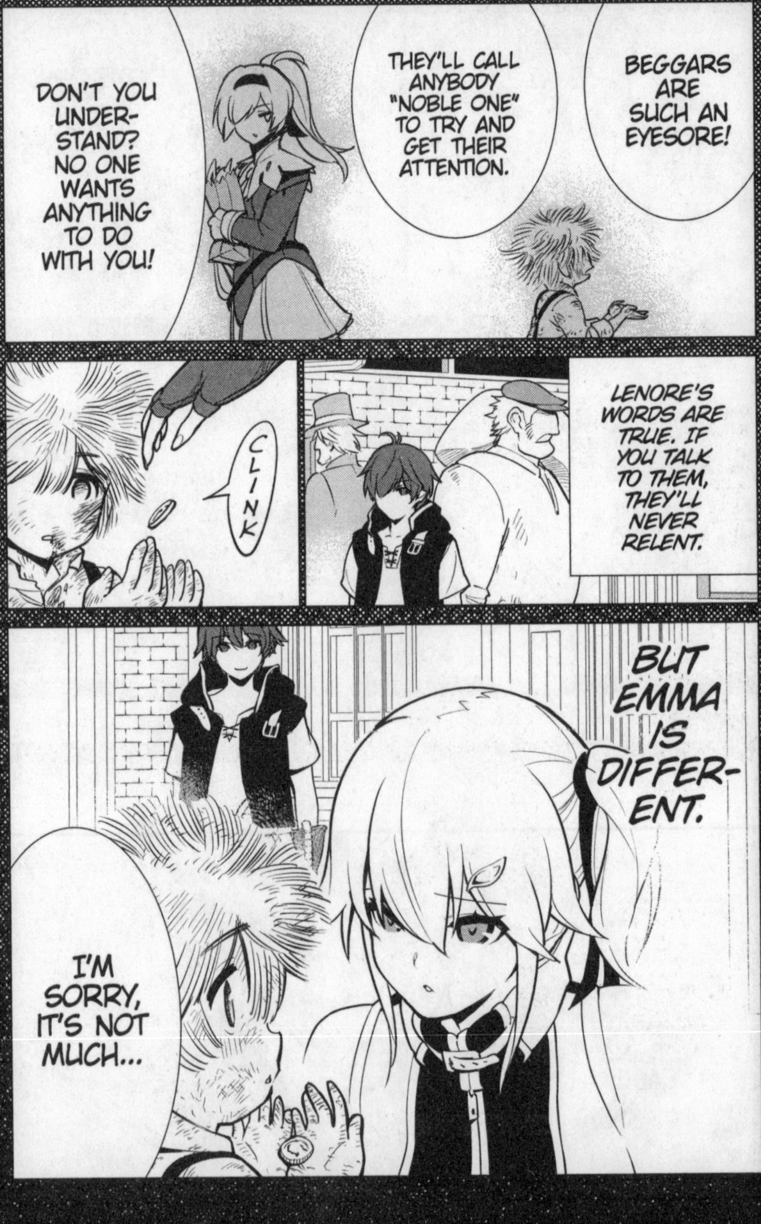
BEGGARS ARE SUCH AN EYESORE!
THEY'LL CALL ANYBODY "NOBLE ONE" TO TRY AND GET THEIR ATTENTION.
DON'T YOU UNDER-STAND? NO ONE WANTS ANYTHING TO DO WITH YOU!
LENORE'S WORDS ARE TRUE. IF YOU TALK TO THEM, THEY'LL NEVER RELENT.
CLINK
BUT EMMA IS DIFFER-ENT.
I'M SORRY, IT'S NOT MUCH...

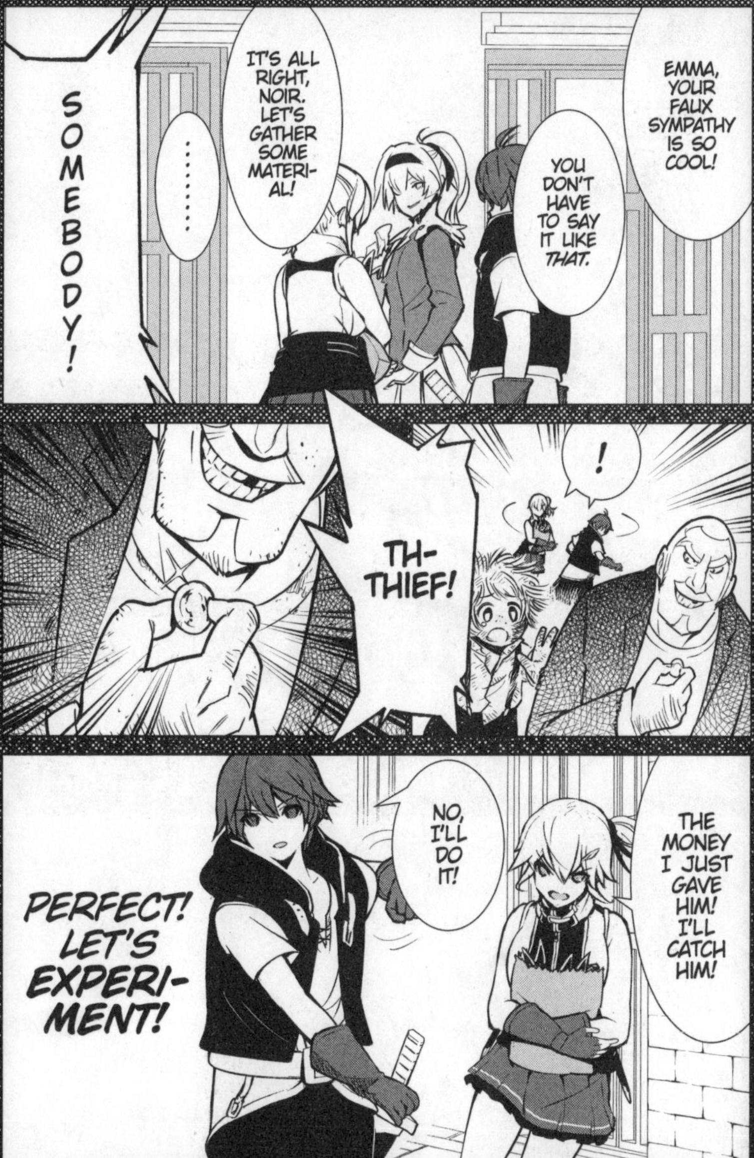
EMMA, YOUR FAUX SYMPATHY IS SO COOL!
YOU DON'T HAVE TO SAY IT LIKE *THAT*.
IT'S ALL RIGHT, NOIR. LET'S GATHER SOME MATERI-AL!
......
SOMEBODY!
!
TH-THIEF!
THE MONEY I JUST GAVE HIM! I'LL CATCH HIM!
NO, I'LL DO IT!
PERFECT! LET'S EXPERI-MENT!

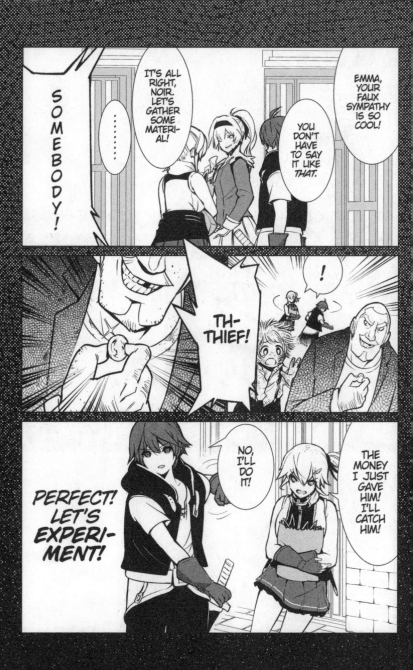

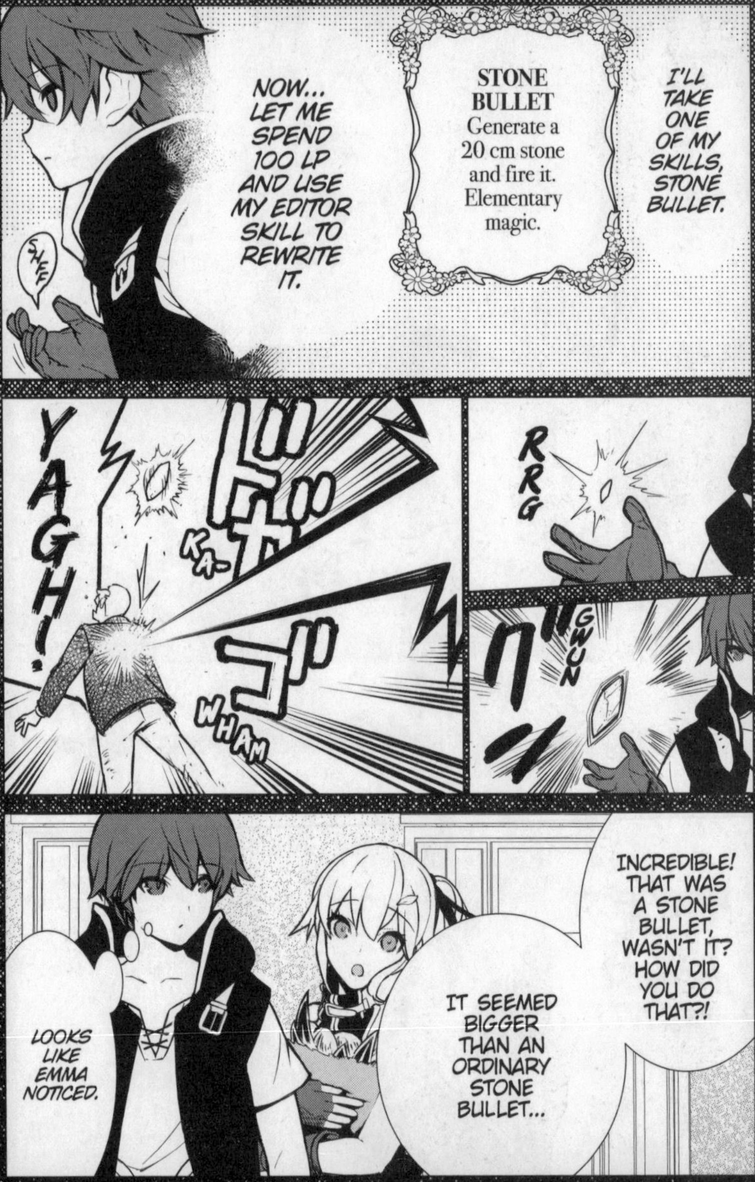
I'LL TAKE ONE OF MY SKILLS, STONE BULLET.
STONE BULLET
Generate a 20 cm stone and fire it. Elementary magic.
NOW... LET ME SPEND 100 LP AND USE MY EDITOR SKILL TO REWRITE IT.
SHFF
RRG
GWUN
YAGH!
KA-
WHAM
INCREDIBLE! THAT WAS A STONE BULLET, WASN'T IT? HOW DID YOU DO THAT?!
IT SEEMED BIGGER THAN AN ORDINARY STONE BULLET...
LOOKS LIKE EMMA NOTICED.

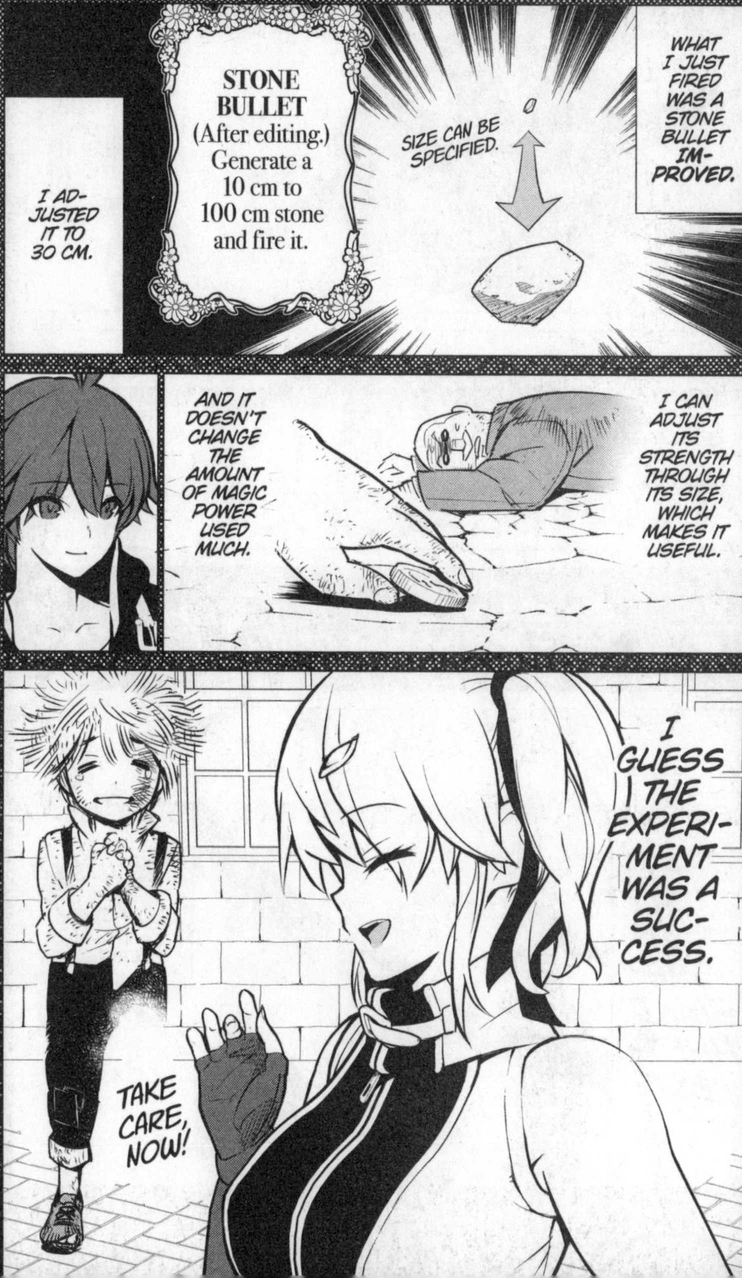
WHAT I JUST FIRED WAS A STONE BULLET IMPROVED.
SIZE CAN BE SPECIFIED.
STONE BULLET (After editing.) Generate a 10 cm to 100 cm stone and fire it.
I ADJUSTED IT TO 30 CM.
I CAN ADJUST ITS STRENGTH THROUGH ITS SIZE, WHICH MAKES IT USEFUL.
AND IT DOESN'T CHANGE THE AMOUNT OF MAGIC POWER USED MUCH.
I GUESS THE EXPERIMENT WAS A SUCCESS.
TAKE CARE, NOW!

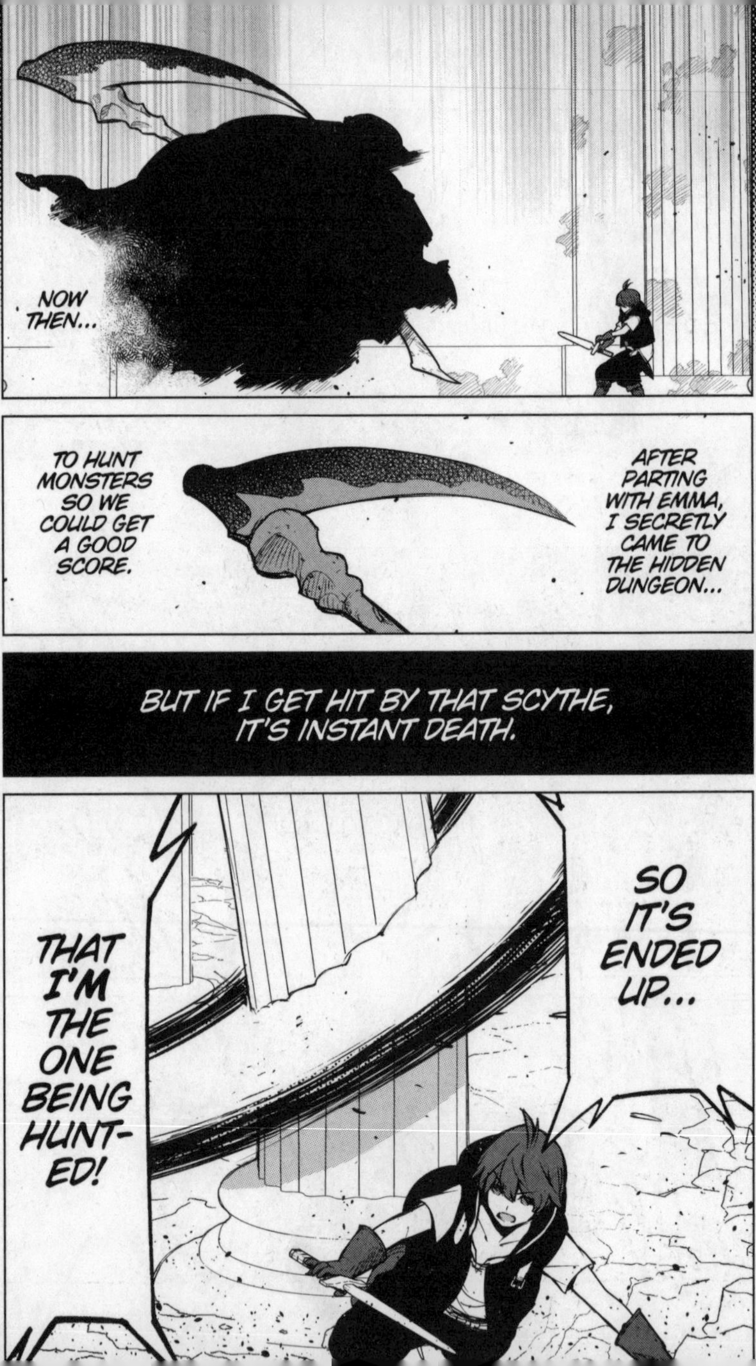
NOW THEN...
AFTER PARTING WITH EMMA, I SECRETLY CAME TO THE HIDDEN DUNGEON...
TO HUNT MONSTERS SO WE COULD GET A GOOD SCORE.
BUT IF I GET HIT BY THAT SCYTHE, IT'S INSTANT DEATH.
SO IT'S ENDED UP...
THAT I'M THE ONE BEING HUNTED!

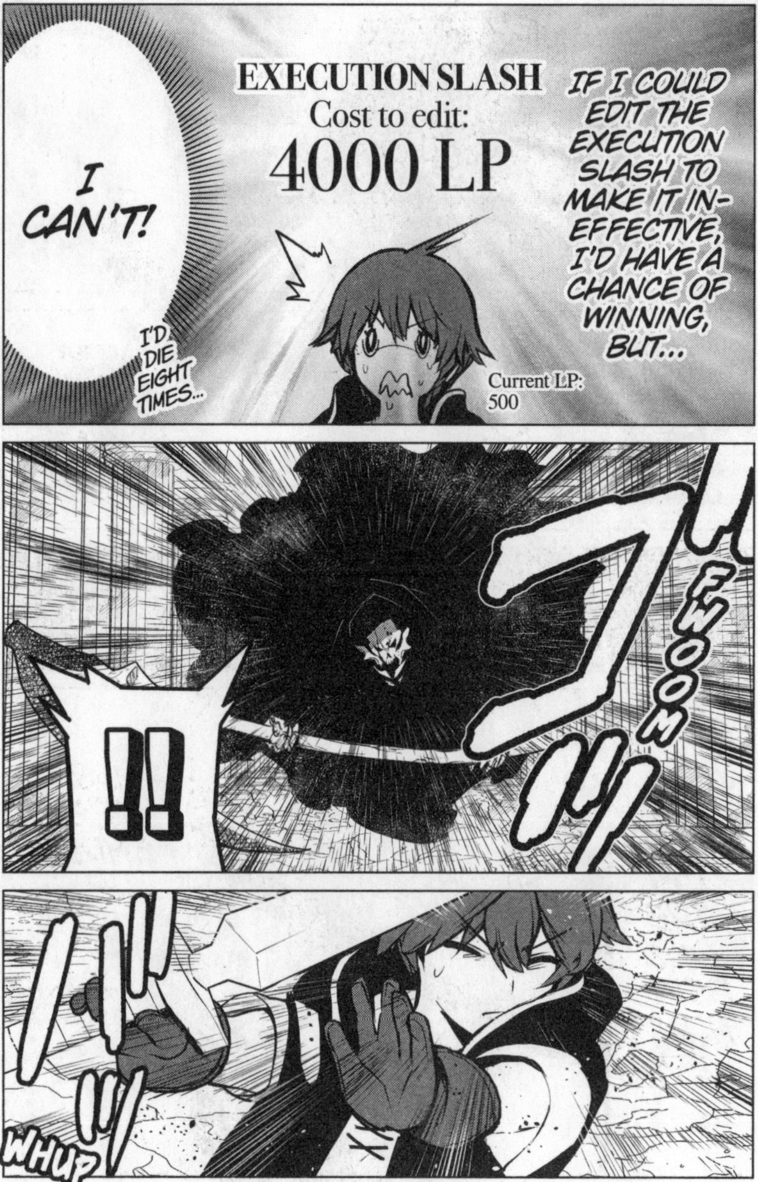
IF I COULD EDIT THE EXECUTION SLASH TO MAKE IT IN-EFFECTIVE, I'D HAVE A CHANCE OF WINNING, BUT...
EXECUTION SLASH
Cost to edit:
4000 LP
I CAN'T!
Current LP: 500
I'D DIE EIGHT TIMES...
FWOOM
!!
WHUP

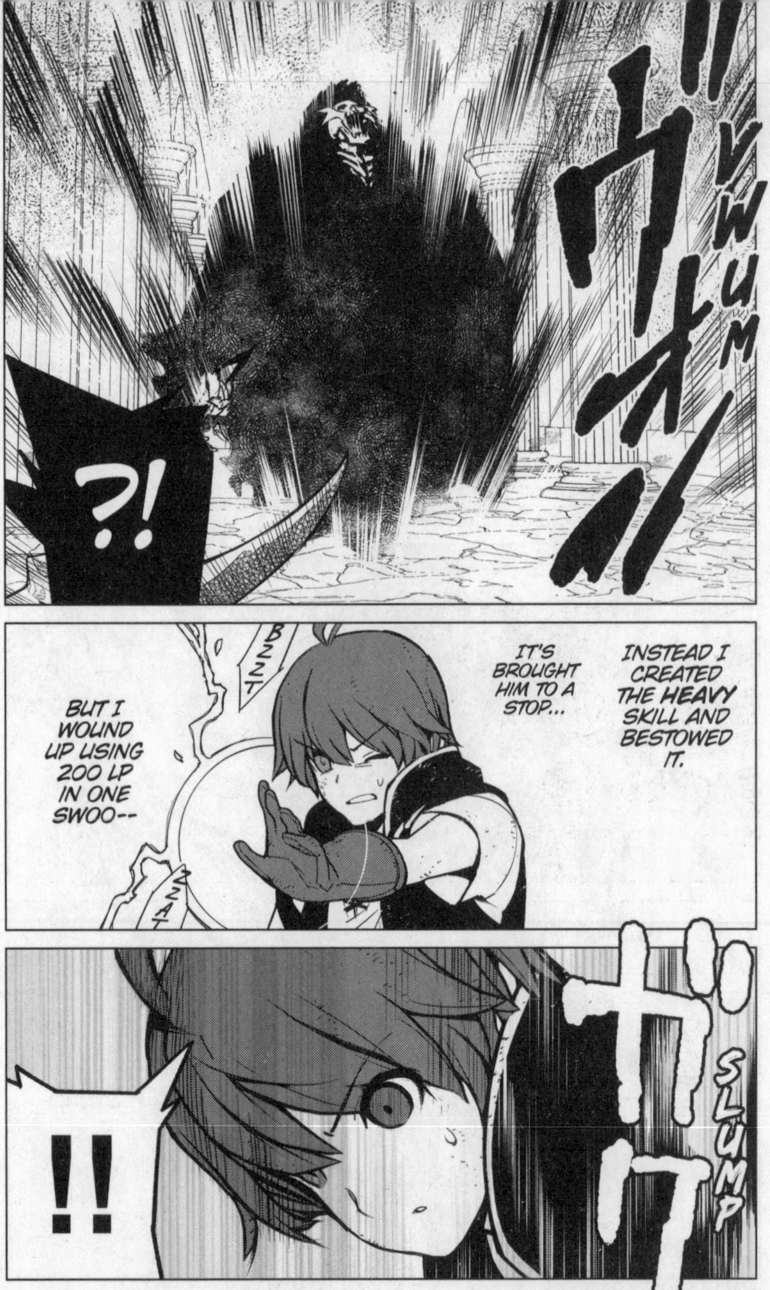
ヴォン
VWUMM
?!
INSTEAD I CREATED THE HEAVY SKILL AND BESTOWED IT.
IT'S BROUGHT HIM TO A STOP...
BZZT
BUT I WOUND UP USING 200 LP IN ONE SWOO--
ZZAT
ガク
SLUMP
!!

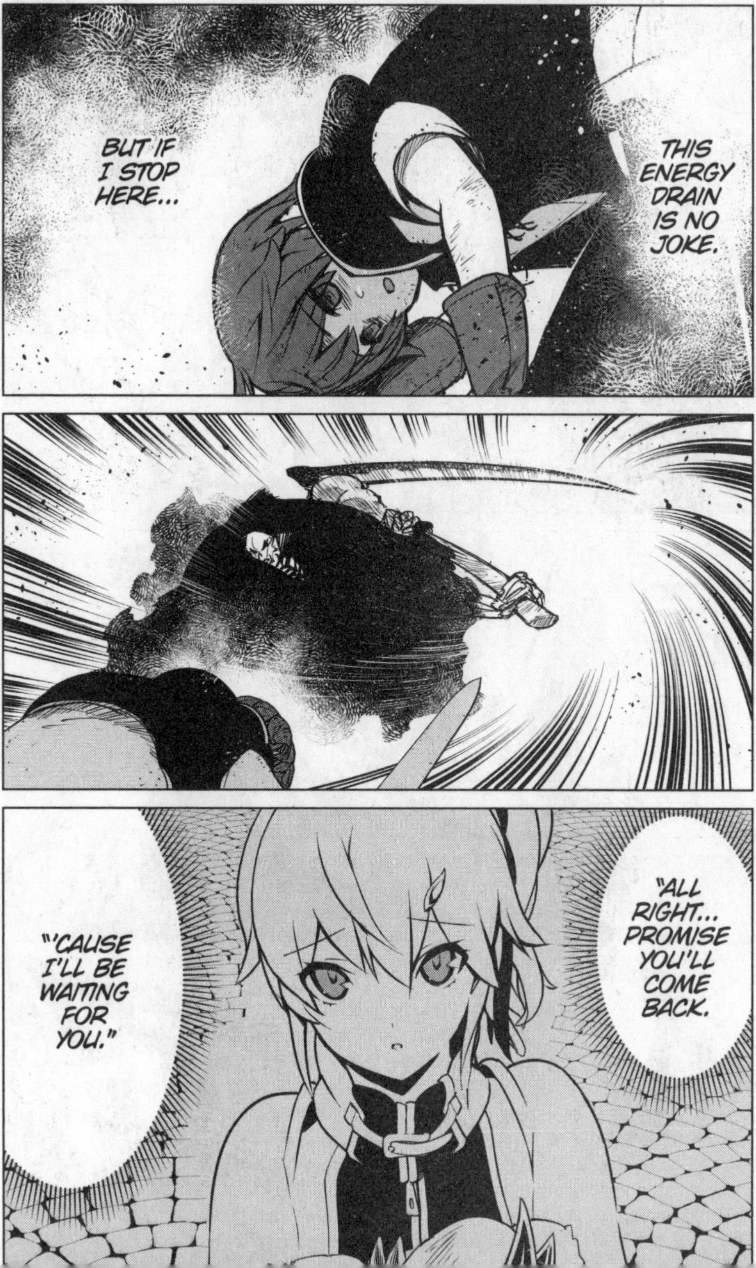
THIS ENERGY DRAIN IS NO JOKE.
BUT IF I STOP HERE...
"ALL RIGHT... PROMISE YOU'LL COME BACK.
"'CAUSE I'LL BE WAITING FOR YOU."

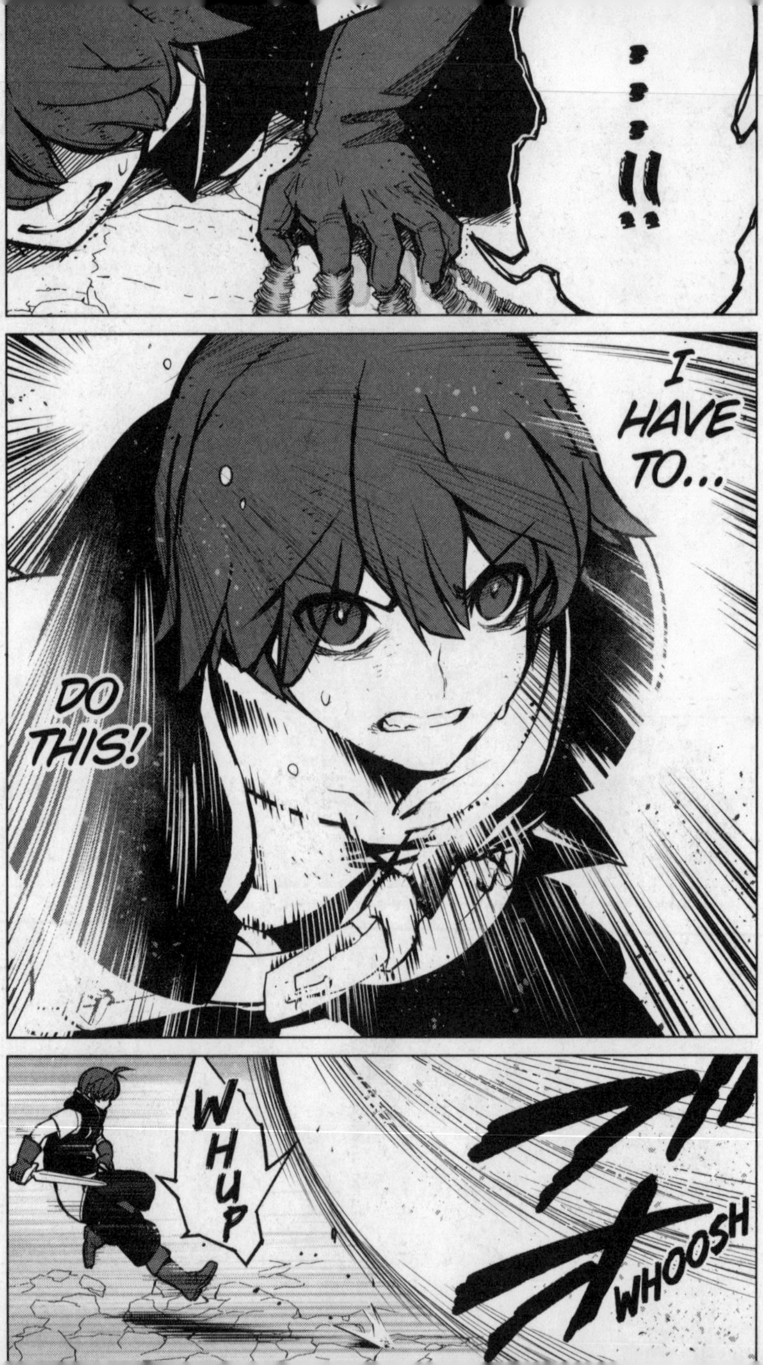
...!!
I HAVE TO...
DO THIS!
WHOOSH
WHUP

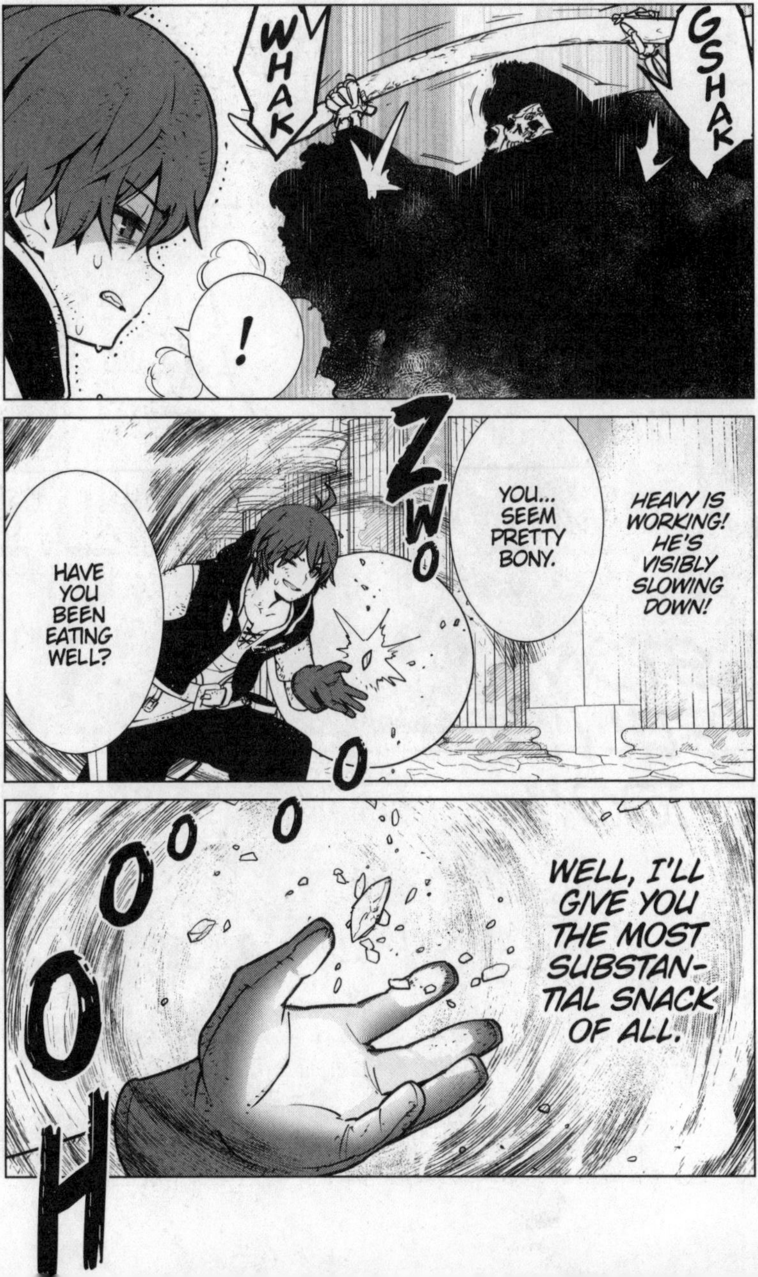
GSHAK
WHAK
!
HEAVY IS WORKING! HE'S VISIBLY SLOWING DOWN!
YOU... SEEM PRETTY BONY.
ZWOOOOOOOH
HAVE YOU BEEN EATING WELL?
WELL, I'LL GIVE YOU THE MOST SUBSTAN-TIAL SNACK OF ALL.

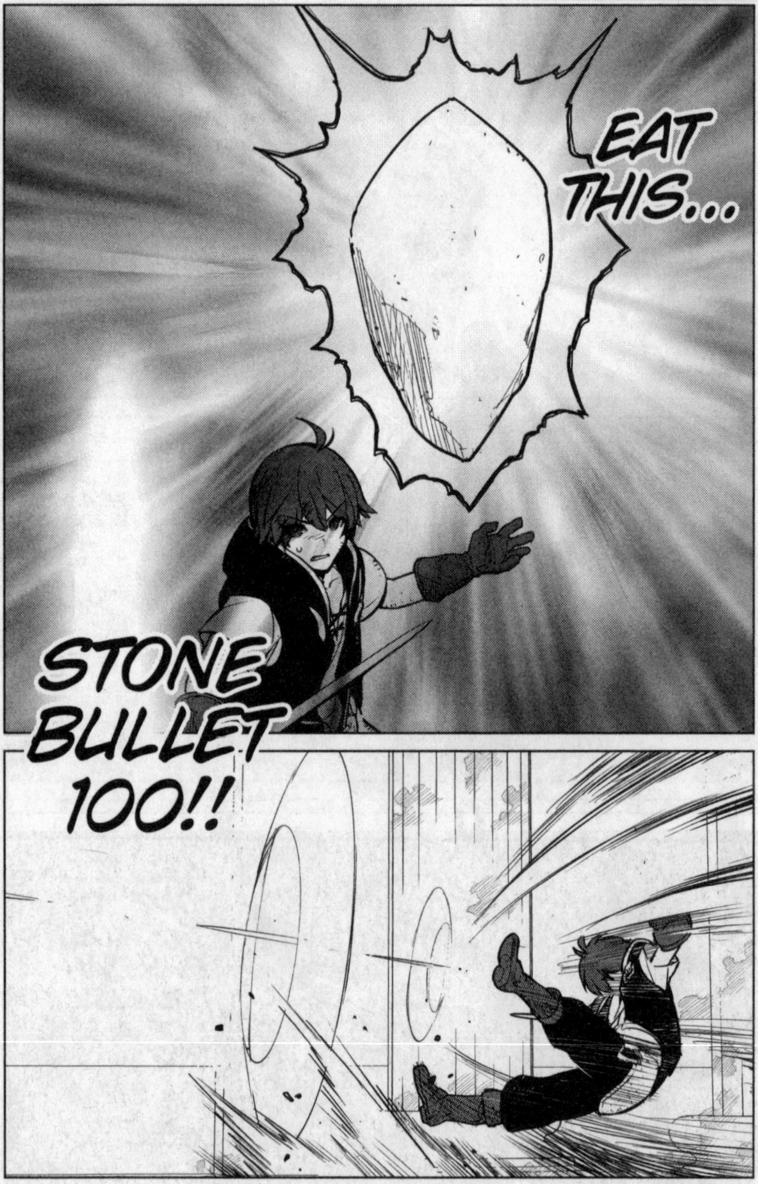
EAT THIS...
STONE BULLET 100!!

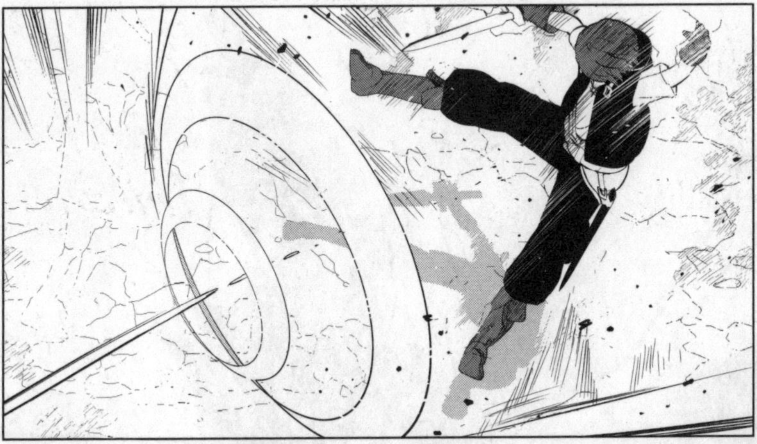
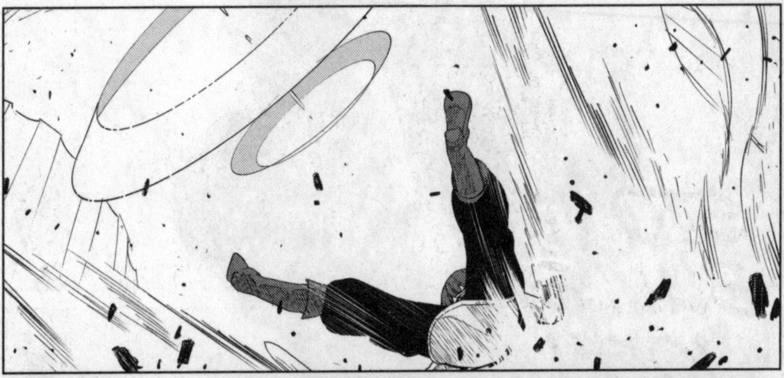
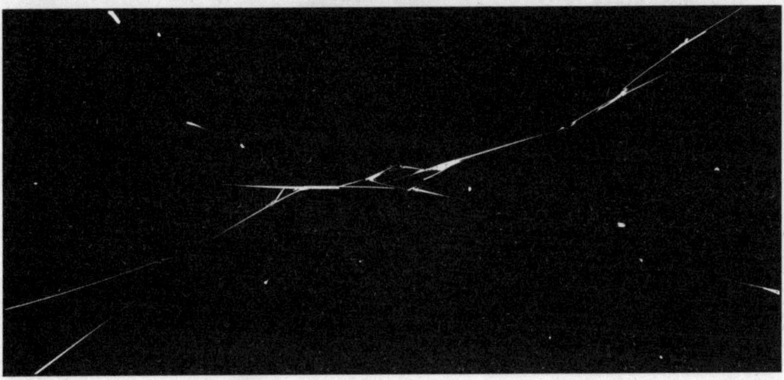

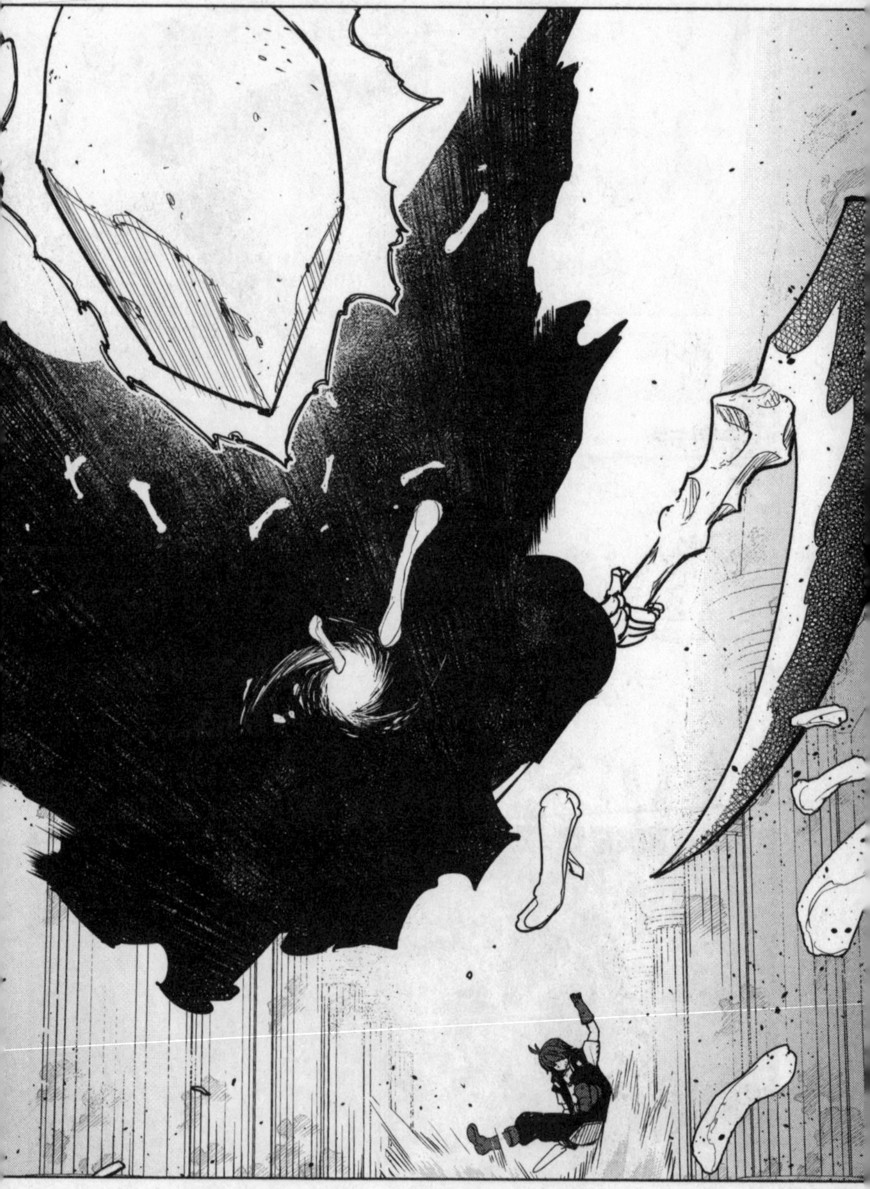

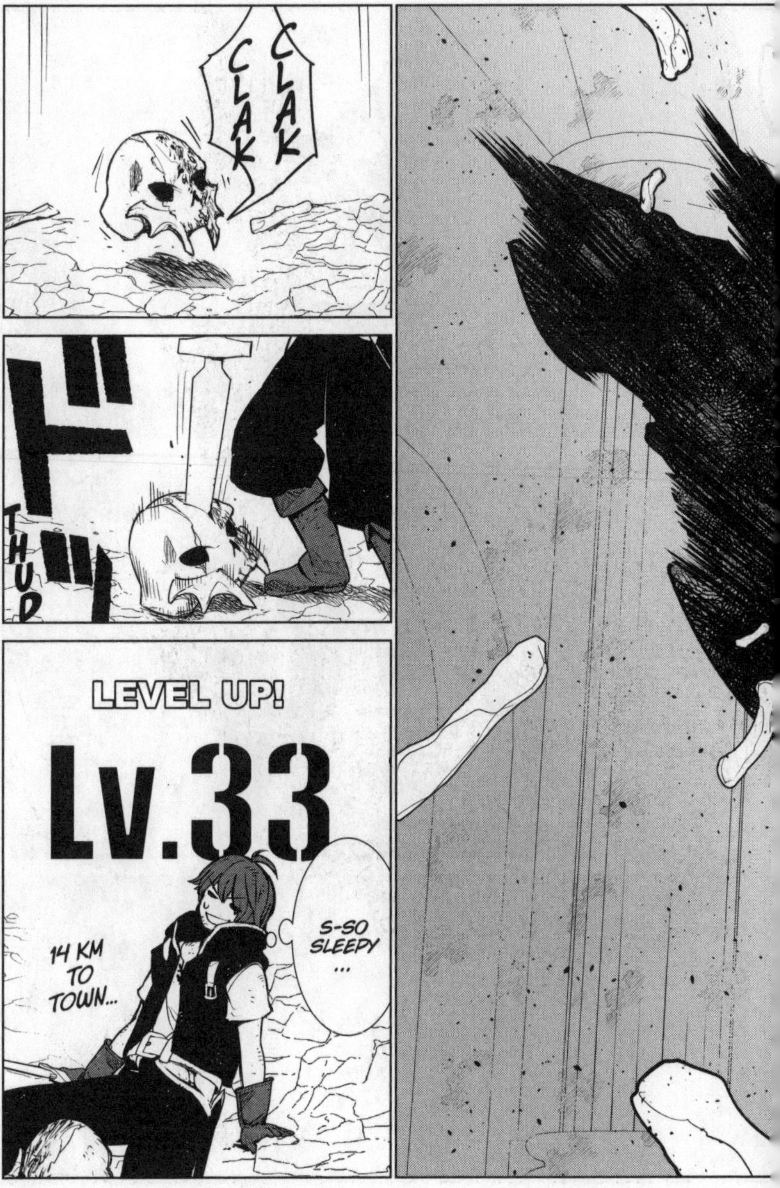
CLAK CLAK
THUD
LEVEL UP!
Lv.33
S-SO SLEEPY ...
14 KM TO TOWN...

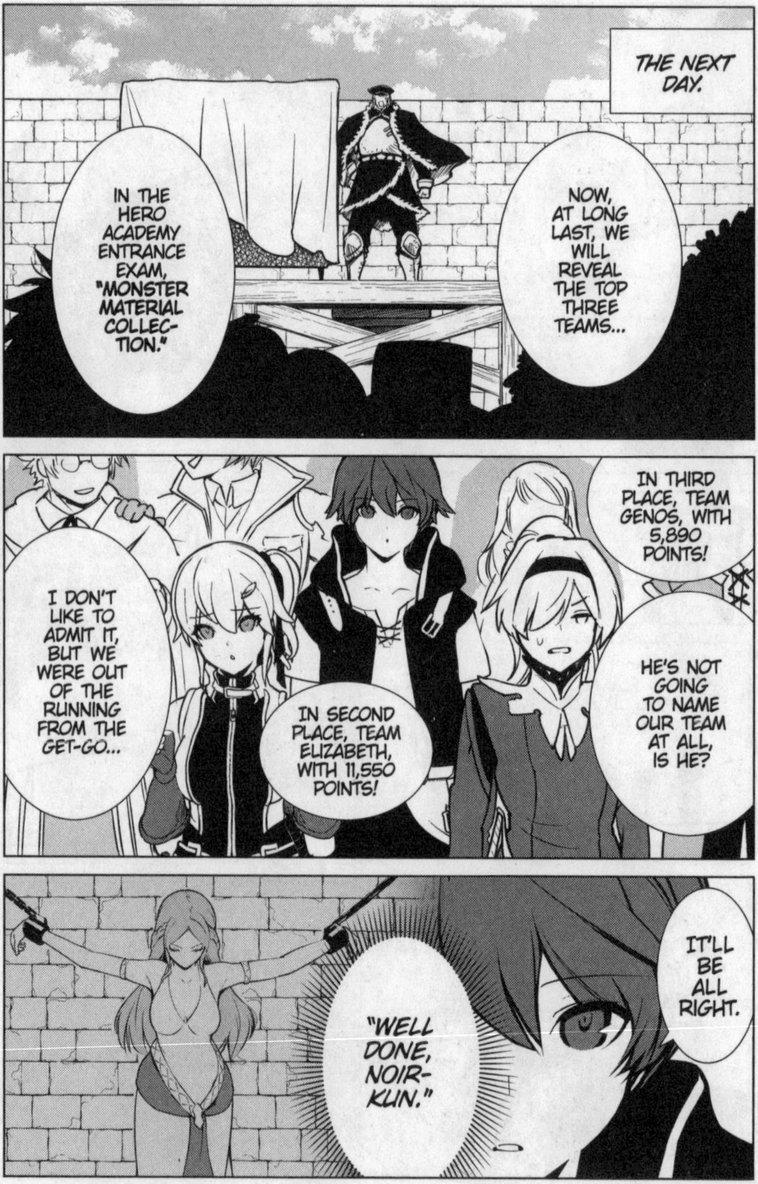
THE NEXT DAY.
NOW, AT LONG LAST, WE WILL REVEAL THE TOP THREE TEAMS...
IN THE HERO ACADEMY ENTRANCE EXAM, "MONSTER MATERIAL COLLECTION."
IN THIRD PLACE, TEAM GENOS, WITH 5,890 POINTS!
I DON'T LIKE TO ADMIT IT, BUT WE WERE OUT OF THE RUNNING FROM THE GET-GO...
IN SECOND PLACE, TEAM ELIZABETH, WITH 11,550 POINTS!
HE'S NOT GOING TO NAME OUR TEAM AT ALL, IS HE?
IT'LL BE ALL RIGHT.
"WELL DONE, NOIR-KUN."

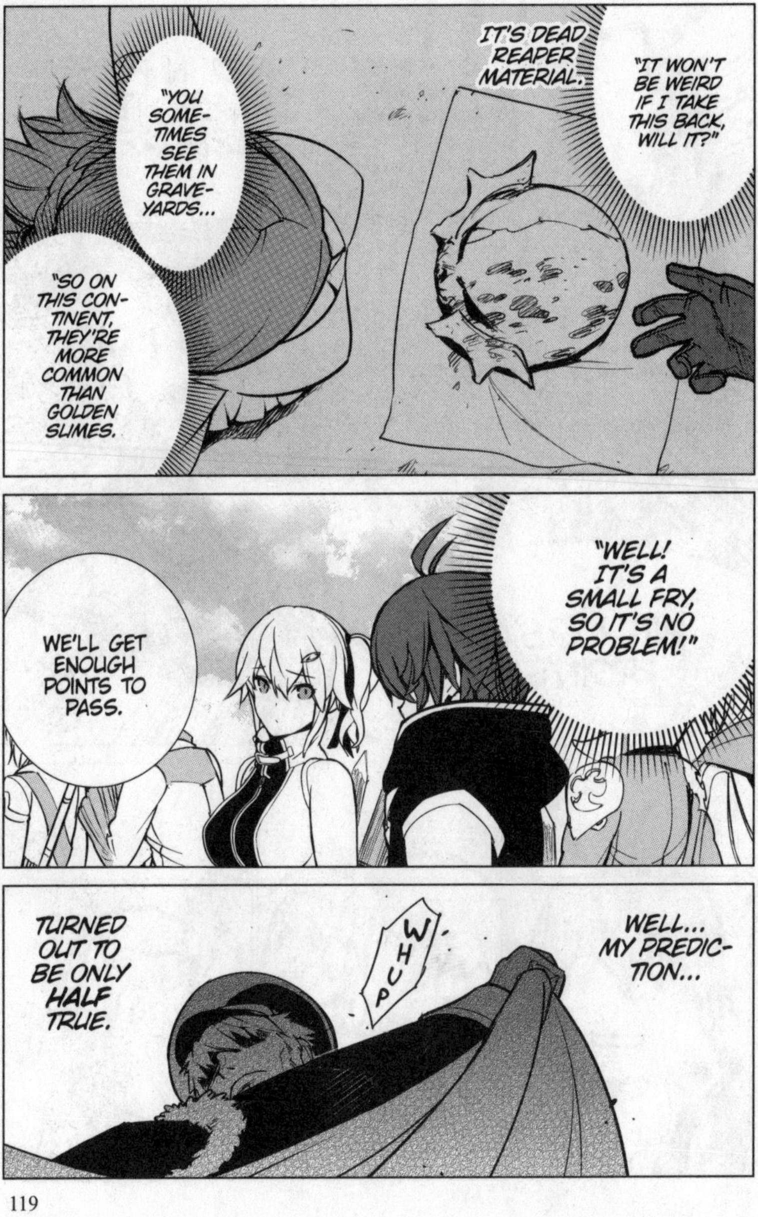
"IT WON'T BE WEIRD IF I TAKE THIS BACK, WILL IT?"
IT'S DEAD REAPER MATERIAL.
"YOU SOMETIMES SEE THEM IN GRAVEYARDS...
"SO ON THIS CONTINENT, THEY'RE MORE COMMON THAN GOLDEN SLIMES.
"WELL! IT'S A SMALL FRY, SO IT'S NO PROBLEM!"
WE'LL GET ENOUGH POINTS TO PASS.
WELL... MY PREDICTION...
WHUP
TURNED OUT TO BE ONLY HALF TRUE.

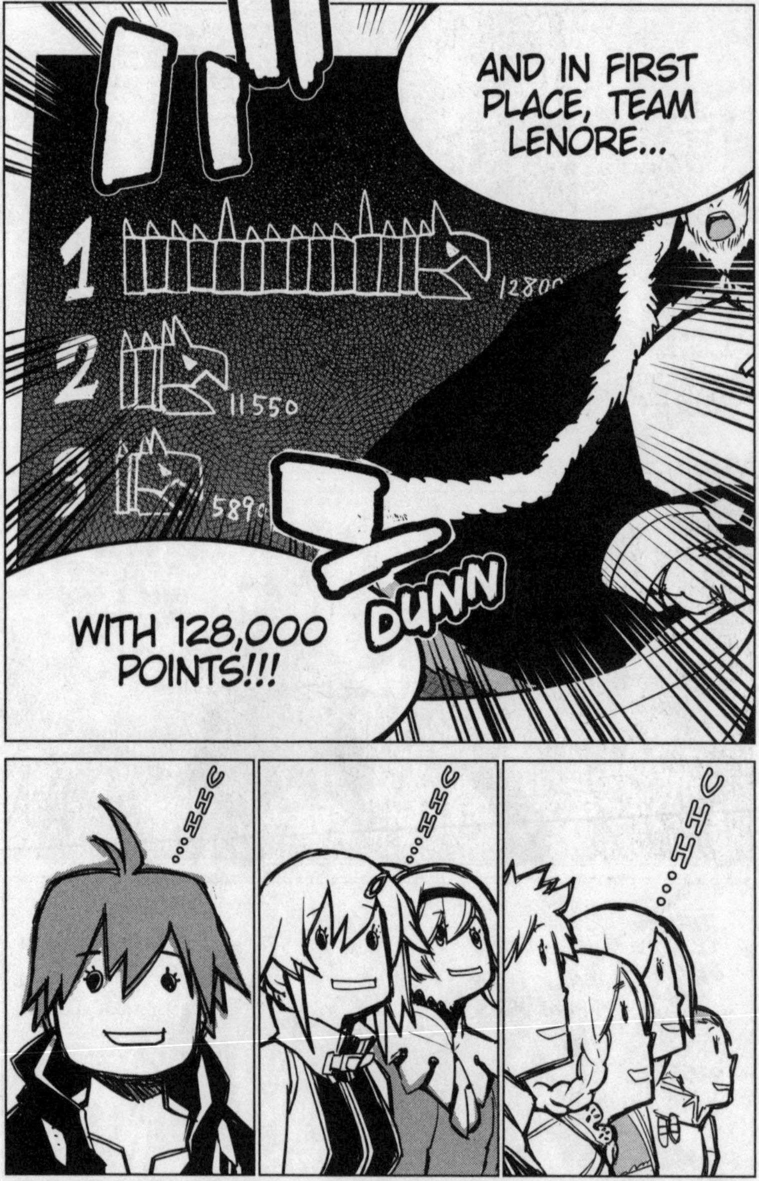
AND IN FIRST PLACE, TEAM LENORE...
11550
WITH 128,000 POINTS!!!
DUNN
...HHC
...HHC
...HHC

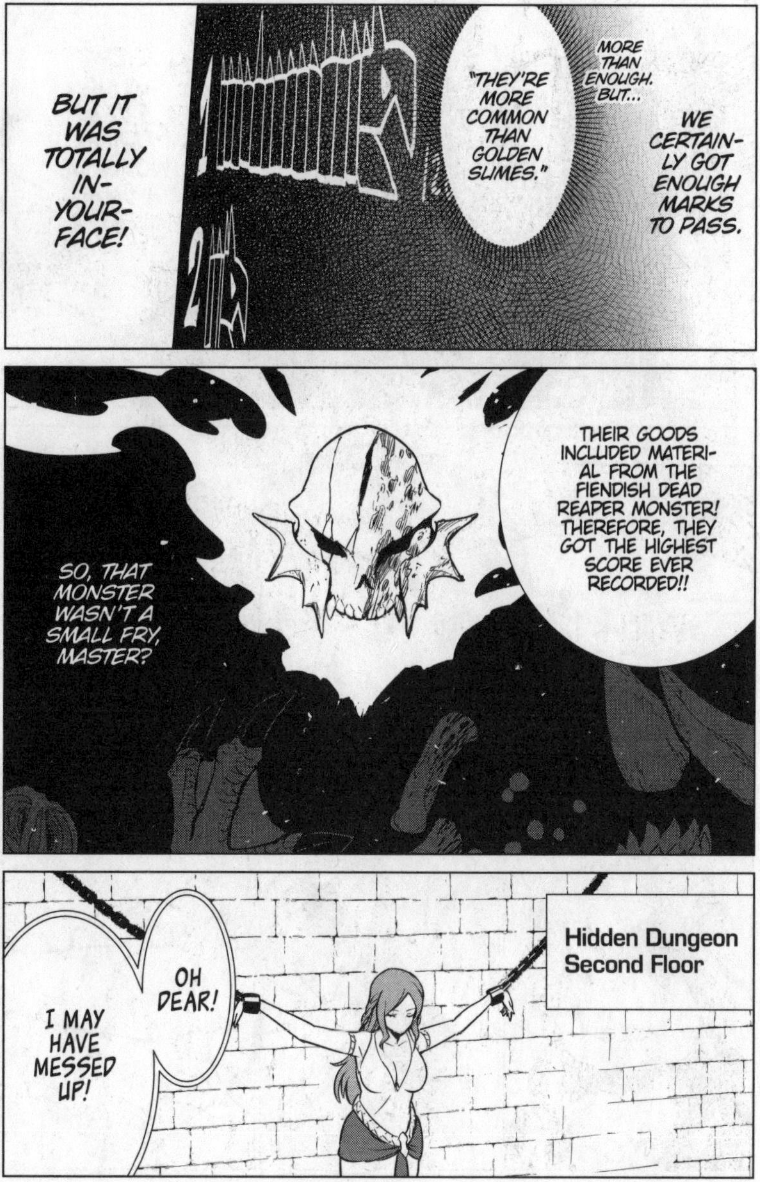
WE CERTAIN-LY GOT ENOUGH MARKS TO PASS.
MORE THAN ENOUGH. BUT...
"THEY'RE MORE COMMON THAN GOLDEN SLIMES."
BUT IT WAS TOTALLY IN-YOUR-FACE!
THEIR GOODS INCLUDED MATERI-AL FROM THE FIENDISH DEAD REAPER MONSTER! THEREFORE, THEY GOT THE HIGHEST SCORE EVER RECORDED!!
SO, THAT MONSTER WASN'T A SMALL FRY, MASTER?
Hidden Dungeon Second Floor
OH DEAR!
I MAY HAVE MESSED UP!

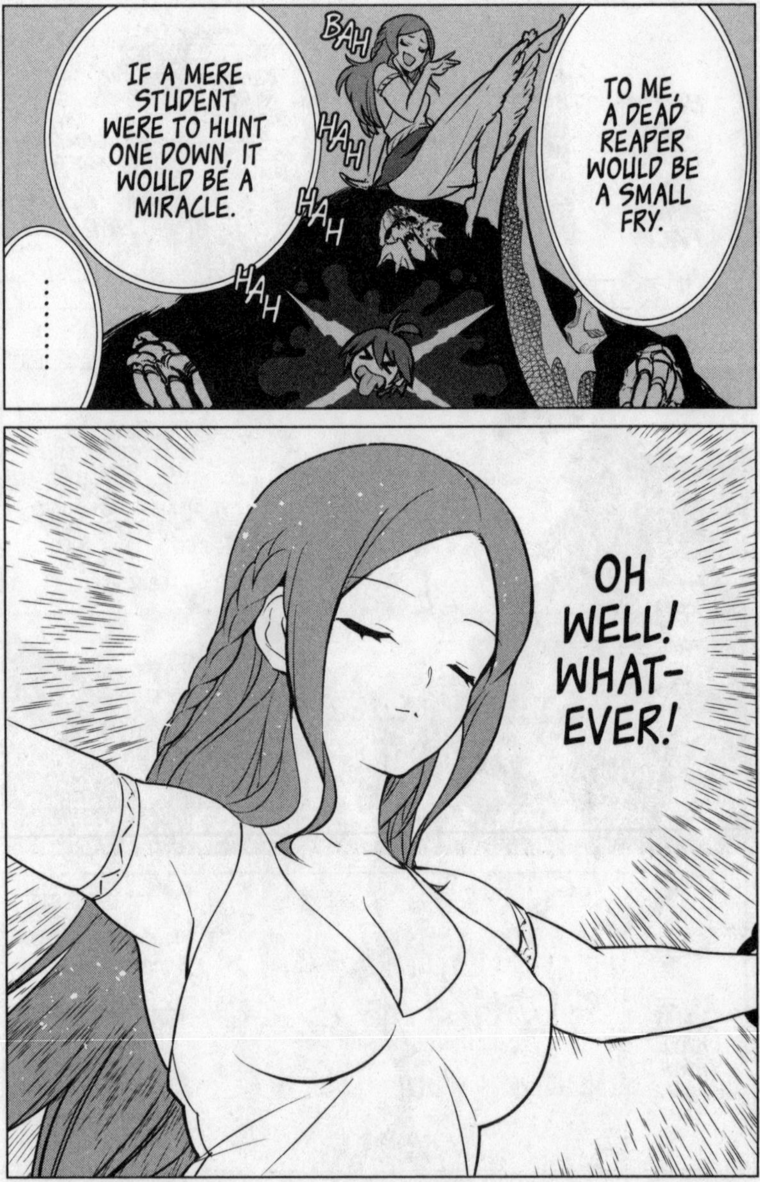
TO ME, A DEAD REAPER WOULD BE A SMALL FRY.
BAH
HAH
HAH
HAH
IF A MERE STUDENT WERE TO HUNT ONE DOWN, IT WOULD BE A MIRACLE.
......
OH WELL! WHAT-EVER!

◆NO REGRETS, NO REMORSE◆

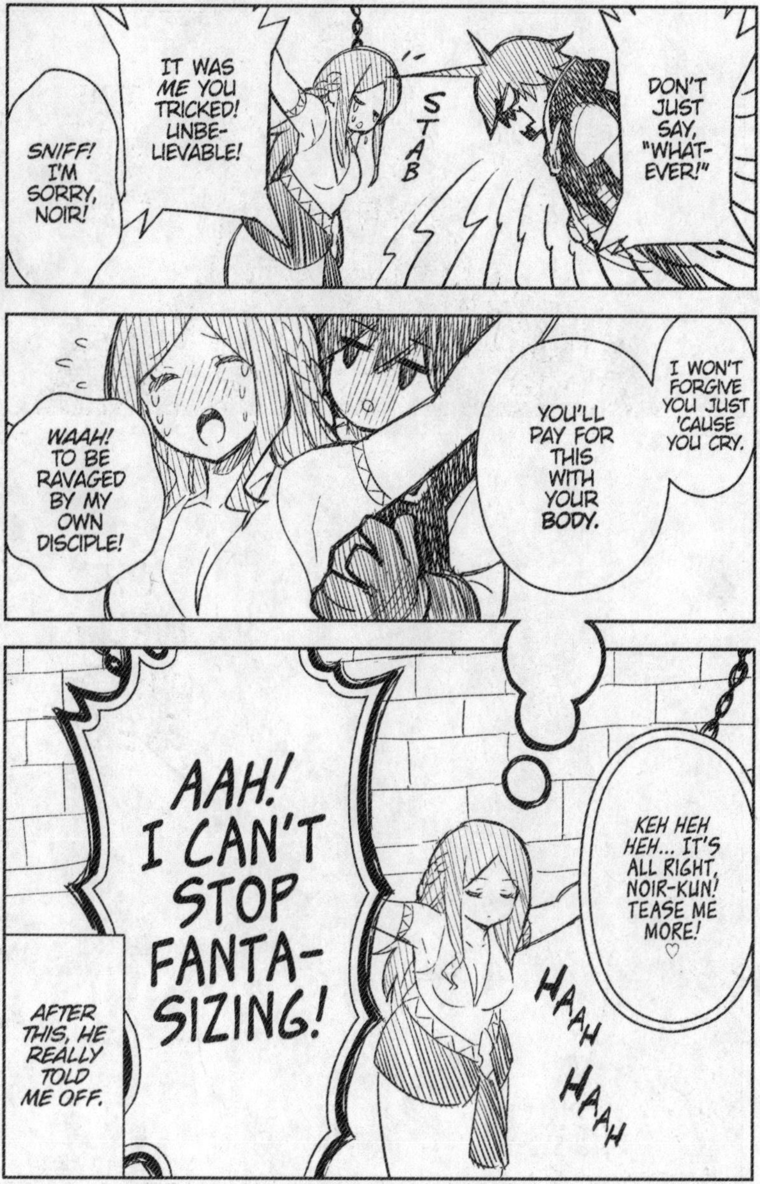

DON'T JUST SAY, "WHAT-EVER!"
STAB
IT WAS ME YOU TRICKED! UNBE-LIEVABLE!
SNIFF! I'M SORRY, NOIR!
I WON'T FORGIVE YOU JUST 'CAUSE YOU CRY.
YOU'LL PAY FOR THIS WITH YOUR BODY.
WAAH! TO BE RAVAGED BY MY OWN DISCIPLE!
KEH HEH HEH... IT'S ALL RIGHT, NOIR-KUN! TEASE ME MORE! ♡
HAAAH HAAAH
AAH! I CAN'T STOP FANTA-SIZING!
AFTER THIS, HE REALLY TOLD ME OFF.

THE HIDDEN DUNGEON ONLY I CAN ENTER

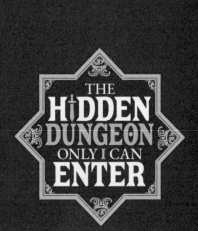

Chapter 5: Headache Immunity

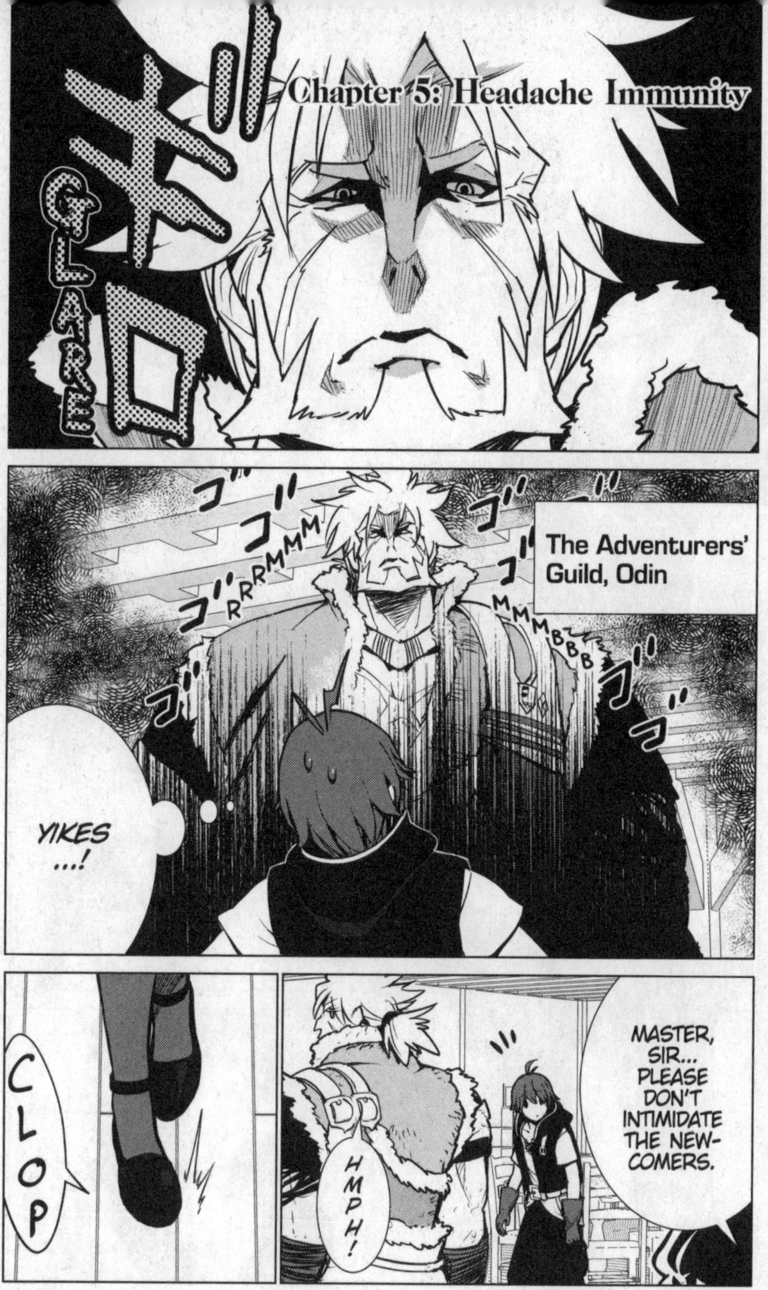
Chapter 5: Headache Immunity
GLARE
The Adventurers' Guild, Odin
RRRMMM
MMMBBB
YIKES ...!
MASTER, SIR... PLEASE DON'T INTIMIDATE THE NEW-COMERS.
HMPH!
CLOP

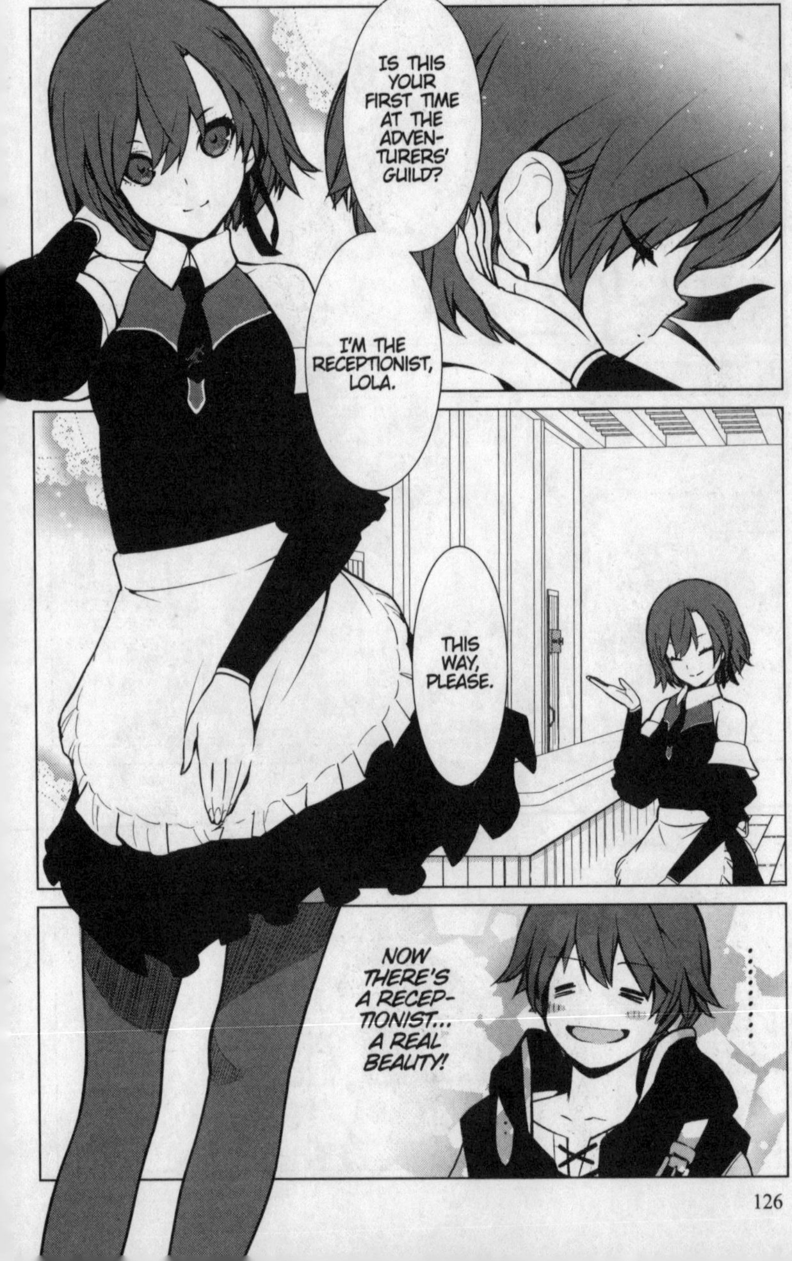
IS THIS YOUR FIRST TIME AT THE ADVEN-TURERS' GUILD?
I'M THE RECEPTIONIST, LOLA.
THIS WAY, PLEASE.
NOW THERE'S A RECEP-TIONIST... A REAL BEAUTY!

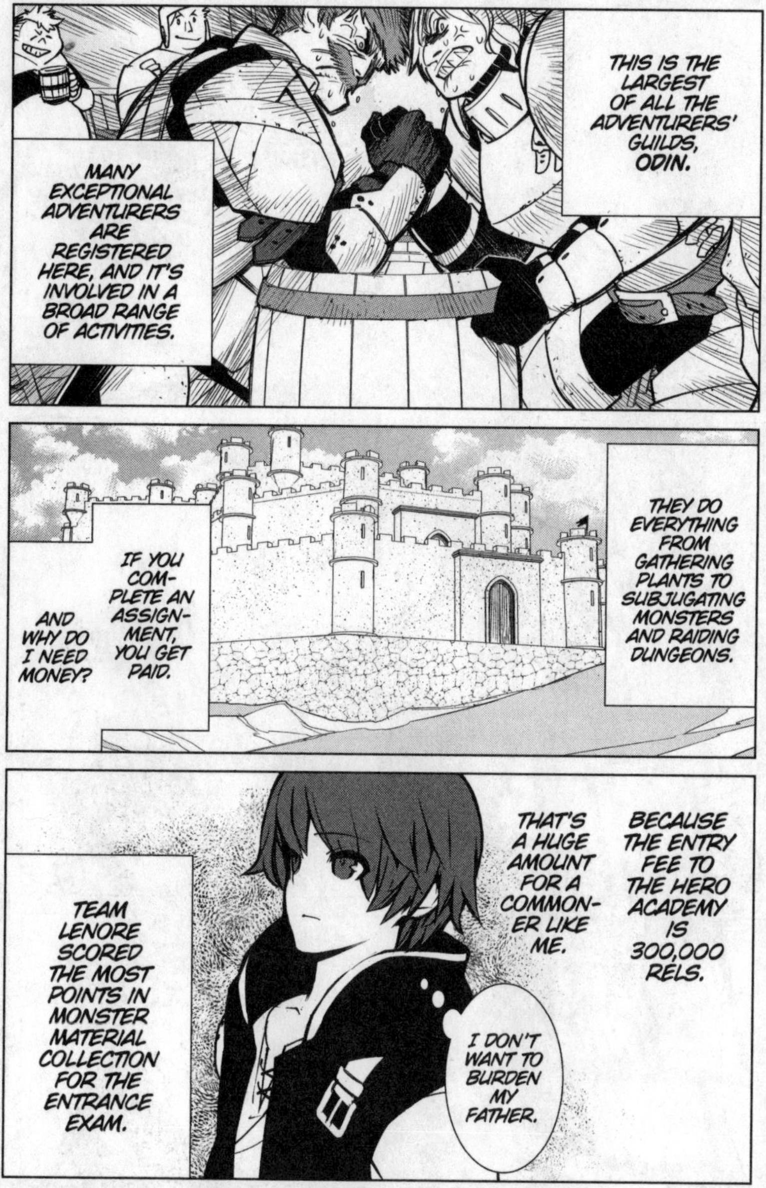
THIS IS THE LARGEST OF ALL THE ADVENTURERS' GUILDS, ODIN.
MANY EXCEPTIONAL ADVENTURERS ARE REGISTERED HERE, AND IT'S INVOLVED IN A BROAD RANGE OF ACTIVITIES.
THEY DO EVERYTHING FROM GATHERING PLANTS TO SUBJUGATING MONSTERS AND RAIDING DUNGEONS.
IF YOU COMPLETE AN ASSIGNMENT, YOU GET PAID.
AND WHY DO I NEED MONEY?
BECAUSE THE ENTRY FEE TO THE HERO ACADEMY IS 300,000 RELS.
THAT'S A HUGE AMOUNT FOR A COMMONER LIKE ME.
I DON'T WANT TO BURDEN MY FATHER.
TEAM LENORE SCORED THE MOST POINTS IN MONSTER MATERIAL COLLECTION FOR THE ENTRANCE EXAM.

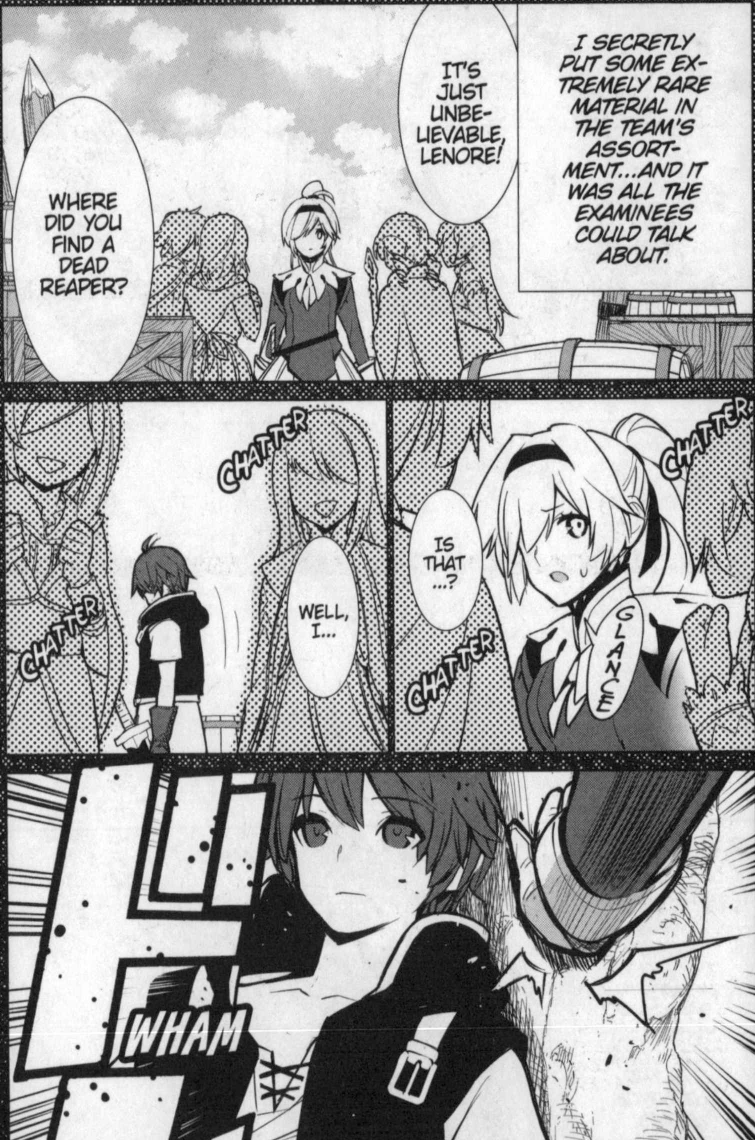
I SECRETLY PUT SOME EXTREMELY RARE MATERIAL IN THE TEAM'S ASSORTMENT...AND IT WAS ALL THE EXAMINEES COULD TALK ABOUT.
IT'S JUST UNBELIEVABLE, LENORE!
WHERE DID YOU FIND A DEAD REAPER?
CHATTER
IS THAT ...?
GLANCE
CHATTER
CHATTER
WELL, I...
CHATTER
WHAM

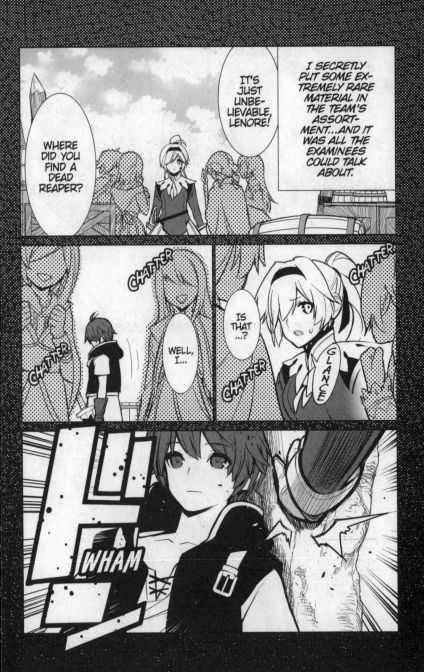

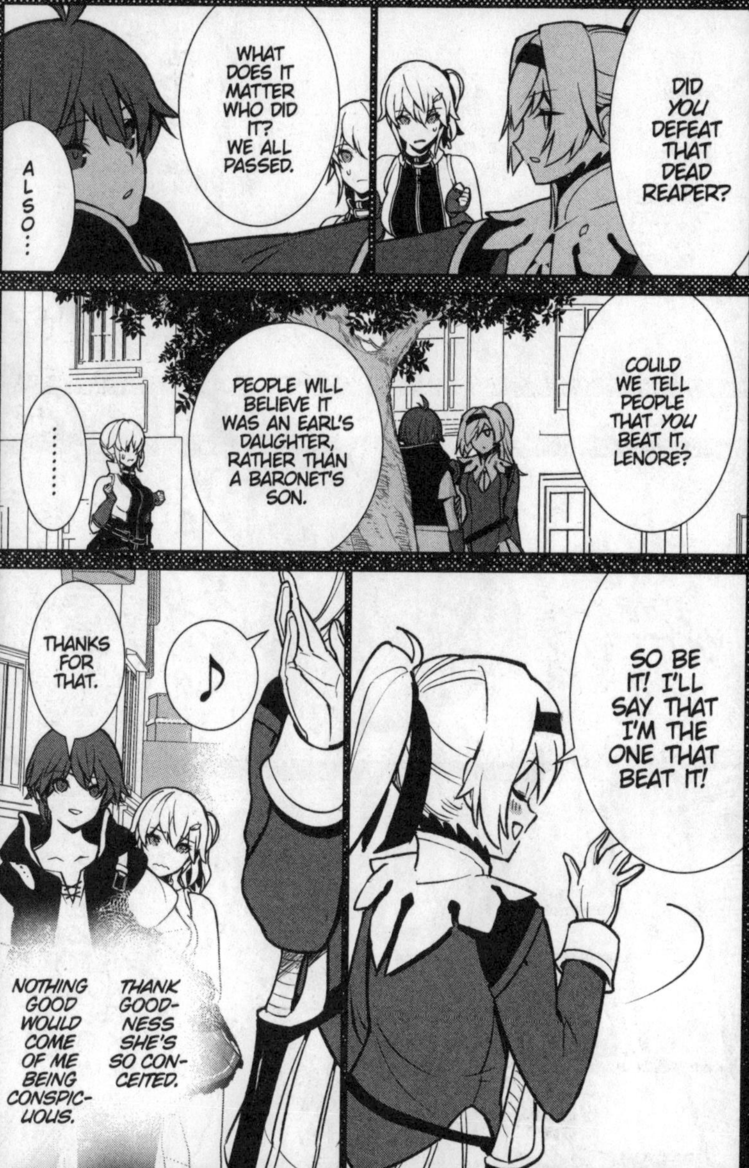
DID YOU DEFEAT THAT DEAD REAPER?
WHAT DOES IT MATTER WHO DID IT? WE ALL PASSED.
ALSO...
COULD WE TELL PEOPLE THAT YOU BEAT IT, LENORE?
PEOPLE WILL BELIEVE IT WAS AN EARL'S DAUGHTER, RATHER THAN A BARONET'S SON.
......
SO BE IT! I'LL SAY THAT I'M THE ONE THAT BEAT IT!
♪
THANKS FOR THAT.
THANK GOODNESS SHE'S SO CONCEITED.
NOTHING GOOD WOULD COME OF ME BEING CONSPICUOUS.

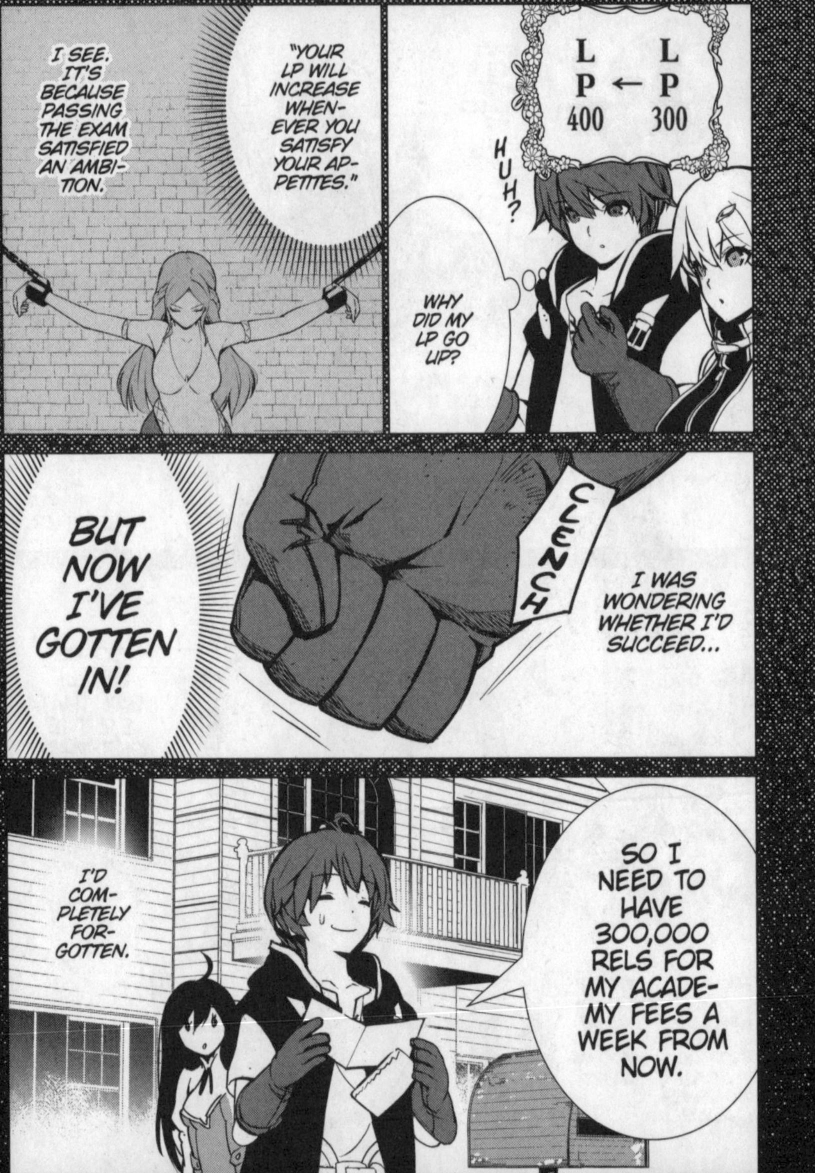
LP 400 ← LP 300
HUH?
WHY DID MY LP GO UP?
"YOUR LP WILL INCREASE WHENEVER YOU SATISFY YOUR APPETITES."
I SEE. IT'S BECAUSE PASSING THE EXAM SATISFIED AN AMBITION.
CLENCH
I WAS WONDERING WHETHER I'D SUCCEED...
BUT NOW I'VE GOTTEN IN!
SO I NEED TO HAVE 300,000 RELS FOR MY ACADEMY FEES A WEEK FROM NOW.
I'D COMPLETELY FORGOTTEN.

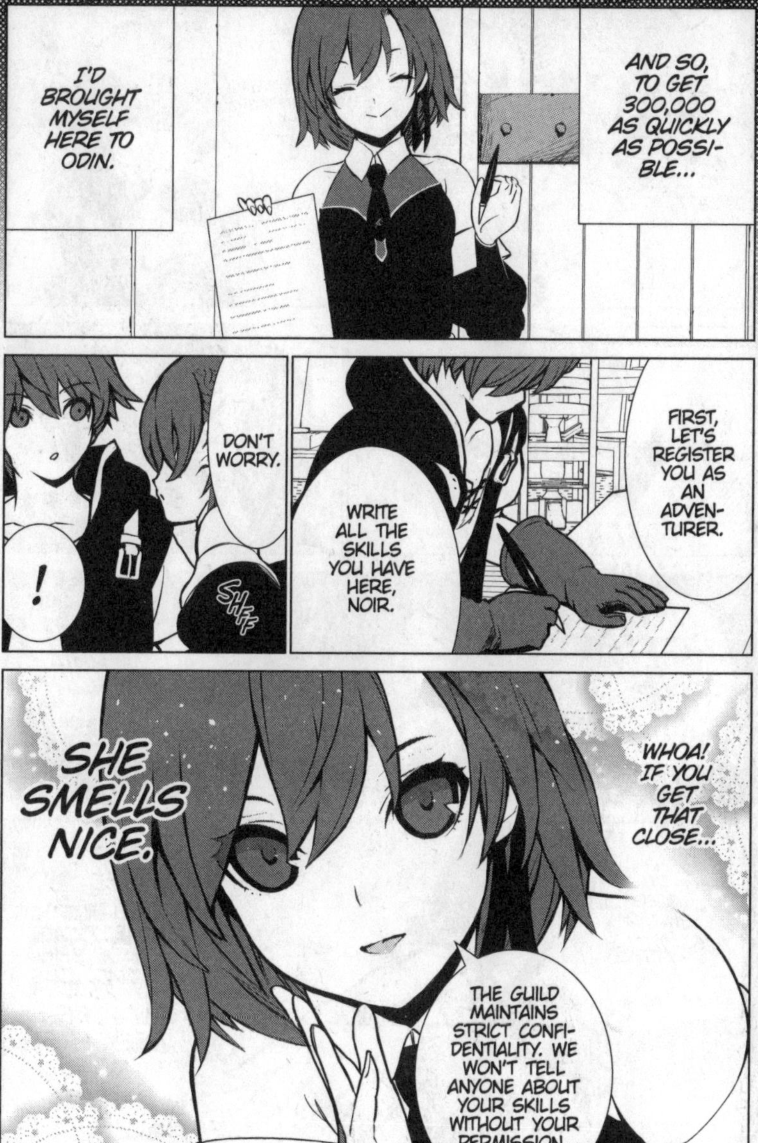
AND SO, TO GET 300,000 AS QUICKLY AS POSSI- BLE...
I'D BROUGHT MYSELF HERE TO ODIN.
FIRST, LET'S REGISTER YOU AS AN ADVEN- TURER.
WRITE ALL THE SKILLS YOU HAVE HERE, NOIR.
DON'T WORRY.
SHFF
!
WHOA! IF YOU GET THAT CLOSE...
SHE SMELLS NICE.
THE GUILD MAINTAINS STRICT CONFI- DENTIALITY. WE WON'T TELL ANYONE ABOUT YOUR SKILLS WITHOUT YOUR PERMISSION.

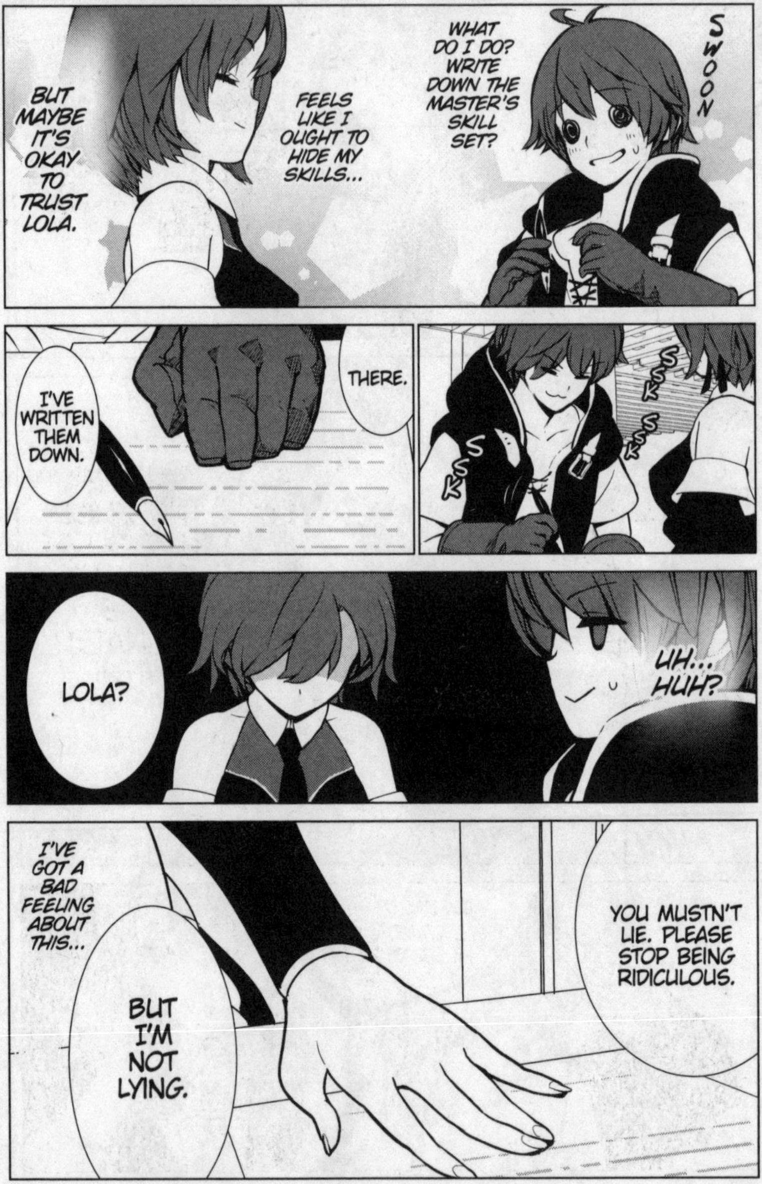
SWOON
WHAT DO I DO? WRITE DOWN THE MASTER'S SKILL SET?
FEELS LIKE I OUGHT TO HIDE MY SKILLS...
BUT MAYBE IT'S OKAY TO TRUST LOLA.
SSK SSK
SSK
THERE.
I'VE WRITTEN THEM DOWN.
UH... HUH?
LOLA?
YOU MUSTN'T LIE. PLEASE STOP BEING RIDICULOUS.
I'VE GOT A BAD FEELING ABOUT THIS...
BUT I'M NOT LYING.

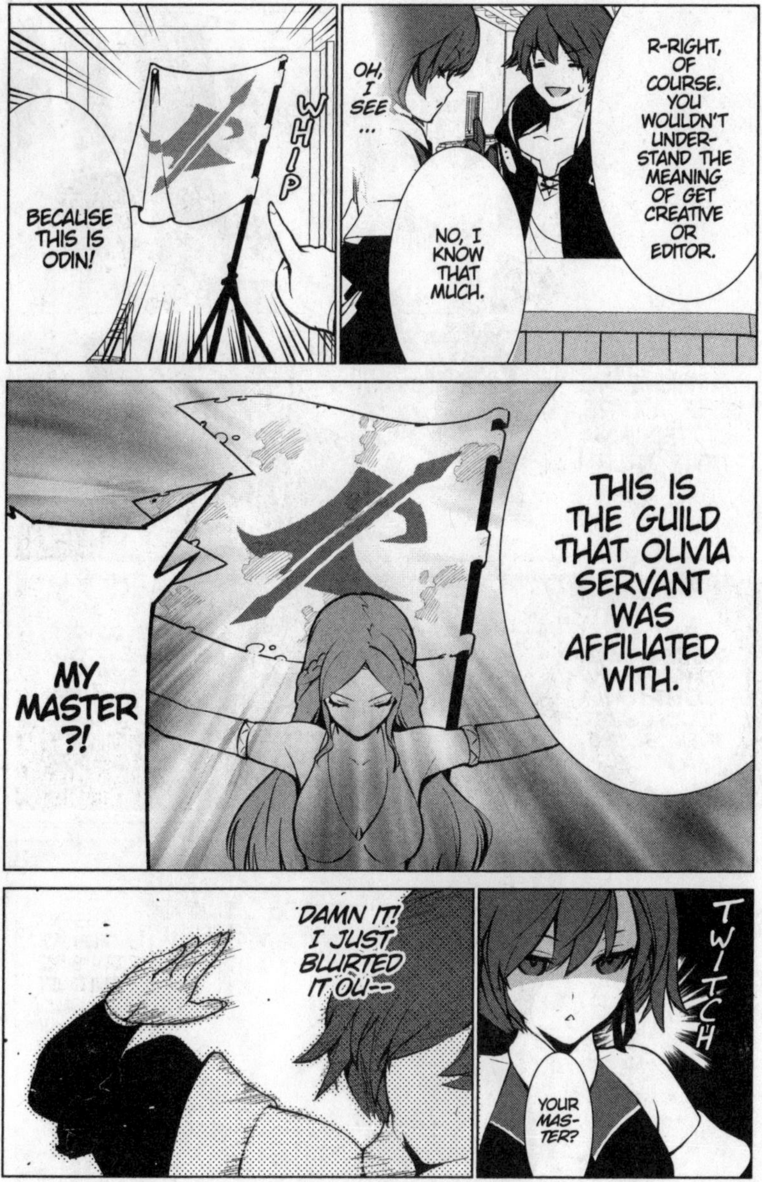
R-RIGHT, OF COURSE. YOU WOULDN'T UNDERSTAND THE MEANING OF GET CREATIVE OR EDITOR.
OH, I SEE ...
NO, I KNOW THAT MUCH.
WHIP
BECAUSE THIS IS ODIN!
THIS IS THE GUILD THAT OLIVIA SERVANT WAS AFFILIATED WITH.
MY MASTER ?!
TWITCH
YOUR MASTER?
DAMN IT! I JUST BLURTED IT OU--

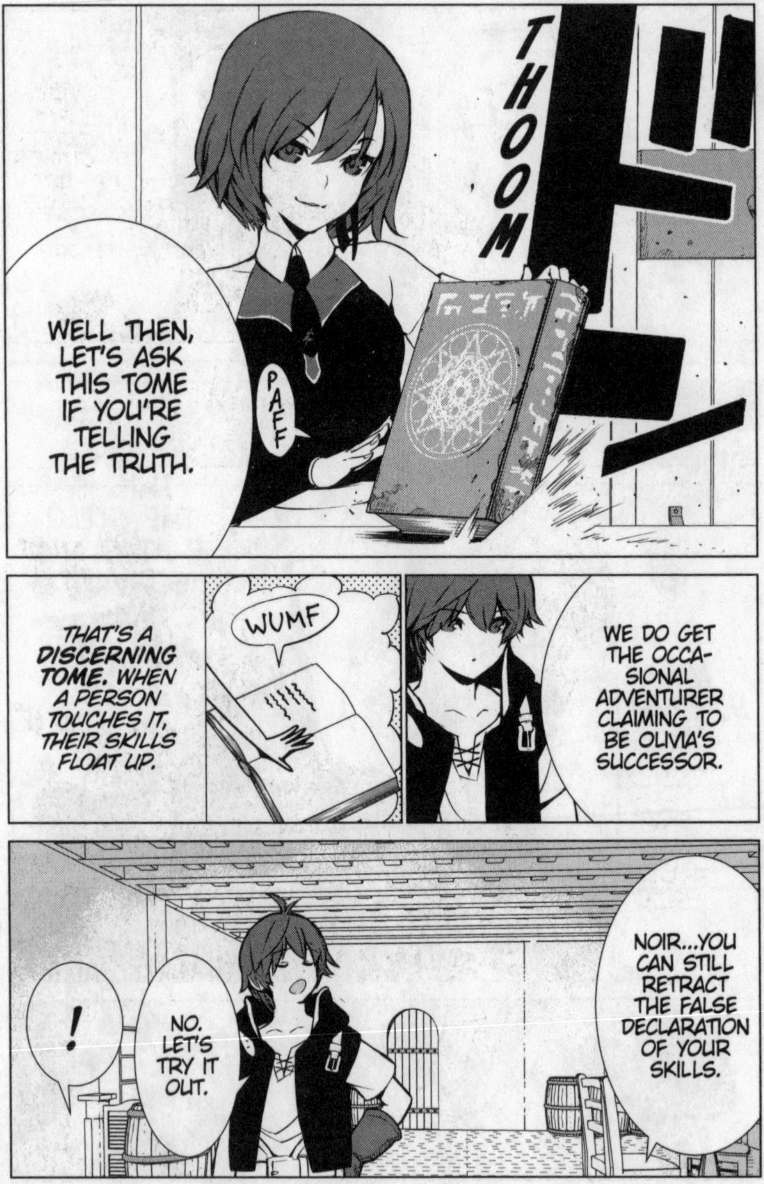
THOOM
WELL THEN, LET'S ASK THIS TOME IF YOU'RE TELLING THE TRUTH.
PAFF
WE DO GET THE OCCA-SIONAL ADVENTURER CLAIMING TO BE OLIVIA'S SUCCESSOR.
WUMF
THAT'S A DISCERNING TOME. WHEN A PERSON TOUCHES IT, THEIR SKILLS FLOAT UP.
NOIR...YOU CAN STILL RETRACT THE FALSE DECLARATION OF YOUR SKILLS.
NO. LET'S TRY IT OUT.
!

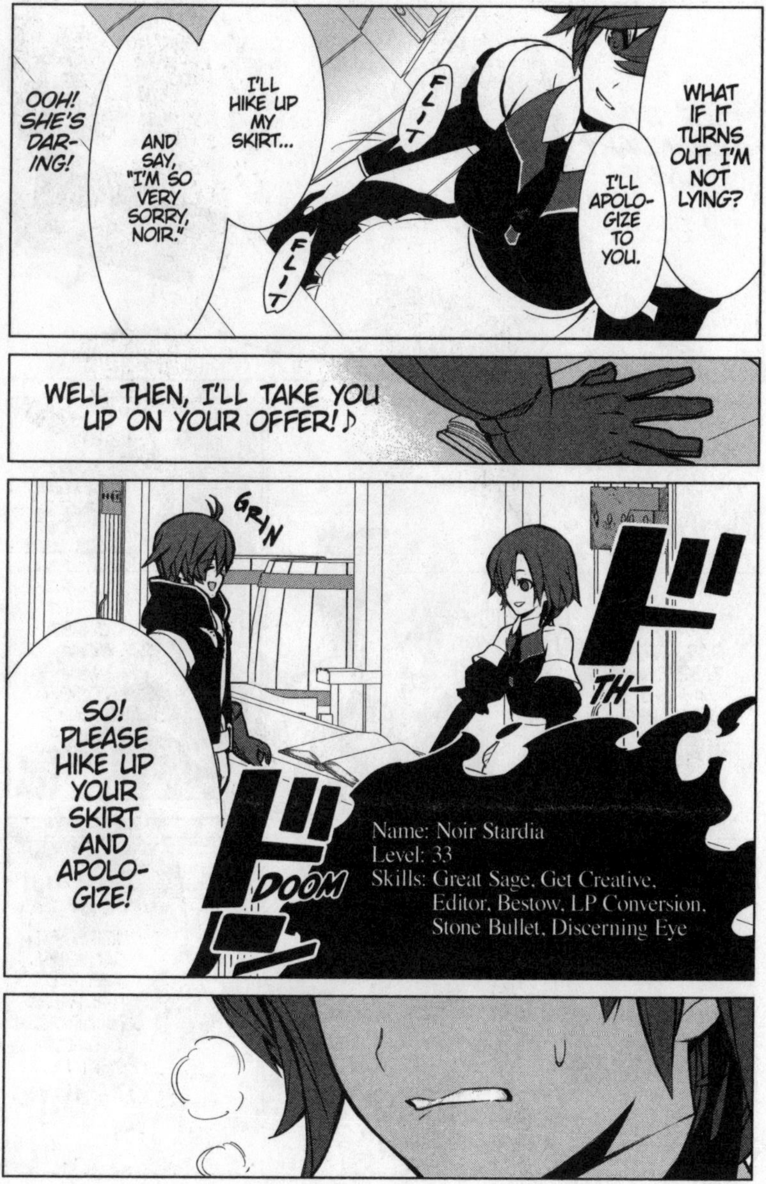
WHAT IF IT TURNS OUT I'M NOT LYING?
I'LL APOLOGIZE TO YOU.
FLIT
I'LL HIKE UP MY SKIRT...
AND SAY, "I'M SO VERY SORRY, NOIR."
FLIT
OOH! SHE'S DARING!
WELL THEN, I'LL TAKE YOU UP ON YOUR OFFER!♪
ド
TH-
GRIN
Name: Noir Stardia
Level: 33
Skills: Great Sage, Get Creative, Editor, Bestow, LP Conversion, Stone Bullet, Discerning Eye
ド
DOOM
SO! PLEASE HIKE UP YOUR SKIRT AND APOLOGIZE!

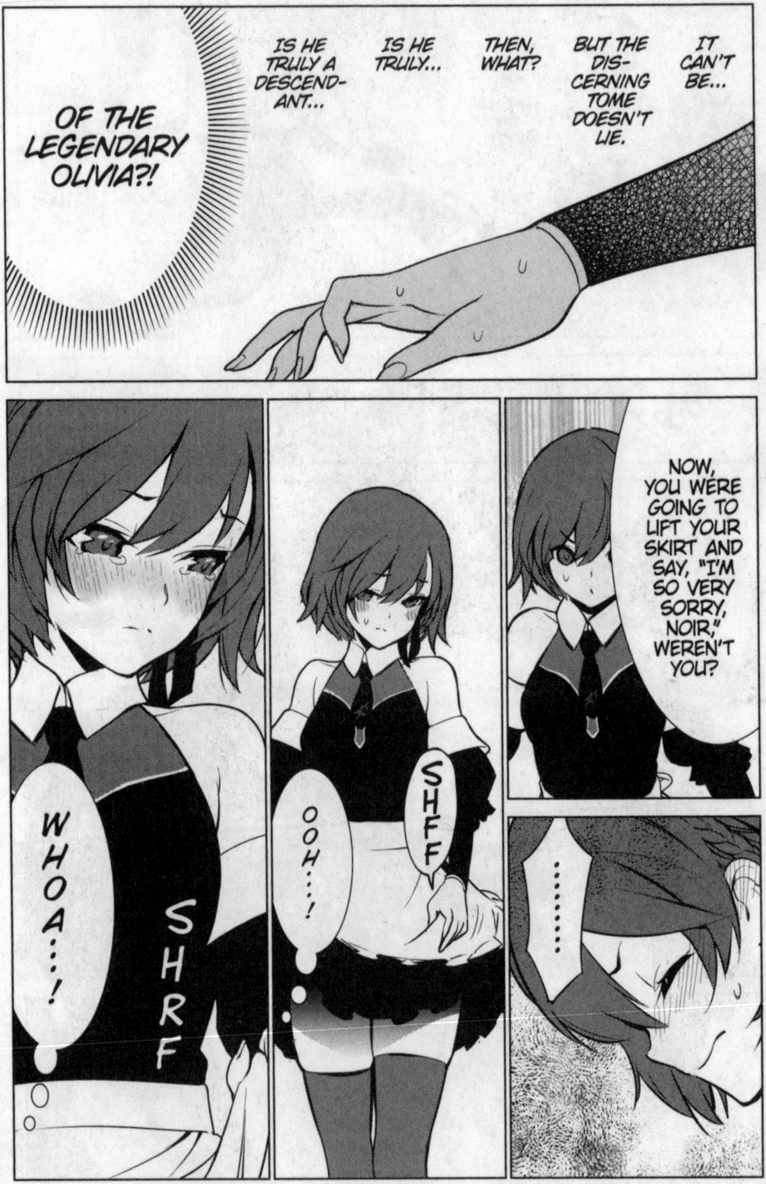
IT CAN'T BE...
BUT THE DIS-CERNING TOME DOESN'T LIE.
THEN, WHAT?
IS HE TRULY...
IS HE TRULY A DESCEND-ANT...
OF THE LEGENDARY OLIVIA?!
NOW, YOU WERE GOING TO LIFT YOUR SKIRT AND SAY, "I'M SO VERY SORRY, NOIR," WEREN'T YOU?
......
SHFF
OOH...!
SHRF
WHOA...!

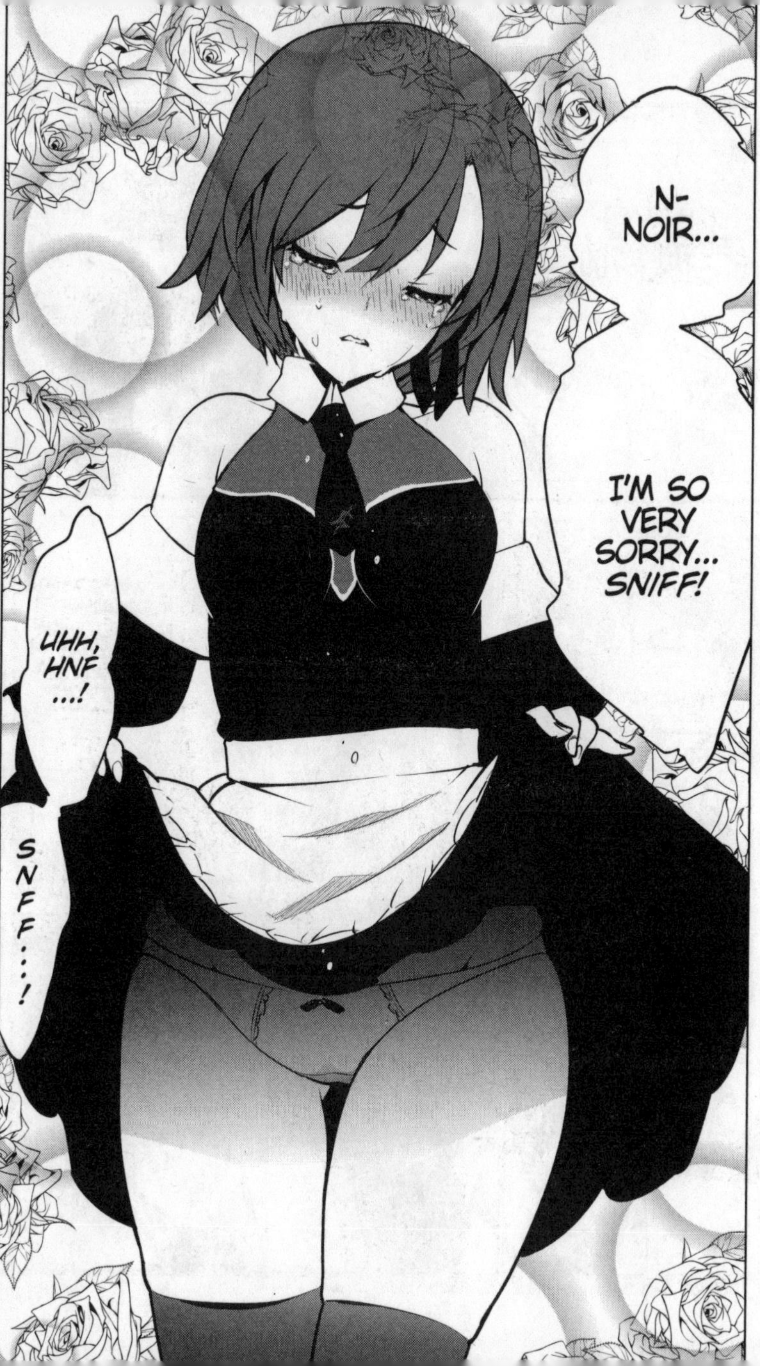
N-NOIR...
I'M SO VERY SORRY... SNIFF!
UHH, HNF ...!
SNFF...!

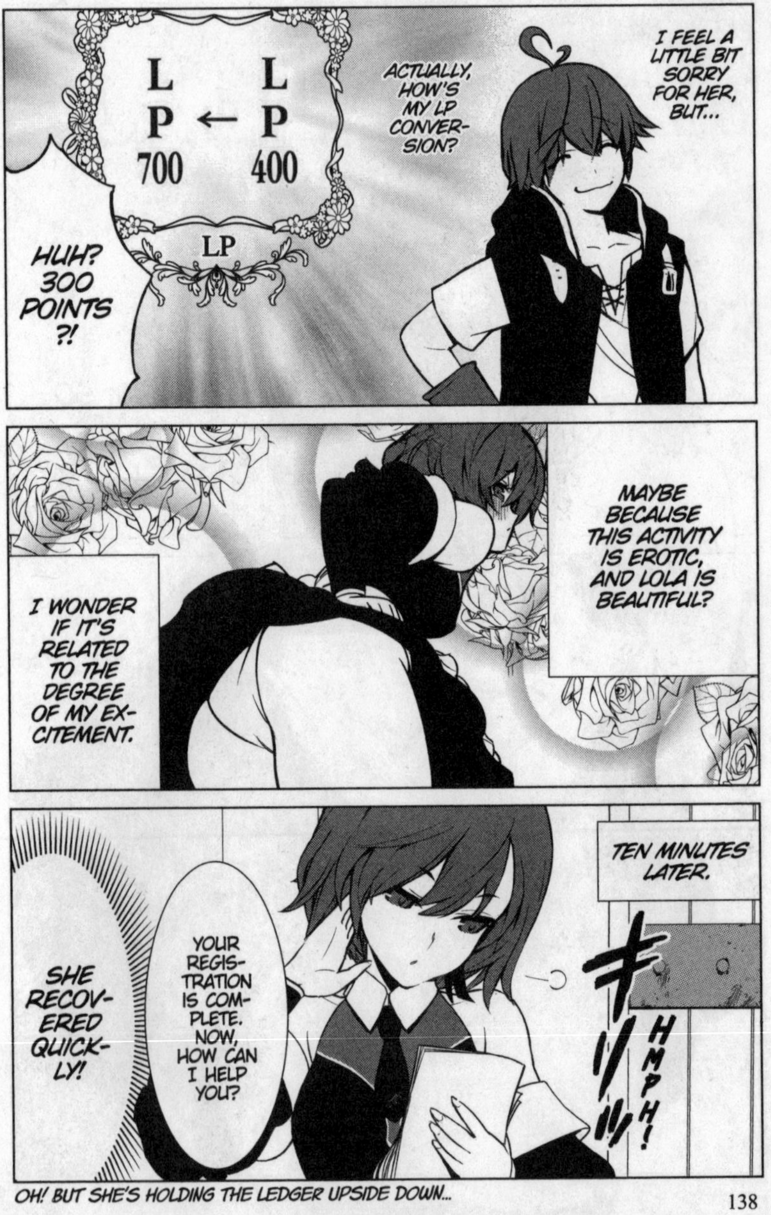

I FEEL A LITTLE BIT SORRY FOR HER, BUT...
ACTUALLY, HOW'S MY LP CONVERSION?
LP 700 ← LP 400
LP
HUH? 300 POINTS?!
MAYBE BECAUSE THIS ACTIVITY IS EROTIC, AND LOLA IS BEAUTIFUL?
I WONDER IF IT'S RELATED TO THE DEGREE OF MY EXCITEMENT.
TEN MINUTES LATER.
HMPH!
YOUR REGISTRATION IS COMPLETE. NOW, HOW CAN I HELP YOU?
SHE RECOVERED QUICKLY!

OH! BUT SHE'S HOLDING THE LEDGER UPSIDE DOWN...

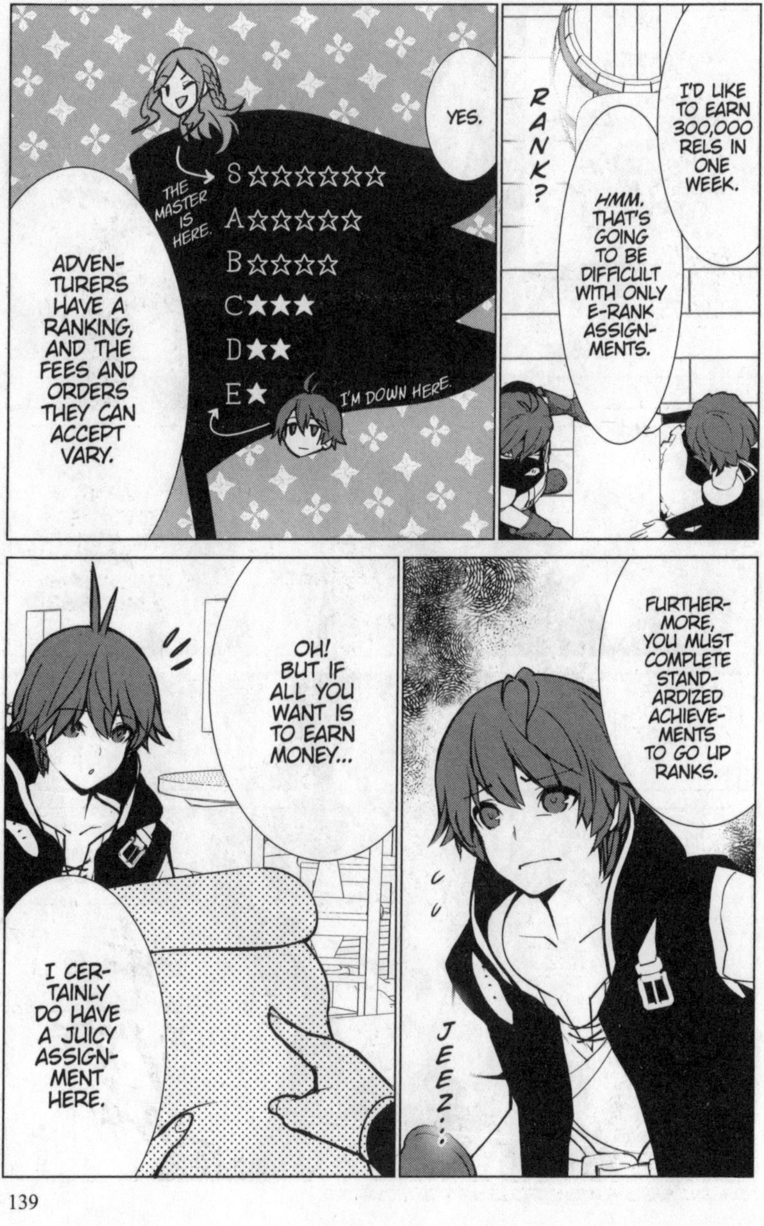
I'D LIKE TO EARN 300,000 RELS IN ONE WEEK.
HMM. THAT'S GOING TO BE DIFFICULT WITH ONLY E-RANK ASSIGNMENTS.
RANK?
YES.
THE MASTER IS HERE.
S☆☆☆☆☆☆
A☆☆☆☆☆
B☆☆☆☆
C★★★
D★★
E★
I'M DOWN HERE.
ADVENTURERS HAVE A RANKING, AND THE FEES AND ORDERS THEY CAN ACCEPT VARY.
FURTHERMORE, YOU MUST COMPLETE STANDARDIZED ACHIEVEMENTS TO GO UP RANKS.
JEEZ...
OH! BUT IF ALL YOU WANT IS TO EARN MONEY...
I CERTAINLY DO HAVE A JUICY ASSIGNMENT HERE.

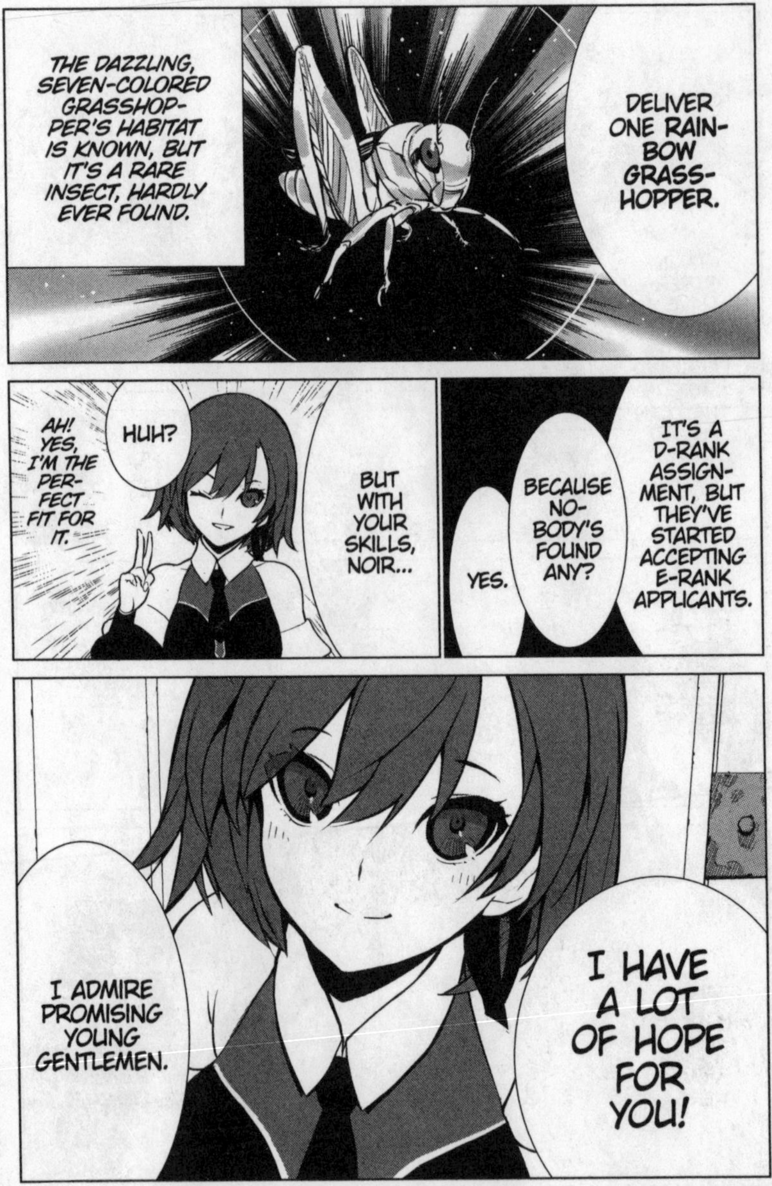
DELIVER ONE RAINBOW GRASSHOPPER.
THE DAZZLING, SEVEN-COLORED GRASSHOPPER'S HABITAT IS KNOWN, BUT IT'S A RARE INSECT, HARDLY EVER FOUND.
IT'S A D-RANK ASSIGNMENT, BUT THEY'VE STARTED ACCEPTING E-RANK APPLICANTS.
BECAUSE NOBODY'S FOUND ANY?
YES.
BUT WITH YOUR SKILLS, NOIR...
HUH?
AH! YES, I'M THE PERFECT FIT FOR IT.
I HAVE A LOT OF HOPE FOR YOU!
I ADMIRE PROMISING YOUNG GENTLEMEN.

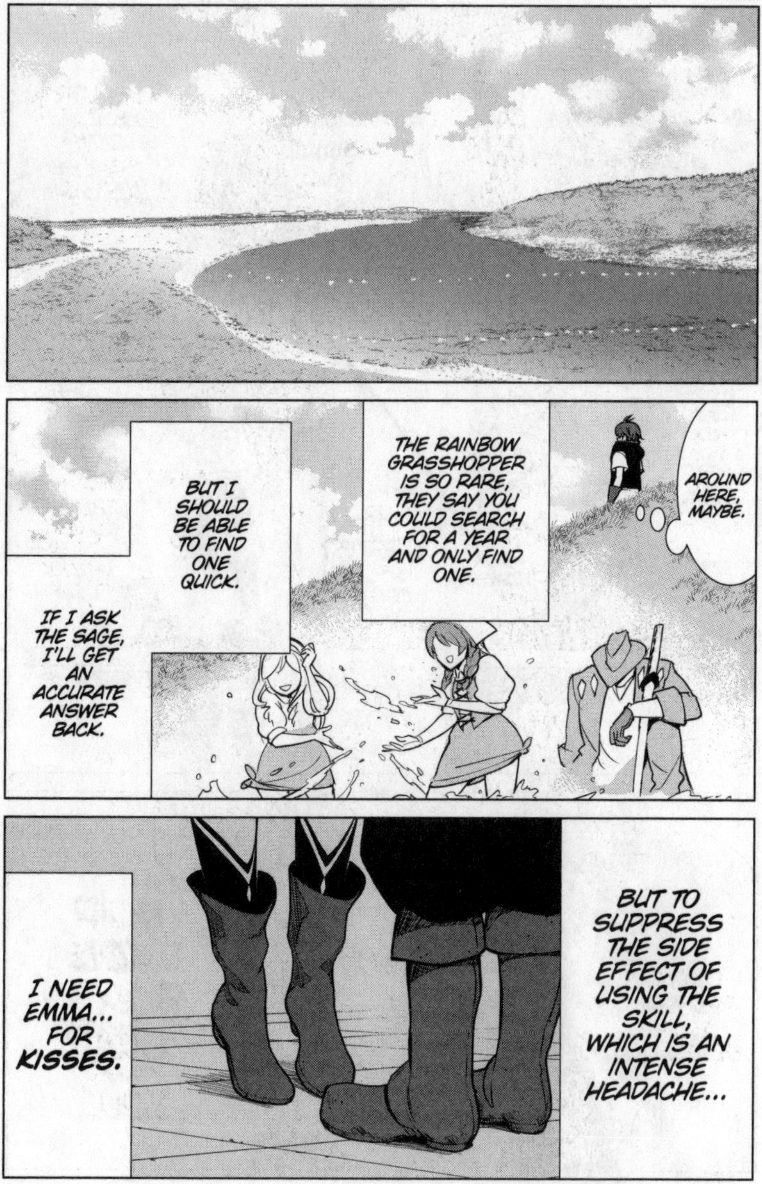
AROUND HERE, MAYBE.
THE RAINBOW GRASSHOPPER IS SO RARE, THEY SAY YOU COULD SEARCH FOR A YEAR AND ONLY FIND ONE.
BUT I SHOULD BE ABLE TO FIND ONE QUICK.
IF I ASK THE SAGE, I'LL GET AN ACCURATE ANSWER BACK.
BUT TO SUPPRESS THE SIDE EFFECT OF USING THE SKILL, WHICH IS AN INTENSE HEADACHE...
I NEED EMMA... FOR **KISSES.**

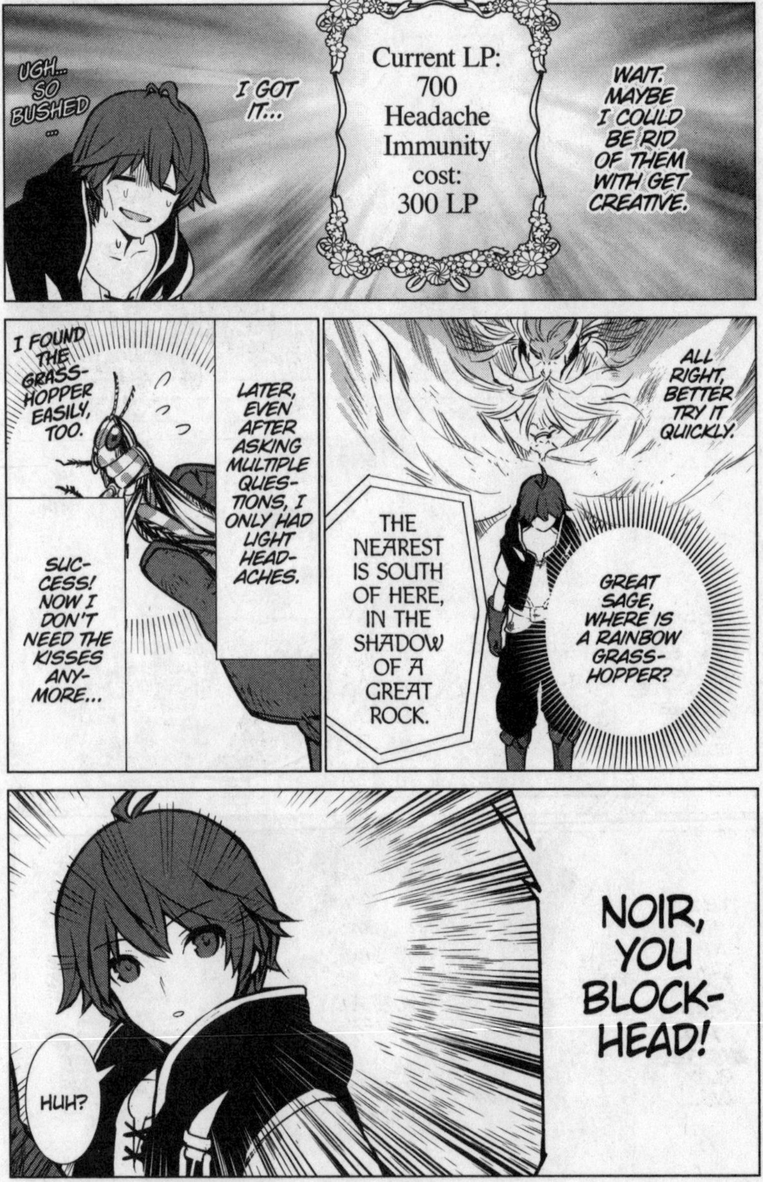

WAIT. MAYBE I COULD BE RID OF THEM WITH GET CREATIVE.
Current LP: 700 Headache Immunity cost: 300 LP
I GOT IT...
UGH... SO BUSHED...
ALL RIGHT, BETTER TRY IT QUICKLY.
GREAT SAGE, WHERE IS A RAINBOW GRASS-HOPPER?
THE NEAREST IS SOUTH OF HERE, IN THE SHADOW OF A GREAT ROCK.
LATER, EVEN AFTER ASKING MULTIPLE QUES-TIONS, I ONLY HAD LIGHT HEAD-ACHES.
I FOUND THE GRASS-HOPPER EASILY, TOO.
SUC-CESS! NOW I DON'T NEED THE KISSES ANY-MORE...
NOIR, YOU BLOCK-HEAD!
HUH?

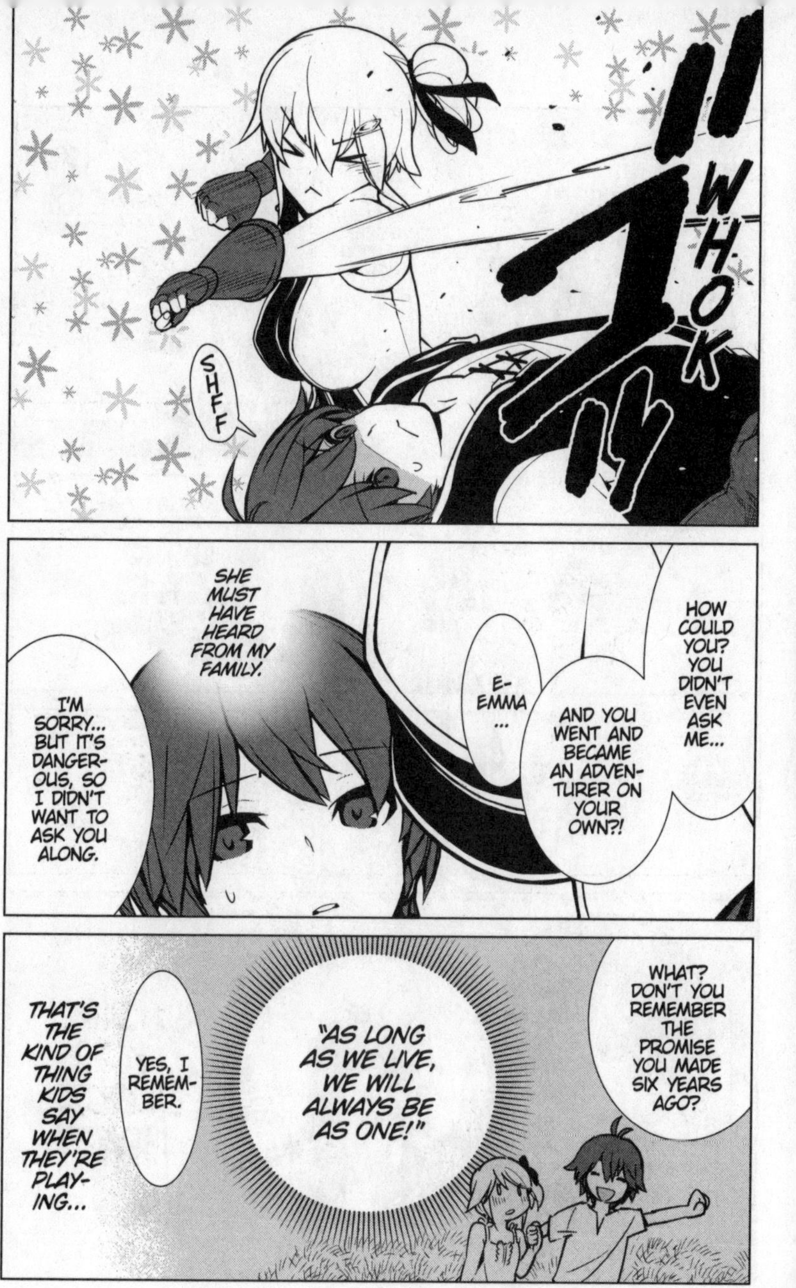
WHOKK
SHFF
HOW COULD YOU? YOU DIDN'T EVEN ASK ME...
AND YOU WENT AND BECAME AN ADVEN-TURER ON YOUR OWN?!
E-EMMA...
SHE MUST HAVE HEARD FROM MY FAMILY.
I'M SORRY... BUT IT'S DANGER-OUS, SO I DIDN'T WANT TO ASK YOU ALONG.
WHAT? DON'T YOU REMEMBER THE PROMISE YOU MADE SIX YEARS AGO?
"AS LONG AS WE LIVE, WE WILL ALWAYS BE AS ONE!"
YES, I REMEM-BER.
THAT'S THE KIND OF THING KIDS SAY WHEN THEY'RE PLAY-ING...

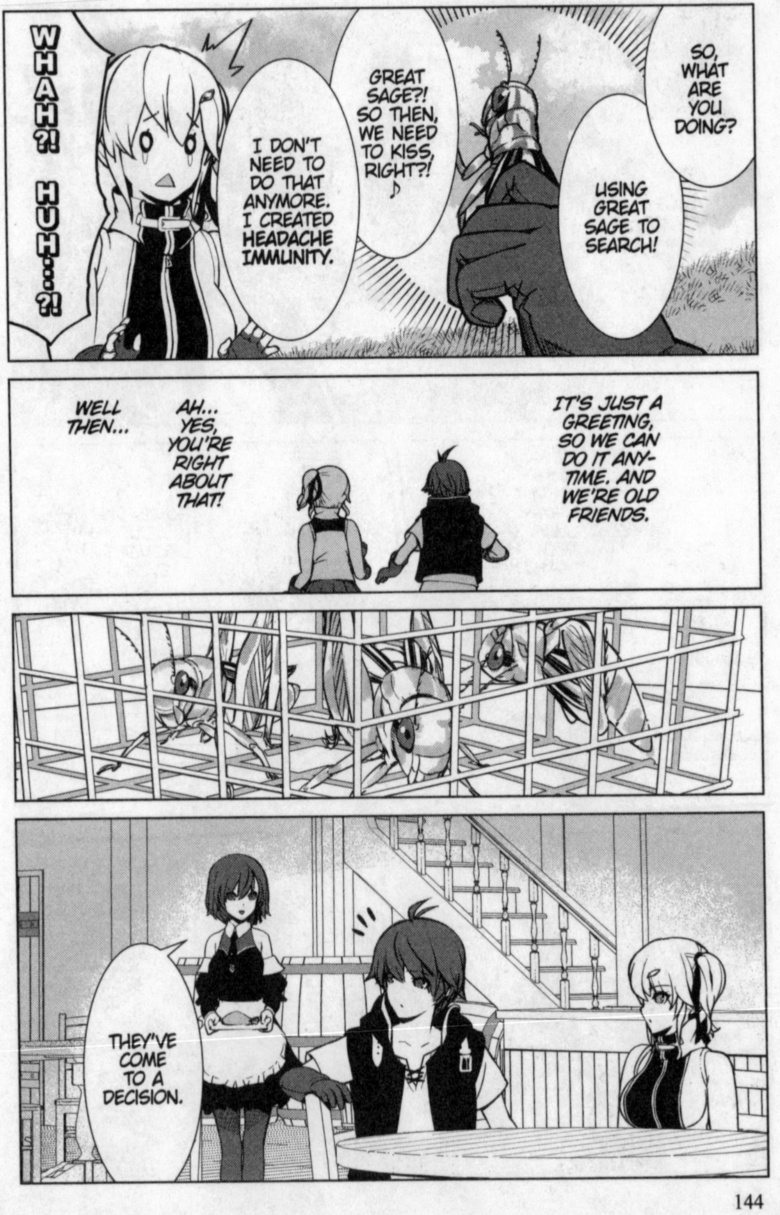
SO, WHAT ARE YOU DOING?
USING GREAT SAGE TO SEARCH!
GREAT SAGE?! SO THEN, WE NEED TO KISS, RIGHT?! ♪
I DON'T NEED TO DO THAT ANYMORE. I CREATED HEADACHE IMMUNITY.
WHAH?! HUH...?!
IT'S JUST A GREETING, SO WE CAN DO IT ANYTIME. AND WE'RE OLD FRIENDS.
AH... YES, YOU'RE RIGHT ABOUT THAT!
WELL THEN...
THEY'VE COME TO A DECISION.

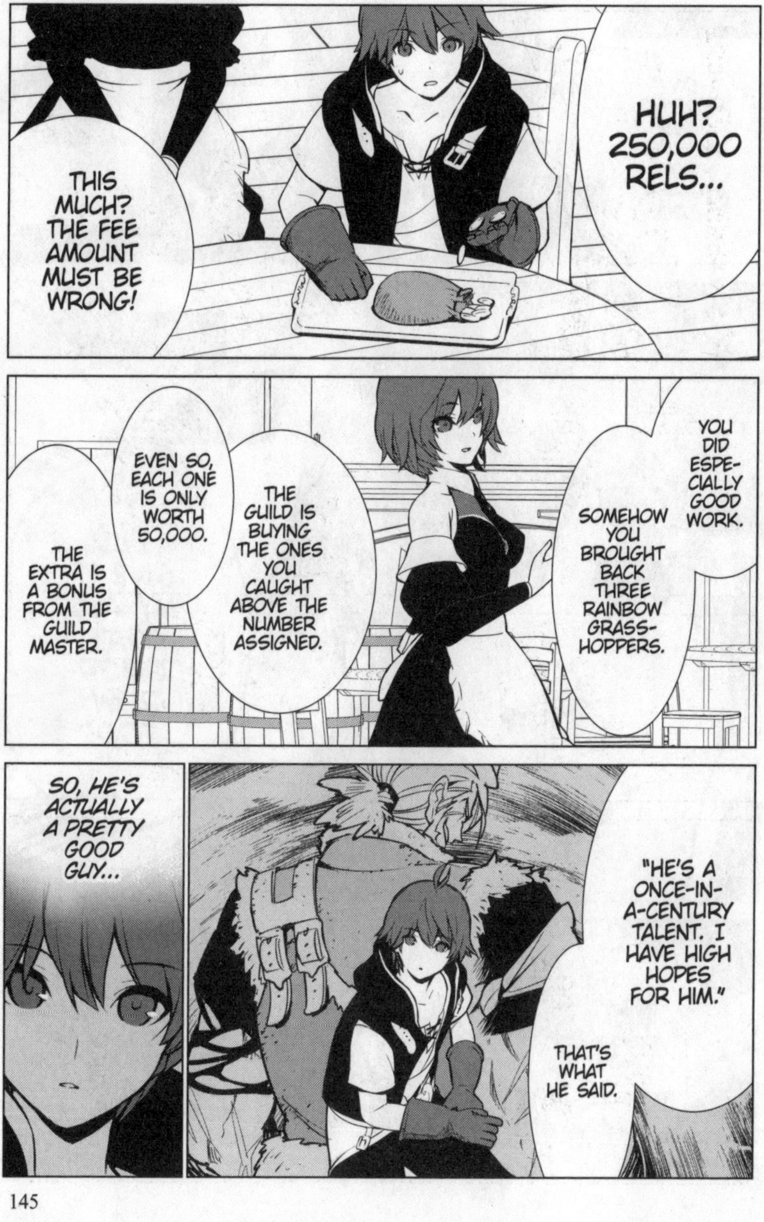
HUH? 250,000 RELS...
THIS MUCH? THE FEE AMOUNT MUST BE WRONG!
YOU DID ESPECIALLY GOOD WORK.
SOMEHOW YOU BROUGHT BACK THREE RAINBOW GRASSHOPPERS.
THE GUILD IS BUYING THE ONES YOU CAUGHT ABOVE THE NUMBER ASSIGNED.
EVEN SO, EACH ONE IS ONLY WORTH 50,000.
THE EXTRA IS A BONUS FROM THE GUILD MASTER.
"HE'S A ONCE-IN-A-CENTURY TALENT. I HAVE HIGH HOPES FOR HIM."
THAT'S WHAT HE SAID.
SO, HE'S ACTUALLY A PRETTY GOOD GUY...

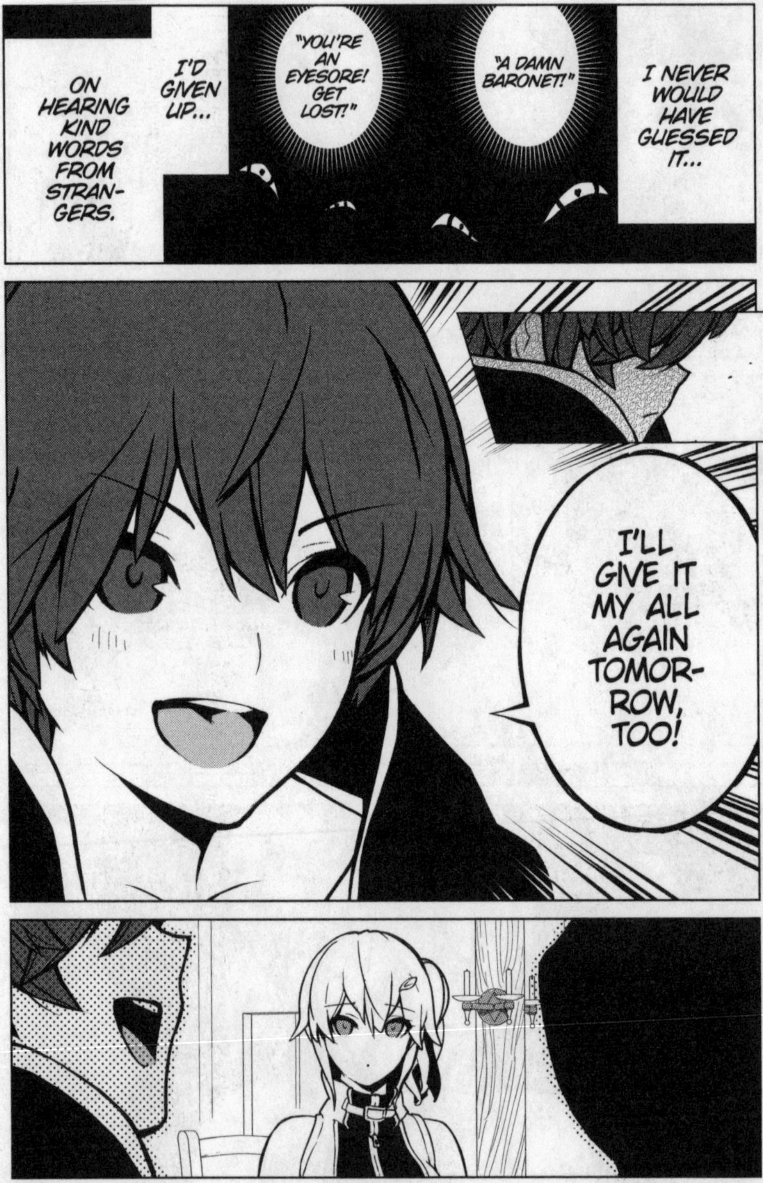
I NEVER WOULD HAVE GUESSED IT...
"A DAMN BARONET!"
"YOU'RE AN EYESORE! GET LOST!"
I'D GIVEN UP...
ON HEARING KIND WORDS FROM STRAN-GERS.
I'LL GIVE IT MY ALL AGAIN TOMOR-ROW, TOO!

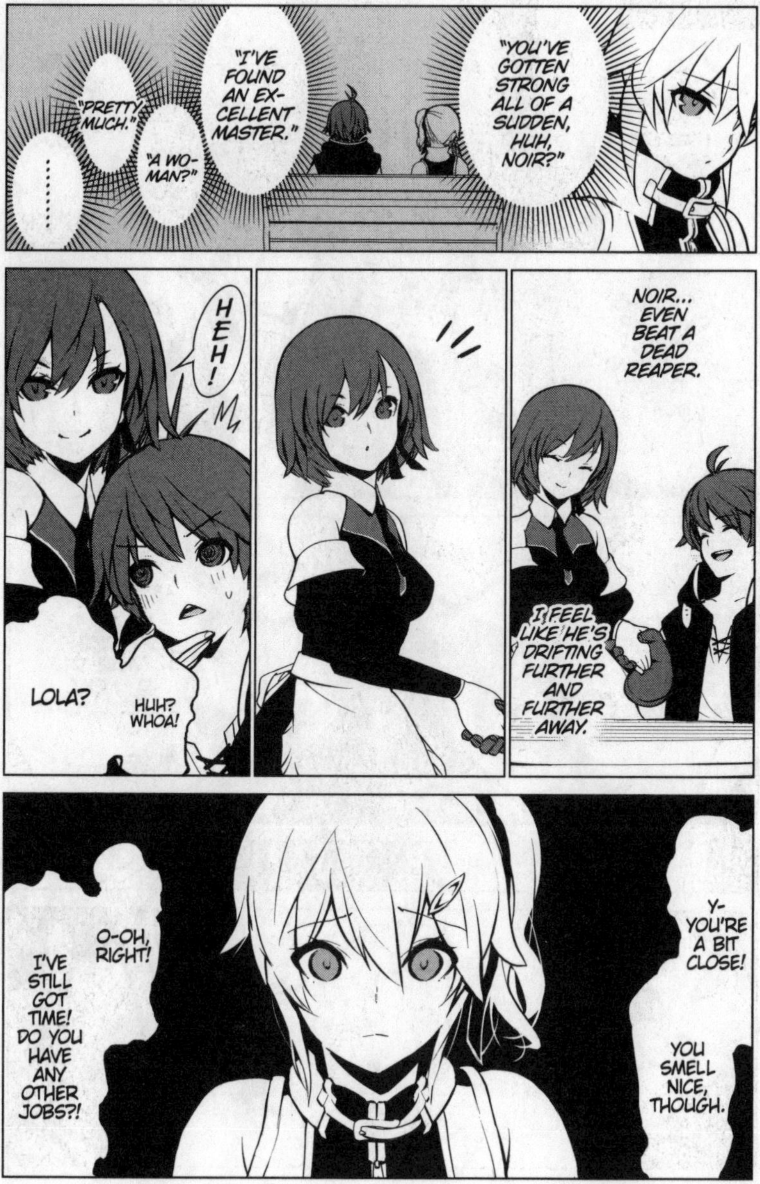
"YOU'VE GOTTEN STRONG ALL OF A SUDDEN, HUH, NOIR?"
"I'VE FOUND AN EX-CELLENT MASTER."
"A WO-MAN?"
"PRETTY MUCH."
......
NOIR... EVEN BEAT A DEAD REAPER.
I FEEL LIKE HE'S DRIFTING FURTHER AND FURTHER AWAY.
HEH!
HUH? WHOA!
LOLA?
Y-YOU'RE A BIT CLOSE!
YOU SMELL NICE, THOUGH.
O-OH, RIGHT!
I'VE STILL GOT TIME! DO YOU HAVE ANY OTHER JOBS?!

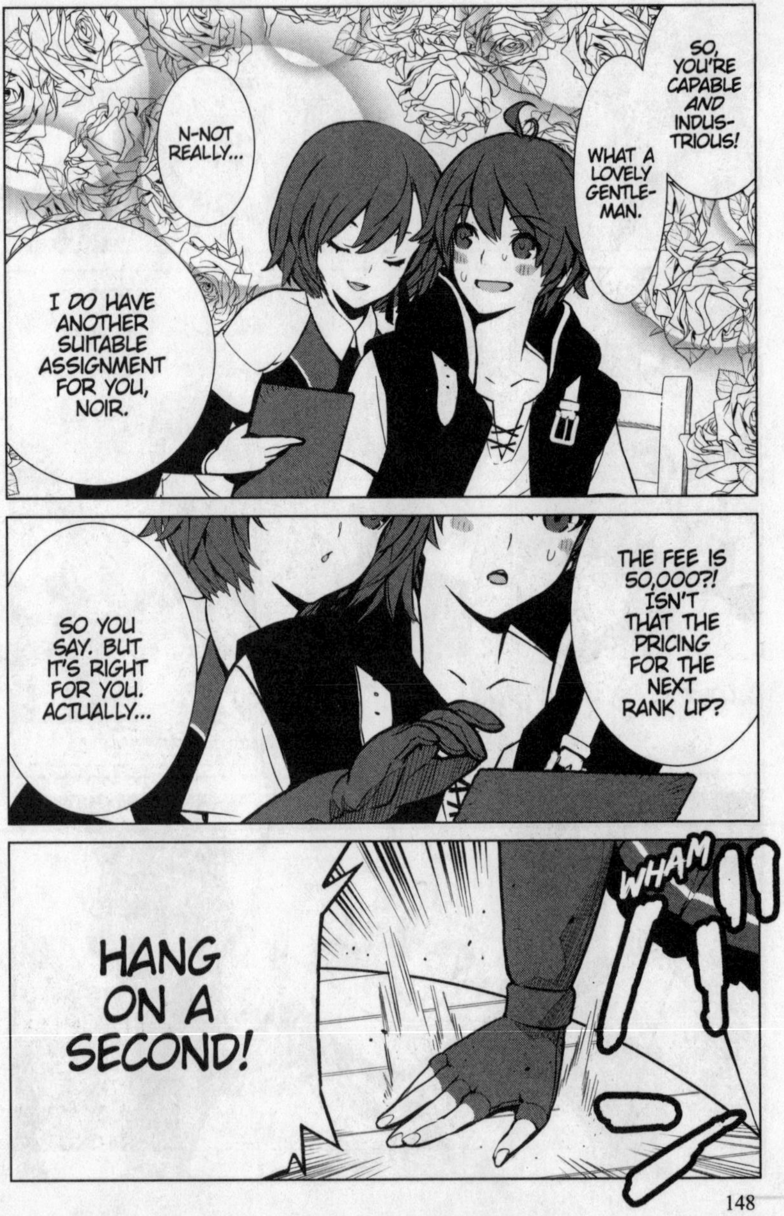
SO, YOU'RE CAPABLE AND INDUSTRIOUS!
WHAT A LOVELY GENTLEMAN.
N-NOT REALLY...
I *DO* HAVE ANOTHER SUITABLE ASSIGNMENT FOR YOU, NOIR.
THE FEE IS 50,000?! ISN'T THAT THE PRICING FOR THE NEXT RANK UP?
SO YOU SAY. BUT IT'S RIGHT FOR YOU. ACTUALLY...
WHAM
HANG ON A SECOND!

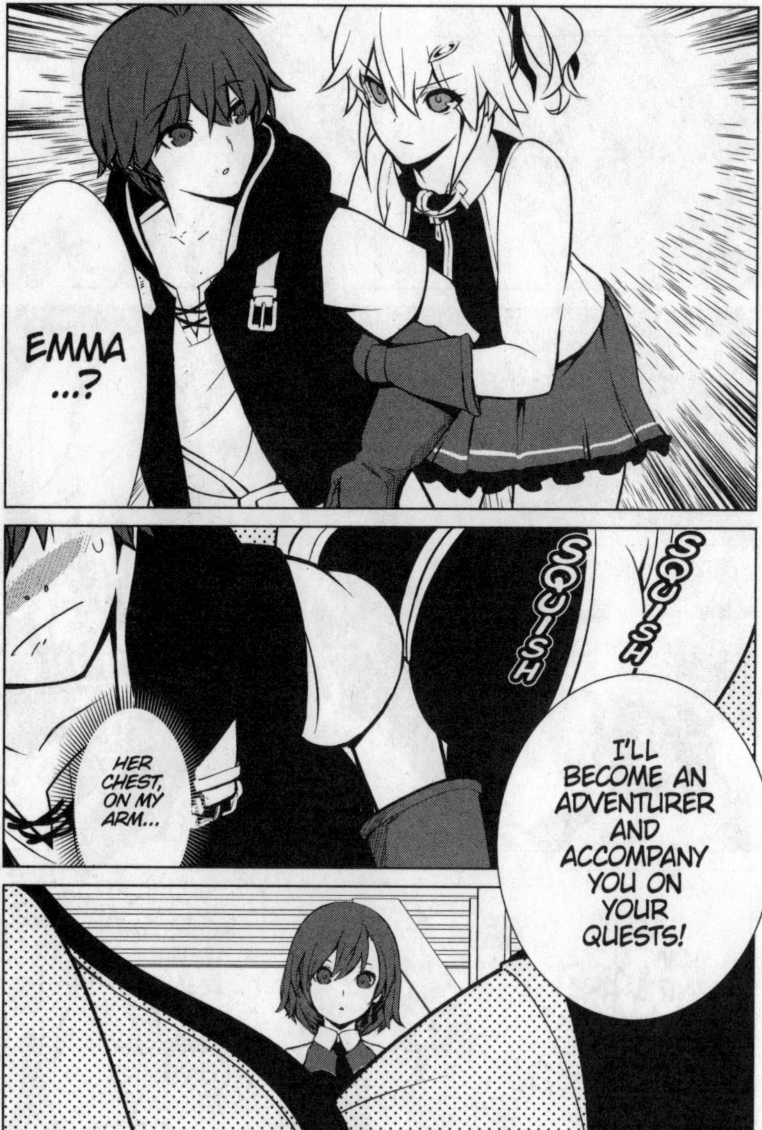
EMMA ...?
SQUISH
SQUISH
I'LL BECOME AN ADVENTURER AND ACCOMPANY YOU ON YOUR QUESTS!
HER CHEST, ON MY ARM...

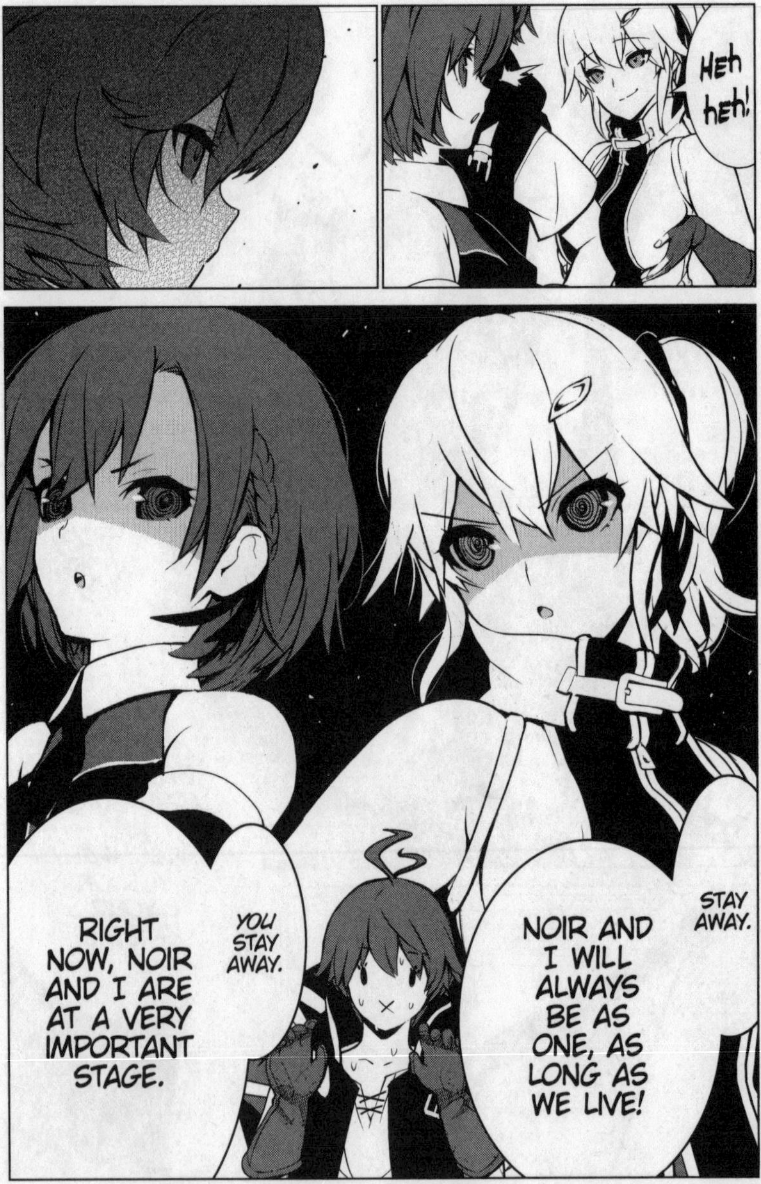
Heh heh!
STAY AWAY.
NOIR AND I WILL ALWAYS BE AS ONE, AS LONG AS WE LIVE!
YOU STAY AWAY.
RIGHT NOW, NOIR AND I ARE AT A VERY IMPORTANT STAGE.

Chapter 5 / End

THE HIDDEN DUNGEON ONLY I CAN ENTER

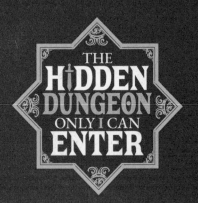

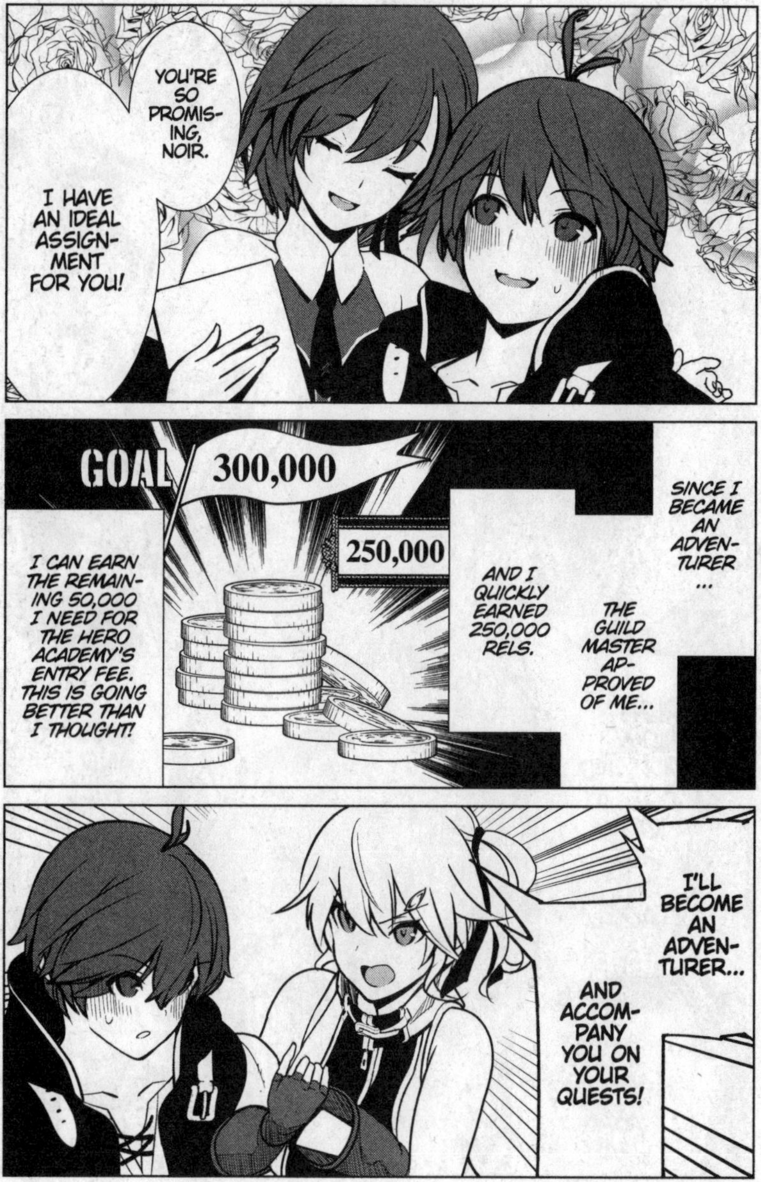
YOU'RE SO PROMISING, NOIR.
I HAVE AN IDEAL ASSIGNMENT FOR YOU!
SINCE I BECAME AN ADVENTURER...
THE GUILD MASTER APPROVED OF ME...
AND I QUICKLY EARNED 250,000 RELS.
GOAL 300,000
250,000
I CAN EARN THE REMAINING 50,000 I NEED FOR THE HERO ACADEMY'S ENTRY FEE. THIS IS GOING BETTER THAN I THOUGHT!
I'LL BECOME AN ADVENTURER...
AND ACCOMPANY YOU ON YOUR QUESTS!

Chapter 6: Dual Wielded Daggers

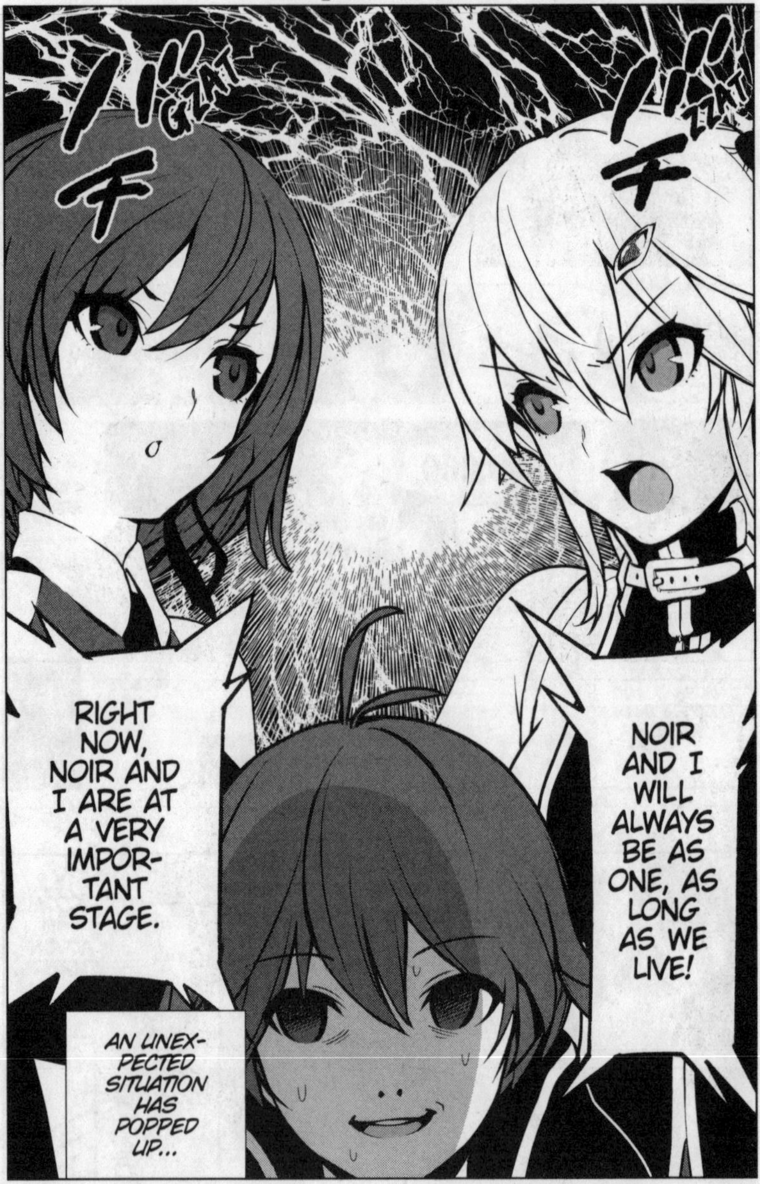
ZZAT
GZAT
NOIR AND I WILL ALWAYS BE AS ONE, AS LONG AS WE LIVE!
RIGHT NOW, NOIR AND I ARE AT A VERY IMPORTANT STAGE.
AN UNEXPECTED SITUATION HAS POPPED UP...

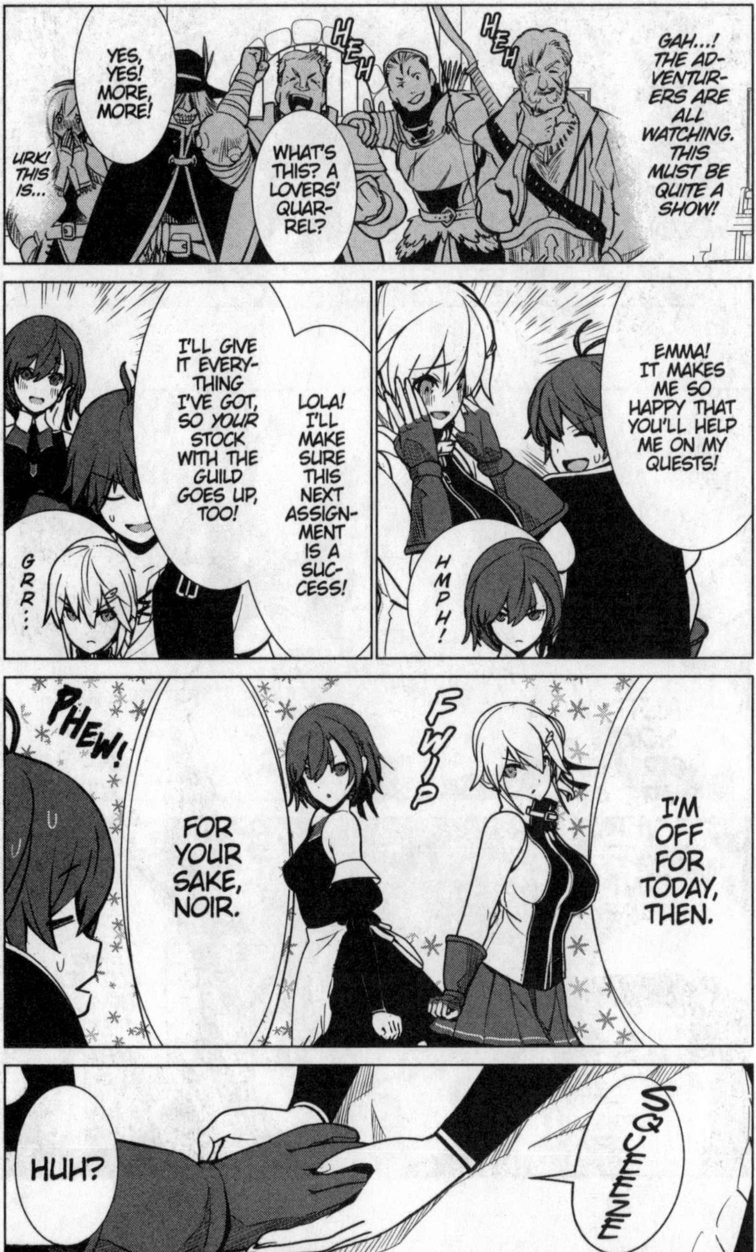
GAH...! THE ADVENTURERS ARE ALL WATCHING. THIS MUST BE QUITE A SHOW!
HEH
HEH
WHAT'S THIS? A LOVERS' QUARREL?
YES, YES! MORE, MORE!
URK! THIS IS...
EMMA! IT MAKES ME SO HAPPY THAT YOU'LL HELP ME ON MY QUESTS!
HMPH!
LOLA! I'LL MAKE SURE THIS NEXT ASSIGNMENT IS A SUCCESS!
I'LL GIVE IT EVERYTHING I'VE GOT, SO *YOUR* STOCK WITH THE GUILD GOES UP, TOO!
GRR...
I'M OFF FOR TODAY, THEN.
FWIP
FOR YOUR SAKE, NOIR.
PHEW!
SQUEEEE
HUH?

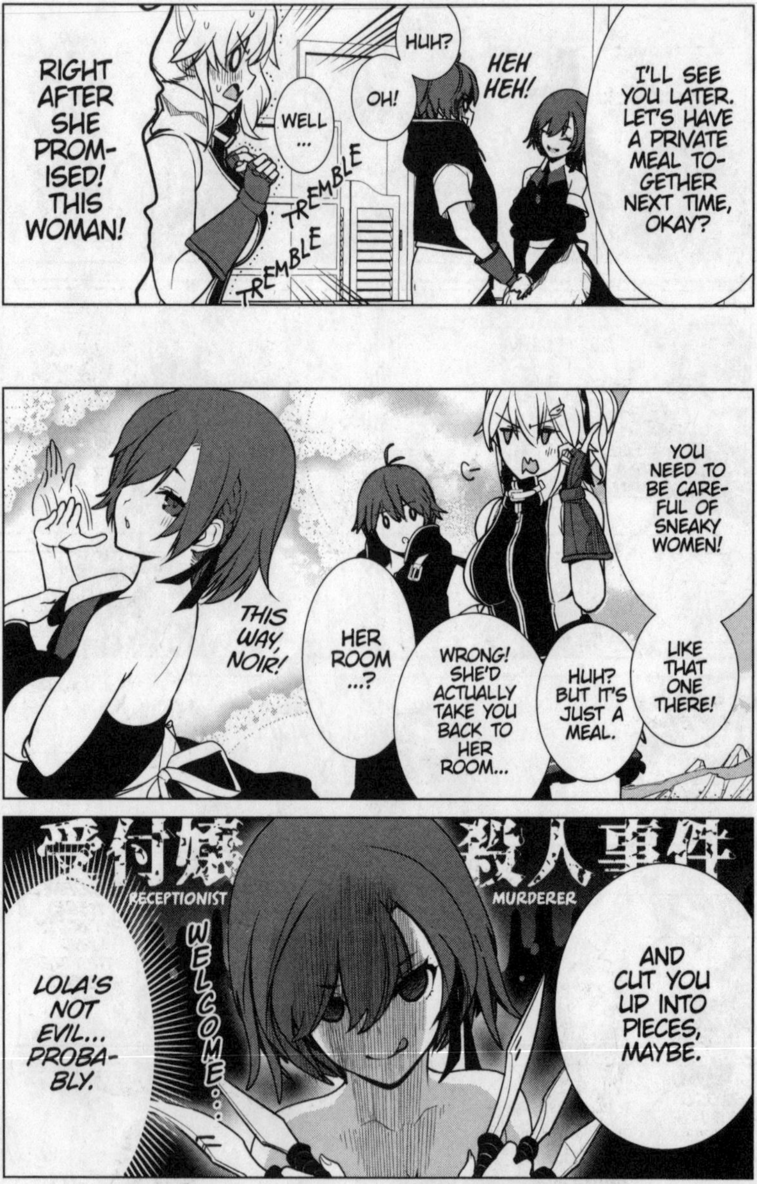
I'LL SEE YOU LATER. LET'S HAVE A PRIVATE MEAL TOGETHER NEXT TIME, OKAY?
HEH HEH!
HUH?
OH!
WELL ...
TREMBLE TREMBLE
RIGHT AFTER SHE PROMISED! THIS WOMAN!
YOU NEED TO BE CAREFUL OF SNEAKY WOMEN!
LIKE THAT ONE THERE!
HUH? BUT IT'S JUST A MEAL.
WRONG! SHE'D ACTUALLY TAKE YOU BACK TO HER ROOM...
HER ROOM ...?
THIS WAY, NOIR!
殺人事件
MURDERER
受付嬢
RECEPTIONIST
AND CUT YOU UP INTO PIECES, MAYBE.
WELCOME...
LOLA'S NOT EVIL... PROBABLY.

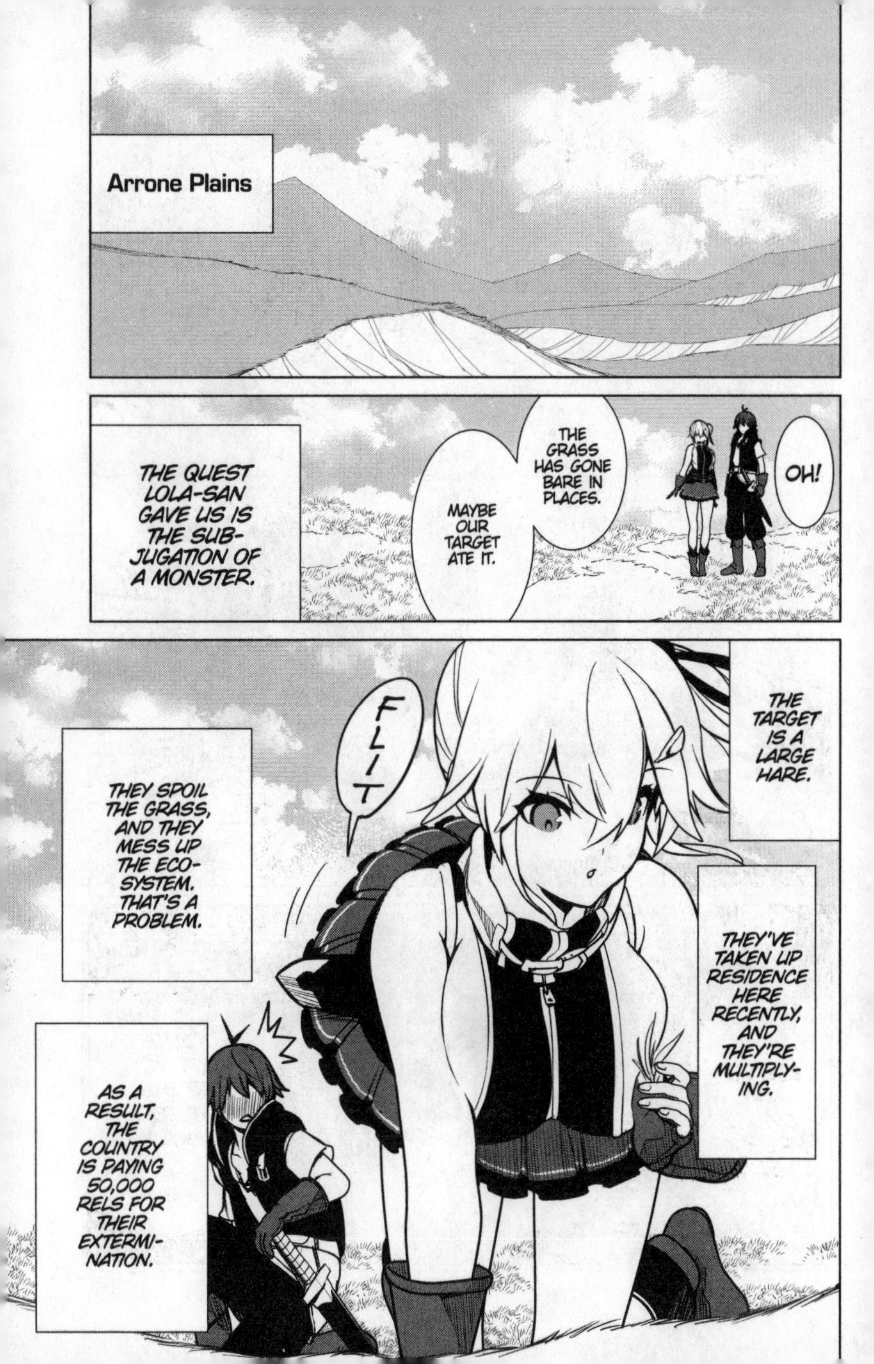
Arrone Plains
OH!
THE GRASS HAS GONE BARE IN PLACES.
MAYBE OUR TARGET ATE IT.
THE QUEST LOLA-SAN GAVE US IS THE SUBJUGATION OF A MONSTER.
THE TARGET IS A LARGE HARE.
FLIT
THEY SPOIL THE GRASS, AND THEY MESS UP THE ECOSYSTEM. THAT'S A PROBLEM.
THEY'VE TAKEN UP RESIDENCE HERE RECENTLY, AND THEY'RE MULTIPLYING.
AS A RESULT, THE COUNTRY IS PAYING 50,000 RELS FOR THEIR EXTERMINATION.

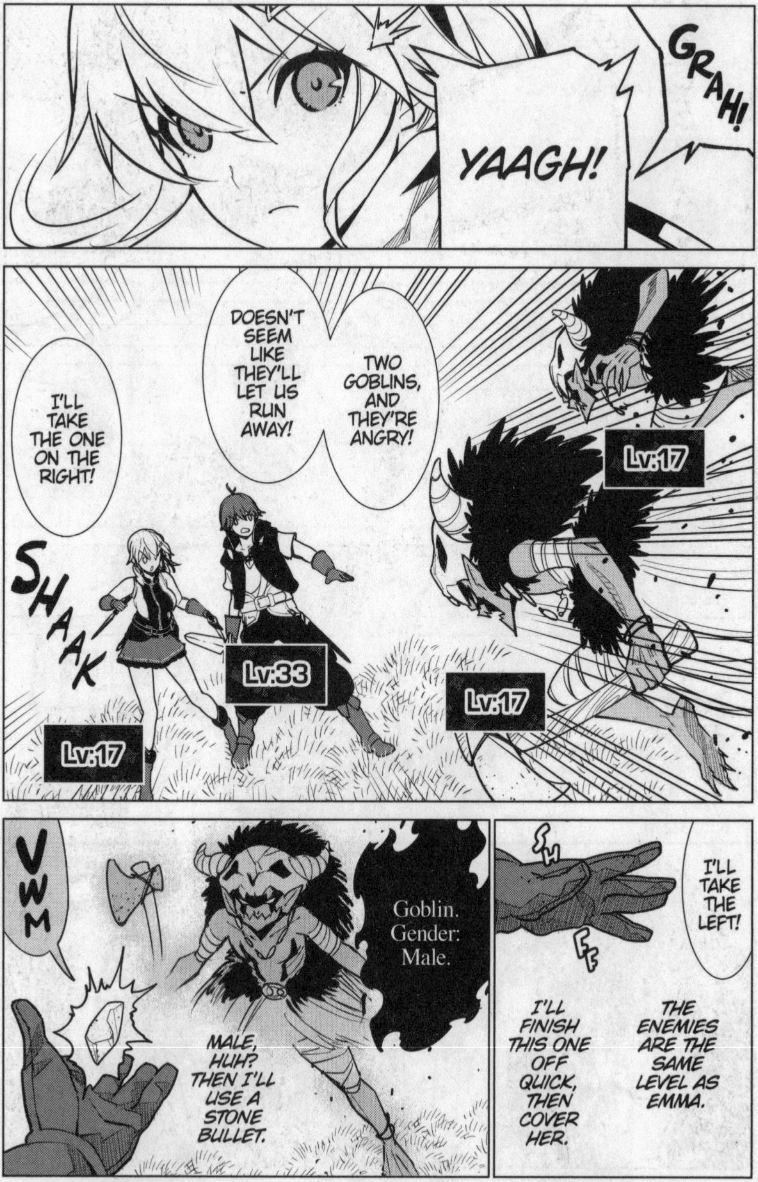
GRAH!
YAAGH!
TWO GOBLINS, AND THEY'RE ANGRY!
DOESN'T SEEM LIKE THEY'LL LET US RUN AWAY!
Lv:17
I'LL TAKE THE ONE ON THE RIGHT!
Lv:17
SHAAK
Lv:33
Lv:17
I'LL TAKE THE LEFT!
SHFF
THE ENEMIES ARE THE SAME LEVEL AS EMMA.
I'LL FINISH THIS ONE OFF QUICK, THEN COVER HER.
Goblin. Gender: Male.
VWM
MALE, HUH? THEN I'LL USE A STONE BULLET.

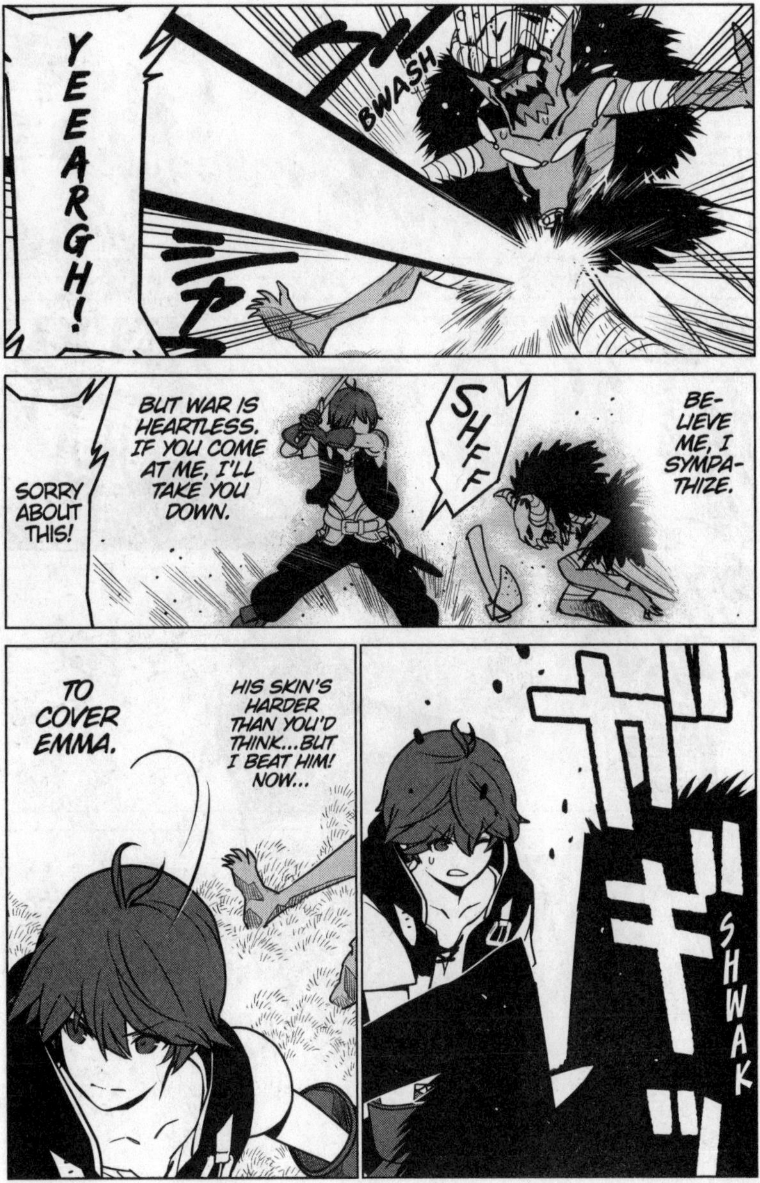

BWASH
YEEEARGH!
BE-LIEVE ME, I SYMPA-THIZE.
SHFF
BUT WAR IS HEARTLESS. IF YOU COME AT ME, I'LL TAKE YOU DOWN.
SORRY ABOUT THIS!
SHWAK
HIS SKIN'S HARDER THAN YOU'D THINK...BUT I BEAT HIM! NOW...
TO COVER EMMA.

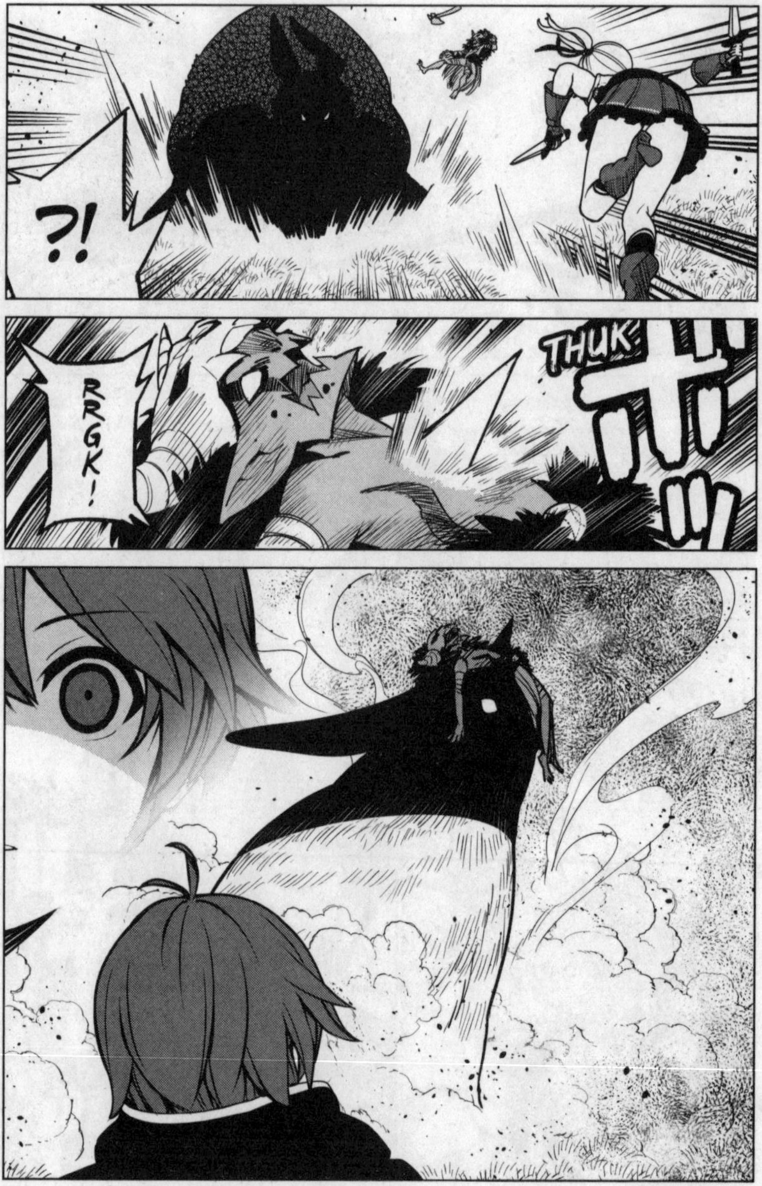
?!
THUK
RRGK!

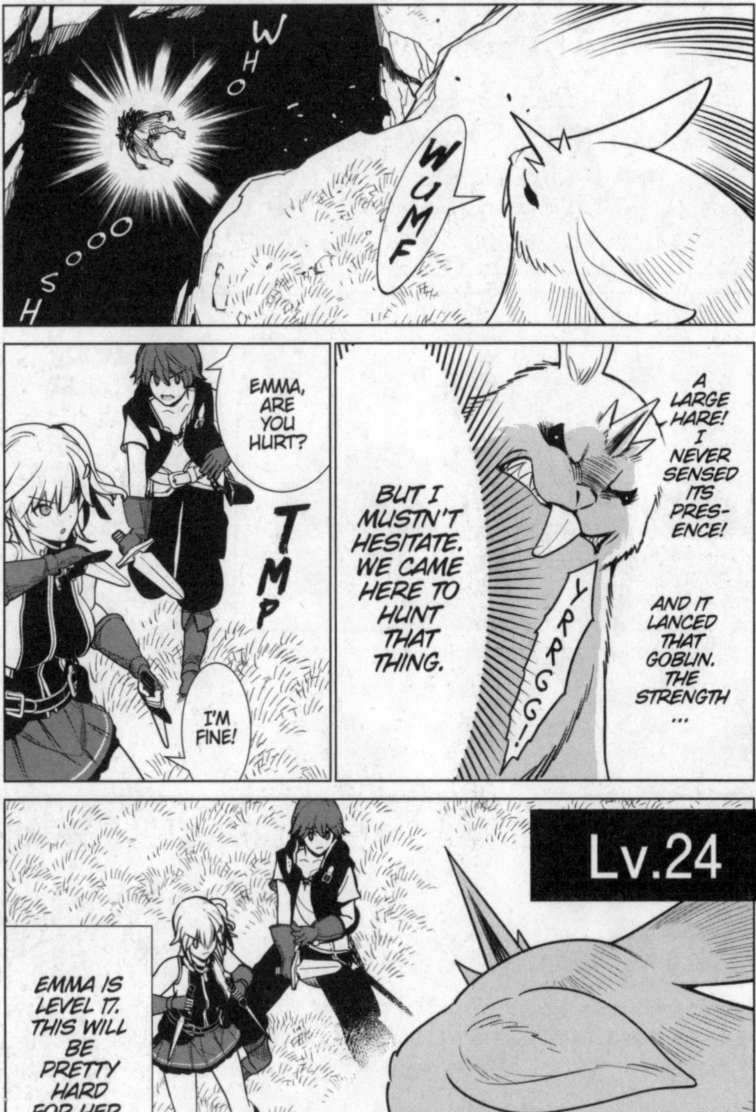
WUMF
WHO
OOOSH
A LARGE HARE! I NEVER SENSED ITS PRESENCE!
AND IT LANCED THAT GOBLIN. THE STRENGTH...
BUT I MUSTN'T HESITATE. WE CAME HERE TO HUNT THAT THING.
YRRGG!
EMMA, ARE YOU HURT?
TMP
I'M FINE!
Lv.24
EMMA IS LEVEL 17. THIS WILL BE PRETTY HARD FOR HER.

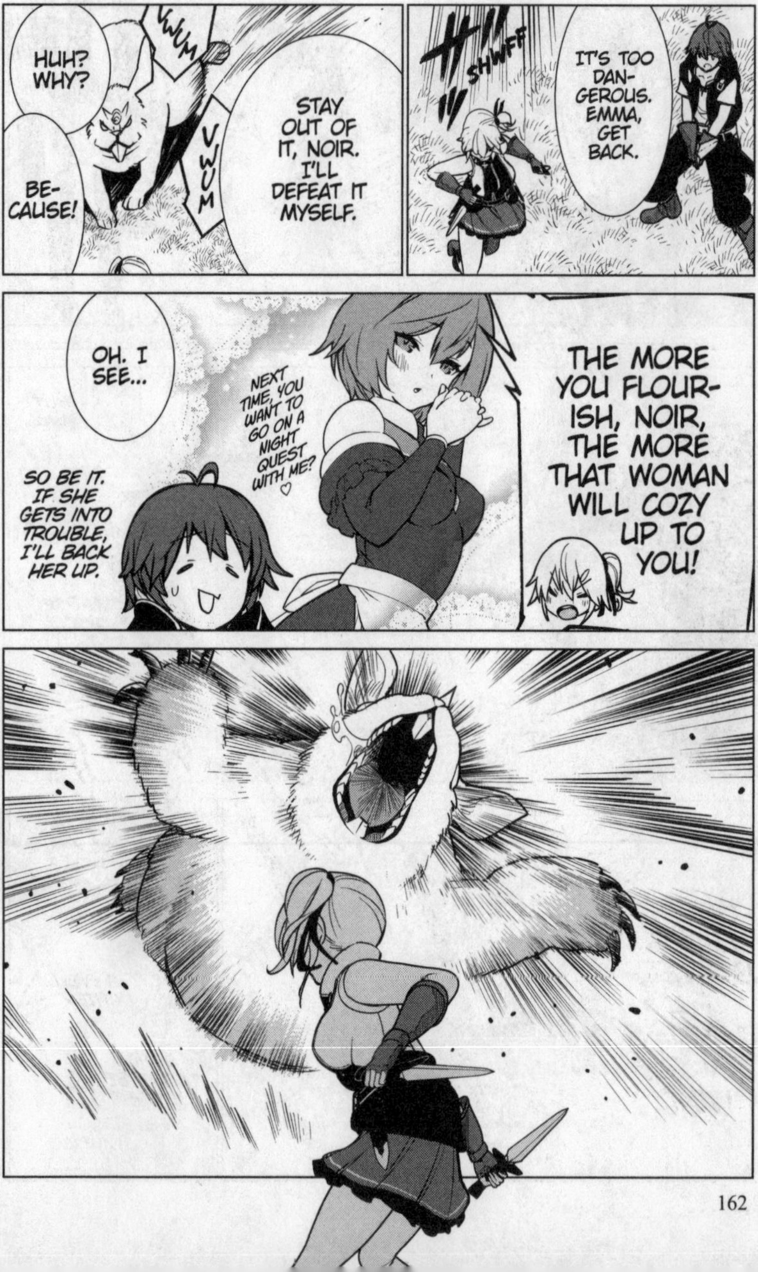
SHWFF
IT'S TOO DANGEROUS. EMMA, GET BACK.
STAY OUT OF IT, NOIR. I'LL DEFEAT IT MYSELF.
VWUM
VWUM
HUH? WHY?
BE-CAUSE!
THE MORE YOU FLOURISH, NOIR, THE MORE THAT WOMAN WILL COZY UP TO YOU!
NEXT TIME, YOU WANT TO GO ON A NIGHT QUEST WITH ME? ♡
OH. I SEE...
SO BE IT. IF SHE GETS INTO TROUBLE, I'LL BACK HER UP.

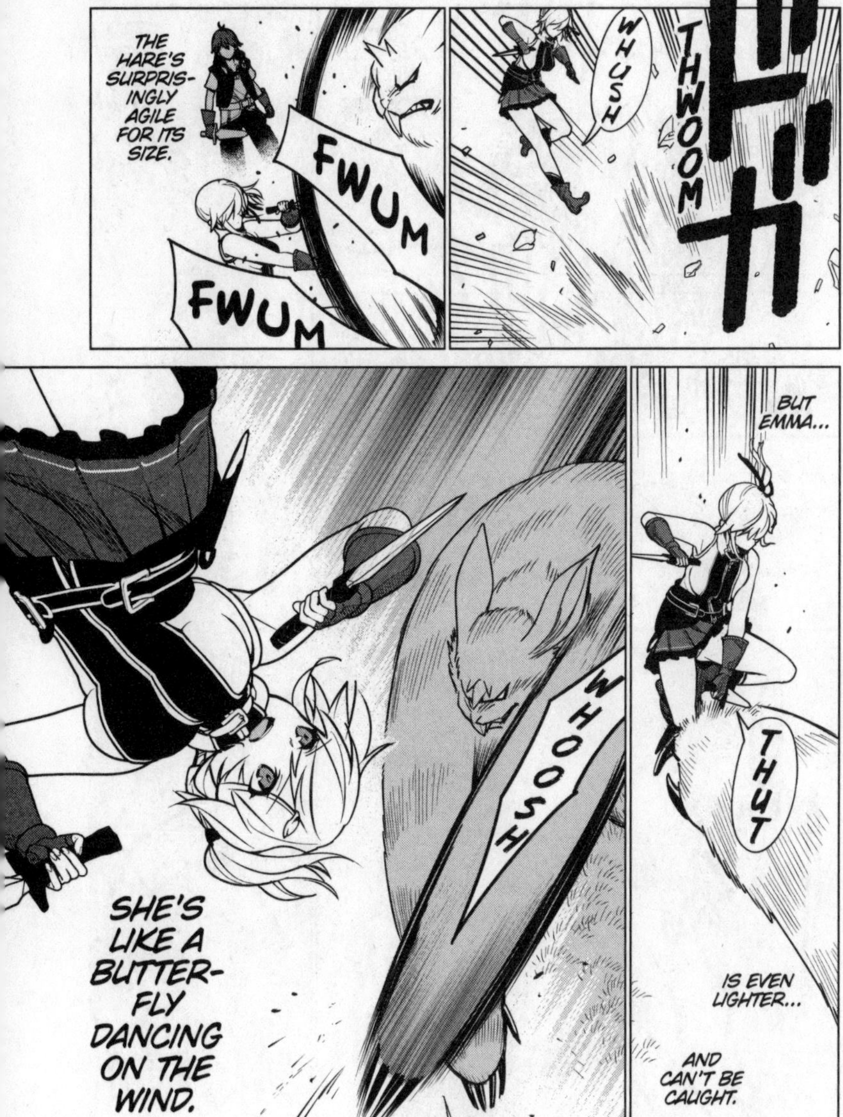
ドガ
THWOOM
WHUSH
THE HARE'S SURPRIS-INGLY AGILE FOR ITS SIZE.
FWUM
FWUM
BUT EMMA...
THUT
IS EVEN LIGHTER...
AND CAN'T BE CAUGHT.
WHOOSH
SHE'S LIKE A BUTTER-FLY DANCING ON THE WIND.

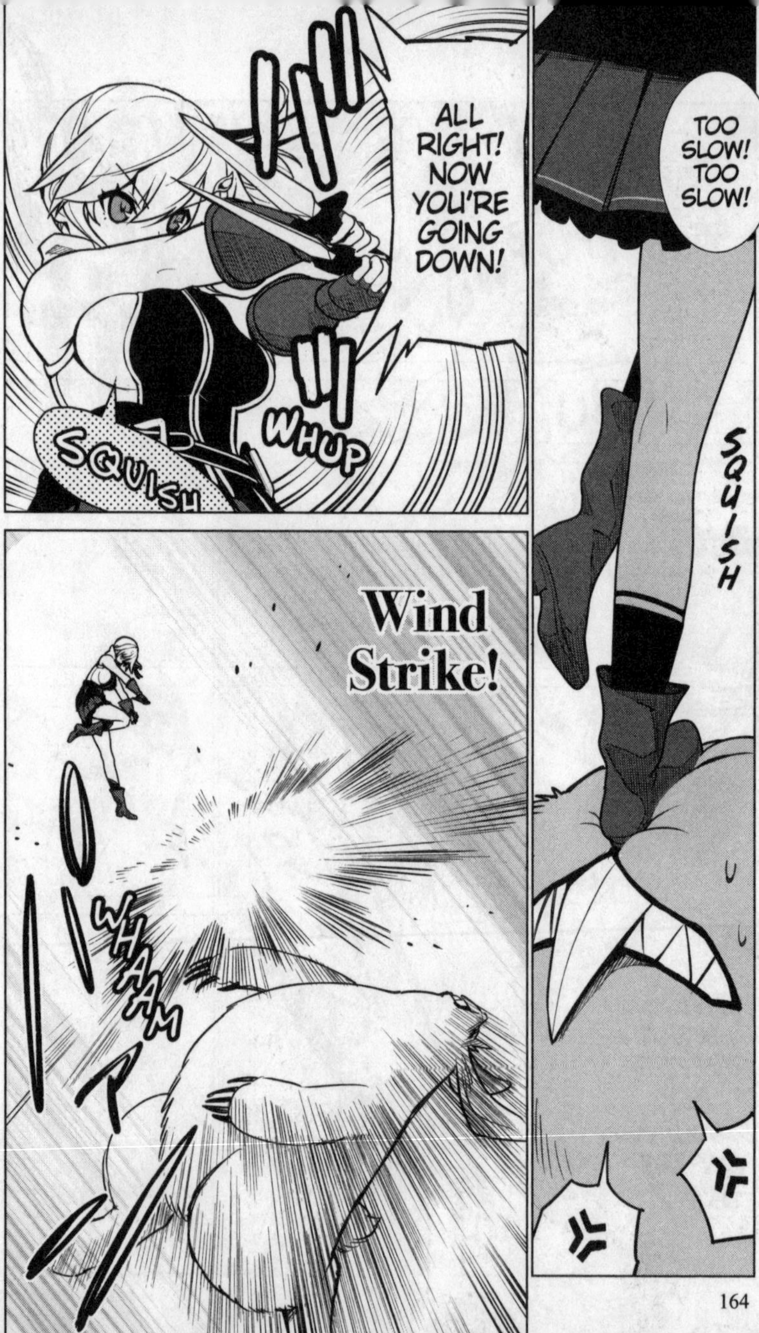
TOO SLOW! TOO SLOW! TOO SLOW!
SQUISH
ALL RIGHT! NOW YOU'RE GOING DOWN!
WHUP
SQUISH
Wind Strike!
WHAAM

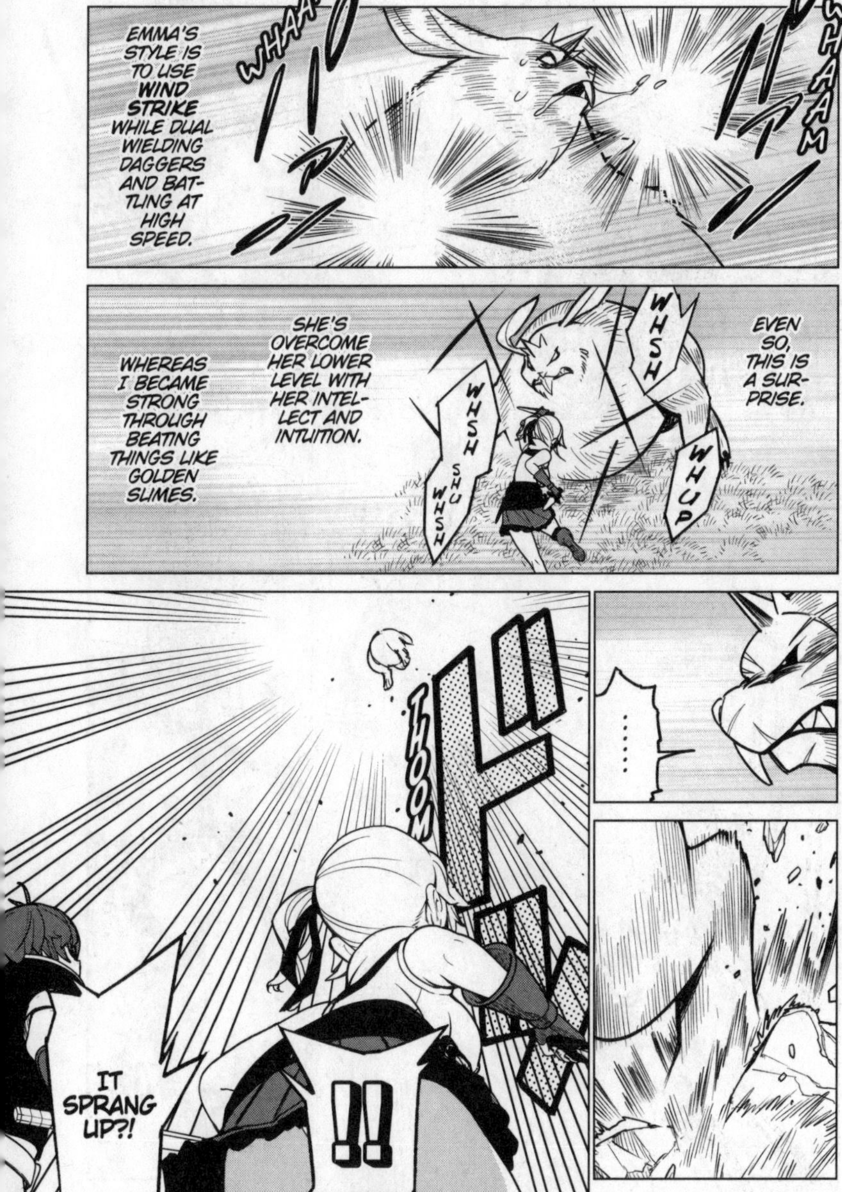

WHAAM
WHAAM
EMMA'S STYLE IS TO USE WIND STRIKE WHILE DUAL WIELDING DAGGERS AND BATTLING AT HIGH SPEED.
EVEN SO, THIS IS A SURPRISE.
WHSH
WHUP
SHE'S OVERCOME HER LOWER LEVEL WITH HER INTELLECT AND INTUITION.
WHSH
SHU
WHSH
WHEREAS I BECAME STRONG THROUGH BEATING THINGS LIKE GOLDEN SLIMES.
......
THOOM
!!
IT SPRANG UP?!

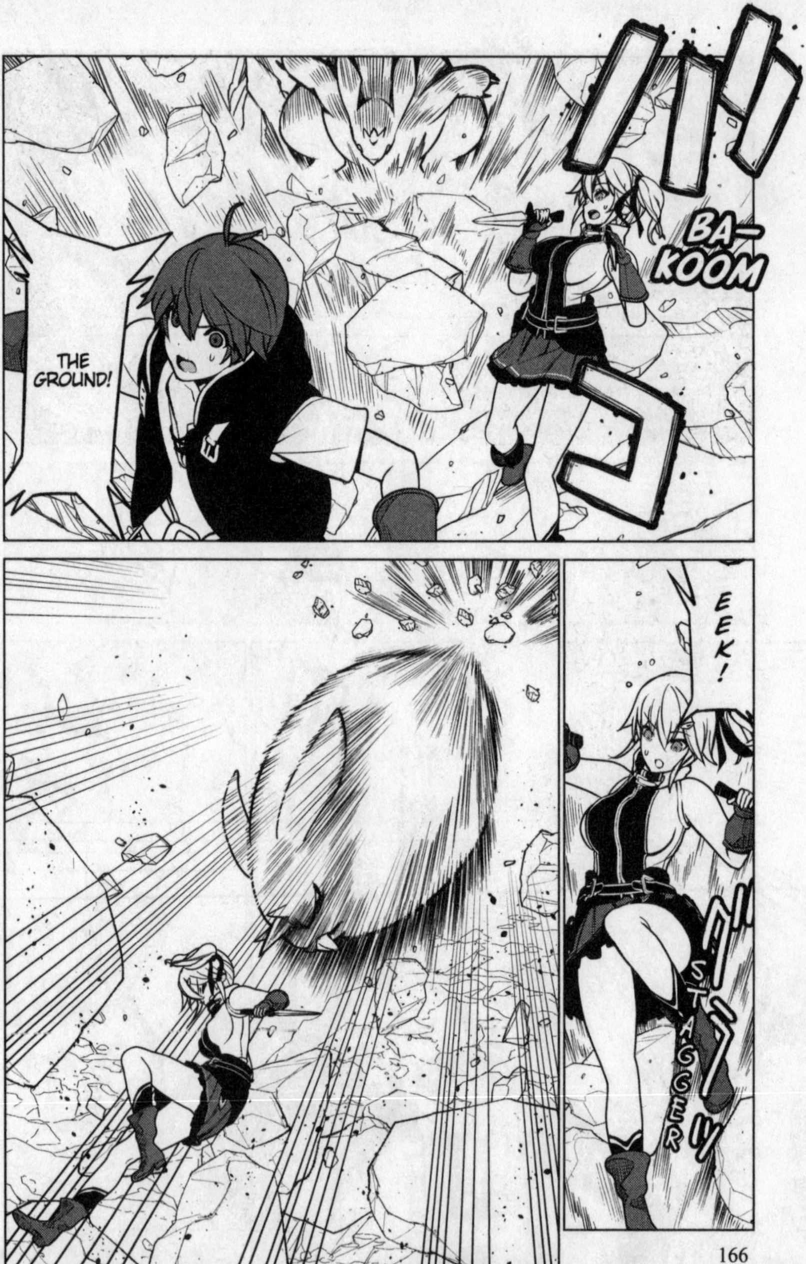
BA-
KOOM
THE GROUND!
EEK!
STAGGER

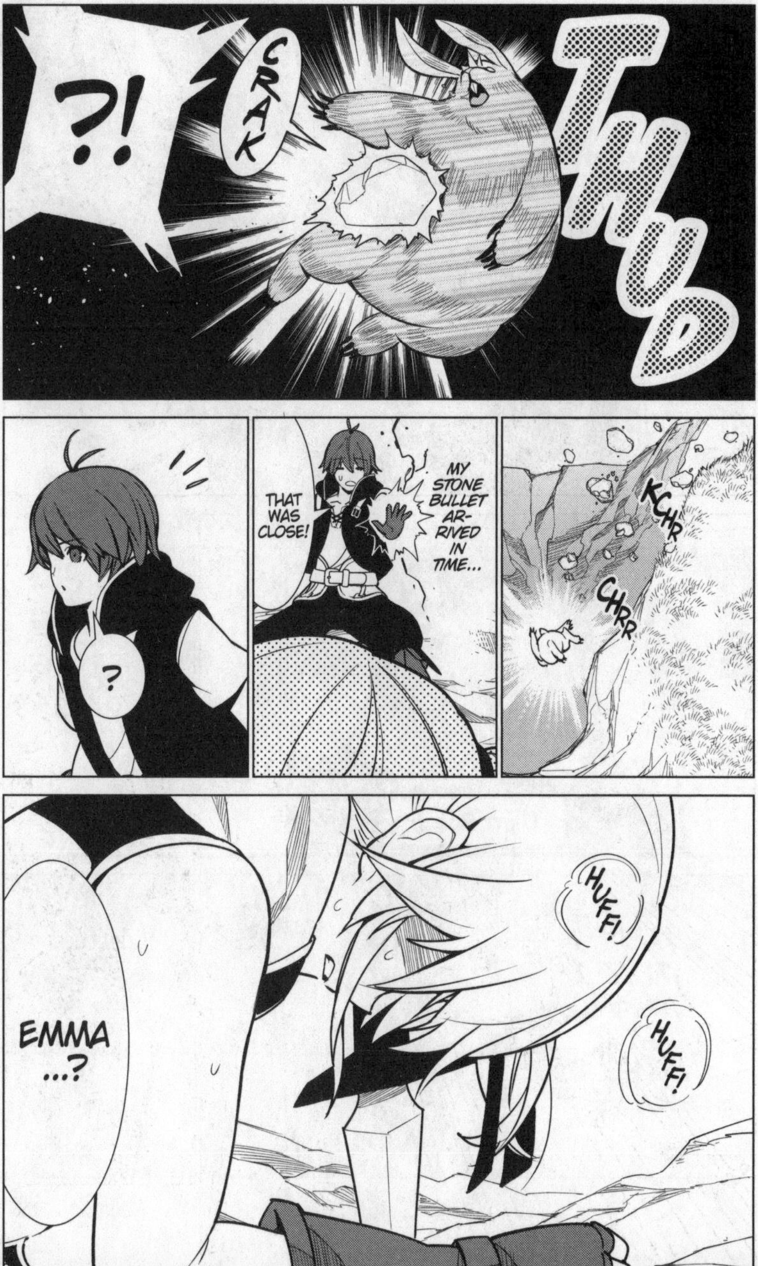
THUD
CRAK
?!
KCHR
CHRR
MY STONE BULLET AR-RIVED IN TIME...
THAT WAS CLOSE!
?
HUFF!
HUFF!
EMMA ...?

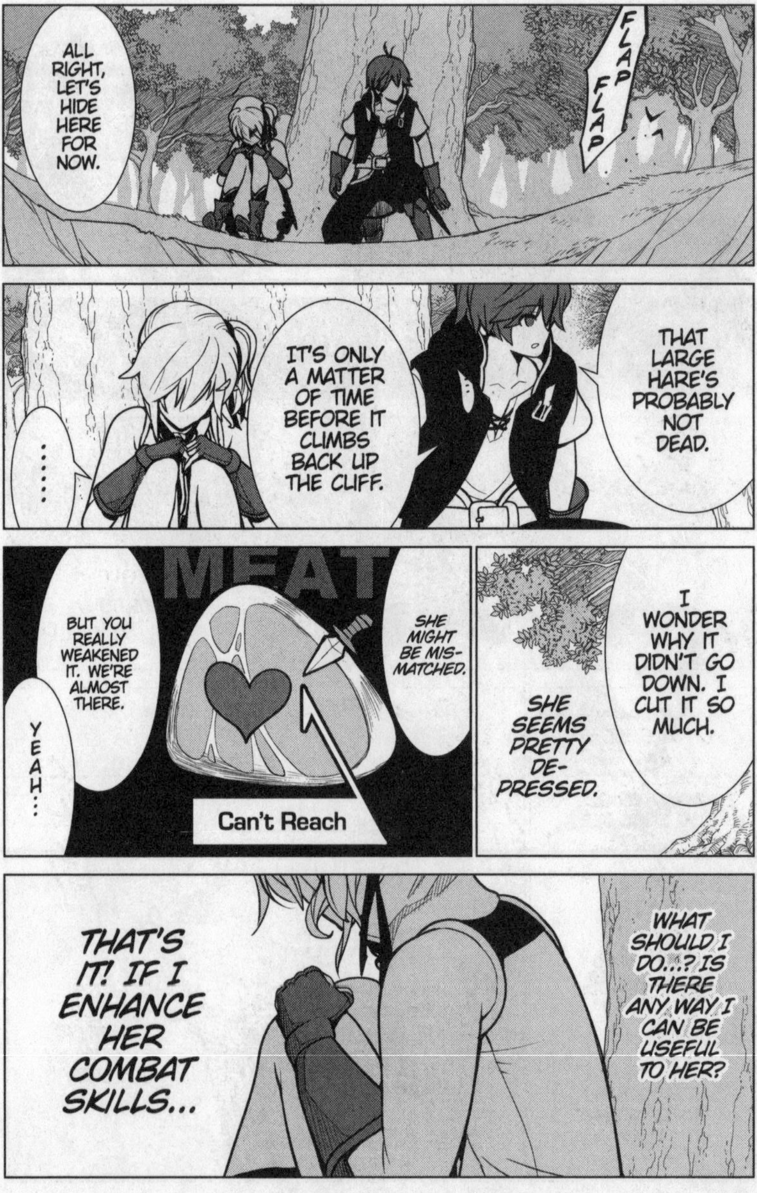
FLAP FLAP
ALL RIGHT, LET'S HIDE HERE FOR NOW.
THAT LARGE HARE'S PROBABLY NOT DEAD.
IT'S ONLY A MATTER OF TIME BEFORE IT CLIMBS BACK UP THE CLIFF.
......
I WONDER WHY IT DIDN'T GO DOWN. I CUT IT SO MUCH.
SHE SEEMS PRETTY DE-PRESSED.
MEAT
SHE MIGHT BE MIS-MATCHED.
BUT YOU REALLY WEAKENED IT. WE'RE ALMOST THERE.
YEAH...
Can't Reach
WHAT SHOULD I DO...? IS THERE ANY WAY I CAN BE USEFUL TO HER?
THAT'S IT! IF I ENHANCE HER COMBAT SKILLS...

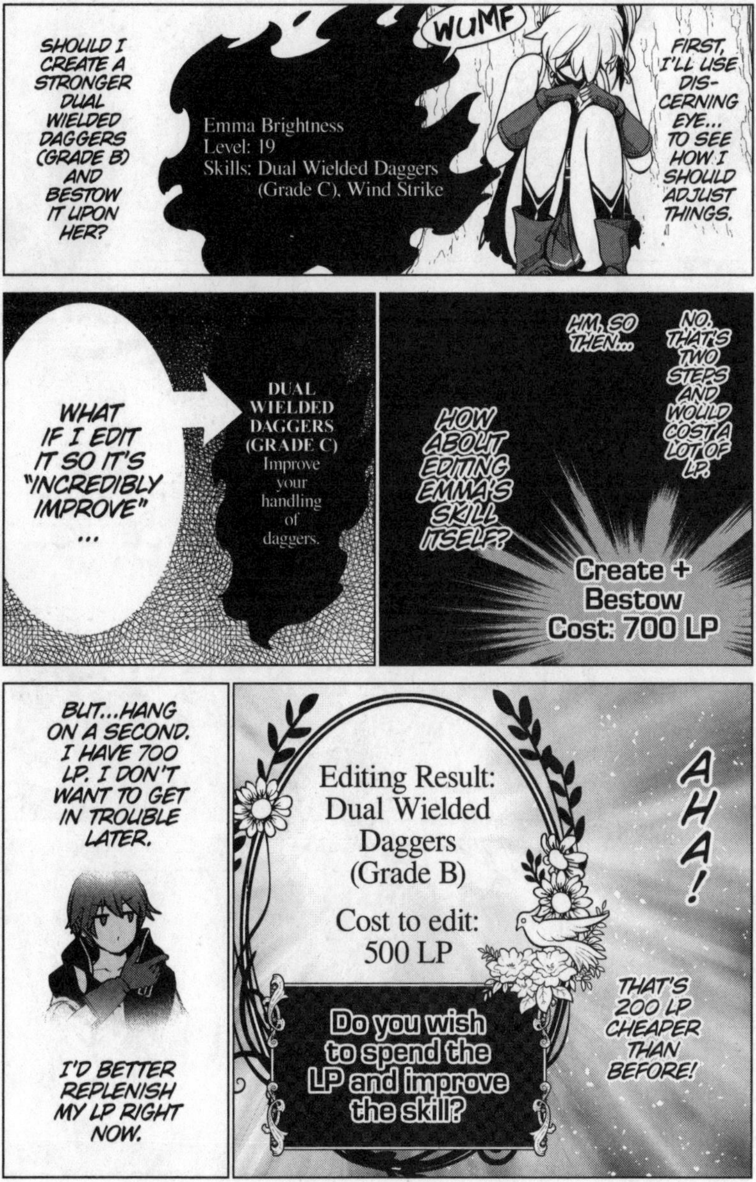
FIRST, I'LL USE DISCERNING EYE... TO SEE HOW I SHOULD ADJUST THINGS.
WUMF
Emma Brightness
Level: 19
Skills: Dual Wielded Daggers (Grade C), Wind Strike
SHOULD I CREATE A STRONGER DUAL WIELDED DAGGERS (GRADE B) AND BESTOW IT UPON HER?
NO. THAT'S TWO STEPS AND WOULD COST A LOT OF LP.
HM, SO THEN...
HOW ABOUT EDITING EMMA'S SKILL ITSELF?
Create + Bestow Cost: 700 LP
DUAL WIELDED DAGGERS (GRADE C) Improve your handling of daggers.
WHAT IF I EDIT IT SO IT'S "INCREDIBLY IMPROVE"...
AHA!
Editing Result: Dual Wielded Daggers (Grade B)
Cost to edit: 500 LP
THAT'S 200 LP CHEAPER THAN BEFORE!
Do you wish to spend the LP and improve the skill?
BUT...HANG ON A SECOND. I HAVE 700 LP. I DON'T WANT TO GET IN TROUBLE LATER.
I'D BETTER REPLENISH MY LP RIGHT NOW.

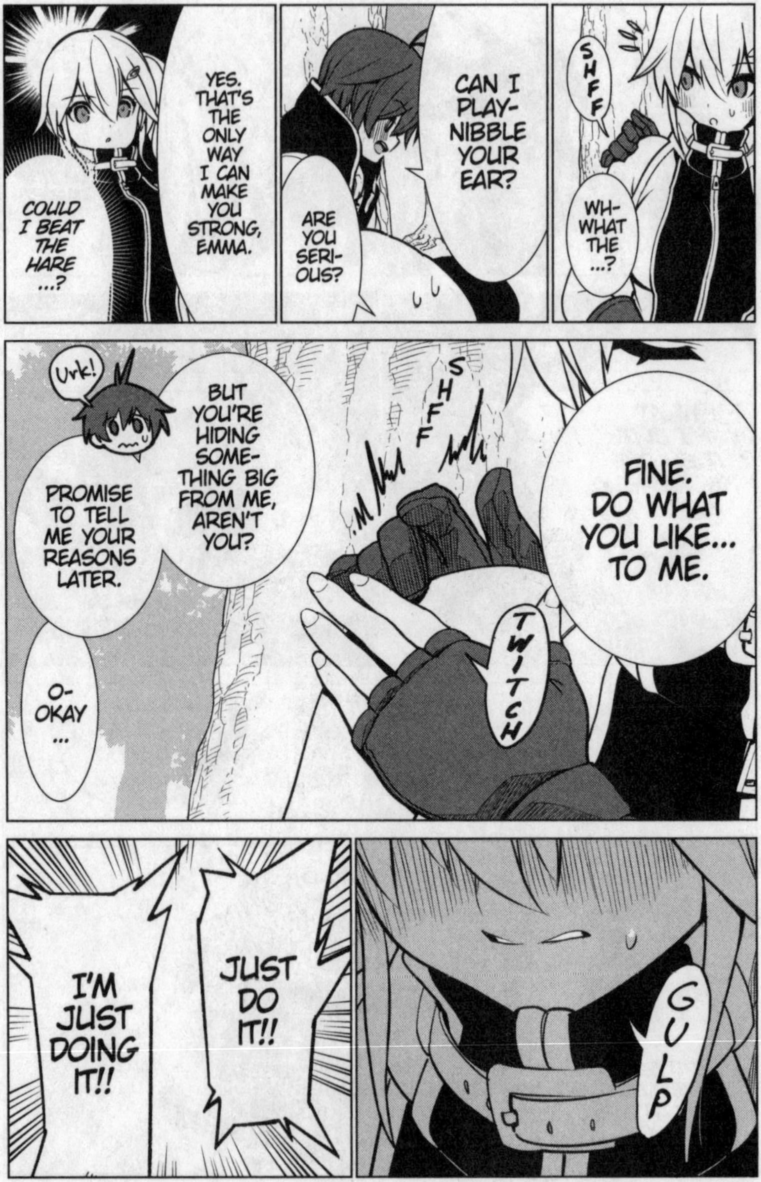
SHFF
WH-WHAT THE ...?
CAN I PLAY-NIBBLE YOUR EAR?
ARE YOU SERIOUS?
YES. THAT'S THE ONLY WAY I CAN MAKE YOU STRONG, EMMA.
COULD I BEAT THE HARE ...?
FINE. DO WHAT YOU LIKE... TO ME.
SHFF
TWITCH
BUT YOU'RE HIDING SOMETHING BIG FROM ME, AREN'T YOU?
Urk!
PROMISE TO TELL ME YOUR REASONS LATER.
O-OKAY ...
GULP
JUST DO IT!!
I'M JUST DOING IT!!

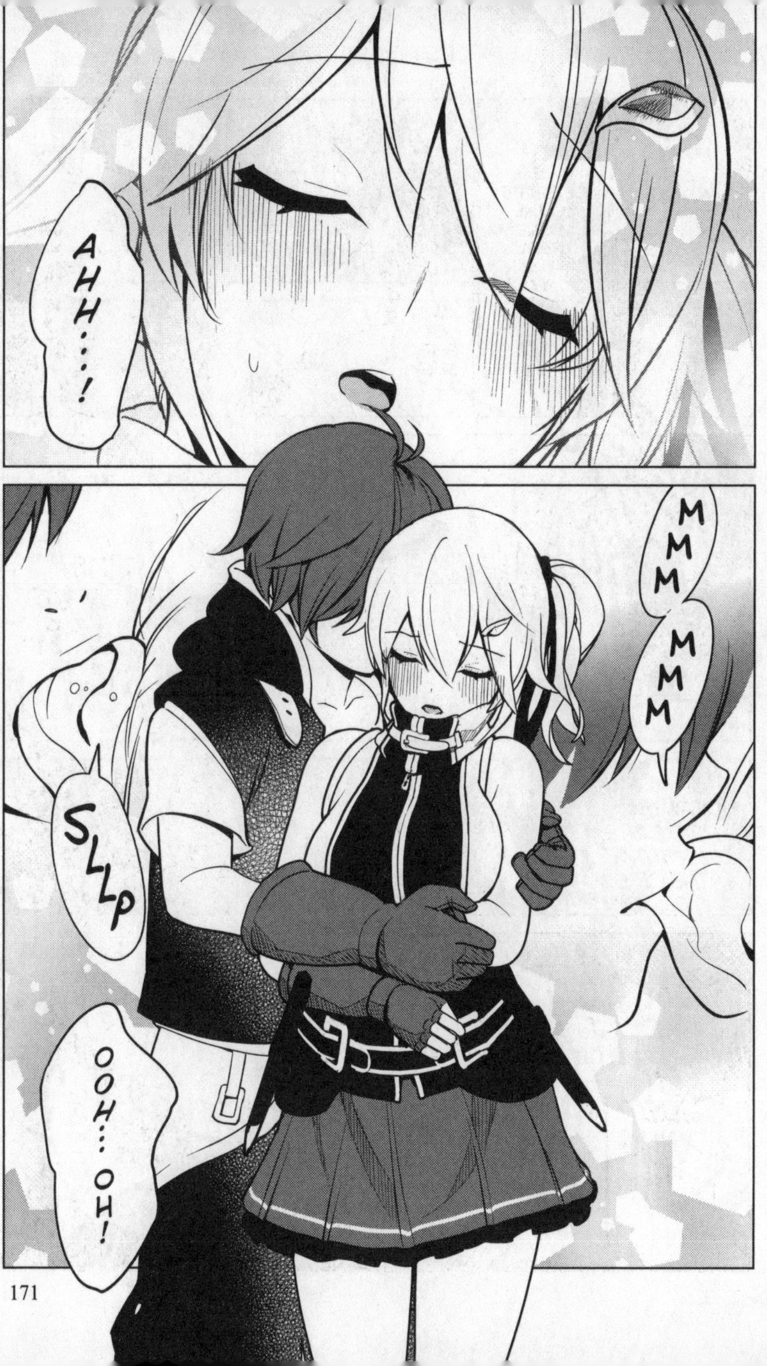
AHH...!
MMM MMM
SLLP
OOH... OH!

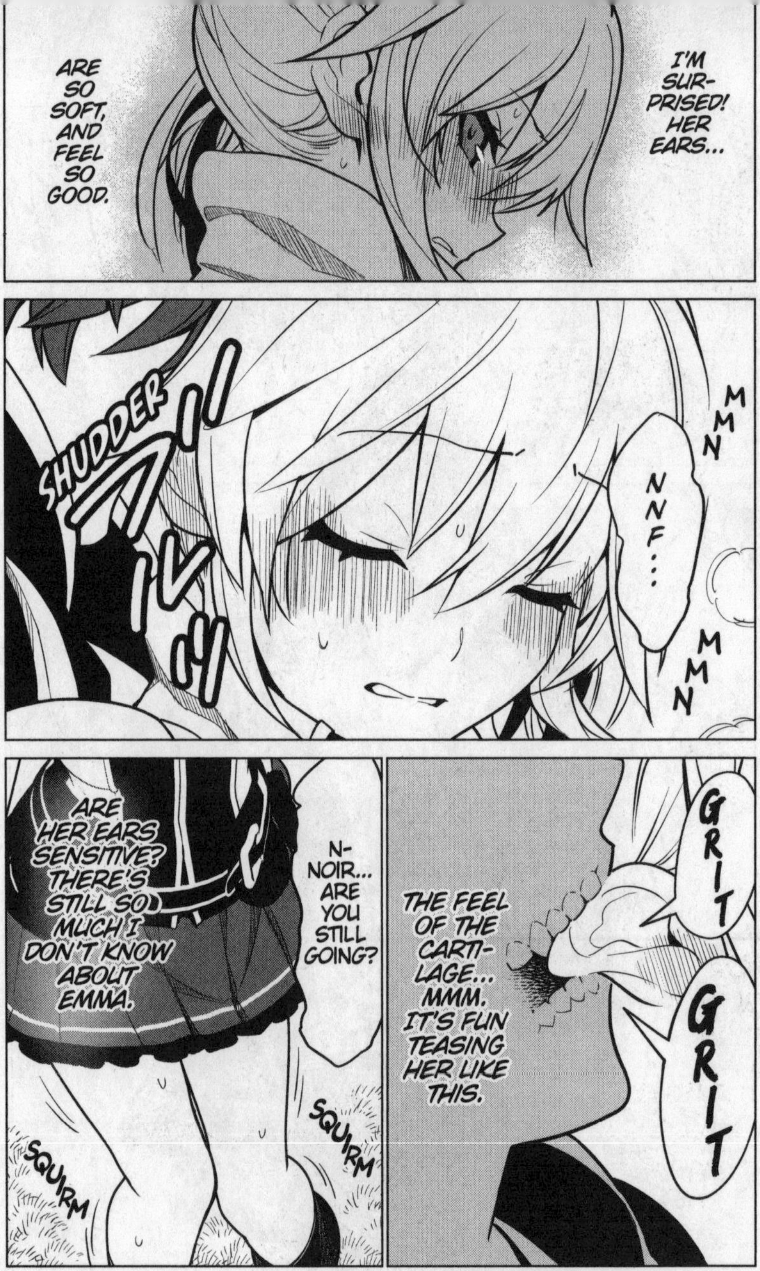
I'M SURPRISED! HER EARS...
ARE SO SOFT, AND FEEL SO GOOD.
MMN
NNF...
MMN
SHUDDER
GRIT
GRIT
THE FEEL OF THE CARTILAGE... MMM. IT'S FUN TEASING HER LIKE THIS.
N-NOIR... ARE YOU STILL GOING?
ARE HER EARS SENSITIVE? THERE'S STILL SO MUCH I DON'T KNOW ABOUT EMMA.
SQUIRM
SQUIRM

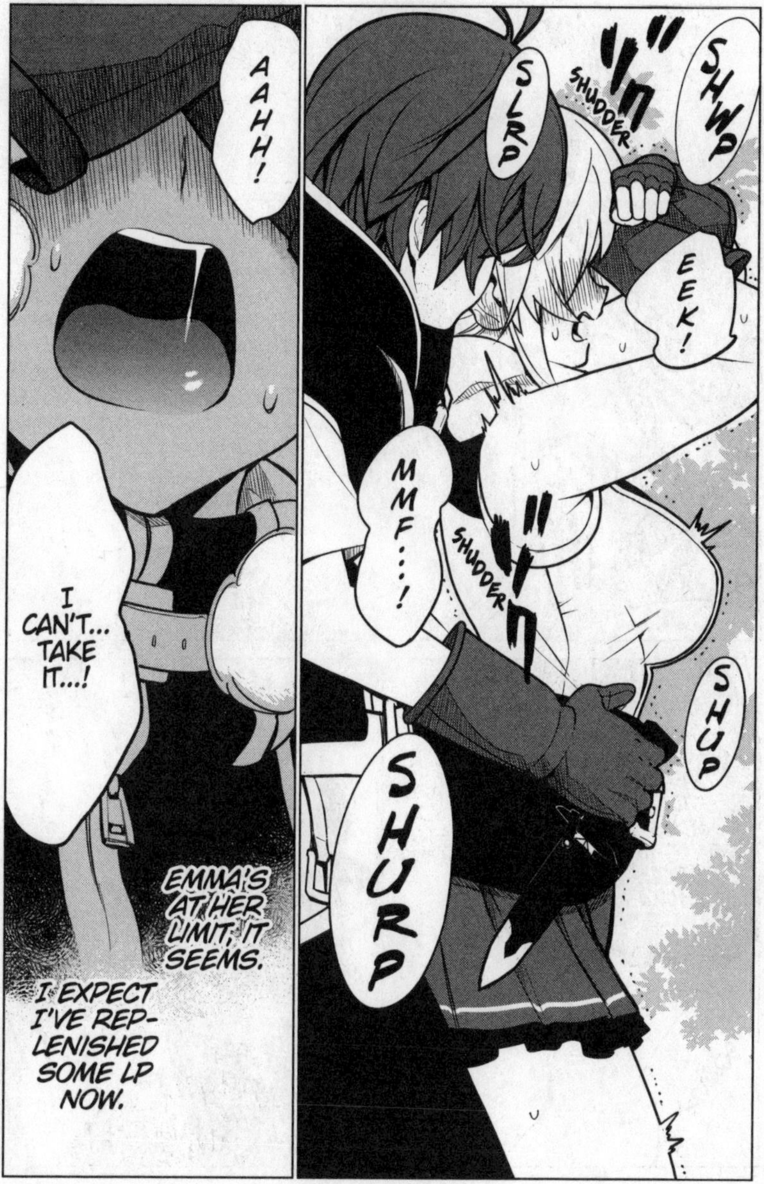
SHWP
SHUDDER
SLRP
EEK!
MMF...!
SHUDDER
SHUP
SHURP
AAHH!
I CAN'T... TAKE IT...!
EMMA'S AT HER LIMIT, IT SEEMS.
I EXPECT I'VE REPLENISHED SOME LP NOW.

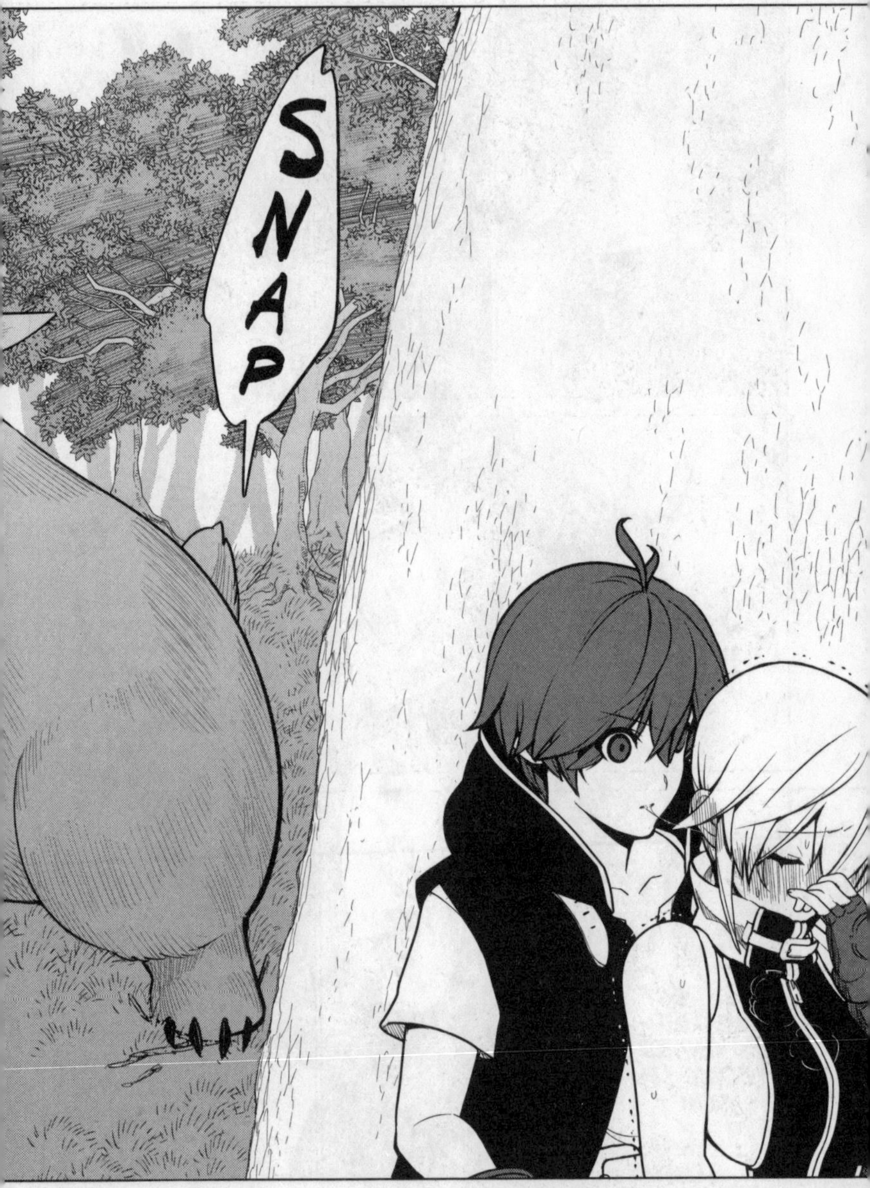
SNAP

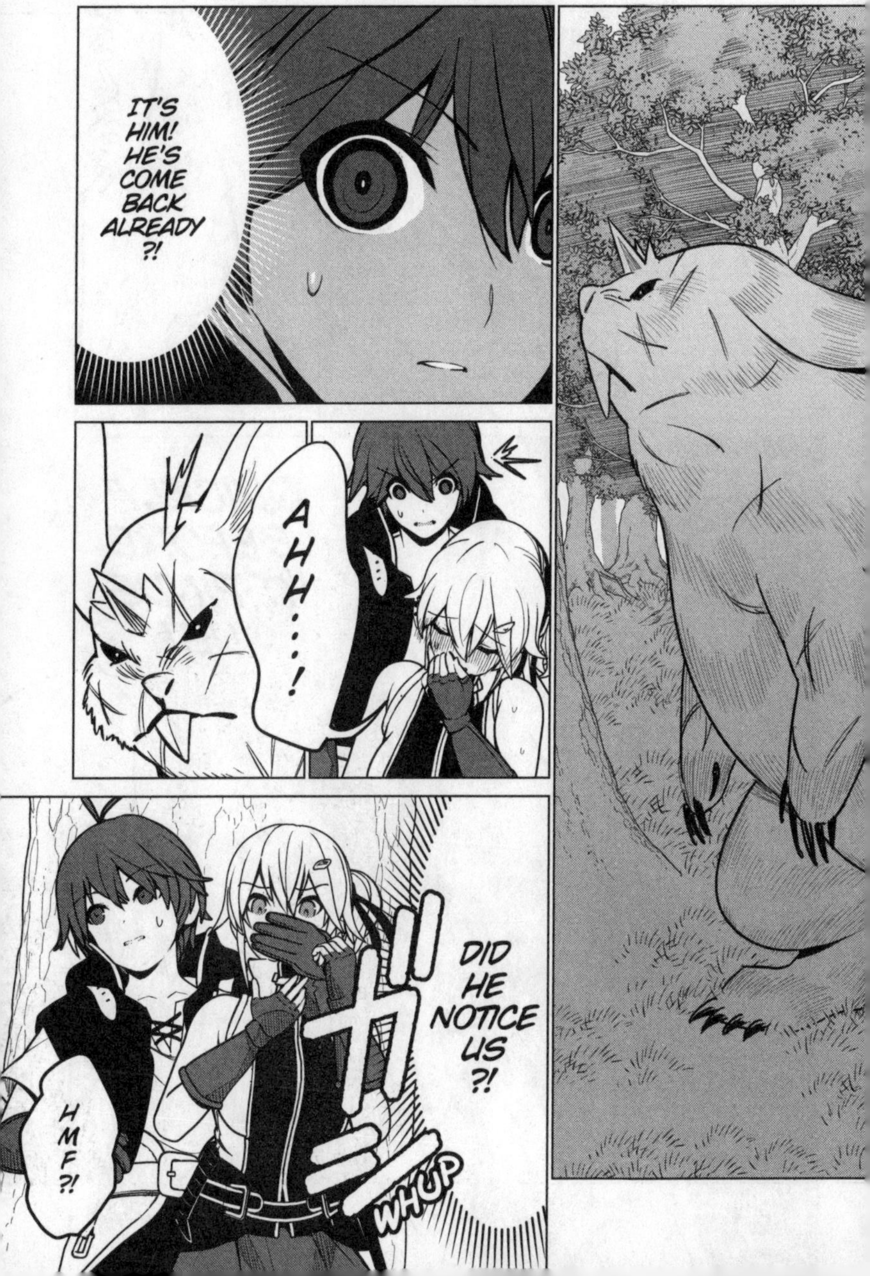
IT'S HIM! HE'S COME BACK ALREADY ?!
AHH...!
DID HE NOTICE US ?!
HMF ?!
WHUP

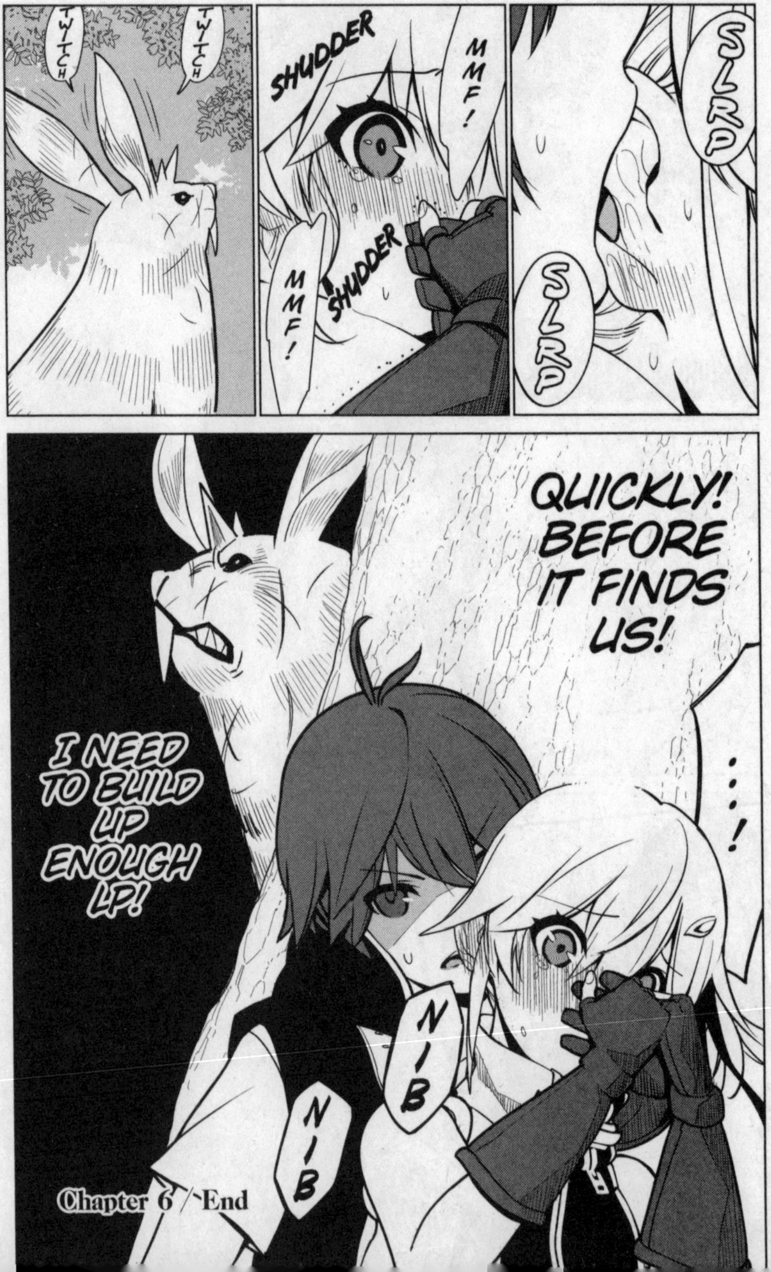
SLRP
SLRP
MMF!
SHUDDER
SHUDDER
MMF!
TWITCH
TWITCH
QUICKLY! BEFORE IT FINDS US!
...!
I NEED TO BUILD UP ENOUGH LP!
NIB
NIB
Chapter 6 / End

THE HIDDEN DUNGEON ONLY I CAN ENTER

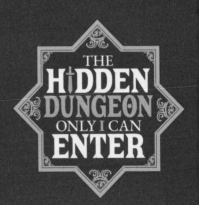

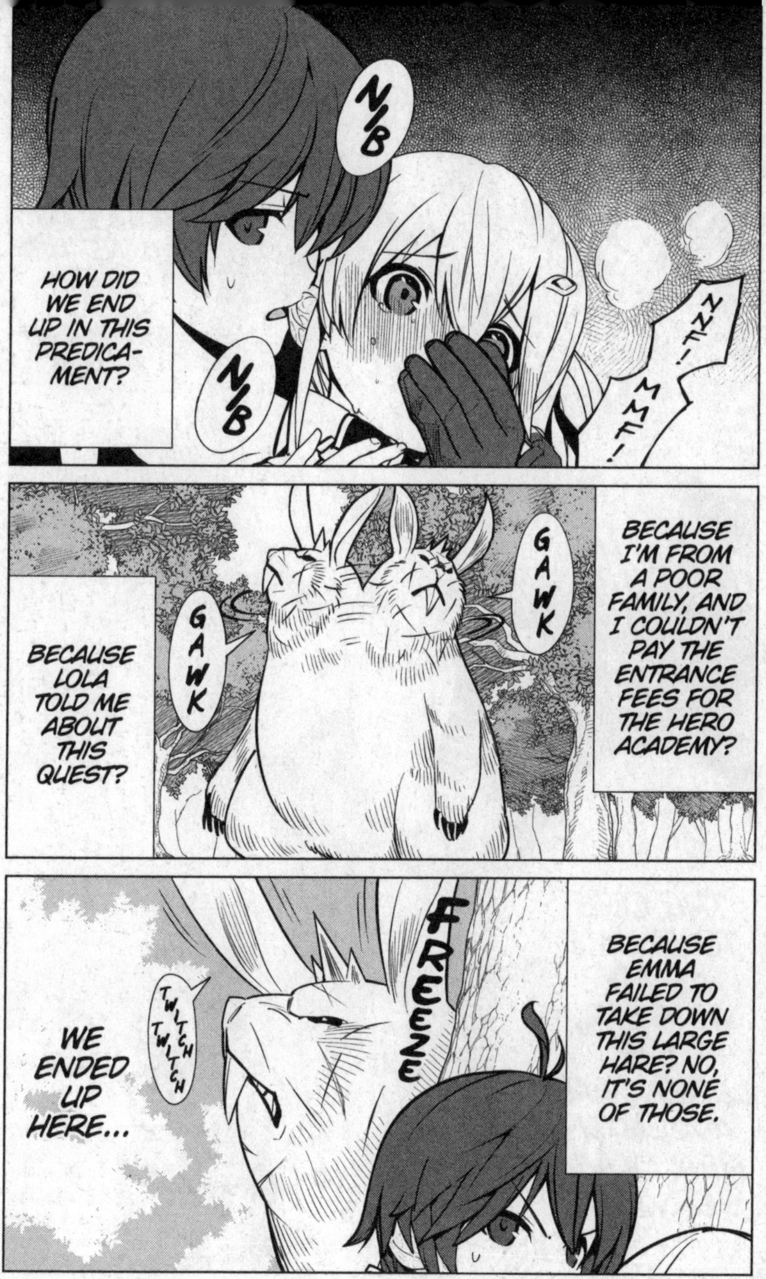
N/B
NNF! MMF!
HOW DID WE END UP IN THIS PREDICA-MENT?
N/B
BECAUSE I'M FROM A POOR FAMILY, AND I COULDN'T PAY THE ENTRANCE FEES FOR THE HERO ACADEMY?
GAWK
GAWK
BECAUSE LOLA TOLD ME ABOUT THIS QUEST?
BECAUSE EMMA FAILED TO TAKE DOWN THIS LARGE HARE? NO, IT'S NONE OF THOSE.
FREEZE
TWITCH TWITCH
WE ENDED UP HERE...

Chapter 7: The Sixteenth Year Death Curse

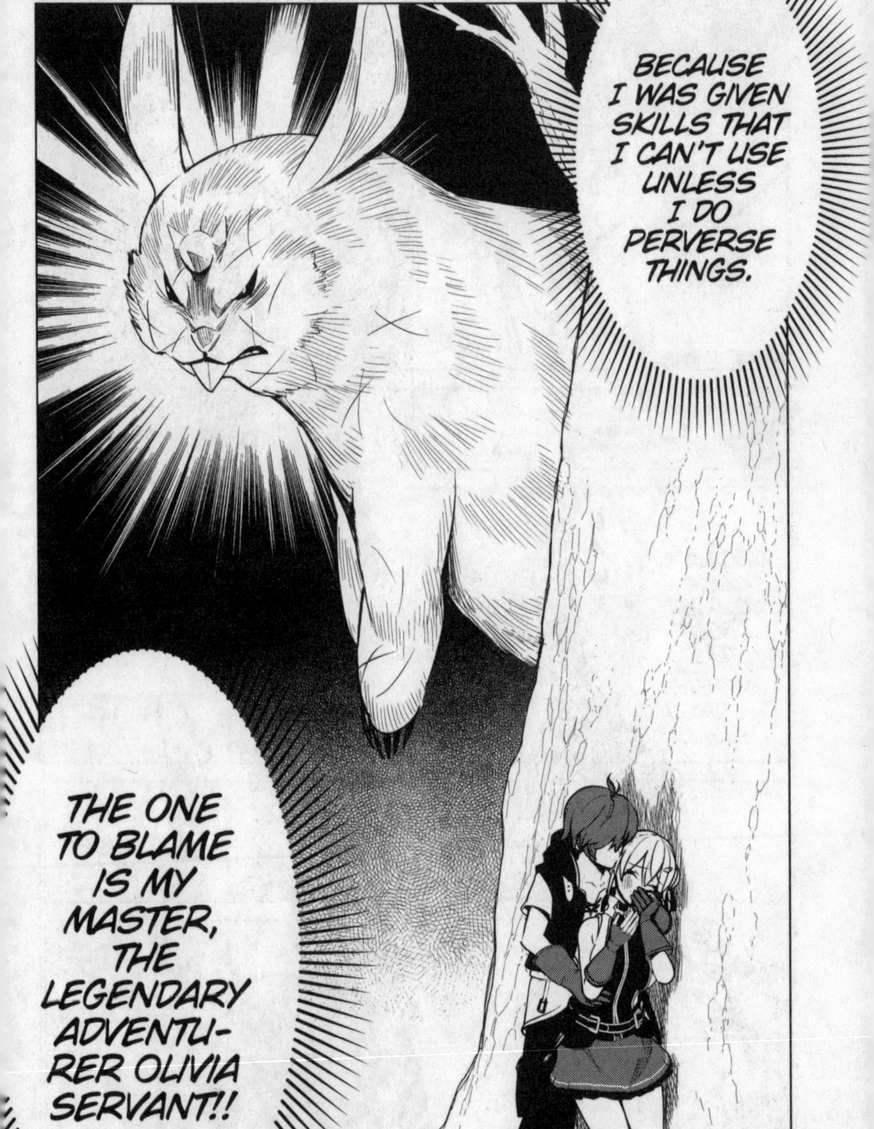
BECAUSE I WAS GIVEN SKILLS THAT I CAN'T USE UNLESS I DO PERVERSE THINGS.
THE ONE TO BLAME IS MY MASTER, THE LEGENDARY ADVENTU-RER OLIVIA SERVANT!!

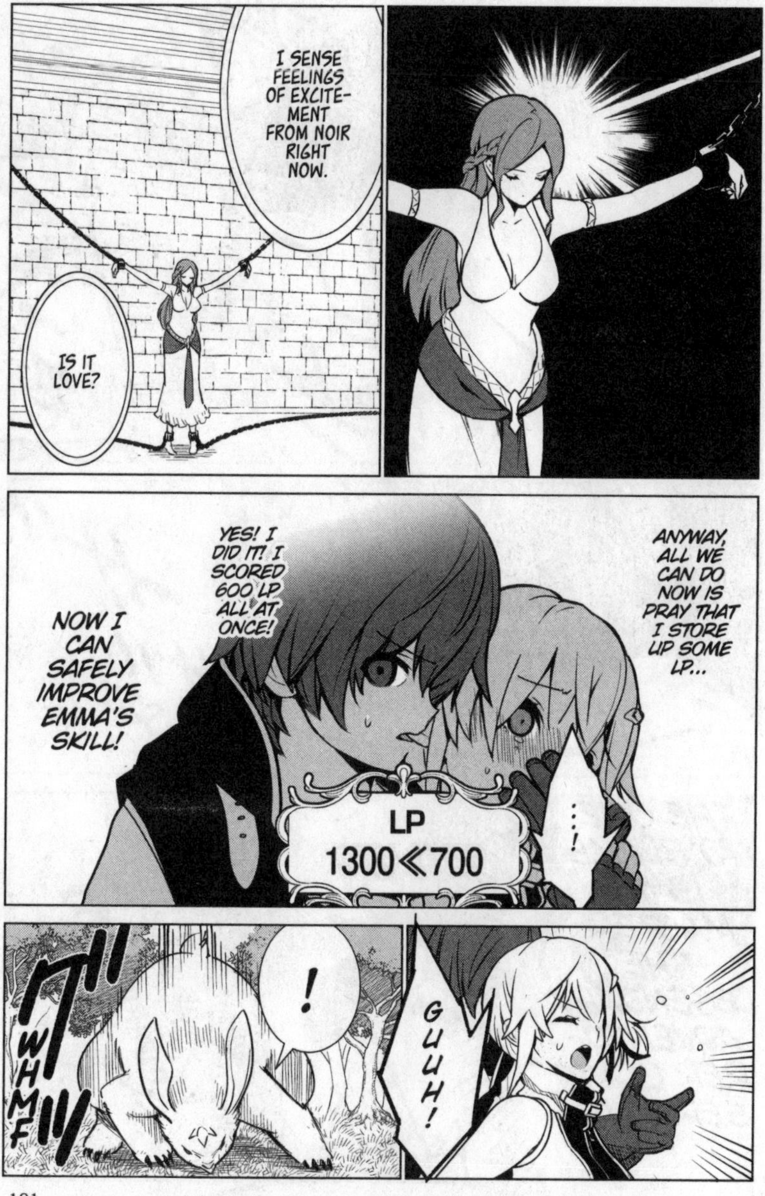
I SENSE FEELINGS OF EXCITE-MENT FROM NOIR RIGHT NOW.
IS IT LOVE?
ANYWAY, ALL WE CAN DO NOW IS PRAY THAT I STORE UP SOME LP...
YES! I DID IT! I SCORED 600 LP ALL AT ONCE!
NOW I CAN SAFELY IMPROVE EMMA'S SKILL!
LP
1300≪700
...!
GUUH!
!
WHMF

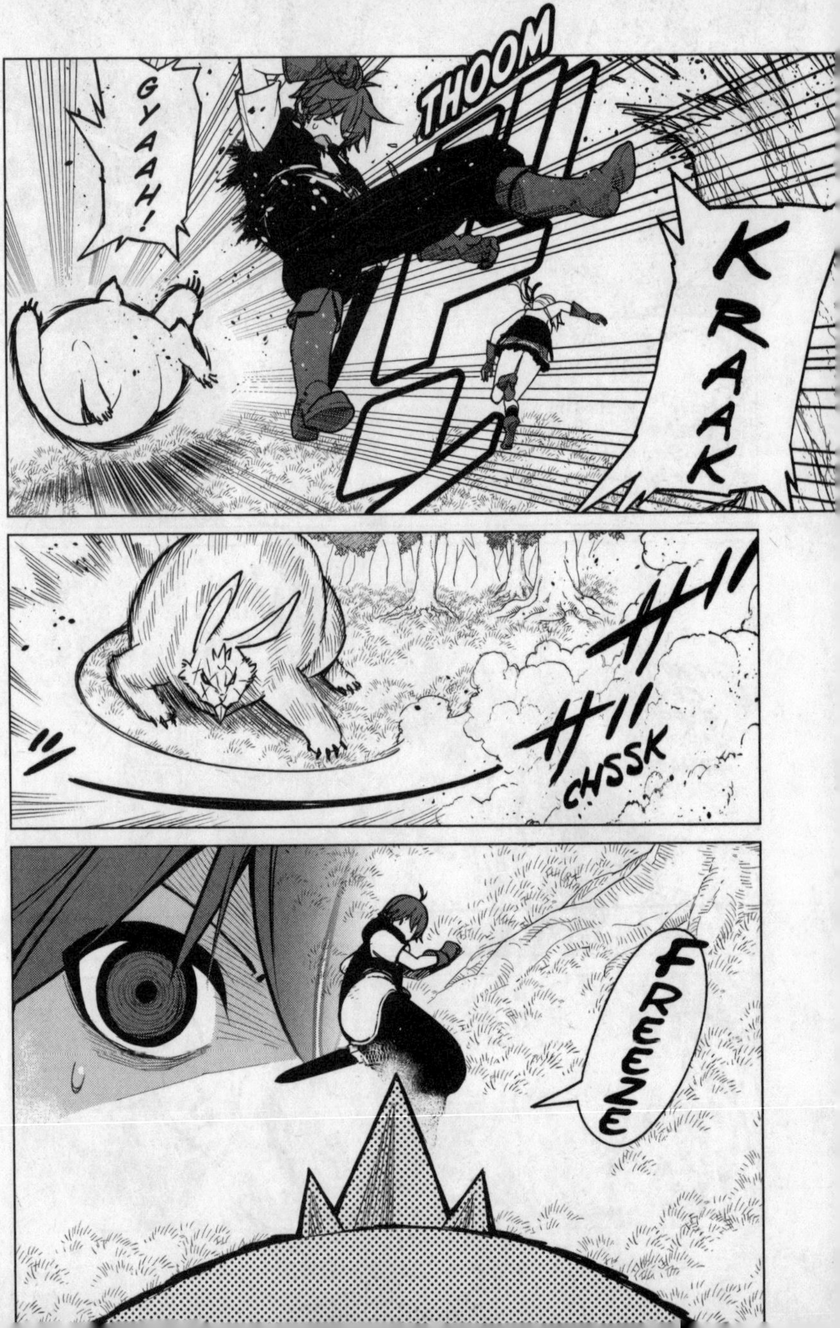
KRAAK
THOOM
GYAAH!
CHSSK
FREEZE

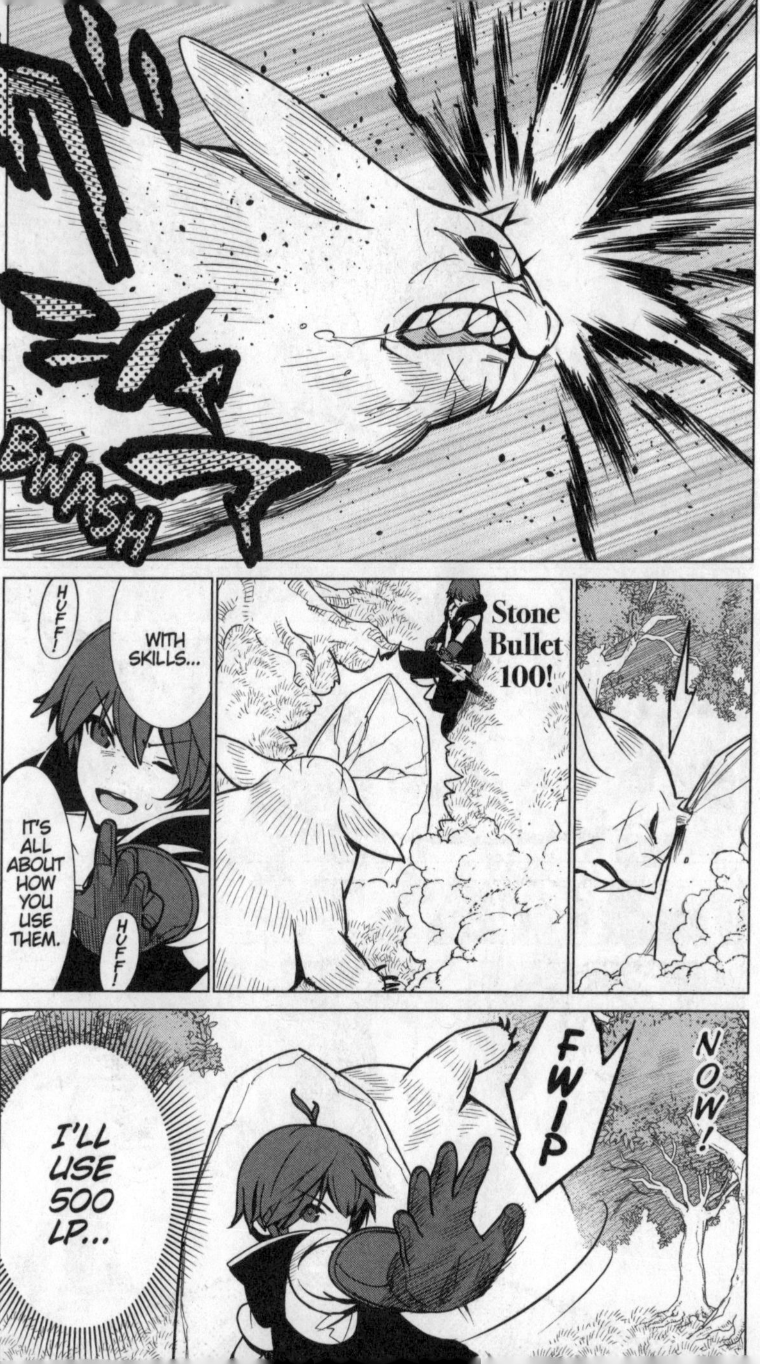
BWISH
Stone Bullet 100!
HUFF!
WITH SKILLS...
IT'S ALL ABOUT HOW YOU USE THEM.
HUFF!
NOW!
FWIP
I'LL USE 500 LP...

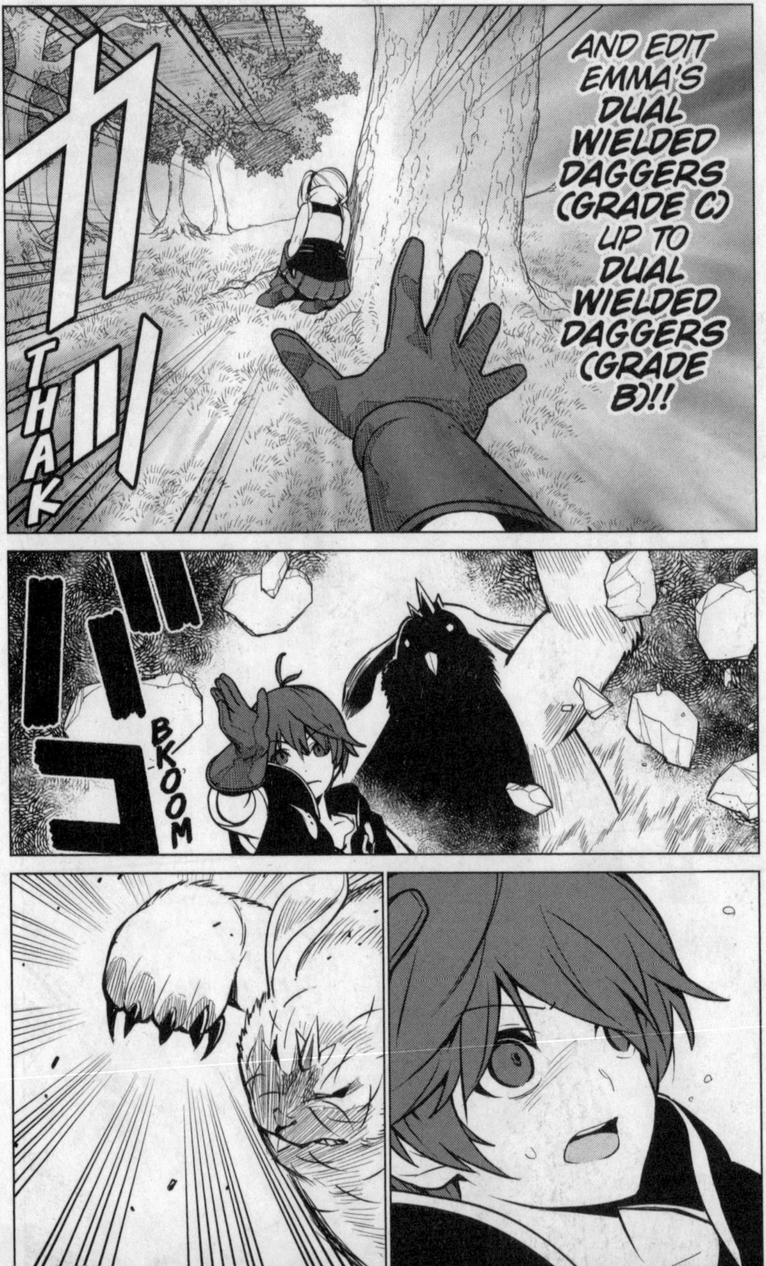
AND EDIT EMMA'S DUAL WIELDED DAGGERS (GRADE C) UP TO DUAL WIELDED DAGGERS (GRADE B)!!
THAK
BKOOM

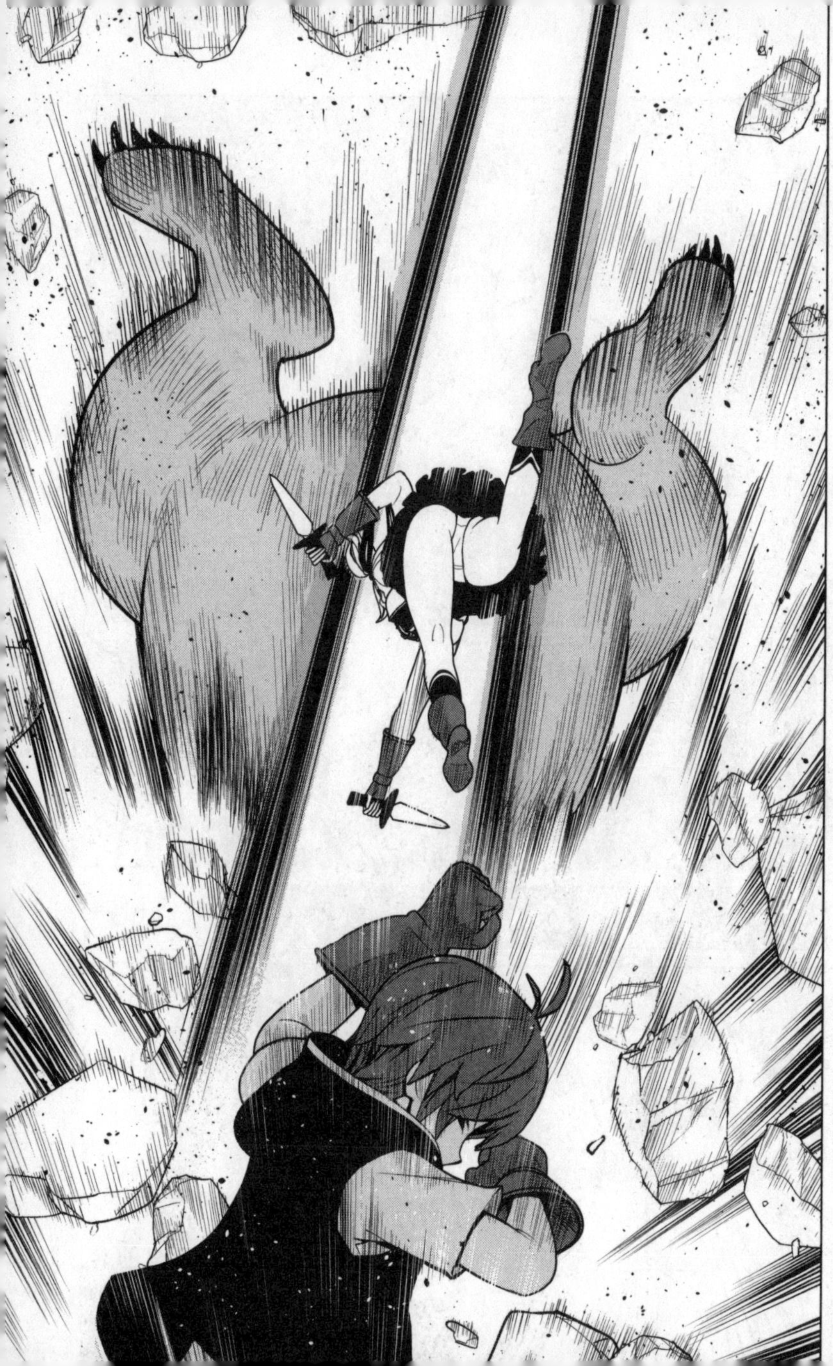

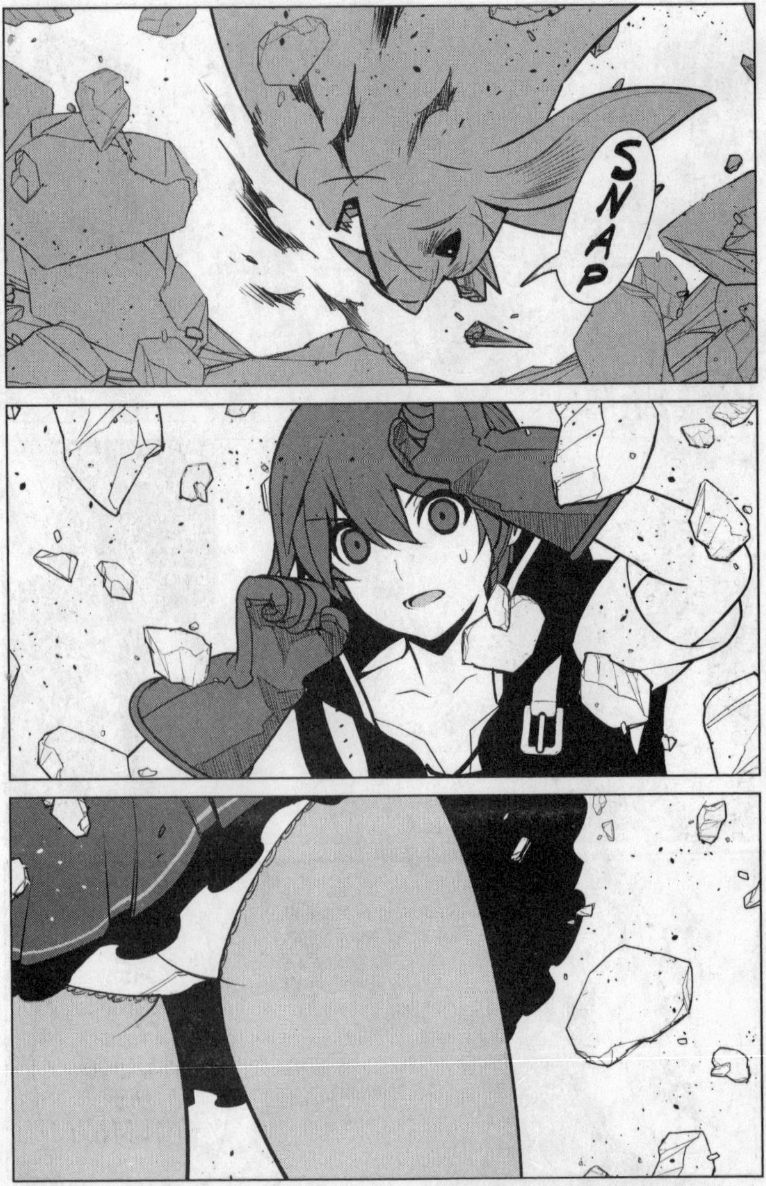
SNAP

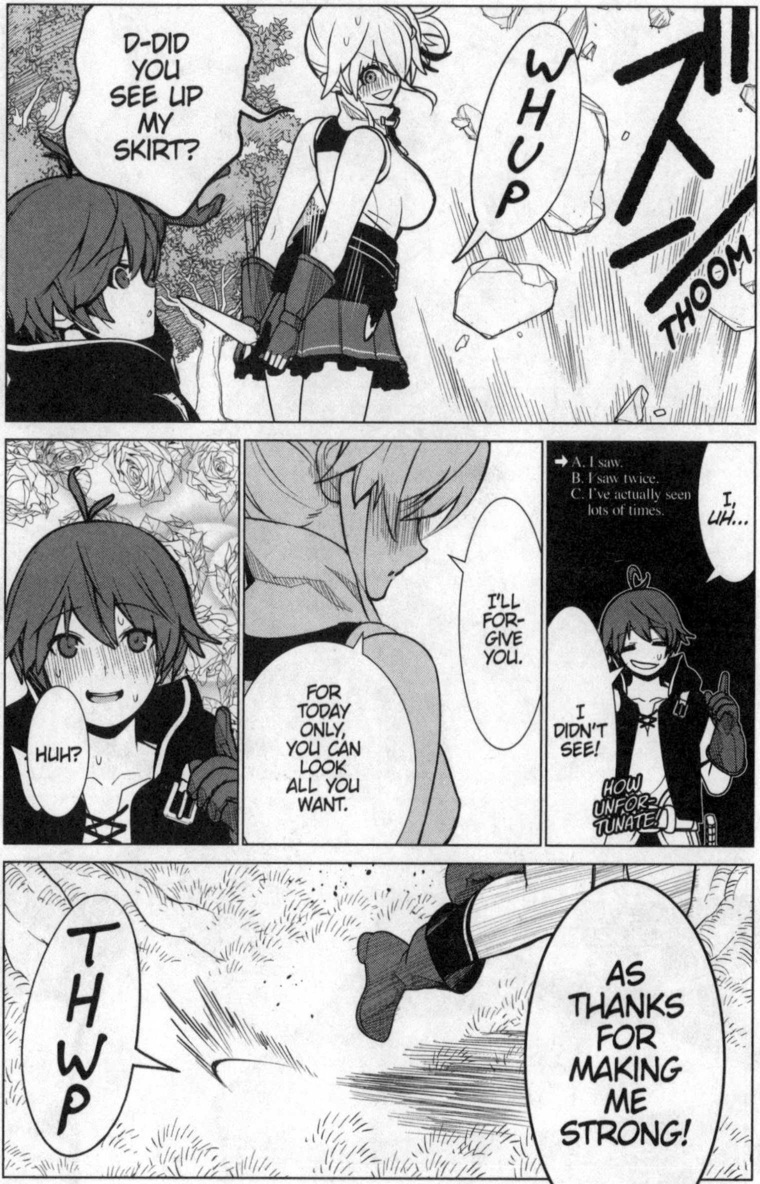
THOOM
WHUP
D-DID YOU SEE UP MY SKIRT?
→ A. I saw.
B. I saw twice.
C. I've actually seen lots of times.
I, UH...
I DIDN'T SEE!
HOW UNFORTUNATE!
I'LL FORGIVE YOU.
FOR TODAY ONLY, YOU CAN LOOK ALL YOU WANT.
HUH?
AS THANKS FOR MAKING ME STRONG!
THWP

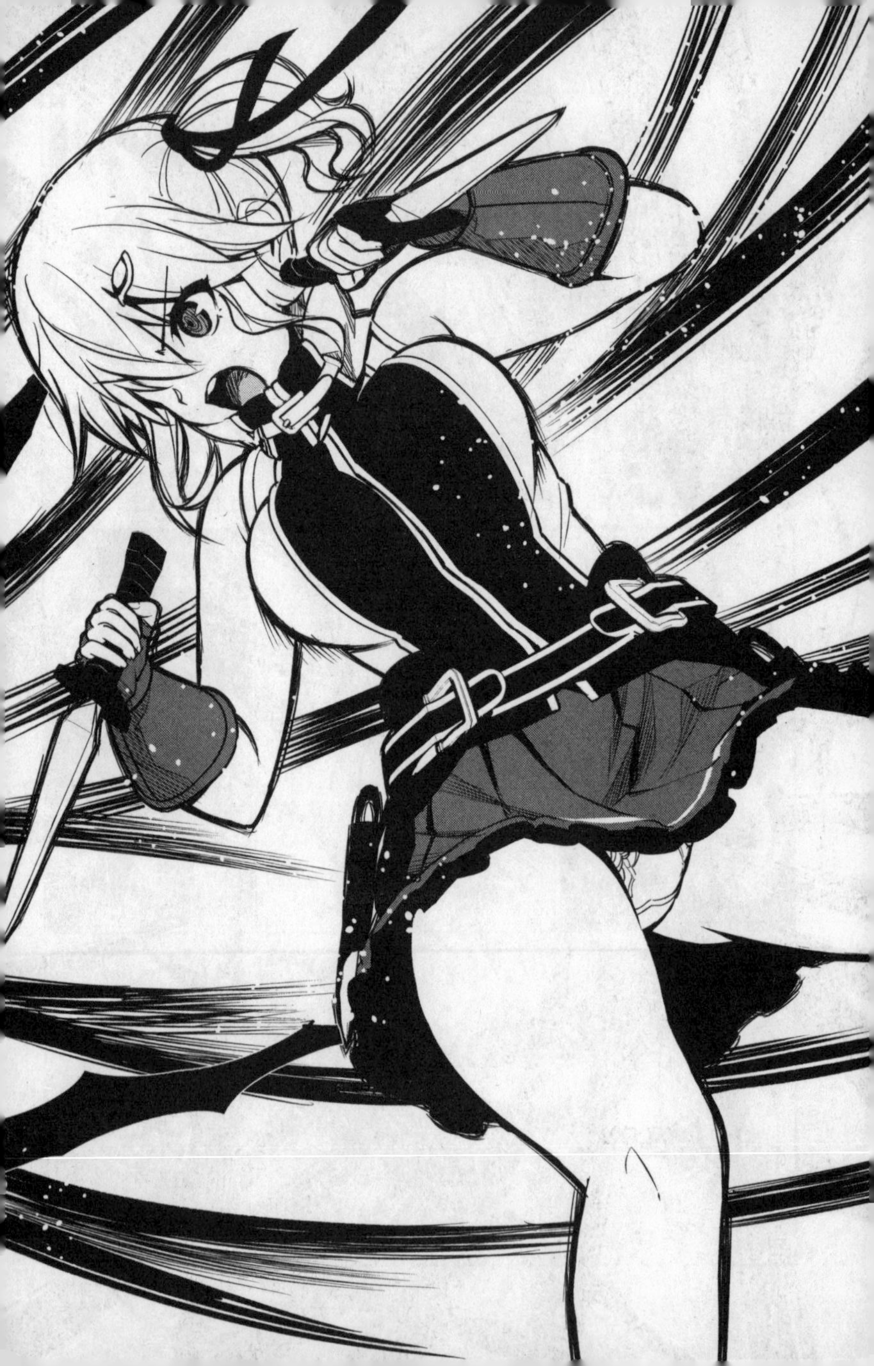

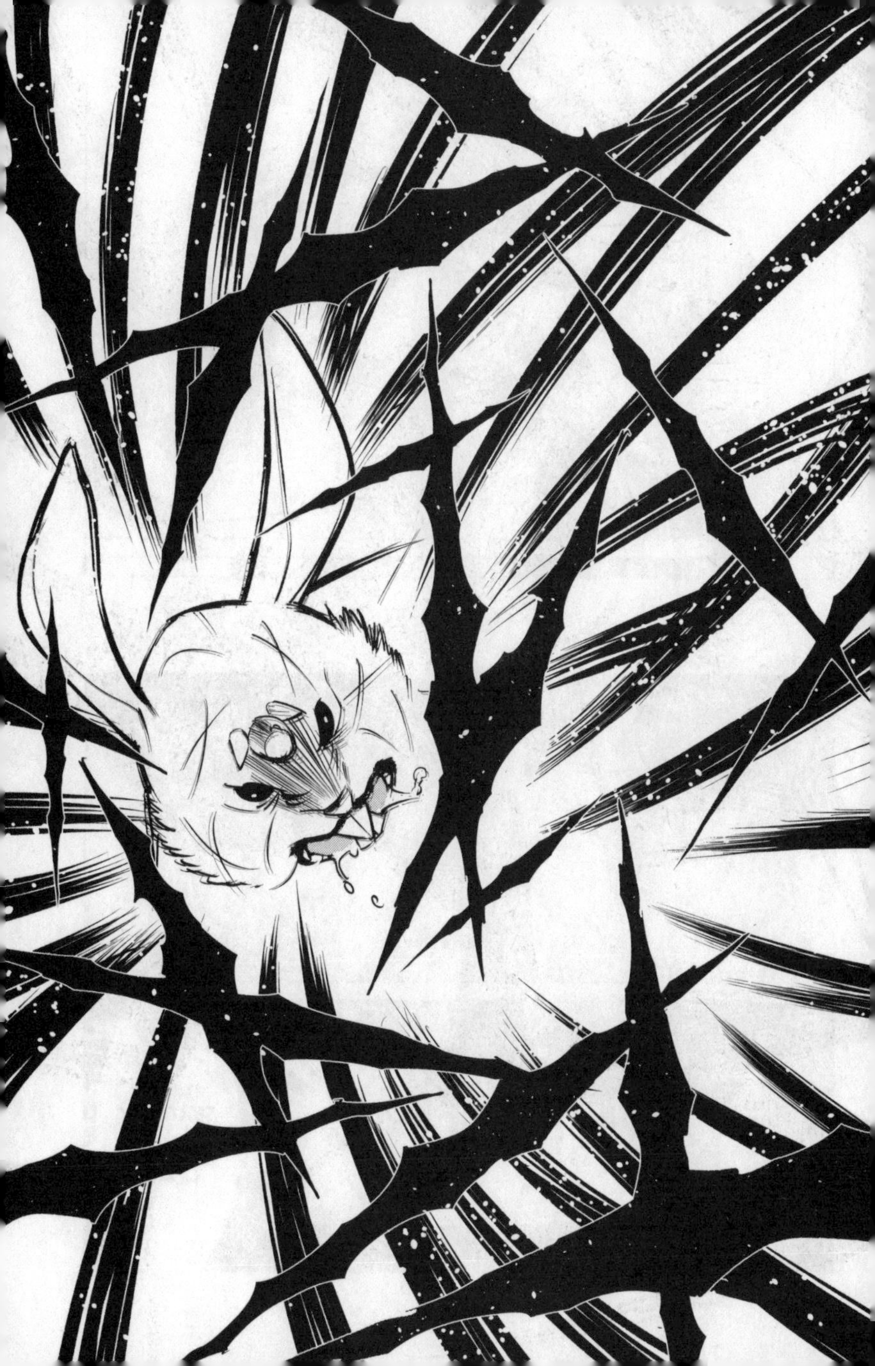

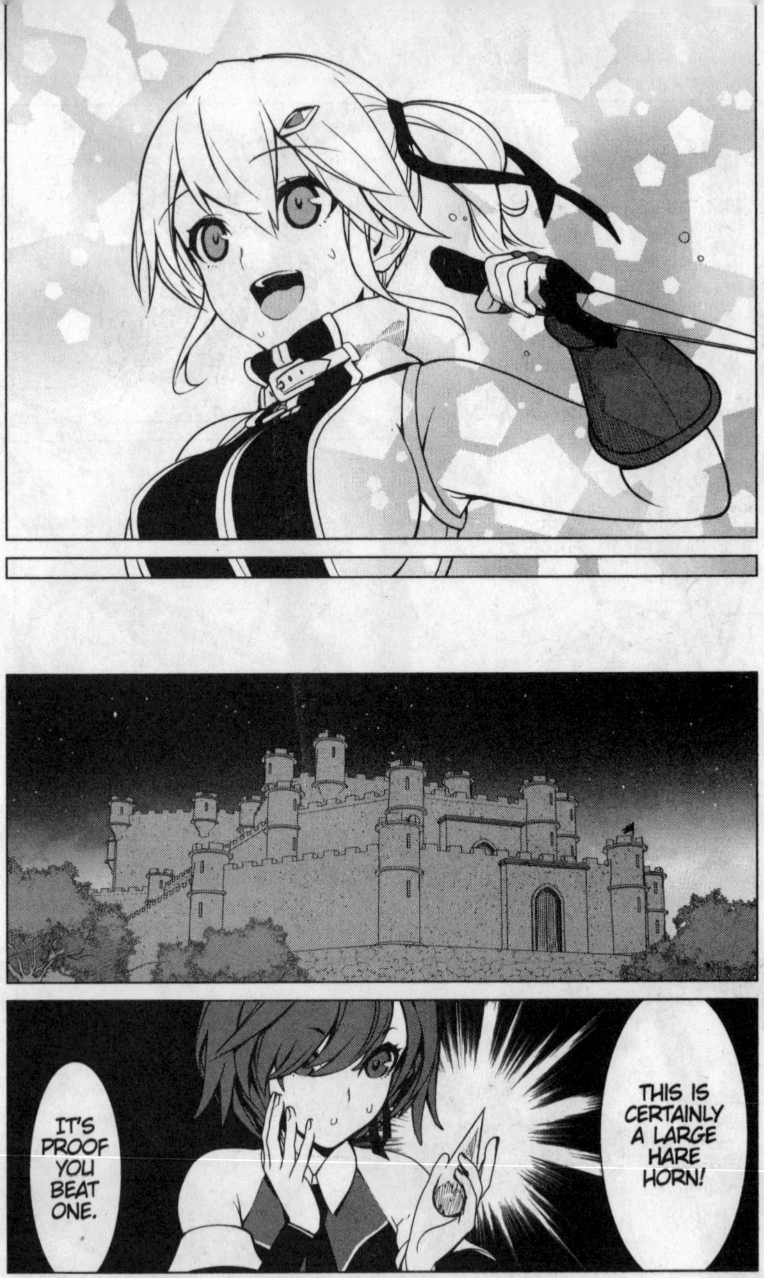
THIS IS CERTAINLY A LARGE HARE HORN!
IT'S PROOF YOU BEAT ONE.

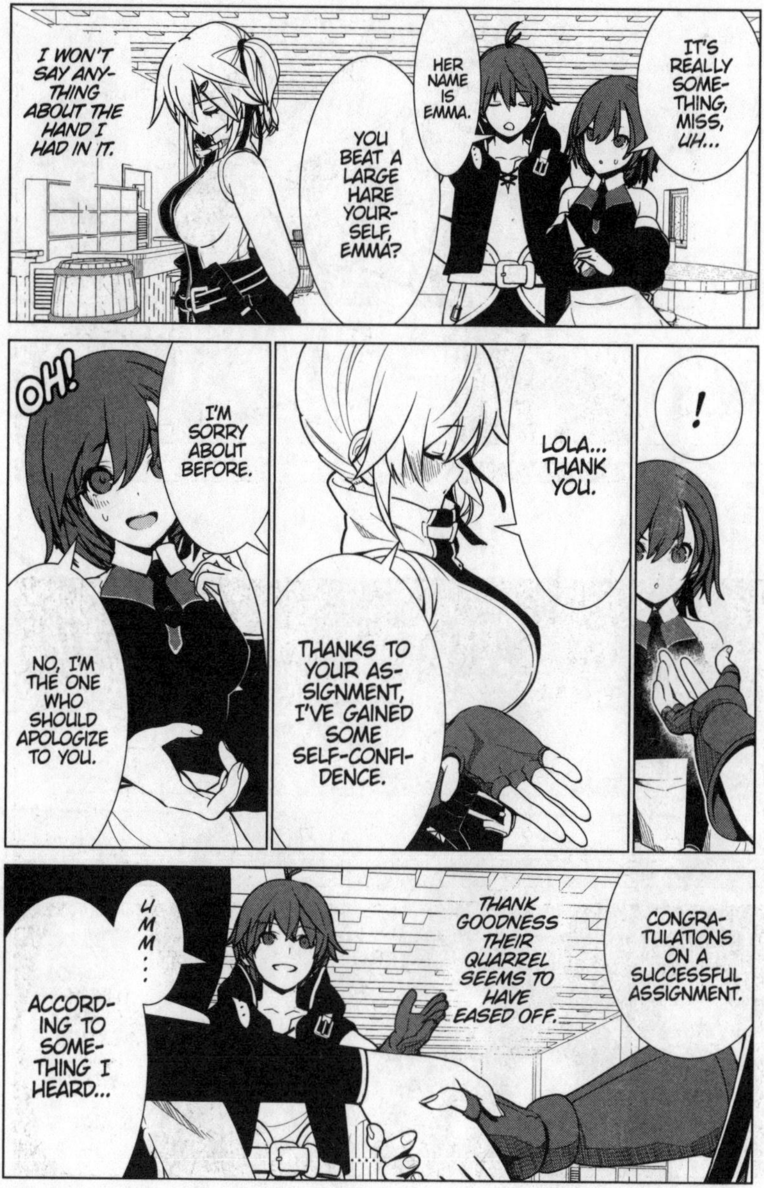
IT'S REALLY SOMETHING, MISS, UH...
HER NAME IS EMMA.
YOU BEAT A LARGE HARE YOURSELF, EMMA?
I WON'T SAY ANYTHING ABOUT THE HAND I HAD IN IT.
!
LOLA... THANK YOU.
THANKS TO YOUR ASSIGNMENT, I'VE GAINED SOME SELF-CONFIDENCE.
OH!
I'M SORRY ABOUT BEFORE.
NO, I'M THE ONE WHO SHOULD APOLOGIZE TO YOU.
CONGRATULATIONS ON A SUCCESSFUL ASSIGNMENT.
THANK GOODNESS THEIR QUARREL SEEMS TO HAVE EASED OFF.
UMM...
ACCORDING TO SOMETHING I HEARD...

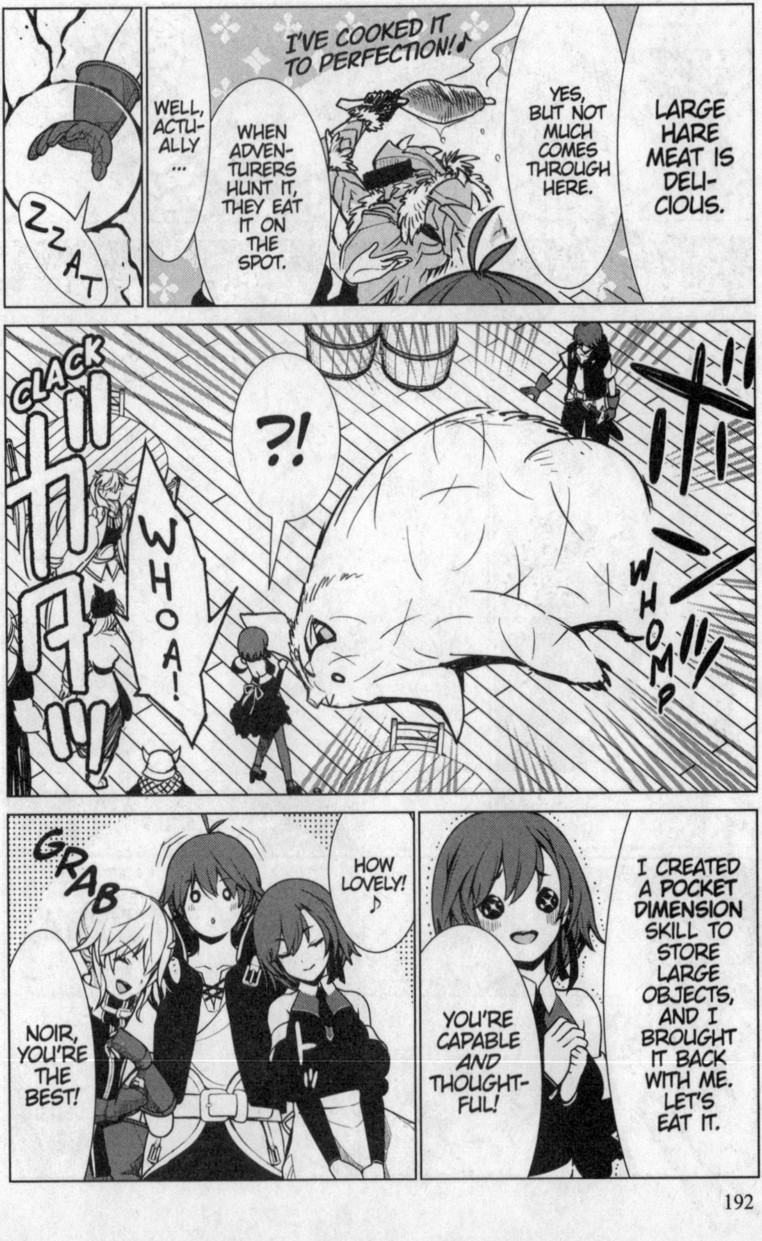
LARGE HARE MEAT IS DELICIOUS.
YES, BUT NOT MUCH COMES THROUGH HERE.
I'VE COOKED IT TO PERFECTION!♪
WHEN ADVENTURERS HUNT IT, THEY EAT IT ON THE SPOT.
WELL, ACTUALLY ...
ZZAT
WHOMP!!
?!
WHOA!
CLACK
I CREATED A POCKET DIMENSION SKILL TO STORE LARGE OBJECTS, AND I BROUGHT IT BACK WITH ME. LET'S EAT IT.
YOU'RE CAPABLE AND THOUGHTFUL!
HOW LOVELY! ♪
GRAB
NOIR, YOU'RE THE BEST!

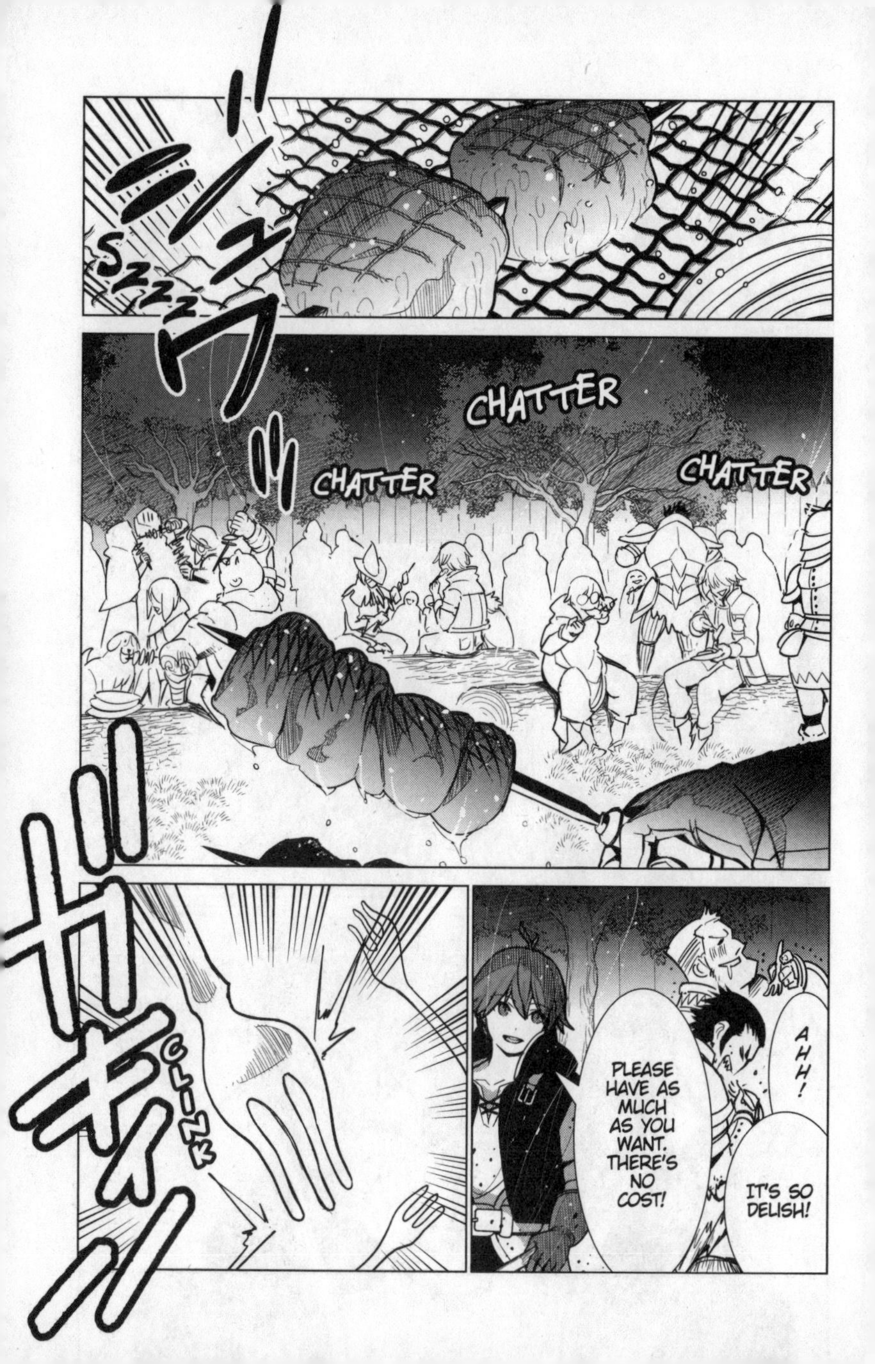
SZZZZ
CHATTER
CHATTER
CHATTER
PLEASE HAVE AS MUCH AS YOU WANT. THERE'S NO COST!
AHH!
IT'S SO DELISH!
CLINK

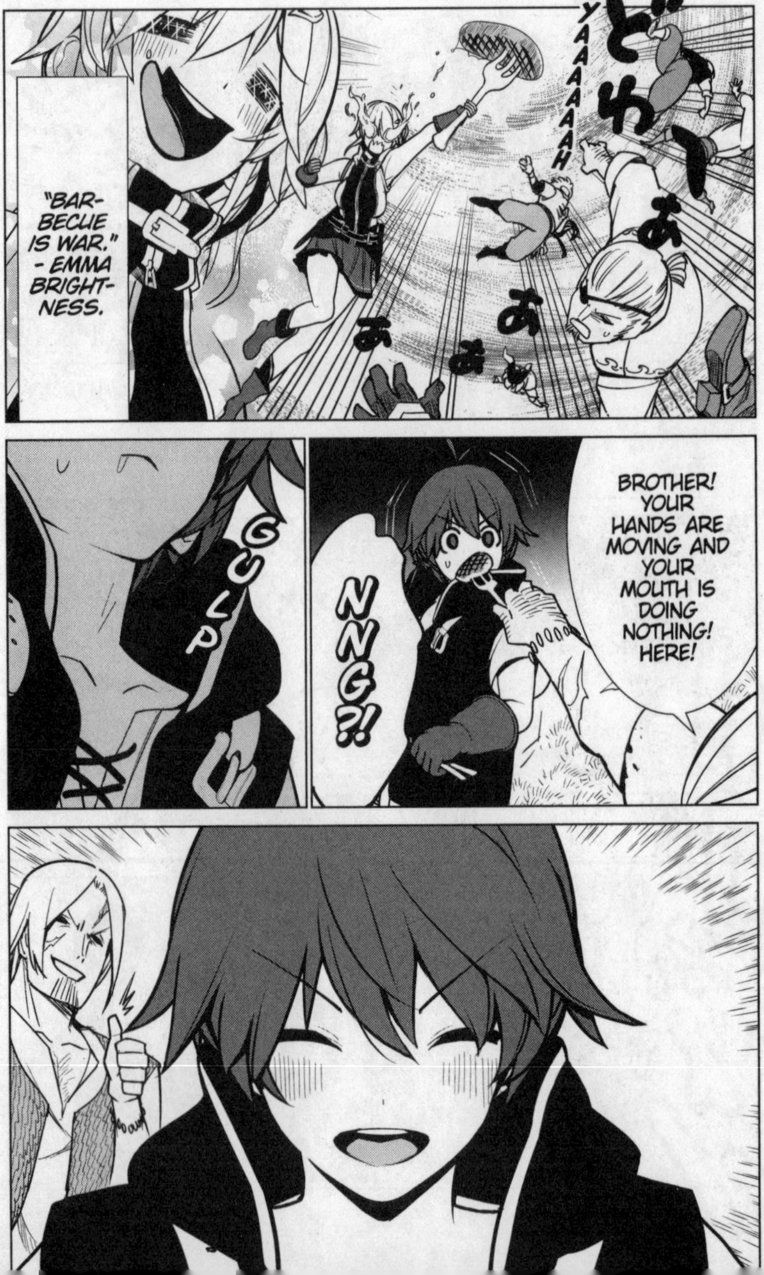
GYAAAAAAAH
"BARBECUE IS WAR." - EMMA BRIGHTNESS.
BROTHER! YOUR HANDS ARE MOVING AND YOUR MOUTH IS DOING NOTHING! HERE!
NNG?!
GULP

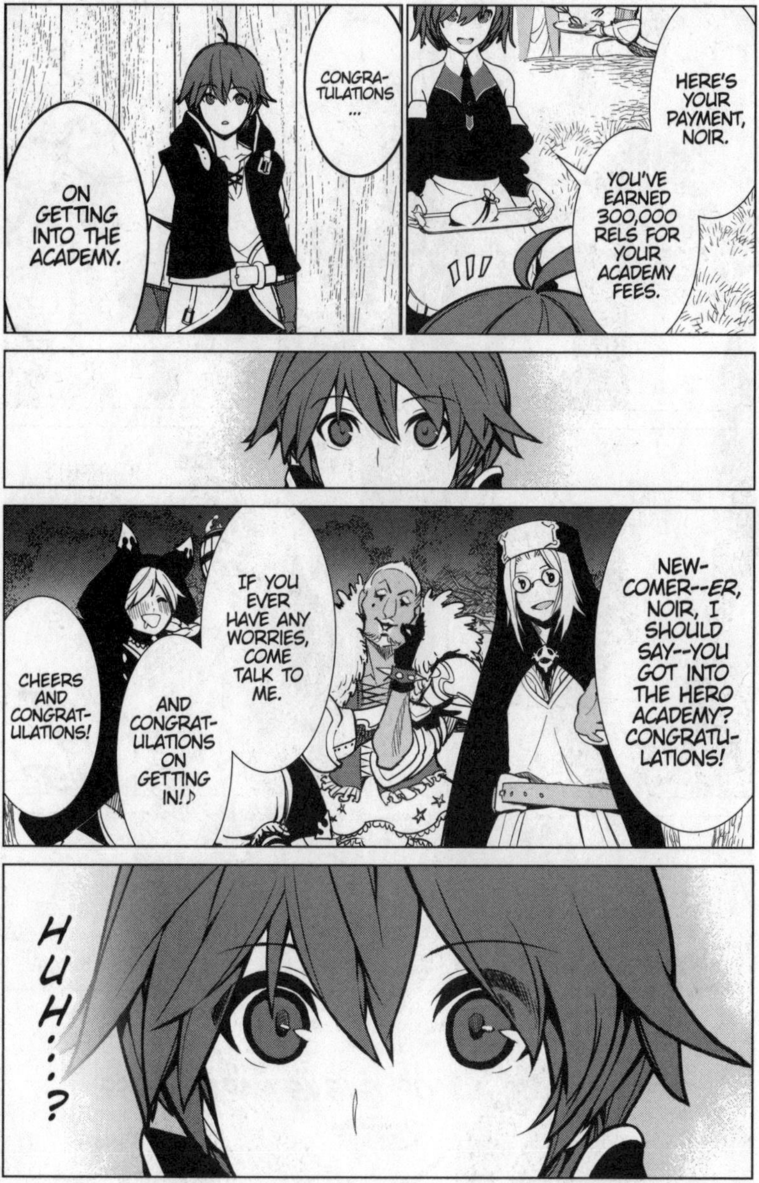
HERE'S YOUR PAYMENT, NOIR.
YOU'VE EARNED 300,000 RELS FOR YOUR ACADEMY FEES.
CONGRATULATIONS...
ON GETTING INTO THE ACADEMY.
NEW-COMER--ER, NOIR, I SHOULD SAY--YOU GOT INTO THE HERO ACADEMY? CONGRATULATIONS!
IF YOU EVER HAVE ANY WORRIES, COME TALK TO ME.
AND CONGRATULATIONS ON GETTING IN!♪
CHEERS AND CONGRATULATIONS!
HUH...?

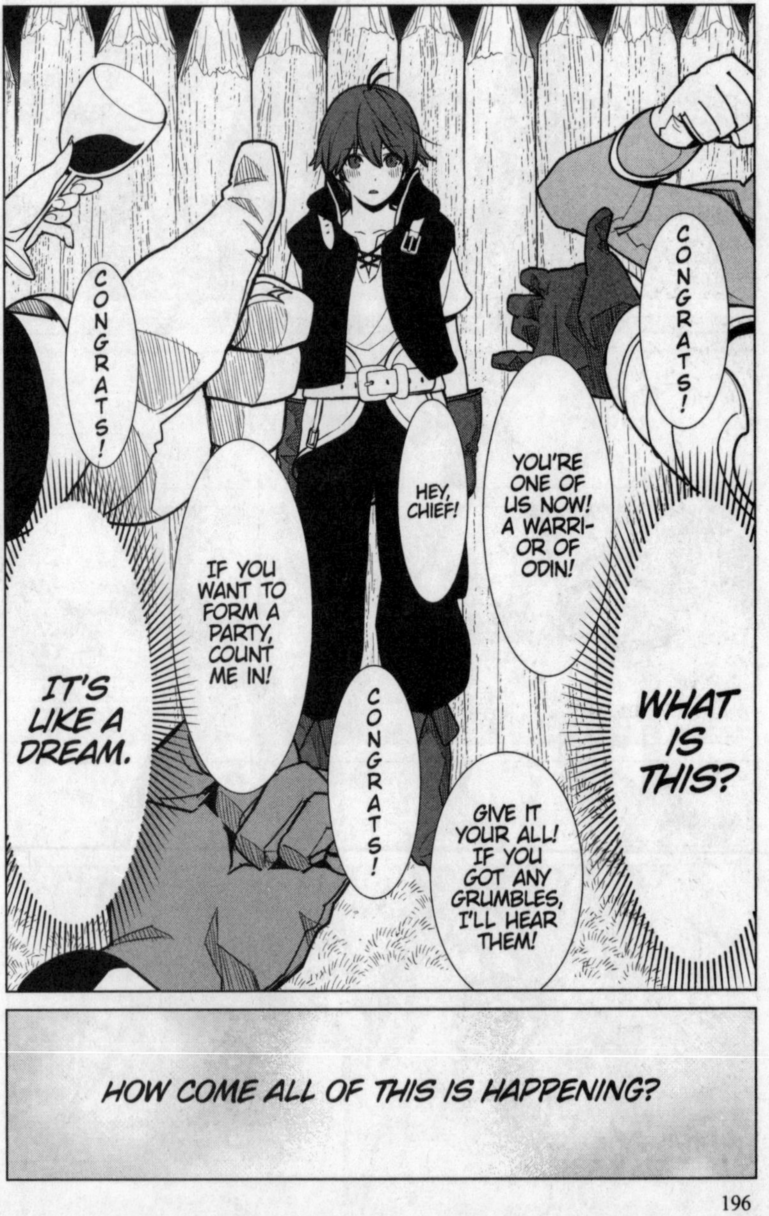
CONGRATS!
CONGRATS!
YOU'RE ONE OF US NOW! A WARRIOR OF ODIN!
HEY, CHIEF!
IF YOU WANT TO FORM A PARTY, COUNT ME IN!
WHAT IS THIS?
GIVE IT YOUR ALL! IF YOU GOT ANY GRUMBLES, I'LL HEAR THEM!
CONGRATS!
IT'S LIKE A DREAM.
HOW COME ALL OF THIS IS HAPPENING?

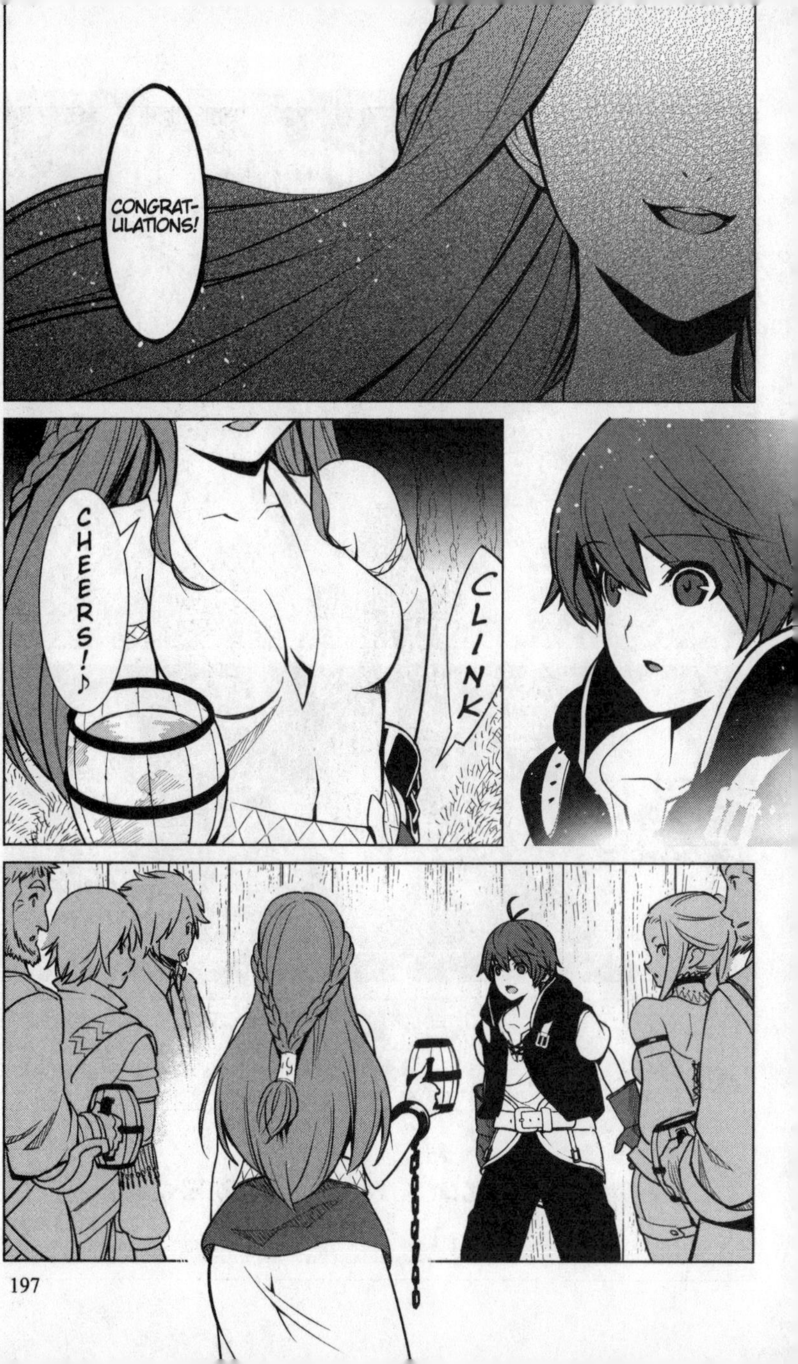
CONGRAT-
ULATIONS!
CHEERS!♪
CLINK

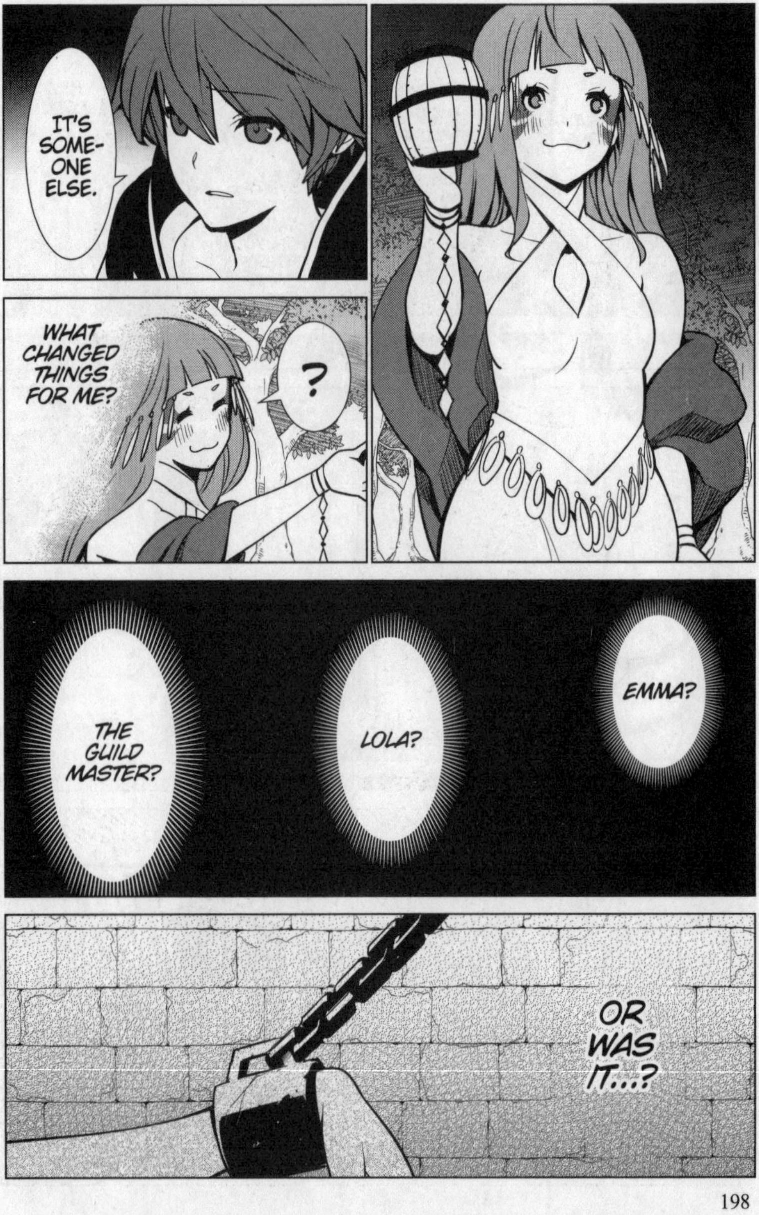
IT'S SOME-ONE ELSE.
WHAT CHANGED THINGS FOR ME?
?
EMMA?
LOLA?
THE GUILD MASTER?
OR WAS IT...?

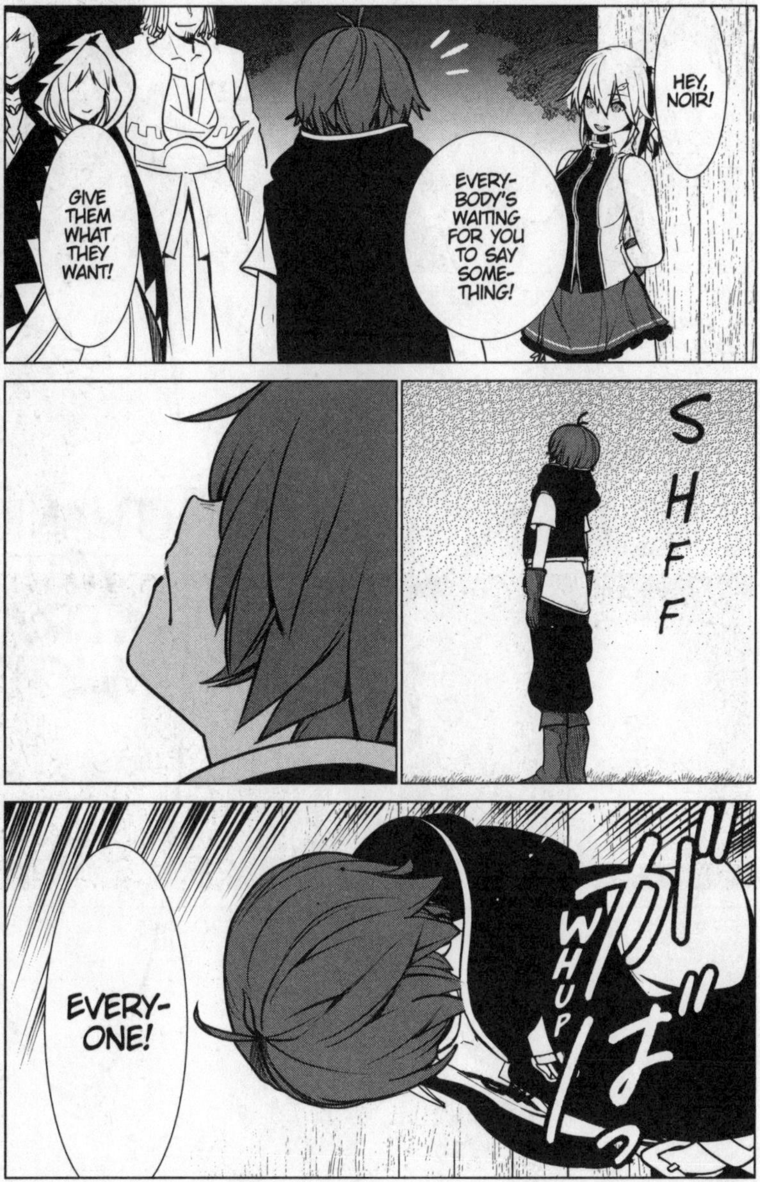
HEY, NOIR!
EVERYBODY'S WAITING FOR YOU TO SAY SOMETHING!
GIVE THEM WHAT THEY WANT!
SHFF
がばっ
WHUP!
EVERYONE!

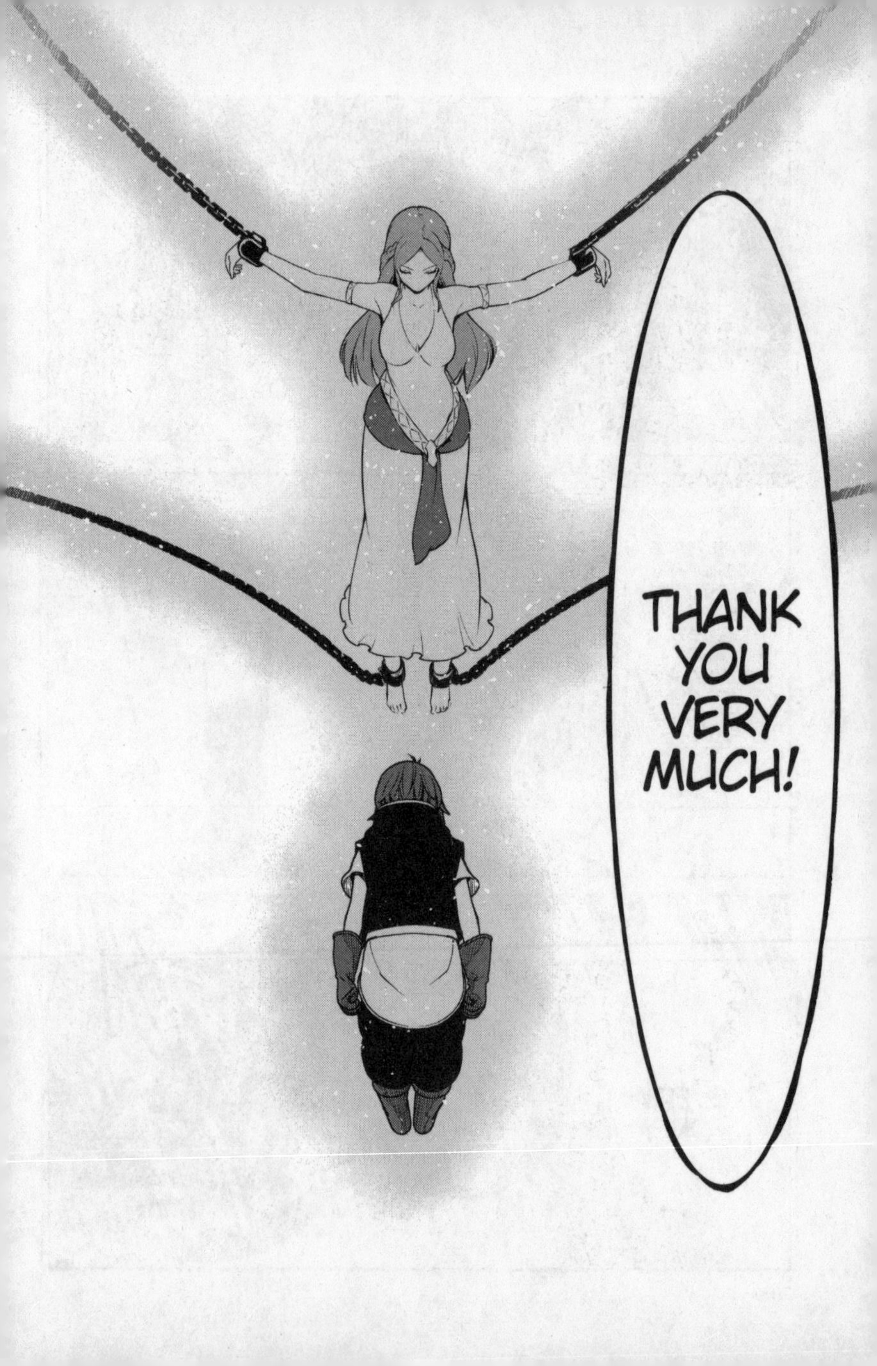
THANK YOU VERY MUCH!

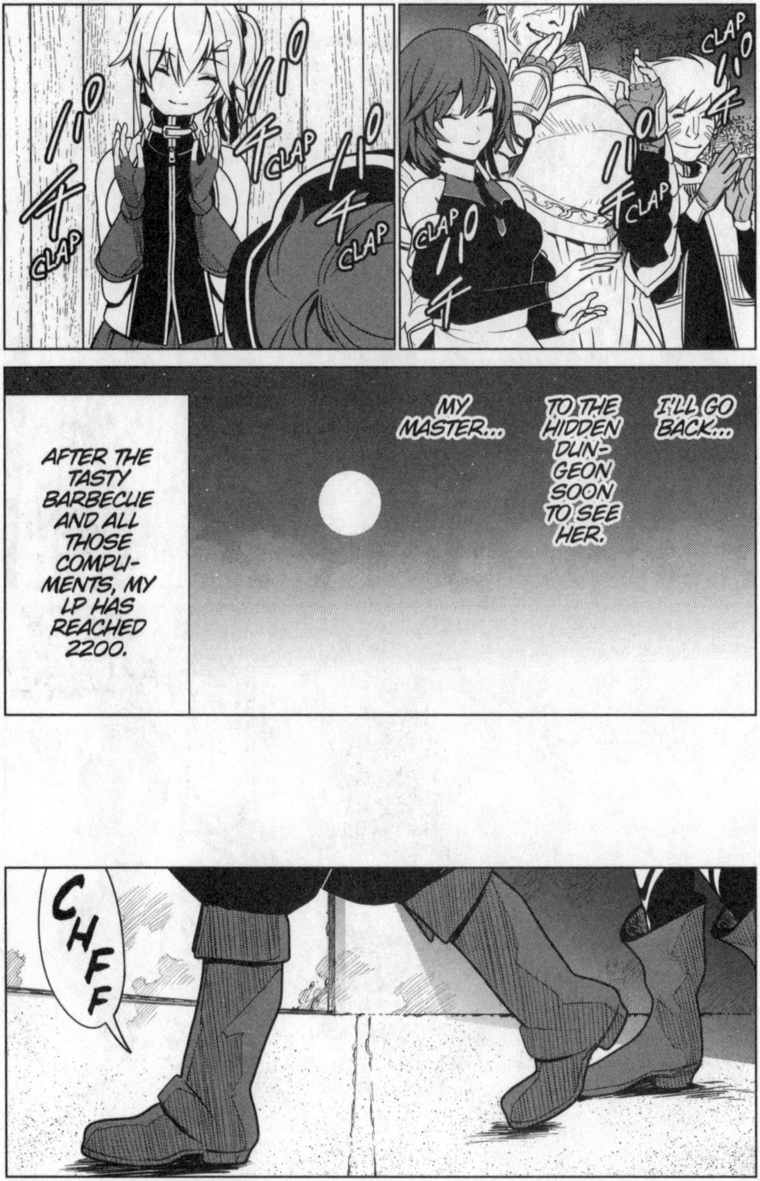
CLAP
CLAP
CLAP
CLAP
CLAP
CLAP
I'LL GO BACK...
TO THE HIDDEN DUNGEON SOON TO SEE HER.
MY MASTER...
AFTER THE TASTY BARBECUE AND ALL THOSE COMPLIMENTS, MY LP HAS REACHED 2200.
CHFF

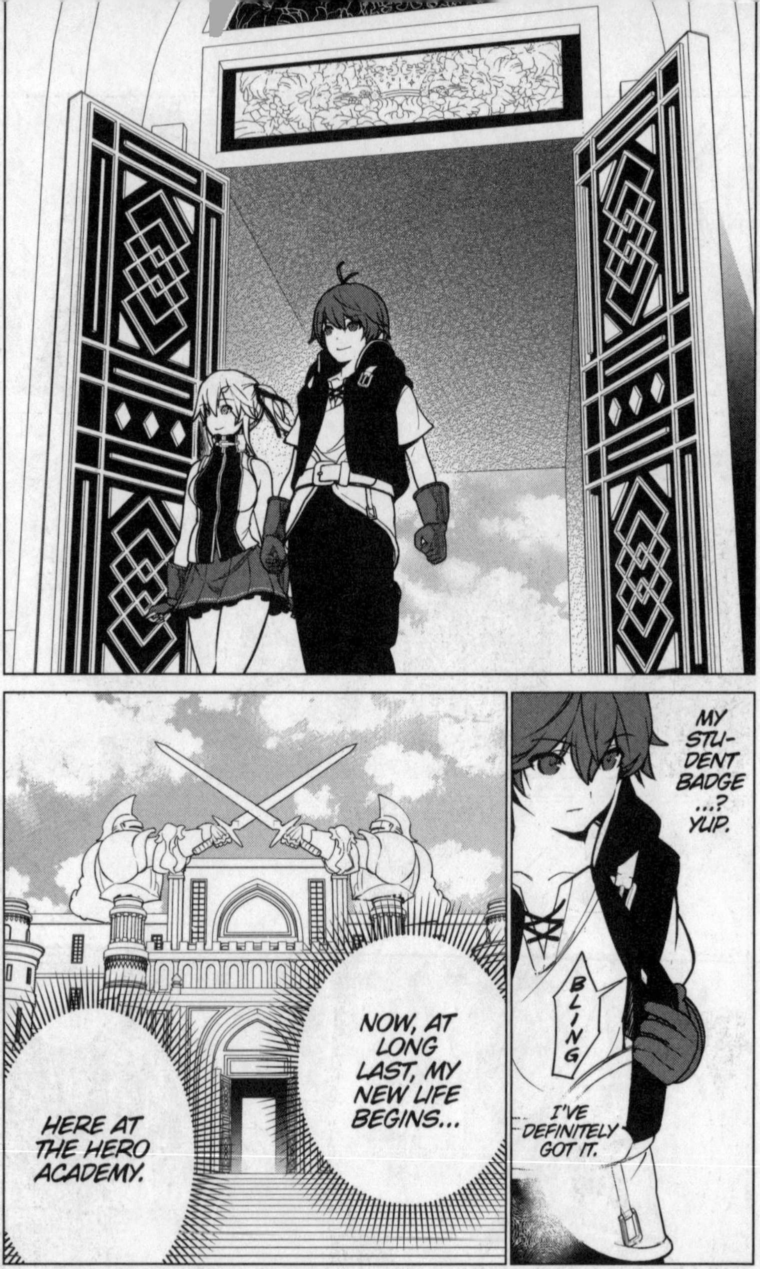
MY STU-DENT BADGE ...? YUP.
BLING
I'VE DEFINITELY GOT IT.
NOW, AT LONG LAST, MY NEW LIFE BEGINS...
HERE AT THE HERO ACADEMY.

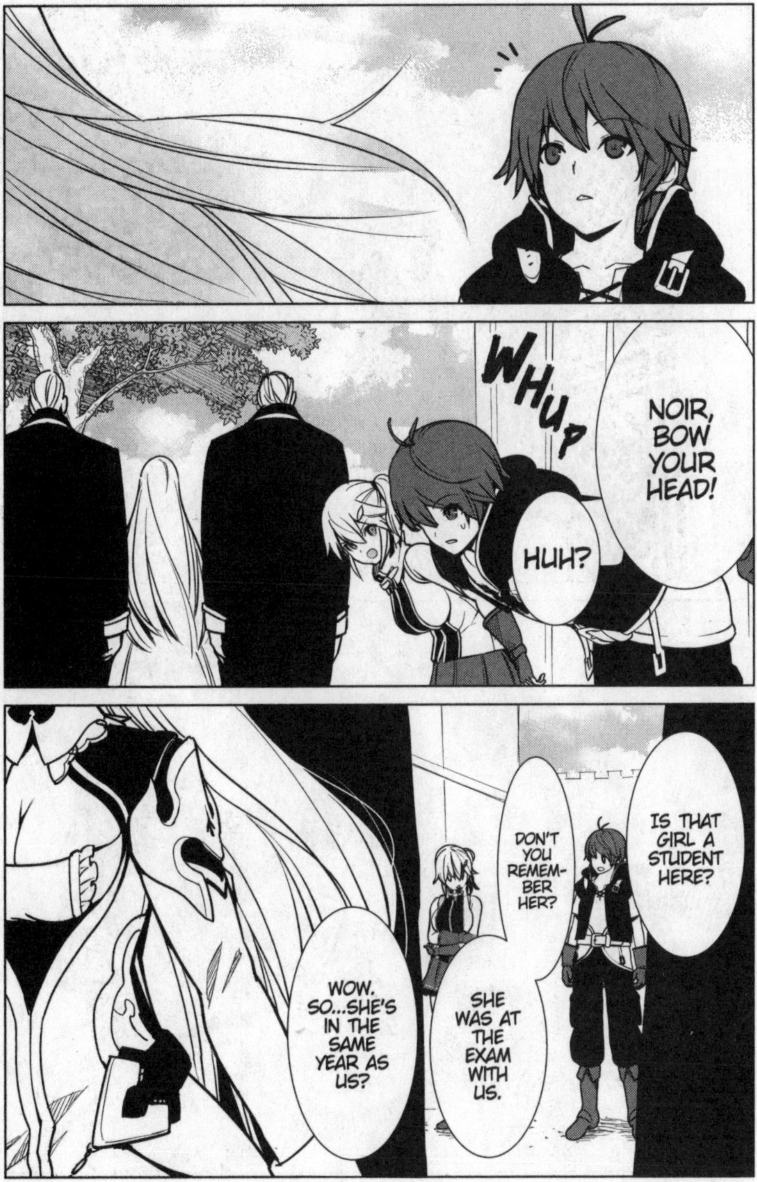
NOIR, BOW YOUR HEAD!
WHUP
HUH?
IS THAT GIRL A STUDENT HERE?
DON'T YOU REMEM-BER HER?
SHE WAS AT THE EXAM WITH US.
WOW. SO...SHE'S IN THE SAME YEAR AS US?

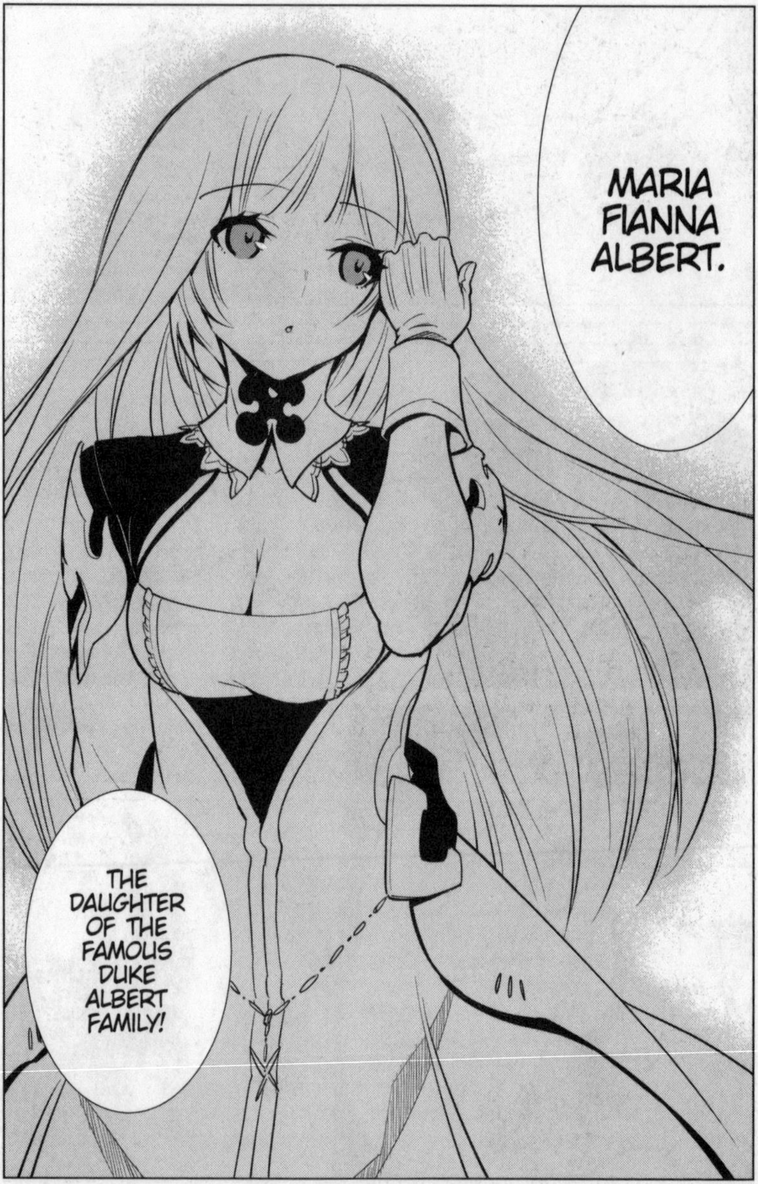
MARIA FIANNA ALBERT.
THE DAUGHTER OF THE FAMOUS DUKE ALBERT FAMILY!

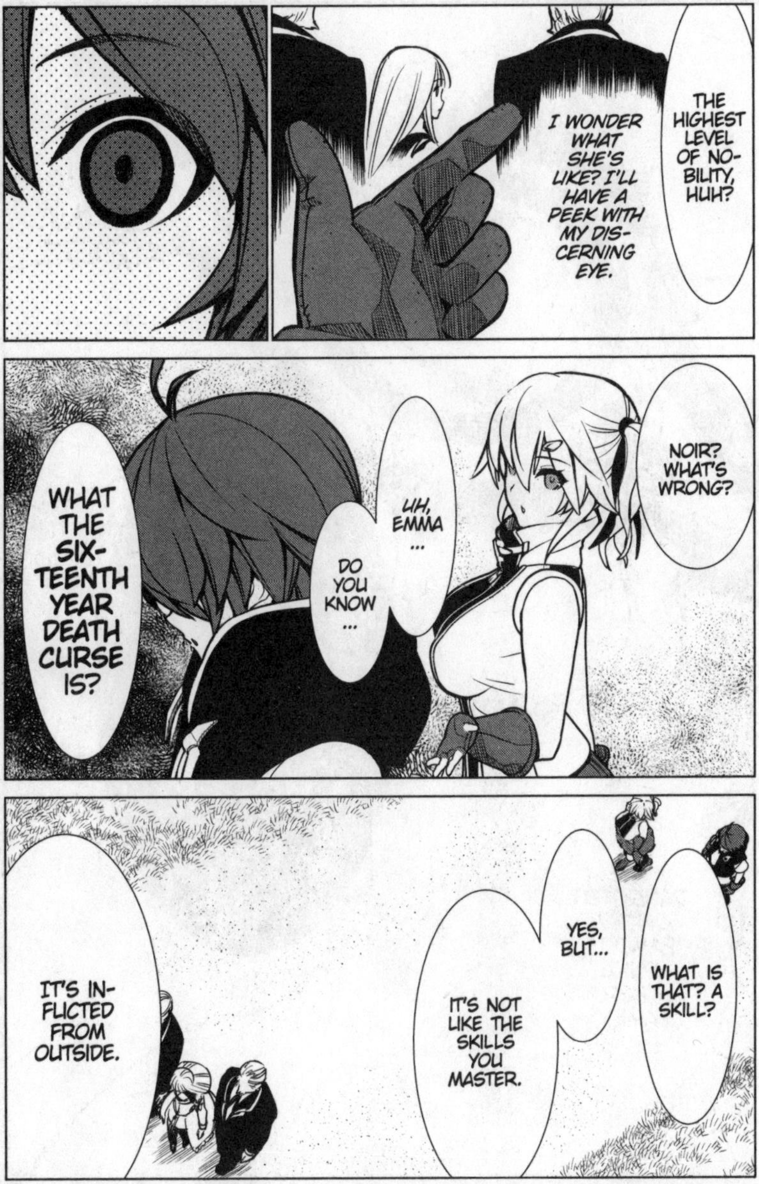
THE HIGHEST LEVEL OF NOBILITY, HUH?
I WONDER WHAT SHE'S LIKE? I'LL HAVE A PEEK WITH MY DISCERNING EYE.
NOIR? WHAT'S WRONG?
UH, EMMA...
DO YOU KNOW...
WHAT THE SIXTEENTH YEAR DEATH CURSE IS?
WHAT IS THAT? A SKILL?
YES, BUT...
IT'S NOT LIKE THE SKILLS YOU MASTER.
IT'S INFLICTED FROM OUTSIDE.

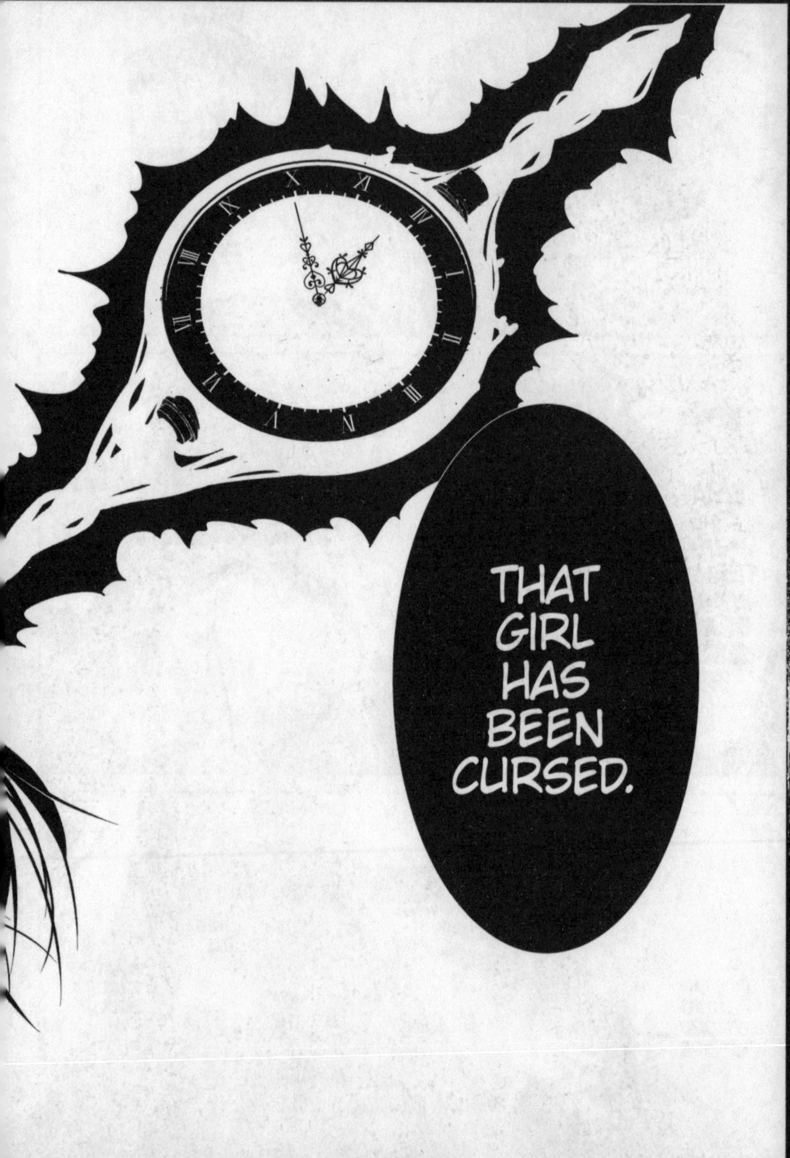
THAT GIRL HAS BEEN CURSED.

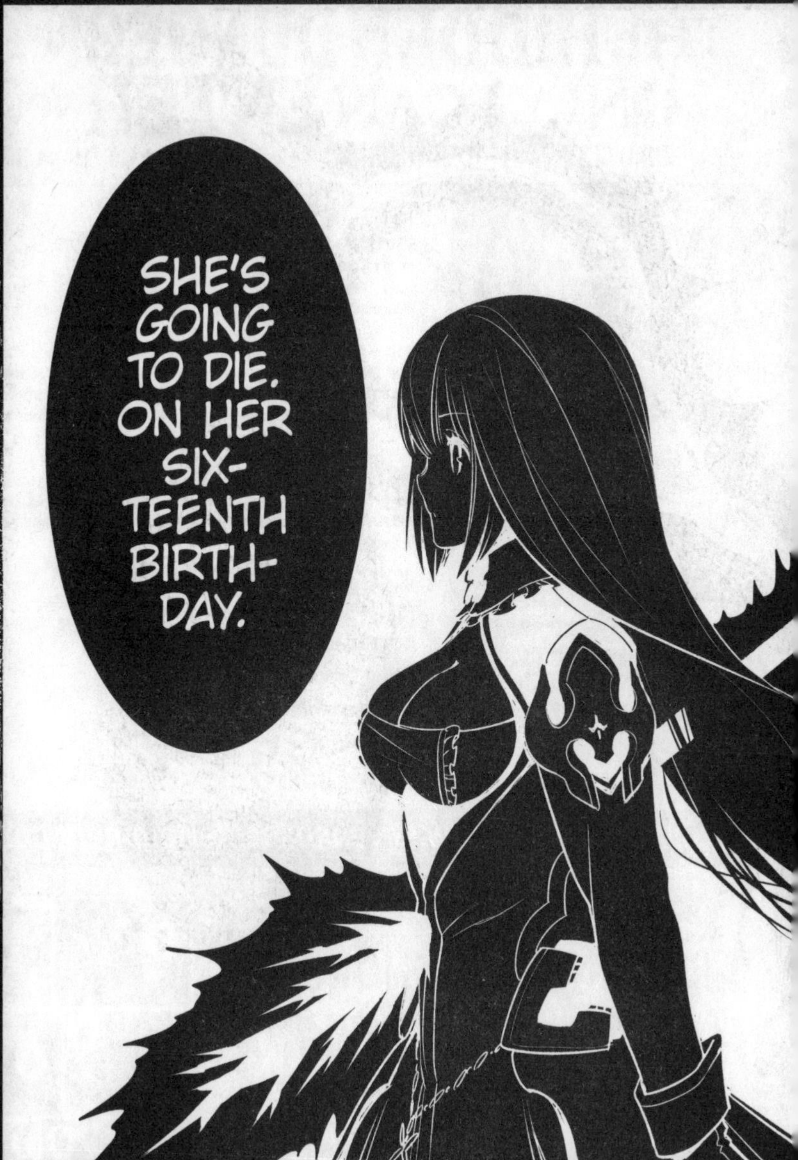
SHE'S GOING TO DIE. ON HER SIXTEENTH BIRTHDAY.

The Hidden Dungeon Only I Can Enter, Volume 1 / End

SEVEN SEAS ENTERTAINMENT PRESENTS

THE HIDDEN DUNGEON ONLY I CAN ENTER VOL. 1

story by MEGURU SETO art by TOMOYUKI HINO character design by TAKEHANA NOTE

TRANSLATION
Kumar Sivasubramanian

LETTERING AND RETOUCH
Rai Enril

COVER DESIGN
Nicky Lim

LOGO DESIGN
Arbash

PROOFREADER
Kat Adler

EDITOR
Peter Adrian Behravesh

PREPRESS TECHNICIAN
Rhiannon Rasmussen-Silverstein

PRODUCTION MANAGER
Lissa Pattillo

MANAGING EDITOR
Julie Davis

ASSOCIATE PUBLISHER
Adam Arnold

PUBLISHER
Jason DeAngelis

THE HIDDEN DUNGEON ONLY I CAN ENTER VOL. 1

First published in Japan in 2018 by Kodansha Ltd., Tokyo.
Publication rights for this English edition arranged through Kodansha Ltd., Tokyo.

Seven Seas press and purchase enquiries can be sent to Marketing Manager Lianne Sentar at press@gomanga.com. Information regarding the distribution and purchase of digital editions is available from Digital Manager CK Russell at digital@gomanga.com.

ISBN: 978-1-64505-843-4

Printed in Canada

First Printing: November 2020

10 9 8 7 6 5 4 3 2 1

FOLLOW US ONLINE: ***www.sevenseasentertainment.com***

READING DIRECTIONS

This book reads from ***right to left***, Japanese style. If this is your first time reading manga, you start reading from the top right panel on each page and take it from there. If you get lost, just follow the numbered diagram here. It may seem backwards at first, but you'll get the hang of it! Have fun!!

1
2
3
4
5
6
7
8
9

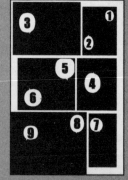

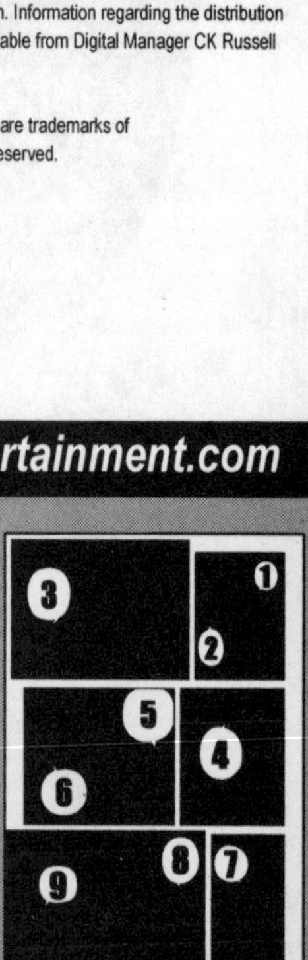